BRADLEY BAKER

and the Pyramids of Blood

DAVID LAWRENCE JONES

BRADLEY BAKER

and the Pyramids of Blood

Amazing Adventures of Bradley Baker

THE PATHYLON TRILOGY – BOOK THREE

Cover illustrated by Abie Greyvenstein

Author's Official Website: bradley-baker.com
Become a fan of Bradley Baker: facebook.com/thebradleybaker

ISBN 978-0-9561499-5-4

1

First published in the UK 2012
Avocado Media - Devon United Kingdom
www.avocadopublishing.co.uk

The author would like to thank

all the school children in Torbay that took part in the

Bradley Baker Literacy Competition 2012

...

The competition was endorsed by the area English Lead, which afforded an opportunity for all schools in Torbay to enter their children's work. The KS2 literary exercise was created by the author and the opening paragraph of a chapter in this book was supplied. The participating children were asked to compose a 350 word written piece that expanded the initial passage. The brief was to describe the main character's journey through an ancient pyramid and invent a new monster to challenge the new boy hero. Extracts from the winning entry have been edited to meet the author's writing style and now appear in this book.

...

Special recognition is afforded to the winner of the competition

Ruth Garner from Torre Primary School

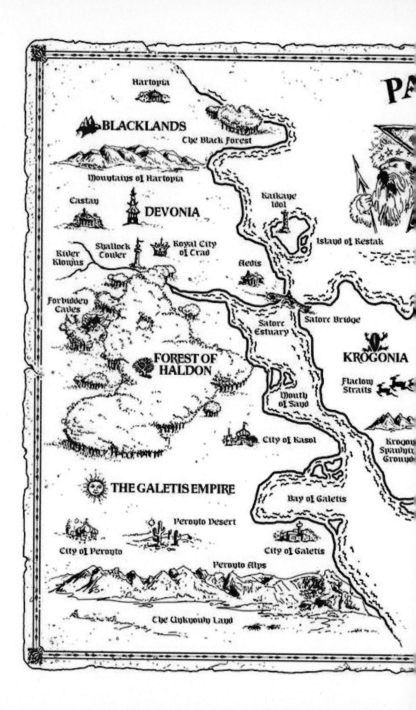

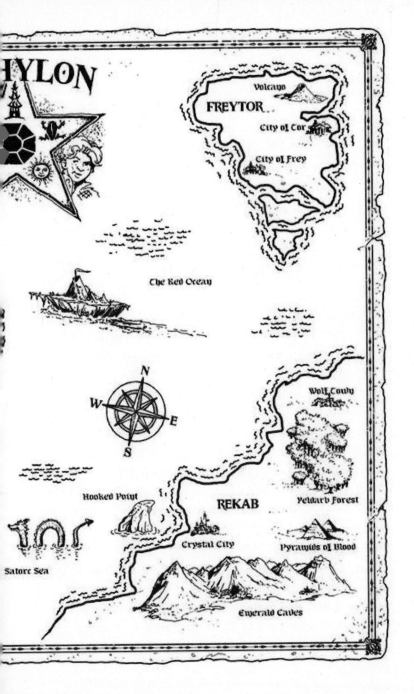

1

The Shadow Druid

The power of the storm intensified and the rain hailed down like a shower of bullets, as the angry waves crashed up against the towering hook-shaped rock. The bottom of a small wooden rowing boat scraped on the shingles, as a tall hooded figure dragged the landing craft to the safety of a nearby cave. The strange being had used the small vessel to ferry himself across the treacherous breakers from a sailing ship, which was anchored just north of the tiny island.

The sinister figure had made the windswept journey across the Red Ocean to Hooked Point with the help of a rogue skeleton crew. Together they had managed to maneuver the vessel along the coastline of Rekab before securing it to the shallow sea bed. The stranger was here to meet an eccentric recluse to collect a special package and his task was to seek self-protection against an impending threat that lurked on the outside world. The mysterious individual was looking for an old spinster, who lived in the stone cottage that was perched a few hundred metres above on the side of the crooked rock.

The uninvited guest made his way over to the base of the three hundred or so sea-carved steps that led up to the entrance of the cottage. He lifted his surly black hood slightly to aid his view and looked skywards to assess the climb, as the foaming waves continued to smash against the surrounding rocks. The rebounding spray drenched his dark leather cloak and the enigmatic visitor brushed the seeping water from his rugged face, as he furrowed his brow to aid his impaired vision. He stared intensely through the overspray of salty water and noticed some green smoke rising from the cottage's chimney. The stranger groaned in anticipation of reaching the rickety house and he could see a flickering light from one of the windows. He pulled his hood down to shield his face from the persistent swell of seawater and placed his foot on the first tread, as he held on to the mollusk exposed hand rail.

The sombre visitor began his long climb up the slippery steps and his feet remained hidden beneath the extensive dark cloak that silhouetted eerily against the rocky structure. His shadow-like figure afforded an impression of gliding effortlessly up the stairwell, as he made the toilsome ascent. Beneath the drenched robes his weighty boots trod heavily, as each fragile step creaked under the weight of his imposing frame.

Inside the cottage, a fragile old lady moved slowly across the stone floor of the parlour and she reached over to retrieve a tall jar of salt from the dresser. She wrapped her long bony fingers around the glass container and held it close to her slight chest with one arm, as she made her way slowly over to a sturdy oak table in the centre of the kitchen.

The haggard Witch used her other arm to support her crooked spine, as she groaned with every shuffled step. "I'm getting too old for this," she cackled and placed her boney knuckle into the small of her back. She then leant forward and held the jar with both hands, as she struggled to position it next to three other containers of differing heights and colours.

The combined ingredients inside the glass vessels would be mixed with the bubbling water in the cauldron next to the open fire. The salt would be added at a later stage for seasoning but firstly the deformed woman straightened her back and picked up the second jar, as she carefully emptied the contents into the iron cask. The thick white wolf fur fizzled when it hit the scolding liquid and soon disappeared beneath the surface, as the Witch stirred the mixture with a large wooden ladle.

A scabby black cat appeared and purred, as it rubbed its body against the spinster's leg. The old lady groaned again, as she bent down to pick up the hungry feline. "Ready for your supper are you, my little friend?" cackled the Witch. "It won't be long now, Truffles... just a few more ingredients to add and I'll be done preparing my new potion - it will need to boil for at least an hour before I can store it and I still need to include the most important ingredient."

The cat purred again and jumped out of the Witch's arms, as she struggled to lift the third jar off the table. The sparkling contents were heavy and she put her hand inside the container to pull out three round gleaming objects. "Ah... my favourites - gemstones from the Emerald Caves that exude from deep within the Mountains of Rekab," exclaimed the Witch, as she held one of the glistening stones out in front of her hoary face. The dancing flames from the fire sparkled through the pure green crystal, as she smiled an evil grin and then cast it into the cauldron.

The sorceress proceeded to add the other two emeralds to the mixture and each glistening stone made a distinct plopping sound, as they hit the water one-by-one. A haze of green smoke steamed up from the surface of the bubbling liquid and she generously added two more gems. "Five of these beautiful jewels should be enough," declared the old lady, as she stirred the liquid again and then replaced the lid back on the jar.

The cat's hunger incensed it to purr repeatedly and the persistent animal spiked the fur along its spine, as it rubbed its arched body against the Witch's leg once more. The old lady relented and delayed adding the contents of the forth container. "Very well, Truffles... you win - anything to please you my precious little fluffy-kins," stated the Witch and she placed the spoilt cat's bowl on the floor. "There you are... freshly caught flax meat - nothing but the best for my little darling!"

The hungry feline tucked its padded feet beneath it's under carriage and settled down contently in a crouched position, as its fur returned to a horizontal lie. The frail spinster resumed her potion-mixing and picked up the fourth jar, as she carefully opened the lid. A strong stale smell of rotten eggs filled the room and the fur on the cat's back stood on end again, as it devoured the raw flesh in its bowl.

The old lady reached for a spoon and scooped out the smelly contents from the glass container. The paste was thick like treacle and dark brown in colour. The putrid mixture was made up of crushed Troglobite eggs, powdered Krogon bones and mixed with Hoffen urine to bind the stock. The dreadful aroma caused the Witch to wretch and she swirled it around the end of the spoon, as she held her wide nostrils together with pinched fingers. Her voice distorted, as she tried to talk through the impeded airway and she murmured an instruction to herself. "Now... I have to be careful not to add too much of this particular ingredient - one level spoonful will be sufficient!"

The Witch released the temporary grip from her nose and tapped the spoon on the side of the cauldron, as the sticky paste dropped into the melting pot. The bubbles grew larger and more intense, as she rinsed the remains of the stock from the spoon and continued to stir the liquid at the same time. The potent smell wafted under her large hooked nose and she closed her eyes to enjoy the smell, as the steaming odour was drawn into her flaring nostrils. "Beautiful... now, just a little salt and we can leave it to simmer," mumbled the Witch, as she took the first jar and emptied all the contents into the mixture. "You can't have enough salt... that's what I say – there, that should do it!"

The Witch stirred the potion for a few more minutes until the stock paste had thickened the mixture. She then placed the ladle on the hearth and made her way over to the parlour window. Her dark clothing and wrinkled skin made her look a lot older than her fifty nine years. The moon lit up her scrawny silhouette, which stood uncomfortably hunched in front of the cobweb covered window panes. "Tomorrow evening will bring a full moon and my potion will be ready for the final addition... but first I will need to venture out to collect the missing ingredient!" she exclaimed and looked over to the twinkling lights scattered like dust over the nearest township known as Crystal City.

The view from the window looked out across the water to the mainland of Rekab, which was a mystical world full of haunted forests and horror torn cities. The Witch only ventured from Hooked Point and across the narrow water inlet to the mainland during daylight hours. At night some of the habitual creatures would prey on any unsuspecting strangers that were brave enough to travel across the open territory of the treacherous landscape.

Truffles interrupted the Witch's concentration. The cat had finished its food and jumped on to the window sill to join her mistress, as the spinster continued to stare out across the water. "Did you enjoy your flax, my dear?" asked the old woman and gently stroked the cats head, as she continued to describe the view to the disinterested animal. "Look over there, Truffles... to the north live the Werebeasts, a species of wolf-like predators who hunt in packs to protect their crudely built homes in a place called Wolf Town – it's one of these creatures that threatens the Shadow Druid's existence and a young hero from another world is destined to join them!" she cackled, as she looked further inland and pointed in the direction of a thick woodland area. "And there in the distance is Yeldarb Forest, where a strange scurry of Black Squirrels cohabit with the gruesome Wood Ogres," explained the deranged old lady. "Together... these two species form a very dangerous alliance and we must be careful to avoid them at all cost!"

The Witch was fully aware that the cat did not understand a word she was saying but she continued to describe the dark landscape despite a lack of response from her nonchalant pet. The bright moonlight illuminated the horizon with a blue wash of splendor and the Witch pointed her boney finger, as the tip of her deformed nail inadvertently scraped the window glass. "Now... you see the mountains in the distance?" she asked, as the cat continued to ignore her with its hind leg vertical to enable it to lick its dark belly fur. "That's where I found my beautiful gemstones... inside the Emerald Caves," continued the Witch. "And let's not forget those magnificent triangular structures that crown the centre ground of Rekab and attract so many unwanted visitors to our land... the Pyramids of Blood!"

The three great pyramids stood due south of Yeldarb Forest and were worshipped daily by the dwarfish inhabitants of Crystal City. Every time one of the tiny creatures from the city died, a grand ceremony would take place and the deceased dwarf would be buried in front of the tallest pyramid, which was named *Talum* because of its aluminum tipped apex. The collective name for the pyramids was associated with blood because of the underground river that flowed beneath the stone structures. Before a dwarf was buried, it would have its head removed to prevent the body returning to back to mortality. The blood from the dead dwarf would run into the river below the pyramids and thus the name for the great landmarks was derived from the ceremonial acts.

The Witch looked away and walked across the cobweb-strewn parlour. She placed the cat on the table and then approached the cauldron again. A quick stir with the ladle and the potion was ready to cool. The light in the room dimmed considerably, as she doused the embers of the fire and left the contents of the round iron vessel to simmer back. "Come along, Truffles... it's time for bed and we have to set off early in the morning - we have to catch the tide when it's out."

The cat obviously understood this particular topic of conversation and leapt off the table straight into the old lady's arms, as the tired hag picked up a rusty oil lamp from the dresser. The Witch yawned, as she cast another look out of the kitchen window and observed the incessant activity on the mainland. "It's nearly midnight and the lights in Crystal City are still shining," she observed and struck the lamp to ignite the flame. "That can only mean one thing... another dwarf has perished today and it's just what we'll need to finish our project - the *Shadow Druid* is due to arrive tomorrow evening and he will be very pleased with this particular potion!" she exclaimed in an excited and croaky voice. "It is tradition that the dwarves bury their dead before the next sunrise so there has to be a burial ceremony tonight... we need to collect fresh blood from the river and we'll have to get to the pyramids and back before nightfall tomorrow - we don't want to be late for the *Master's* arrival and the blood has to be warm when we collect it," she explained and concluded the self-appraisal. "There has to be a full moon when we add the dwarf's blood to the mixture!"

Everything was in place and the timings were perfect for the Witch, as she closed the door behind her and left the parlour. With the cat still purring in her arms, the old lady stroked the skinny animal and then made her way upstairs to the only bedroom in the cottage. "Sleepy time for Truffles," she whispered and entered the room.

Suddenly, the stifled sound of crashing waves against the rocky isle was eclipsed by a loud banging noise that emanated from the front door of the cottage. The Witch jumped in a startled manner and gently placed the cat carefully on the mattress. She made her way to the top of the landing, as the persistent thudding continued to pound at the door. "Alright, alright... I'm coming - wait a minute!" she shouted and held on tightly to the hand rail, as she climbed down the narrow staircase sideways. "Patience... patience!"

The thumping on the door continued and was briefly interrupted by intermittent lightning bolts that lit up the hallway through the tiny round windows. The ugly wart-covered facial features of the Witch were highlighted by the flashing strikes, which were quickly followed by the deep rumbling of thunder.

The Witch pushed the metal spy-hole cover aside and peered through at the strange hooded figure that was waiting impatiently on the doorstep. The stranger had his arms folded and both were hidden by the sleeves of his dark cloak, as the frightened old lady bent down and shouted through the keyhole. "What do you want?" she cackled and took a step back from the door.

No reply came, as she approached the door again and peered through the spy-hole. The Witch focused her line of sight, as another bolt of lightning lit up the porch area. The hooded figure had disappeared from view. "Where are you?" she shouted and proceeded to slowly turn the latch. "Who would be visiting me at this time of night... and on such a stormy evening?"

Before she had chance to answer her own question the door burst open and the dark stranger stood with his arms still permanently folded, as a sheet of rain poured down over his heavy cloak. The stranger stepped forward beneath the shelter of the porch and a waterfall of cascading rainwater poured down behind him creating a translucent backdrop to his shadowy figure. The visitor's head was bowed to shield his face and the Witch was transfixed by the powerful presence of the ghost-like being.

The uninvited guest took a few steps forward and entered the cottage, as the old lady took a few steps back. The hinges on the door creaked, as it slammed shut and the whistling noise of the storm ceased. An eerie quietness filled the hallway and the muffled silence was interrupted by the slow dripping of water from the stranger's cloak. The Witch lowered her head and focused her attention on the droplets of water, which formed miniature-rivers that trickled through the dust on the worn oak floorboards. She was momentarily transfixed by the movement of the salty water, as the tiny streams of liquid merged into one large puddle.

The old spinster shook her head to clear the momentary trance and looked up again to face the stranger, as another flash of lightning lit the hallway. She finally plucked up enough courage to ask the mysterious visitor to reveal his identity and was interrupted by the cat, as it meowed from the top flight of the stairs. "Be quiet, Truffles!" she shouted and turned her attention back to the hooded figure. "Who are you and want do you want?" she asked in a nervous tone, as the cat leapt down the staircase and brushed up against the druid's wet cloak. The rain water caused the smitten animal's fur to stand up like electrical spikes, as it meowed softly again to welcome the hallowed guest and the Witch commented. "It would appear that Truffles likes you... she's normally very particular about who to approach!" she explained, as the shadowy figure pulled his worn hands out of the rain-sodden cloak sleeves.

The Shadow Druid lifted his arms and held the side of the hood that shielded his face. The old woman watched in anticipation, as he drew the hood back to reveal his true identity. The Witch placed her wart-covered hands across her mouth and drew a sharp intake of breath, as she screeched out a shocking revelation. "It's you!" exclaimed the hag, as a raw smile developed across her dry wrinkled face. "So *you* are the mysterious Shadow Druid!"

2

Bullying in the Shower Block

The Yorkshire air was icy fresh on a cold Saturday morning in December. Christmas day was just under two weeks away and the chilling frost clung tightly to the blades of grass that covered the Maulby Grammar School playing fields. The ground was very hard and the frozen surface provided a layer of hard core that simulated concrete. The school term had just finished for the holidays and the last rugby match of the year had still gone ahead as planned, even though the weather conditions were far from suitable.

The referee's decision to go ahead with the game had proved to be the correct one. The studs from the players boots had successfully ploughed through the surface of the soil to gain the necessary grip needed to ensure a soft landing to accommodate any over-committed tackles. The whistle had long been blown to end the bitterly contested game between Maulby Grammar and Ecklington Comprehensive with many cuts and bruises covering the legs and arms of the exhausted participants.

The mood between the war-torn players was a mixture of disappointment from the away team and a celebration of victory from the Maulby boys over their local school rivals. With gum shields now removed, a reprise of adrenalin-lined conversation ensued and the parade of mud soaked gladiators made their way down the path that led away from the playing fields. At last they reached the sports hall building within the grounds of the Grammar School and the stamping of muddy boots on concrete removed any unwanted soil. The sound from their aluminum studs produced a metallic clatter, as they walked over a mesh grid and entered through the main doors of the building. The two teams welcomed the warm air that hit their frozen faces, as they hustled and bustled their way inside the entrance foyer. The two opposing teams continued their competitive spirit and pushed forward like a herd of raging bulls, as they displayed their adolescent nature against each other to cause a stubborn commotion. The sound of their metal studs on the wooden polished floor now echoed to a more pronounced pitch, as they made their way along the narrow corridor that led to the changing rooms.

The Maulby boys recurrently peeled away from the unceasing stampede, as they approached the entrance to the changing room that proudly adorned the *'Home Side'* plaque. The foot plate of the spring-loaded door was repetitively kicked open, as the weary band of victorious brave-hearts single filed into the whitened room and continued to congratulate each other on their achievements in such extreme wintry conditions. The exhausted boys had just won a record tenth league game on the trot and they chanted a chorus of sports related anthems, as the sound of their studs adopted a higher pitch by clattering on the porcelain floor tiles. The stale air within the crowded room began to exude a combined stench of sweat and earthy aromas, as the young athletes discarded their wet clothing following the year seven's grudge match with their neighbours.

Bradley Baker kicked off his muddy boots and peeled back his sodden sports socks to reveal an unusual covering of coarse hair on his pale shins. He then stripped off his number nine shirt and removed his *Canterbury* emblazoned shorts, as the exhausted boy reached out for a towel. He utilized the large bath sheet as a protective screen and loosely held it affront in a defensive manner. He casually concealed his privacy and blushed slightly, as he made his way into the communal shower area to join some of his more confident and mature team mates. The newly appointed scrum-half ignored the inquisitive eyes of his fellow rugby players and plucked up enough courage to discard the temporary shield. He then cast his towel over the nearest rail and proceeded to turn one of the chrome handles to release a cold torrent of water from the domed shower head above.

Bradley stood back for a few seconds and waited for what seemed an eternity but it did not take long for the water to heat sufficiently. He then stepped beneath the skin-routing torrent, as a concentrated haze of steam began to fill the harried bathing area. The visibility within the shower block continued to deteriorate and the bathing area became a shapeless chamber filled with an eerie foggy mist. The uneasy boy was unable to see more than a metre ahead of his outstretched arms and could just make out a few formless figures, as they moved along the line of shower bays.

At last, Bradley was able to relax, as the hot water powered out of the shower head and hit his spine with the force of a tropical rain storm. He tried to ignore the two sniggering prop forwards that had now joined him in the next cubicle.

The teasing jibes continued to resonate through the falling droplets of water and Bradley outstretched his arms again, as he placed the palms of his hands against the white tiled wall. A warm sensation rushed through his cold body, as the heat penetrated his aching pre-teenage muscles and he tried to ignore the childish taunts. A sharp pain shot through his chest and worked its way down to his abdomen. Bradley raised his knee and crouched slightly to disguise the throbbing twinge that was now rushing through his body. The kratennium infecting the boy's physique was now flowing proficiently through his bloodstream and working its way into his skeletal structure via his swollen muscle tissue.

One of the *prop forwards* noticed the discomfited boy reeling in pain. Ethan Darke was a mature heavy-built and very tall thirteen year old with jet black hair, better known as *'Ed-Case'* to rest of the forward pack because of his initials spelling out ED. The muscular thug broke the silence by shouting across to the stricken boy and started to tease him. "Hey, *Baker Boy*... I see you can't take the pressure of the physical game - you should have stayed on the subs bench where you belong!" he taunted. "And what's with all the hair on your legs and down your back... you wimp – you turning into a chimpanzee or something?" he joked and took advantage of Bradley's predicament by flicking his towel at the boy's leg. "Maturing a bit too soon for a twelve year old... aren't you?"

The recoiling action of the towel just reached the top of Bradley's left leg and a stinging sensation shot through his thigh. The pain in his stomach was replaced with a burning sensation in his upper leg and he instinctively turned his head. Bradley's normally mild temper started to boil and he scowled at his overweight team mate, as his eyes shone with a feint glow of red deep inside his pupils. "Do that again *Darke* and I'll take that towel and wrap it round your fat neck!"

"Ooooooooo... just listen to her!" tormented Darke. "Steady on now, Bradders old son... you don't have to take things quite so seriously – I'm only playing with you!" replied the thuggish boy, as he prepared to flick the towel again. "Come on then... let's see what you're made of – little hairy man!"

Bradley arched his back and looked down at his hands, as his fingers became rigid. He noticed his nails had grown somewhat since the end of the rugby match and he felt a rush of adrenalin pump through his aching body. The rage he felt inside caused his top lip to rise and he displayed his teeth to the provocative prop forward, who was now pulling back the towel again in readiness for a second flick at his leg.

Another team mate witnessed what was about to happen and he launched himself in front of Bradley, just as Ethan Darke prepared to release his next act of provocation. The brave defendant was the squad's gangling *full back* Jefferson Crabtree, an African-American boy who had moved to England from New York with his parents a few years ago.

Jefferson dutifully took the painful lash of the towel's whipping action across his buttocks, as he fell to the floor clutching his rear in agony. Ethan and the other forwards started to laugh uncontrollably, as Bradley focused his attention on the felled boy at his feet. He instinctively pulled his towel from the rail and covered Jefferson to protect his dignity. Bradley's rage heightened, as he prepared to launch himself at the sniggering brute. "Now you've asked for it, Darke... it's time someone taught you a lesson in manners – you're not getting away with your bullying ways anymore!"

"Come on then *Baker Boy*... let's be having you!" threatened the ruffian, as the veins on his neck bulged with a throbbing pulsation.

Bradley curled his upper lip again to bare his teeth and readied himself to pounce but his next move was thwarted by a familiar ear-piercing sound that emanated from the far end of the changing room. The distinct high-pitched whistle had been blown by the rugby coach and Mr. Flowers the games teacher approached the scene. "What on earth is going on here, you lot?" he demanded and reached over to turn off the water supply to Bradley's shower head, as Jefferson still lay hunched beneath the towel on the wet floor. "What's all the commotion about... who's responsible for this unacceptable behaviour – and what's happened to young Crabtree?"

Ethan Darke was quick to explain his version of events to the displeased P.E. teacher and attempted to cover up his goading, as he attempted to plead his innocence. "Sir, its Baker's fault... he was mouthing off about the Ecklington Comp's scrum half – so I asked him to be quiet and have more respect for his opposing number nine!"

Mr. Flowers glared at Bradley. "Well... what do you have to say for yourself, Baker?"

Bradley's uncharacteristic anger had now subsided and his nails had drawn back into his fingertips, as he crouched down to help Jefferson get to his feet. He looked up at his rugby coach and offered him an honest stare, as he spoke calmly. "Sir, Darke is telling lies... I did nothing of the sort – he flicked his towel at me and then Jeffers bravely got in the way of the next one."

The rugby coach cast a distrusting gaze at the flustered prop forward, as Bradley's eyes momentarily glinted with a red glow again. "Is this true, Darke?"

Ethan Darke pulled his towel from the rail and wrapped it around his waist, as he grunted a faint reply. "Baker is making it up, Sir... I knew you wouldn't believe me!" he concluded in a disgruntled manner and brushed past the teacher.

"Get back here, Darke... I haven't finished talking to you yet – Baker, you and Crabtree get yourselves dressed," he ordered, as he prodded his finger in the lofty teenager's chest. "You've been at this school for less than three weeks and you're acting as though you own the place... now get your uniform on then I'll see you in my office before you leave – I knew you were trouble from the day I set my eyes on you."

Bradley helped Jefferson to his feet and they walked slowly past the teacher and made their way over to the changing pegs, which hung their waiting school uniforms. Ethan Darke grunted again, as Mr. Flowers passed him by with a glancing nudge. The annoyed teacher then turned to leave the shower block, as he headed off in the direction of his office. The changing room was filled with the noisy hum of newly broken male voices, as the whole rugby team started to murmur their whispered opinions.

"Are you okay, Jeffers?" asked Bradley, as he pulled his black V-neck sweater over his head. "It looked like Darke caught you pretty bad with that last flick."

Jefferson replied in a defined Manhattan tone and examined the bruised area of his ebony coloured skin. "Yeah, thanks Bradley... I'm fine now – still stings a bit but I'll be okay."

"Thanks for stepping in like that... it was very brave of you – not many other boys would have stood up to *Ed-Case* like that," acknowledged Bradley, as he patted his new best friend on the shoulder. "It's still a mystery how he ended up at our school but hopefully Mr. Flowers will sort him out."

"Think nothing of it… thugs like him should spend a few days in the Bronx back home - he'd be pulled down a peg or two that's for sure - anyhow, you'd have done the same for me," retorted the humble boy. "And hey, it's a good job I did intervene… you were like a man possessed – you looked like you were about to turn into a raging animal and kill the big brute!"

Bradley laughed and felt the piercing pain in his midriff again. "Arrrrrrrrrgggghhhh!" he exclaimed.

"You alright, Bradley?" asked Jefferson, as the noise from the other boys in the changing room doused the howling sound of Bradley's excruciating outburst.

Bradley disguised his pain and played down the incident. "Let's finish getting dressed and get out of here," he replied and looped his tie over his head then proceeded to place it under his collar. "Is it still okay if I get a lift home with your Dad?"

Jefferson nodded and decided not to push his friend for a further explanation. "Yeah, no problem… come on – he'll be waiting outside in his car at the school gates."

Bradley picked up his sports bag and followed Jefferson towards the changing room exit. Ethan Darke had his back to them, as they passed him by. The burly prop turned round quickly and grabbed the arm of Bradley's blazer. "This isn't over, Baker… we have unfinished business and *Yankee* boy here can consider himself a marked man too!"

Bradley stared at Ethan's reddened face and then down at the clenched hand that had secured a strong grip on his jacket. "Take your hand off my blazer, Darke," he replied calmly, as the red glint reappeared deep within his eyes again. "And don't even think about harming my friend!"

The aggressor smirked and then let go immediately, as if to be warned off by the persuasive stare from Bradley's bewitching eyes. "Like I said… *Baker Boy* - this isn't over!"

Bradley brushed his hand down his arm to straighten the wrinkles from his clothing and then turned away in a nonchalant manner, as he muttered to himself. "I'm quite sure it isn't, Darke."

The two boys made their way out of the changing room to the sound of patronizing chants from the rugby team's forward pack, led and orchestrated by Ethan Darke. Jefferson offered his friend an inquisitive smile and asked Bradley the obvious question, as they walked through the foyer. "What do you think Ethan meant by… it's not over?"

"Ah, nothing… don't worry about what Darke threatens – let's just find your Dad," replied Bradley in an unruffled manner and he reached into his pocket to locate the sacred *grobite*. "He'll end up getting expelled if he continues with that sort of behaviour… it's probably what happened to him at his last school – it's just a shame Maulby Grammar ended up with him," he assumed. "Anyhow, what he has to say doesn't bother me… I've got more important things to worry about – no time to waste thinking about thugs like him."

"Such as?" asked Jefferson.

"Not now, Jeffers… I don't mean to be rude but I just want to get home – apparently my Mum and Dad are going to make some sort of an announcement to me and Frannie tonight," responded Bradley, as he forced open the main exit doors to the sports hall and the cold winter air instantly bit into the boys faces.

"What do you think it is?" enquired Jefferson, as he avoided the sprung loaded door coiling back in his face.

Bradley walked a few steps ahead and then turned to face his inquisitive friend, as he hesitated slightly before replying. "I don't know… I just hope they haven't planned anything stupid like a holiday over the Christmas period or something else that's equally as dumb – there are things in Ravenswood that I have to do!"

"I can't believe you're saying that… I'd love it if me and my family went away for Christmas – especially somewhere warm or even back to Hudson Valley to visit my cousins!" quipped Jefferson, as Bradley offered no indication that he was prepared to expand upon his comment any further.

Bradley's silence was maintained and he put his hand back in his pocket to hold the gold coin, as they walked away from the sports hall. His thoughts were on Grog and planning the Krogon's release from the vortex below the old cenotaph near his house. In his mind, this had to take precedence over any other plans. The last thing he wanted was to be away from Ravenswood when the full moon was due to appear.

Jefferson shrugged his shoulders to acknowledge his troubled friend's unwillingness to divulge any more information. He pointed at the school gates and spoke clearly, as he blew out a cloud of warm breath. "There's my Dad's car… let's get you home so you can hear the important announcement."

3
The Return of the Gatekeeper

Meanwhile back in the parallel world on the island of Freytor, victory celebrations continued following the recent close encounter with the kratennium filled ice-cloud. The danger had passed some months prior but the heroic exploits of Bradley Baker from the outside world were a constant topic of enthused conversation. A huge sense of relief was evident on the snow-covered streets and the news of Admiral Norsk's death ensured a vote of confidence for the island's leadership inside the senate. The ice-bear populous was finally getting back to some kind of normality and there was plenty of positive activity in the capital city of Frey, as the Freytorians went about their usual business.

An ice-carved balcony with an ornate balustrade protruded an upper floor at the ocean-facing side of the senate building. The golden thread from a royal crest stood proud on a purple velvet flag and reflected beams of sunlight, as it draped over the side of the gallery to signify the continued presence of the Pathylian hierarchy on the remote island.

The magnificent parliament building stood proud and resilient above the harbour. The senate edifice resembled a grand palace from the Galetis Empire but instead of glistening sand, the structure was fashioned from blocks of carved ice and a multitude of tall snow-capped towers with sparkling domed roofs reflected the dancing sun beams that streamed through the morning clouds.

A group of very important delegates stood on the balcony looking out at the panoramic views of the Red Ocean and Frey's bustling port directly below. King Luccese and Queen Vash were joined by General Eidar, as they waved their farewells to Turpol the Gatekeeper. The royal couple's exile on the arctic island of Freytor continued, as the evil Varuna sat unlawfully on the Pathylian throne with the disloyal sorceress Flaglan still by his side.

Luccese pondered over the current situation in Pathylon, as Vash and the Freytorian ice-bear continued to wave at the dwarf. The King turned to his Queen to make polite conversation. "It is good that Turpol can now return to Krogonia, where he still holds the temporary position of High Priest to lead the embattled and depleted Lizardmen," he stated. "I am so pleased that Pavsik and the armies of the Galetis Empire have succeeded in driving Varuna and Flaglan's Tree Elves from that particular region and at least we have secured Krogonia from the Pathylian mainland."

Vash looked up into her husband's sad eyes and offered some words of reassurance. "We *will* return to Pathylon soon, my love... Meltor is recovering well and I am sure his plans to seek help from the mysterious land of Rekab will prove fruitful."

General Eidar could not help but overhear the royal couple's conversation and he politely interjected. "Excuse me for interrupting, your highnesses... it is great news that Pavsik has led the Galetians into victory over the Tree Elves in Krogonia," he agreed and then paused momentarily to deliver a concerned opinion. "However, with the remaining legions of Galetian soldiers stationed in Krogonia... it means that the Galetis Empire is now vulnerable from attack!" explained the General in a concerned tone. "It is important that the Krogon armies are quickly rebuilt so the Galetians can return to their own region to defend it against Varuna's battalions of archers based on the outskirts of the great forest... with Haldon being their homeland – it is a perfect base for them to launch another attack and gain overall control of the Galetis Empire!"

King Luccese nodded. "I agree, General... but don't forget that we have Guan-yin to help Pavsik and Turpol – she has been banished from the Blacklands and I have received news that she is waiting in Krogonia for Turpol's arrival to help him rebuild the Krogon army." The King sighed and concluded his reply. "Apparently, Varuna has now appointed a new High Priest for the Blacklands and the weasel-like creatures are now being led by an experienced Hartopian Lieutenant called Ulan-dem."

Eidar groaned. "I have heard of this veteran Hartopian you speak of... he has a bad reputation and I believe he is from the old regime that fought against the Galetians back when Meltor's Granddaughter was supposedly sacrificed by Basjoo Ma-otz!"

"That is correct," agreed King Luccese. "Meltor will be none too pleased when he finds out that yet another member of that unlawful regime is now in charge of the Blacklands."

Queen Vash interrupted the conversation between her husband and the General and tried to make light of the situation by diverting their attention back to the ice-ship that was making its way slowly out of the harbour. "Look... Turpol is still waving."

The little Gatekeeper was standing on a crate to elevate him above the icy rails that surrounded the viewing gallery of the Freytorian iceberg ship and he continued to wave back at the royal couple who had now been joined by a recovering Meltor.

The Galetian High Priest bowed to acknowledge the King and Queen, as he nodded to the General. "Good morning everyone... I see our dear friend Turpol has finally set sail for Krogonia."

Luccese expressed a warm welcome to the ailing High Priest from the Galetis Empire. The King's attention was diverted by his Queen and he looked out to sea just as the wind caught the gigantic ice-sail that caused Turpol's vessel to leave the confines of the harbour. Luccese sighed, as the iceberg ship built up speed and eventually faded into the distance. The King then turned to face his old friend and opened his arms to embrace the fragile Galetian. "Ah, Meltor... it is good to see you up and about, my dear friend – we were just talking about you," he stated and released his strong hold to offer his hand.

"I thought I could feel my ears burning," laughed Meltor, as he took a firm grip of the King's hand and shook it confidently. "So tell me, my lord... what was the topic of your conversation that included me?"

Vash afforded her husband a caring glance and moved forward to hold on to Meltor's arm. She was keen to avoid a situation that would upset the old Galetian and for now at least she was determined to stop him finding out about the newly appointed leader of the Blacklands. The Queen quickly diverted the conversation to talk about the plans to seek help from Rekab. "General Eidar tells us that you have a strategy to overthrow Varuna so we can all return to Pathylon?"

Meltor nodded and smiled admiringly at the beautiful Devonian. "Yes, your highness... there is a group of nocturnal creatures that frequent a magical forest, which is blanketed with a dense cover of mysterious silver trees located next to the great pyramids on Restak - a race of Black Squirrels who, if they decided to help us, would be a great match for the Tree Elves because of their knowledge of forest life."

King Luccese asked. "What is the name of this magical forest you speak of?"

"Yeldarb, your majesty!" replied the old Galetian, as he held tightly to the icy hand rail in order to steady his balance. "And if we act quickly we could also secure the help of the Wood Ogres, who also frequent Yeldarb Forest," concluded Meltor, as he held his forehead to clutch a sudden bout of dizziness.

"Are you feeling alright, Meltor?" asked Queen Vash and took a tighter hold of the High Priest's sleeve.

Meltor sighed and replied. "I'm alright, my lady... I'm just feeling a bit tired following the operation - Rathek's heart still beats strongly inside my chest so I'm confident that my health will improve and I'll be able to face Varuna and his sorceress ally again!"

General Eidar approached Meltor. "May I suggest you get some rest?" He proposed and offered to escort the ailing Galetian back inside the senate building. "Even though the sun beats down beautifully from the skies... it's cold out here and it can't be good for your condition."

Meltor reluctantly agreed and Queen Vash helped him away from the balustrade. They then made their way across the balcony to the warm confines of the royal suite inside the senate building. The King followed closely behind and it was agreed that they should all meet again later when the ailing High Priest had rested for a while.

General Eidar insisted on taking Meltor's arm from the Queen and he suggested that he should escort the Galetian back to the Ice Hospital for some routine checks. Luccese and Vash agreed that this was a good idea, as the General chaperoned Meltor out of the royal chamber.

The stubborn High Priest insisted that he did not need to return to his health pod. "Why are you taking me there?"

General Eidar explained. "I'm not... I just wanted to get you away from the King and Queen - I think it would be best if we meet alone later."

"Why?" asked the Galetian, as the General released his grip on the High Priest's robe.

"Because I don't believe that Luccese is in the right frame of mind to organize an effective attack on Varuna's army!" stated the Freytorian. "The King's emotions are running too high and this will definitely affect his judgment... I feel it would be best if you and I work together closely to coordinate the attack - do you agree?"

Meltor stopped in the middle of the ice carved corridor and paused before replying. "I have known Luccese all my life and he has never made rash decisions... but I do agree with you, in this instance he is showing signs of emotional stress!"

"Then it is agreed... you and I will lead the mission to regain control of Pathylon from the evil clutches of Varuna?" insisted Eidar.

Meltor hesitated for a moment and scratched his long white beard. Finally the wise old Galetian answered. "Very well... but I don't want to discuss this any further, whilst standing in a corridor - it's not very private and anyone could overhear us!" He declared, as he looked from side to side. "We should get together later so I can give the task ahead some more thought... where do you suggest we should meet?"

The General smiled and replied confidently. "Come to my office... it's located on the fifth floor of this building - turn left when you get out of the vertical transporter and it's the last door at the end of the passageway!"

"Very well!" replied Meltor, as the two strong-minded individuals struck hand and paw together in a dominant grasp. "I'll see you in about three hours!"

"My office in three hours it is then... and bring some maps of Pathylon - we'll need them!" insisted the General, as he succeeded in securing the last word and they simultaneously released their grip on each other.

Luccese appeared in the corridor just as Meltor nodded to the General. The King looked surprised to see the two of them still outside his quarters and questioned their motives. "Is everything in order... I wasn't expecting to see you still talking outside my door - are you struggling to walk, Meltor?"

General Eidar offered an explanation. "Everything is fine, your majesty... Meltor felt a little weak, so we waited for a minute - he has rested though and is well enough to continue now."

The King noticed the embarrassed Galetian High Priest looked uncomfortable with the Freytorian's reply and he queried the General's response. "You look troubled, my friend... do you disagree with what the General says?"

Meltor hesitated before answering and afforded Eidar a slight glare. The Freytorian had made him look weak in front of his King but he knew he had to refrain from exposing their plans. The High Priest altered his demeanor and responded appropriately. "Yes... it's true, my lord - just another slight pain in my chest but nothing to worry about."

The King looked unconvinced but felt no more information would be forthcoming so he gave them both a final look of slight disapproval before returning to the royal chamber.

Meltor hated lying to his King but he knew it was in the best interests of Pathylon. He did not want to be seen as weak either and he glared at the General again before turning quickly, as the trajectory of his heavy robe flowed in motion with his act of disparagement.

Eidar knew he had upset the High Priest so he did not attempt to make any effort to justify his actions. The Freytorian General slumped his broad shoulders and turned slowly. The two proud commanders moved away from each other, as they paced the corridor in opposite directions and no more words were spoken.... for now at least.

4
Flashing Blue Lights

Meanwhile back in Ravenswood, a thick fog had developed since the school rugby game had finished and it hung heavy over the mining village like a leaden blanket. Mr. Crabtree revved the engine of his Vauxhall Astra, as he struggled to focus through the misty weather conditions. The poor visibility ahead was curtailing his attempts to make the final left turn of the short journey from Maulby Grammar and he waited patiently inside the white-chevrons located in the central area of the main road.

The oncoming traffic was relentless and it took a while before a safe gap-to-cross appeared. Jefferson's father glanced in his rear view mirror and quipped a predictable cliché in a very broad accent that mirrored the inhabitants of Brooklyn. "I think half the population of Sheffield are passing through here today… we'll never get you home at this rate Bradley – so near but yet so far away!"

Bradley was not amused and he sat quietly in the back of the car holding his abdomen. The pain in his stomach was still intense and he was getting very worried about his health. His rugby team mate starred open-mouthed and waited for his friend to respond. Hardly a word had been spoken since the boys left the school gates and the incident in the shower block with Ethan Darke had obviously engaged a downbeat effect. There was an uncomfortable feeling in the air and Mr. Crabtree's son attempted to disguise the uneasiness by replying to his father on Bradley's behalf. "I think Bradley's a bit tired after the game… it was a pretty hard fought affair and the Ecklington guys really tested our back line towards the end of the match."

Mr. Crabtree paid no attention to Bradley's silence, as he accepted his son's retort and continued. "I still can't get the hang of this game you call *Rugby Union*... you should adopt the real game of football like ours back home in the New York - come to think of it, I wonder how the Giants faired against the Steelers this week?"

Jefferson corrected his father. "American Football is already played in some parts of the UK, Dad... but Rugby Union is the preferred game here in Yorkshire," he explained. "I must admit, though… I do miss going to the *MetLife Stadium* back home to watch the Giants!"

"Well maybe we can take a vacation in the spring... I'm sure your Ma would be keen to take a stroll in Central Park and shop in Macy's department store - and it will give us an opportunity to check out the house in Hudson Valley to make sure our tenants are looking after the place for when we return to the States for good in the summer," summarized Mr. Crabtree. "Anyhow, I wish I could have been there to watch you this morning, lads… but I had to go to the hardware store to pick up some light bulbs – I told your Ma not have spot lights in the kitchen but she wouldn't listen to me," he waffled. "I warned her that the G10 halogen bulbs don't last two minutes… it's much better to have the twelve volt transformer units – they last a lot longer than the ones fed straight from the mains!" replied Mr. Crabtree tediously, as he wiped the inside of the windscreen with the back of his hand and looked ahead at the oncoming traffic again. "Come to think of it… florescent tubes would have been even more economical - there's one particular brand that I like…"

Jefferson rolled his eyes and stopped his father in mid-sentence before he had the chance to rattle off the entire range of light fittings in B&Q. "Okay, Dad... I think we've just about got the drift," he confirmed and looked to his distracted friend for a reaction.

Bradley was not paying any attention to what either Jefferson or Mr. Crabtree was talking about. His sensitive hearing had picked up an annoying sound from behind the dashboard, as it clicked in accompaniment with the left-hand indicators. The light on the instrument panel continued to flash incessantly and he was alarmed to feel yet another change to his aching body. He held his hands over each side of his head to smother the irritating sound and used the opportunity to probe his fingers through his hair. The startled boy felt two pointed shapes that now tipped both his ears with coarse bristles and he began to panic inwardly. He was careful not to reveal the latest features of his transformation and ruffled his thick locks to disguise the evidence.

At last a sufficient gap appeared in the traffic and Jefferson's father stopped riding the clutch, as he lifted his foot off the brake then started to turn left into the Silvermoor housing estate. He made another attempt to stimulate a polite conversation. "Well, that's the last game before Christmas…

so plenty of time to relax and recuperate over the holiday period - hey boys?"

Jefferson smiled politely but there was still no response from Bradley and he stared out of the window in the direction of war memorial. The car passed by the cenotaph and approached an uncustomary scene, which fronted the garden of number 127 Braithwaite Road. The sight of blue flashing lights atop a stationary police car alerted Bradley's attention and he shouted an assured instruction to the driver. "Please, Mr. Crabtree... stop the car!"

The brakes squealed, as Jefferson's father heeded the boy's request and Bradley flung open the rear passenger door, as a blast of wet fog smothered his face like a cold flannel. He jostled respectfully through the crowd of worried onlookers and made his way over to where his parents were crouching around a panting animal on the ground. He looked down to see Frannie weeping uncontrollably, as she held her slender arms around the dog's broad neck.

"K2!" cried Bradley in a stunned tone, as he fell to his knees and felt his mother's protective arm envelope his shoulder.

Margaret consoled her son and spoke softly. "We've called for the vet and he's on his way."

"What happened?" asked Bradley, as his voice croaked and Frannie continued to weep hysterically. "Was he hit by a car?"

Patrick rubbed his daughter's back in an attempt to stem the tears and he looked at Bradley, as the Burnese Mountain Dog continued to pant heavily. "We're not sure what happened, Son... there's a slight mark on his back leg but there doesn't appear to be any blood coming out of the wound - we'll have to see what the vet has to say when he gets here."

"Who found him?" asked Bradley, as he leant over to stroke his faithful pet.

"Mrs. Knowles from across the road heard a loud yelp and the next thing we heard was her knocking on our door," replied Patrick. "We came outside and he was just lying here in the middle of the road."

An elderly woman lent down and positioned her head between Bradley and Patrick. It was Mrs. Knowles and she spoke softly. "My husband said he saw a black car pull up outside your house and two hooded men got out."

"What kind of car was it?" asked Bradley.

Mrs. Knowles turned to her husband and indicated for him to come over. The ageing man acknowledged his wife's request and adjusted his walking stick, as he approached steadily. Mr. Knowles crouched down and asked his wife. "Did you tell them what I saw?"

"Yes dear, but the young fella has asked if you noticed what kind of car it was... you know, the one that the two hooded men got out of," yelled the old lady.

Mr. Knowles held his hand over his ear. "No need to shout you silly old bat... I've got my blooming hearing aid on full blast – you're deafening me woman!"

Patrick interrupted and calmed the conversation, as he repeated his son's question. "Please, Mr. Knowles... do you know what make of car it was?"

"I'm afraid not... it was so foggy but I did see one of the men walking across your front lawn," replied the elderly neighbour. "That's when your dog appeared... he just stood his ground and kept barking at the stranger."

Bradley kept stroking K2's head and his father asked Mr. Knowles if he saw what happened next. "Did the men hurt K2?"

Mr. Knowles paused and his wife put her hand over her mouth, as she replied on his behalf. "My husband's view of the incident was hindered slightly by the car… but I did see your dog chase the hooded fella into the road!" she continued. "And then I saw the man lift some kind of bar-like object above his head… the next thing I heard was the sound of your dog yelping - so I assume he must have struck the poor thing."

The old man held on to his stick for support and agreed with his wife's account by concluding. "That's right and then both men jumped back in the car and sped off… they were going far too fast, though!" he shouted and adjusted the volume on his ear piece. "The car skidded across the road and I tried to read the registration number… but it was just too foggy!"

"Thank you, Mr. and Mrs. Knowles… I'd appreciate it very much if you could tell the police officer what you just told us," requested Patrick, as he placed the palm of his hand to support the back of his son's head.

Bradley instinctively shook off his father's caring gesture in fear of his unusual-shaped ears being discovered. This was not the time for any more mysterious explanations and he proceeded to rest his face on the dog's puffing cheek. He then whispered in K2's ear, as steam began to rise from the injured canine's body. The dog's stomach moved up and down in time with his heavy panting and Bradley pleaded with his loyal pet. "Stay with me old boy... don't you dare die on me."

The tip of the dog's pink tongue appeared at the front of his snout, as he swallowed deeply. Then to Bradley's surprise he heard K2 reply with a faint and strained human voice. The startled boy lifted his head away to refocus his attention, as he quickly repositioned his mouth near to the dog's ear again and spoke slowly. "Did you just speak to me, pal?"

K2 blinked an eye and raised the corner of his slobbering mouth. "Yes, but no one else can hear me, Bradley... you are able to understand me because your animal instincts are developing and your human form is deteriorating!" explained the hound. "Your body is starting to transmute into a Werebeast and have to seek help to reverse the effect of the kratennium!"

Bradley looked around to see if anyone else was listening to the conversation. The crowd was totally detached from the surreal connection between him and his wounded pet, as he lowered his head again to whisper. "I guess that explains why my body is getting hairs all over it and I even noticed my ears changing shape in the car," he confirmed and diverted the topic of conversation, as he asked bluntly. "Are you going to die?"

K2 blinked again and swallowed slowly, as he prepared to deliver the devastating news to his young master. "My life is being taken away against my will and it's time for my soul to enter the vortex beneath the blue light... but my death will create the opportunity for Grog's release – your Krogon friend is needed back in Pathylon, to help Turpol and the others lead the depleted Lizardmen against Varuna's armies."

Bradley gulped and found it difficult to accept the tragic news. "K2, I don't want you to go... Grog's return will be welcomed and as you know his release was our primary objective on the date of the next full moon - but why do *you* have to be sacrificed to save the trapped Krogon?"

The brave hound twitched his front paws and replied. "You thought that you, Henley and your friends from Sandmouth were the only ones able to recall the incredible journeys into Pathylon," he whimpered. "Well, now you know you weren't alone... I also remember being one of the twelve chosen one's that created the circle around the Kaikane Idol - when the eight prisoners from Freytor were released!"

"This is weird... I thought you were just my pet dog caught up in all this amazing stuff," replied Bradley, as the sound of another vehicle approached the scene. "That will be the vet... what do you want me to do?"

K2 groaned and advised his young master. "Let the animal doctor do his bit for I'm ready to go now, so prepare yourself because he will diagnose my death imminently... please make sure Frannie is okay and you must make the necessary arrangements for my body to be buried beneath the cenotaph when there is a full moon – as you rightly stated, it's the only way to enable Grog's release from the vortex."

"I can't believe this is happening... I am so proud of you – but I still don't want you to die," consoled Bradley, as he stroked the dog's thick coat. "Before you go… at least tell me - why you were barking at the hooded men?"

K2 breathed heavily. "They were *Shade Runners* from a place called Rekab on the other side… they were sent by the *Shadow Druid* to kill you and I tried to stop them – I knew you were due home at any minute and I did all I could to warn them off."

"Why were they sent to kill me?" he asked.

The dog closed his heavy eyelids to gather his thoughts and blinked again to reveal more information about the ritual on the Island of Restak. "You recall I told you that I remembered the ceremony around the Kaikane Idol?"

"Yes... but what's that got to do with the Shadow Druid?" asked the puzzled boy.

"Something strange happened during the ritual... there was an evil presence of some sort!" explained K2. "Turpol noticed it, as well... I could tell he felt it too - because of the horrified look on his face."

Bradley pleaded with the dog to recall more detail of the event. "What did you see?"

"Not sure, exactly... but the incident definitely relates to the Shadow Druid that is now seeking your demise!" explained the panting hound, as his failing heart skipped a beat. "All I know is that your special powers are deteriorating because of your transformation and this will enable the Shadow Druid to defeat you!" he warned. "You must drink the antidote to restore your formidable status… as the eternal chosen one!"

Bradley looked around to see if his parents were watching but they were still too busy talking to the vet. Tears started to roll down his cheeks and he placed his hands either side of the dog's head, as he turned it slightly so he could look into K2's dying eyes. "How do you know about these things, old fella?"

The dog curled his slobbering cheeks and smiled, as he quietly answered the inquisitive boy's question. "Turpol the Gatekeeper told me everything I needed to know… he is aware that I am looking out for you here in the outside world – that's why you have to find him when you go back to Pathylon," explained the weakened hound. "He will be able to help you on the other side and explain why the Shadow Druid is seeking you dead!"

"What about you… it's another week till Christmas Day – how am I going to stop them burying you before the next full moon?"

"Don't worry… your Uncle Henley will take care of everything – just make sure you get back to Pathylon, as soon as you can," explained K2 and then offered his young master a final statement of sincerity. "I love you very much Bradley Baker… remember you are the *eternal chosen one* and you still have much to do to protect yourself and the arcane world of Pathylon," confirmed the ailing canine. "Hopefully you will seek comfort in my spirit living on inside Grog!" he gasped and uttered a final pledge to the adoring boy. "We will meet again, someday… I promise!"

Bradley felt a final wheeze of breath from the canine's mouth and his eyes began to well up with more tears. He tried to ask K2 to explain more about the Shadow Druid but it was too late. The dog's eyes closed and the vet tapped the distraught boy on the shoulder and placed a stethoscope on the dog's chest. He then delivered the sad news that Bradley was expecting. "I'm afraid that he's gone... I'm so sorry for your loss!"

5

A Secret Tunnel

Back in Rekab, the stormy seas had produced a tirade of crashing waves that persistently battered the tall rocky structure throughout the night. Hooked Point had survived the relentless onslaught and it remained hauntingly erect just off the main coastline. The crimson skies on the horizon marked the dawning of another eerie morning, as the dark clouds hung heavy to spoil what would have been a perfect start to the new day.

The thunderous clouds started to drift slowly towards the unforgiving stretch of ocean known as the Satorc Sea and the receding waters exerted their last feeble attempts to crash against the base of rocky mount. The retreating tide had not yet produced the safe passage needed for the Witch and her strange companion to cross the short distance on foot to the mainland. The landing craft used by the Shadow Druid had been flounced from the small cave and swept away by the unforgiving sea.

Truffles issued a soft outburst of discontent, as the Witch coveted the scraggy cat under her arm and led the way down the last few steps at the base of the crooked rock. She trod carefully onto the protruding boulders that had now formed a landscape of rock pools at the base of the structure. The Shadow Druid peered downwards through his hood and utilized his staff to steady his footing. The ghostly figure followed the Witch's steps and then grabbed her clothing, as he pulled her towards his leather cloak. His ghostlike mouth conversed a haunting message to the trembling hag. "You must not reveal my identity to anyone... what happened back in the cottage must remain our secret and no-one must know who I am - especially Bradley Baker and his meddling band of allies!"

The Witch shrugged her shoulders and pulled her arm free from the Shadow Druid's chilling grip. She adopted a more secure grasp on the frightened cat and nodded, as she continued to guide the intimidating stranger over the rocks below the cottage at Hooked Point. "Do not worry, my dear dark lord... your true identity is safe - it would not serve any purpose for me to reveal it."

"Well remember this old woman!" warned the threatening tall figure. "You will not return to your precious little cottage if my identity slips your tongue!" The Witch cowered and lowered her stare to acknowledge his warning, as they stepped over more rocks and made their way to the blind side of isolated isle. "What's that?" exclaimed the Shadow Druid, as the side of a small sea-battered shack appeared.

The abandoned hut was positioned just above the sea level on a raised decking area that was made from old drift wood. The cat jumped down onto the worn boards, as the Witch climbed up sluggishly onto the decking and approached the entrance to the shack. She reached into one of her pockets and retrieved a rusty key from her thread bare cardigan. "This will get us to where we need to go!" she cackled and pushed away some seaweed, as she forced the ancient key into the keyhole.

The Shadow Druid refused to join the Witch and stood on the rocks, as he maintained an intimidating hand hidden stance. The sleeves of his dark cloak hung heavy to reveal only the lower part of his rugged face. He revealed one of his hands and tapped the end of his long staff on the decking before reluctantly stepping onto the small terrace, as the Witch pushed the door open to reveal the sparse interior of the shack.

The dark warlock became more inquisitive and followed the hags lead, as he approached the doorway. The Shadow Druid declared his disappointment in a sarcastic tone. "It's empty... there's nothing in here - you're wasting my time you stupid old woman!" he expressed as a threatening outrage. "We have to reach the great pyramids to collect the blood so we can finish the potion... why are you wasting my time?" he fumed, as the sea spray crashed against the rocks and showered the back of his cloak. "Every minute we spend in this hut means the boy from the outside world gains an advantage!" He thundered. "You know very well that there is a secret chamber hidden deep inside the great *Talum* pyramid... if Bradley Baker discovers the contents inside the ancient tomb - he will be able to reverse the transformation that is turning him into a Werebeast," explained the Shadow Druid, as he struck the end of his shaft on the decking again. "The boy must not be allowed to find the antidote otherwise our efforts to destroy him will prove futile!" he growled. "And if we don't collect the final ingredient for your potion that will help protect me, I will be rendered powerless against him should he succeed... we must collect the dead dwarf's blood and get back to your cauldron before he reaches the pyramid!" The grumbling figure concluded. "Then and only then will I be able to defeat the boy in the *duel of destiny* and take back control of Rekab... as well as Freytor!" he declared. "And let's not forget the main prize... control of Pathylon!"

The Witch approached the irate Shadow Druid and placed a calming hand on his cloak, as she spoke in a confident manner. "You worry too much about the pathetic boy hero, my lord... you have to trust me and I will not let you down – the potion will be ready for you to drink in time for the *duel of destiny*," she assured and then scurried around inside the shack. The Witch opened the lid of a small sea chest and lifted out a glass container with a rounded base. "And to prove to you that I am one step ahead... there won't be any need to return to my cottage either," she explained, as she reached inside her black cloak. "I brought enough of the unfinished potion with me in this tube!" she revealed and poured the contents of the tube into the sturdier glass container. "So all I have to do is add the dwarf's blood to the mixture when we get to the underground river beneath the pyramids... now stop fretting and help me!" she concluded and paid no more attention to the ramblings of the impatient hooded being.

The Shadow Druid was pleased with the Witch's foresight but offered no praise. He watched the old woman, as she tied the glass container to her belt and asked. "What do you want me to do... how can I help?"

The Witch held out her boney hands and started to feel the vertical ridges on the wooden panelling. "We need to find a hidden hole in one of these walls!" she replied. "Now, are you going to just stand there... or are going to help me find it?"

"Very well, you ugly hag... I'll start looking over this side!" replied the Shadow Druid in a disgruntled tone, as the Witch continued her search and ignored his retort. "There's nothing on this wall... we are wasting time – now hurry up and find this blasted hole!"

The Witch held her hand over her mouth and cackled quietly, as she sniggered a sigh of satisfaction. Unbeknown to her raging accomplice, she had already found the hole but was revelling in the frustration of such a prominent figure. The Shadow Druid's impatient attitude was amusing her and she deliberately slowed her pace. "Patience, patience... dark lord - these things can't be rushed and you have to trust my judgment."

"What are you doing, woman?" demanded the Shadow Druid, as he turned and started to pace back-and-forth across the dusty boards. A small crab scuttled sideways along the floor and suffered its fate, as the merciless heavy laced boot of the dark figure crushed down. The sound of the cracking shell caused the Shadow Druid to lift his boot and he smeared the remains of the sea creature onto the boards. "That's going to smell if I don't wash it off... keep looking for the hole!" he declared, as he stepped out of the hut and walked across the decking towards the water.

The Witch cackled again and watched on intently, as her cat followed the hooded figure through the doorway of the shack and over to the water's edge. The cat moved to one side, as the Shadow Druid sat on the jetty and dipped his boot into the adjacent rock pools. He shook his wet foot and completed the task of removing the remains of the dead crab from his boot, as he stepped back on to the decking.

The Witch quickly turned to face the wooden panels again and pretended to continue her search for the hole, as the cat returned to the confines of the hut. The light inside the shack was suddenly diminished, as the Shadow Druid's darkened frame filled the doorway. "Well... have you found it yet?"

"Ye of little faith!" screeched the Witch, as the hairs on the cat's back stood on end in response to her owner's high-pitched outburst. "Here it is!" exclaimed the old hag, as she pushed her forefinger into an empty knot hole to trip a small lever that was hidden behind the panel. The grinding mechanical sound of moving cogs vibrated beneath the floor and a hidden trap door sprang up from the dusty boards. "There... I told you to be patient!"

The Shadow Druid re-entered the shack and approached the square opening that had been created by the Witch's prolonged probing. The tall figure waited for the dust to settle and pulled his hands from the safety of his robe. He leant his staff against the door casing and knelt down, as he placed his outstretched fingers on the floor to support his dark frame. He peered into the hole and grunted a faint sound of laughter, as he lifted his covered head to address the smug old lady. "An underground rail track and small coal wagon... I assume this primitive mode of transport will take us to where we need to go?"

The Witch cackled again and replied; as the cat jumped down to inspect the trap door. "Of course... the track runs through an old mining tunnel that will take us directly beneath Crystal City to a time portal – once safely through the vortex, we can follow the underground river that flows through the foundations of the great pyramid!" she confirmed and invited the tall figure to descend the narrow staircase that led down to the disused tunnel. "The dwarf's blood will still be warm by the time we get there and I'll be able to add it to the potion immediately... then you will have the serum you need to protect you against the new boy hero," she declared and pointed to the opening in the floor. "Now... after you and mind the first step - it's a bit rotten!"

The warning from the over-confident Witch was too late, as the Shadow Druid placed his full weight on the first tread. The cat meowed loudly, as the tall figure's foot snapped the step in half and a loud cracking sound echoed down the entrance to the tunnel. He fell forward and instinctively reached out to protect himself, as he crashed through the handrail and tumbled down the full flight of steps. His embarrassing fall came to a thudding end when he landed heavily against the side of the wagon some ten metres down. "Arrrrrrrrrghhhhh!" he groaned in a muffled tone and carefully flicked back his tousled robe to reveal the lower part of his face.

The Witch scurried down the staircase followed by the inquisitive cat and they both stood in front of the dishevelled warlock. The amused old woman cackled a faint snigger and stated the obvious. "I told you to mind the top step... now, come on - get to your feet you clumsy thing!"

The Shadow Druid stood up and brushed down his dusty clothing, as he growled a disgruntled reply. "You could have warned me a bit earlier... you stupid old bat!"

"Now, now... a little bit more courtesy wouldn't go a miss," the Witch replied calmly, as she inspected the contents of the wagon and checked the operation of the release handle. "This looks like it's working okay... it's been a while since I last used it but everything seems to be in order - jump in and we'll soon be on our way."

The Shadow Druid was totally bemused by the Witch's erratic manner and he decided not to comment further on the primitive mode of transport. He disappeared back up the broken staircase to retrieve his staff and then quickly returned with an eerie flight, as his robes drifted effortlessly down the wooden steps. Without paying the Witch any attention, he completed his graceful descent and carefully climbed into the wagon. The dark being was very conscious of his stature and made sure that he did not make any more embarrassing slip-ups in front of the ageing sorceress. He checked his footing was secure at all times and settled into the coal wagon.

The cat sprang onto the rim of the cart, as the Witch struggled to climb back up what was left of the staircase. She secured the entrance to the shack and closed the trap door before reappearing a few moments later in front of the wagon. The old woman held out her scrawny hand. "Could you help me in?"

"You are trying my patience!" shouted the Shadow Druid, as his deep voice echoed along the tunnel. "Here... take the end of my staff and I will pull you up!"

The Witch took hold of the wooden shaft and the Shadow Druid strenuously hauled her into the carriage. All three passengers were now seated in the wagon and the hag pulled the handle to release the brake. There was a dull creaking noise, as the wheels struggled to turn and the Shadow Druid grabbed the edge of the cart to thrust his large frame from side to side. At last, a distinct metallic clunking sound emanated from the axles below the carriage and the wheels started to rotate.

"Hold on!" shouted the Witch, as the wagon moved away and soon picked up speed down the slight incline in the tunnel. "Snuggle in here, Truffles... it won't take long to get to the vortex!" she encouraged, as the scabby cat pounced into her open cape and the sorceress wrapped her scrawny arms around the frightened feline.

The Shadow Druid afforded the Witch a nonchalant look and then focused his attention on the narrow roadway ahead, as the vibration from the rail track jolted his body at every joint. The fast pace of the wagon wheels had now fully dispersed the last traces of rust from the drive shafts and the carriage moved smoothly, as it turned along the dark twisted tunnel.

6

An Important Announcement

Meanwhile back in the outside world there was a hive of activity on the Silvermoor housing estate, as a concerned crowd of onlookers continued to congregate in front of Bradley Baker's house. The weather conditions were still quite misty and the twinkling lights from decorated Christmas trees illuminated in every other lounge window along Braithwaite Road. The mood was very sombre and the neighbours stood with their heads slumped along the edge of the pavement, as they took turns to offer their condolences to the heartbroken members of the Baker family.

The loss of K2 under such mysterious circumstances held a puzzling effect and Patrick asked the vet for an explanation, as it started to snow lightly again. "What was wrong with him... one of our neighbours said he might have been hit with a stick or something?"

A stray flake of snow rested on the end of the vet's nose and he brushed it away with the back his hand, as he answered Patrick's question in a solemn tone. "There's no sign of any broken bones, so he definitely wasn't hit by a moving vehicle... I guess the mark on his back leg may have had something to do with it but I think his ticker just decided to stop working and he must have had a heart attack - it's one of those things I'm afraid!"

Bradley knew differently, as a chorus of weeping echoed through the foggy air and Frannie clung even more tightly to the dog's neck. Margaret put her arms around Bradley and whispered, as more snowflakes began to fall on the deceased animal. "Come on, Son... let's get K2 inside and out of the cold."

Bradley nodded and held back his tears. He stood to one side, as the vet and one of the police officers helped his father to carry the heavy stricken hound into the house. The distraught boy instinctively cried out in a desperate tone. "I want him buried under the cenotaph on Christmas Day!"

Margaret sighed and cast a friendly glance in the direction of Mrs. Knowles. The old lady obliged with a friendly nod and shouted. "Don't worry, Bradley... I'm sure the neighbours won't have a problem with that!" She announced and looked around for support from the other onlookers. There was a unanimous reply of agreement and Mrs. Knowles issued a promise to the Baker family. "I'll get in touch with the local authorities first thing on Monday… my daughter works for the council - so I'm sure there won't be any issues!"

The weather was starting to turn for the worse and the snowflakes increased in size, as K2 was carried into the Baker's house. The crowd started to disperse, as Mr. Crabtree retrieved Bradley's sports bag from the boot of his car and gave it to Jefferson. "You'd better take this to Bradley and then we'll get on our way... looks like the snow is settling again and I don't want us to get caught in this bad weather – the roads are treacherous enough as it is!"

Jefferson carried the hold-all over to Bradley's mother, who was still consoling Frannie on the front doorstep. "Here you are Mrs. Baker... this is Bradley's rugby gear – the weather is getting worse so me and my Dad best be on our way now."

Margaret looked up at the boy and thanked him. "Please thank your Dad for bringing Bradley home safely... and tell your Mum I'll give her a call tomorrow – I have something important news to discuss with her."

"Is this anything to do with the announcement you were going to make this evening to Bradley and Frannie?" asked Jefferson, as he put his hand to his mouth having just realized that Frannie was sat on her knee. "Oops... sorry, Mrs. Baker!"

"That's alright Jefferson... we've already told Frannie and yes – it is the reason I need to speak with your Mum," she explained, as Mr. Crabtree approached to see what was keeping his son. Margaret welcomed Jefferson's father, as Frannie snuggled her face into her mother's polo-necked jumper. "Oh hello, Charles... I was just telling Jefferson that I'll call Marian tomorrow - she has been a great friend to me, whilst you guys have been staying in England and I need to let her know that we will be moving away from Ravenswood for a while," she explained. "It's even more appropriate now K2 has gone... a new start in a new part of the country will hopefully heal the loss of him much more quickly for the children."

Mr. Crabtree offered his condolences and then asked. "I'll tell Jefferson's Ma you'll give her a call... and may I ask where you are moving to?"

Margaret ushered Frannie inside and rose to her feet. "Patrick has negotiated the purchase of a small Victorian hotel but it's located down in Devon… so we'll be living near my sister in Sandmouth – we used our savings for the deposit on the hotel so that meant we didn't need to sell this house," she explained. "So in the meantime, we're going to rent out our home in Ravenswood... just in case we want to return to Yorkshire one day," she confirmed and looked up at the house. "I'll arrange to meet Marian for a coffee before we go… I know she's working every day till Christmas but hopefully I'll be able to meet up for a chat during lunchtime one day - then I'll be able to tell her all about our move to Devon."

"I'll let Marian know," replied Jefferson's father. "She'll be quite shocked and upset that you are going but we'll be moving back to the States next summer... so a parting of ways would have been on the cards, anyhow."

"Oh, how wonderful... I know Marian misses New York and that gives us even more to talk about when we meet up," replied Margaret. "And I'm sure she will understand us leaving at such short notice... we've known for a little while about the new venture but it was always going to be a last minute decision by Patrick's company, as to when we moved - the news of his resignation from E.M.M.C.O. was officially announced yesterday and it only leaves us a week to prepare for the move down south."

"That's a bit inconvenient… a few days before Christmas and all!" responded Mr. Crabtree, as Jefferson stood open-mouthed and his father voiced his disappointment again. "The school rugby team are going to miss Bradley… he's turned into a really good scrum-half – anyhow, I'm starting to waffle on a bit and I'm keeping you from your family," stated Jefferson's father, as he took a few steps back. "You'd better go inside and get out of the cold."

Margaret nodded. "Yes, Charles… you're right – Bradley and Patrick will be wondering where I've got to," she surmised and turned to walk into the house. "Moving home the day before Christmas isn't ideal but our Vera has offered to help us move in to the hotel... hopefully Bradley will be pleased – he loves Amley's Cove and the hotel is just up the hill from the bay!"

Jefferson took the opportunity to offer his commiserations, as he started to walk down the path behind his father. "Please tell Bradley how sorry I am about K2 and hopefully I'll speak to him before you leave for Devon... can you ask him to call me?" he requested and ran back to offer Margaret a piece of note paper. "This is my new mobile number… an early Christmas present – Mum and Dad got me the new *iPhone4*."

"Thank you, Jefferson… I'll make sure he gets it – although you do know Bradley lost his *new* mobile phone during Halloween, don't you?" replied Margaret, as the snowflakes fell heavier from the grey skies above. "Probably had his head in the clouds again at the time!" she surmised, unaware that Bradley actually used the device to steer the ice-cloud away from Freytor and save Pathylon from destruction. "We gave it to him for his birthday a few months ago and we still haven't found it... never mind, he'll have to use the landline – I'll get him to speak to you tomorrow after I've spoken to your Mum!"

Mr. Crabtree walked towards the pavement, as he turned to leave and encouraged his son to follow him back to the car. The police officer appeared from the house and brushed past Jefferson, as he tipped his hat to acknowledge Margaret.

"The dog is lying peacefully in the conservatory Mrs. Baker... I'll file the report when I get back to the station – I've taken a statement from Mr. and Mrs. Knowles but the vet confirmed that there doesn't appear to be any suspicious circumstances surrounding the animal's death."

"Thank you, officer... and goodbye Charles - bye Jefferson," responded Margaret, as she closed the front door to prevent the snowflakes from falling into the hallway and made her way into the house. The distant sound of Mr. Crabtree's car engine moved away, as she made her way into the lounge to witness Bradley sitting on the settee staring at the floor. Margaret sat down beside him and rubbed her consoling hands across her son's knee. "Where's the vet?" she asked.

"He's still in the conservatory with Dad... Frannie's gone upstairs – I think you better go up and see if she's okay," replied Bradley, as his mother stood up and started to walk back towards the living room door. "Oh, Mum... what did you and Dad want to talk to me and Frannie about?"

Margaret returned and knelt in front of her disheartened son. "It's not important right now... K2 leaving us like that has put a bit of a downer on it all – we'll talk when the vet has left," she suggested. "I'll go and see if Frannie is okay... why don't you go into the kitchen and stick the kettle on - there's a good lad!"

Bradley looked up into his mother's loving eyes and nodded. "Yep... no problem, Mum – and ask Frannie if she wants anything."

Margaret smiled at her son's rare display of kindness towards his four year old sister and then left the room. Bradley waited for the door to close and thought to himself out loud. "The *Shadow Druid*... now he's a new one – I can't wait to tell Muzzy and Sereny about him." He stood up and made his way over to the window and stared down the road at the war memorial. "Losing K2 is real kick in the teeth but I guess meeting Grog again is going to be a blast!" he avowed and cast a look at the nails on the ends of his fingers. The sharp tips were growing out again and the blue light at the top of the cenotaph flickered momentarily, as Bradley thought to himself. "I've got to get back into Pathylon and find Turpol before it's too late!"

Bradley made his way into the kitchen and flicked the switch on the kettle. The sound of the element inside the device roared into operation and the noise of the boiling water drowned out the conversation between his father and the vet, who were concluding their deliberation about the cause of K2's death. The two men were standing inside the adjoining conservatory and stood ominously where the deceased pet lay, as Patrick shook the vet's hand over the dog's lifeless body.

Bradley recalled his role as the *Eternal Chosen One* and stared at the peaceful hound, who was lying full-length and motionless across the soft cushions that adorned one of the wicker settees. He summoned a feeling of strength and honour, as he muttered. "Don't worry, K2... your sacrifice will not be in vain - I won't let you down my old friend!"

7
Building Bridges

The weather in Freytor reciprocated the cold conditions on the outside world. The ice-caps were covered with a thick layer of new fallen snow and the glaciers sparkled like diamonds beneath the soft flakes. Meltor had been inside General Eidar's office for some time and the incident in the corridor earlier had received no mention. They were busy working together to prepare the strategy needed to launch the newly built fleet of ice-submarines. The Freytorian commander was showing the interested Galetian some blue print schematics detailing the design of the improved state-of-the-art submersible vessels.

The pitch of the conversation suddenly changed and Meltor noticed the General pause for a moment, as they studied the drawings. The High Priest asked in a concerned tone. "What's wrong, Eidar?"

"Looking at these prints has brought back memories of my deceased brother," replied the General. The recent death of his twin filled the ice-bear with immense sadness but he was very proud of Admiral Norsk's nautical prowess following his valuable input into creating the original underwater vessels that could travel at a much greater speed than the surface-designed iceberg ships. Plans to build more of the seaworthy craft had been hastened by the senate's approval, in readiness for an attack on Varuna's illegal hold over the kingdom of Pathylon.

Luccese was eager to remove the evil Hartopian and his treacherous sorceress wife Flaglan from the throne, as quickly as possible. The frustrated King's refuge on the remote arctic island had proved to be a good safe haven and whilst in Frey, his power of authority had been put to good use. The persuasive Devonian had successfully negotiated with the Freytorians to help the launch of a new naval super-fleet. The negotiations had taken place during long drawn out meetings in the senate and had paid dividends. The King was keen to return to Pathylon to lead the attack but the General had already expressed his concerns to Meltor. The two strategists now had to come up with a battle plan without Luccese knowing about them meeting in private.

Meanwhile a floor above the General's office, King Luccese sat in a soft chair on the royal balcony and looked out to sea. He sighed and offered his thoughts aloud. "Back home in Pathylon... the armies from the Galetis Empire, the noblemen from Devonia and the Lizardmen from Krogonia have been heavily depleted following many hard fought battles," he declared and rose to his feet, as he took a few steps forward towards the ice-carved balustrade. "Varuna is displaying all the characteristics of a blood thirsty leader... the ruthless thug is showing no mercy and his cleansing of the kingdom has sent a chilling message to all those that would consider challenging his rule over Pathylon's mainland regions," retorted the angry monarch. "However, he underestimates my resolve and I will do everything within my power to remove that heartless Hartopian and his sorceress Tree Elf traitor from the throne!" Luccese was frustrated at the amount of time he was spending on the remote island of Freytor and that Varuna had been allowed to take a secure hold over Pathylon. Unbeknown to the true King, his senior aides were still busy planning to bolster the offensive lines on the floor below.

Back in the General's office, Eidar and Meltor were putting their final touches to the battle plan to regain control of Pathylon. An orchestrated attack on Varuna's army of Tree Elves and Hartopians looked possible just as soon as the super fleet of ice-vessels were ready to set sail.

"Turpol should have arrived in Krogonia by now," assumed the General, as he pointed to the map of Pathylon on his desk. "His first task will be to secure an alliance between the depleted armies of the Galetis Empire with the remaining Lizardmen and Devonian noblemen."

Meltor leant over the desk and pointed to the bridge that connected Krogonia with the mainland. "If I was in Varuna's shoes... I would blow the Satorc Bridge to pieces in order to isolate Krogonia and prevent any invasion across that route into Devonia - I suggest we anticipate this and inform Pavsik and Guan-yin to help the Gatekeeper to deploy some troops to the Flaclom Straits."

The General grunted and rubbed one of his huge paws across his beard. "Why do you suggest that we deploy troops to the south?"

Meltor pointed to the map of Pathylon and placed his ageing finger at the narrowest stretch of water that separated the Galetis Empire from Krogonia. "That's why, General!" he declared.

Eidar lifted his head with an open-jawed appreciation of High Priest's plan. He knew immediately what the Galetian was inferring and growled, as he thumped his white furry fist on the desk. "That's brilliant, Meltor... I see now why your King holds you in such high regard!"

"Then you obviously know what I'm referring to?" assumed Meltor, as he stood upright and stretched his aching back.

"Of course... you want to build another bridge - that is an excellent idea and Varuna will never suspect such a huge project to be completed in time to become a threat to him!" exclaimed the Freytorian. "Speaking of which, constructing such a large structure to support a charging army *will* take time *and* great strength... we must we get word to Turpol, Pavsik and Guan-yin immediately - they will need to instruct the Lizardmen to start gathering the heavy materials needed to support the bridge!"

Meltor suggested sending the last remaining Klomus Hawk to deliver the important message. "Ploom will get there quicker than any ice-ship... but we will have to inform Luccese of our plans - the royal bird belongs to the King and if we don't let him know what we are doing and send Ploom without his authority, we could face a charge of treason!"

"You may face treason... but not I - I'm a Freytorian General and your King has no authority over me!" roared Eidar and thumped his fist on the desk again.

"Stop being so pompous and arrogant!" replied Meltor and reasoned with the angry ice-bear. "Your rank or creed doesn't come into this... we have to work together to save Pathylon!"

General Eidar did not reply and calmed his demeanor immediately, as he raised his furrowed brow. He nodded and reluctantly agreed, as they concluded the meeting by arranging a time to meet with King Luccese to inform him of their plans. Before they departed the General's office the Galetian High Priest reminded the Freytorian about his previous suggestion. "Let's not forget about our potential allies in Rekab... I'll need to make arrangements to travel across the Red Ocean to meet with them."

The General had calmed down by now and he acknowledged Meltor's request. "Yes of course... I'll speak with my most experienced sea captain and arrange an ice-ship to transport you," assured Eidar. "Hopefully, by the time we next meet with King Luccese... you will feel well enough to travel to Rekab and seek out the reinforcements we need."

The two strategists were of the same opinion that the Black Squirrels, as well as a reclusive clan of Wood Ogres that frequented Yeldarb Forest could play a vital role in reclaiming the mainland of Pathylon from Varuna's illegal hold.

Meltor made his way over to the door and turned to face the General, who had now relaxed enough to light a large cigar and he was leaning back heavily in his leather chair. The High Priest hesitated for a moment and then spoke quietly. "If all else fails... we do have another call we can make."

"What would that be, Meltor?" asked the General, as he held the flame in front of the cigar to bolster the embers at the end of the curled brown tobacco leaves. He sucked the tab aggressively, as swirls of smoke escaped from his snout and created a series of thin parallel wisps above his head.

"Well, I'd like to make it clear that this would be a final resort and only if it looked like our attack was about to fail... but we could summon Bradley Baker from the outside world - *the eternal chosen one* has the power to help us destroy Varuna!" declared Meltor.

The General shrugged his shoulders, as he stubbed the cigar butt into an ice-glass ashtray on his desktop and confidently rebuked the Galetian's suggestion. "Let's not be too defeatist... like you said - that would be our last resort and I don't think we're going to need the *new boy hero* to help us this time!" retorted the agitated ice-bear. "It's not as if we have a giant ice-cloud hovering in the sky or an evil curse being cast over your arcane kingdom!"

Meltor smiled. "I guess you're right... anyhow, you've got some nerve mentioning evil curses!"

The General roared a short burst of laughter in an agreeing tone. "Yes, you do have a point, my friend... and that certainly won't happen again - you have my word!" he declared and then shocked the Galetian by mentioning something that Turpol had told him before departing for Krogonia. "It's weird that you should speak of Bradley Baker though... it so happens that the dwarf said that the boy would be making a return to our world very soon - for quite a different reason!"

"What did Turpol say?" asked Meltor in an excited tone, as he approached the desk and placed his bony knuckles on the thick slab of blue ice.

"To be fair, I wasn't really taking much notice... but I did overhear the little Gatekeeper talking to Luccese about some kind of transformation that is taking place inside the boy?" the General explained. "Probably best if you speak with your

King about it when we see him later... I'm sure it's nothing too serious!"

Meltor nodded and pinched his furrowed brow, as he walked back towards the office door. "Hopefully you're right... but for Bradley to even contemplate returning to Pathylon without my knowledge must mean there is something seriously wrong."

Eidar could see the Galetian was looking very concerned but did not comment further on the matter. He decided to change the subject with a brief reminiscence of their previous encounters with Varuna. Meltor's eyes looked glazed and the General sensed that his thoughts were very much elsewhere. The Freytorian cleared his throat. "Er'hermmm, right then... let's wrap things up here - I think we're just about done!" he concluded, as Meltor mustered a raw smile and they finally agreed to meet later to inform Luccese of their plans.

8

A New Adventure

Meanwhile back in Ravenswood, Bradley Baker was sitting in front of a blank computer screen in his bedroom. He was waiting patiently for the hard drive to power up and his eyes sparkled with excitement, as the desktop containing a number of familiar icons burst into life. He placed his hand nervously on the wireless mouse and took a deep breath before starting to navigate the cursor across the screen.

Bradley's parents had told him about the family's imminent move to Devon and he couldn't wait to email his friends in Sandmouth to inform them of the exciting news about the hotel purchase. "Muzzy and Sereny won't believe me!" he exclaimed out loud, as the internet icon appeared on the monitor. He positioned the curser arrow over the *Firefox* logo and clicked the left mouse button. "I'm so glad I set up a *hotmail* account on here," he professed, as he typed in his username and password. "Since I lost my mobile phone in the ice-cloud… it's been a real pain picking up my messages quickly - still, it was worth it in the end and I wouldn't have missed that particular adventure for the world!"

Bradley accessed his inbox and then opened a new email, as he started to type Musgrove's address into the space provided; *muzzythesurfingdude@live.co.uk*. He copied Sereny into the message and then thought for a few seconds before typing the subject heading. "What shall I put?" He pondered and then smiled, as he continued to type and talk out loud. "This should get their attention... *a new adventure*!"

In Sandmouth, Musgrove Chilcott lay on his bed complete with latest *'must-have'* headphones parting his long blonde hair. They snuggled tightly around his ears and the teenager was totally oblivious to the world around him. The gangly boy had his customary shades hooked into his hairline and was listening to a *Jack Johnson* music compilation that he had just downloaded online.

Musgrove's computer was still connected to the internet and his attention was aroused by an orange-coloured square icon flashing on the bottom task bar. "I've got mail!" he shouted and instinctively sat up, as he launched himself off the bed. The athletic boy landed perfectly in the seat of his computer chair and he pushed his foot against the desk. The chair swivelled round in a three hundred and sixty degree circle, as he confidently tapped the keyboard on returning to a forward seating position. His mail homepage opened up onto the huge wide-screen TV and the pitch of Musgrove's voice heightened, as he cried out in an excited tone. "It's from Brad... *a new adventure* - what's all this about!" he exclaimed and opened the message, as he read it aloud in an excited tone;

To: muzzythesurfingdude@live.co.uk
Cc/Bcc: serenyugbrooke@aol.com
From: bradleybaker1@hotmail.co.uk
Subject: "A New Adventure"

....

Hi Muzzy and Sereny,

Hope you guys are ok. This is a quick message to let you know that I will be moving to Devon! Yep... you read it right! And you're not going to believe this... it's happened so quick, I'll be down at the weekend. Mum and Dad have only gone and bought a hotel. I've so much to tell you. I've got some sad news about K2 though... he's been killed and you're not going to believe what happened. Everyone's still shaken up about it but I have some exciting news to tell you both. Anyhow, I'll be arriving in Sandmouth on Saturday afternoon so make sure you're both around... looks like we're going on another adventure! Tell you all about it when I see you.
Bradley :)

p.s. I've got a new facebook page... it would be great if you checked it out and "liked" it... here's the link;
http://www.facebook.com/thebradleybaker

Musgrove sat back in his chair and thought hard for a moment. He tried to absorb the contents and context of Bradley's message. He felt a strange sadness for the loss of K2 and was eager to learn more about the dog's death. Then the realization that the eternal chosen one would be moving to Sandmouth permanently inspired him to fling his arms upwards, as he punched the air with both fists. "Wicked!" he exclaimed in a gleeful tone, as he reached over to pick up his mobile phone. "That's awesome... Bradley Baker is moving

70

down here - I must call Sereny to see if she's picked up the message!"

Sereny was brushing her teeth and heard the faint ring tone that replicated a hit song from her favourite boy band. She quickly rinsed her mouth and rushed into her bedroom to search for her mobile, as a muffled soundtrack rang out from beneath the unmade bed sheets.

The frustrated girl was expecting a call from Jules. Simon's girlfriend had agreed to meet her in Sandmouth town centre to enjoy some last minute Christmas Shopping. Sereny had an eye for the perfect gift and she was looking forward to helping Jules pick out something nice for Musgrove's older brother. "There you are!" she exclaimed, as she pulled back the quilt to reveal the phone's flashing screen. "Oh... it's not Jules - it's Muzzy!"

Sereny answered the call and listened intently to what the excited teenager on the other end of the phone had to say. Musgrove informed her about the email and they agreed to meet in town later. "That's really sad news about K2... Bradley must be going through hell!" she declared and wiped a stray tear from her cheek. "Still it's brilliant news that he's going to be living in Sandmouth... any idea which hotel his Mum and Dad have bought?"

Muzzy replied. "Not sure... the hotel at the bottom of the sea road leading down to Amley's Cove has been on the market for a while - it might be that one."

Sereny instinctively nodded. "Yeah, come to think of it there is a sold sign on the for sale board... wow, that would be great if they've bought the Haytor Hotel - it's so close to the sea and Bradley will love it there, especially being so near to Amley's Cove!" she exclaimed and then remembered

71

her meeting with Jules. "Hey, listen we're just speculating... and I've got to get ready to do some shopping in town, so why don't we meet at Costa inside the HMV store - let's say three o'clock so we can talk more then?"

They agreed to meet at the designated coffee house and the conversation ended, as Sereny placed her phone down gently. She felt her face glowing and a strange rush of adrenalin filled her body. The thought of Bradley Baker living so close made her feel quite nervous. She would find it even more difficult to hide her feelings for the eternal chosen one, especially as they would both be attending the same school in Sandmouth and most probably sharing some of the same classes.

Back in Ravenswood, Bradley was unaware of his two friends' subjective conversation and he waited patiently in front of his computer screen for a reply email from either Musgrove or Sereny. At that moment, a short bleep sounded out from the speakers to indicate that he had incoming mail. He clicked the mouse to open the inbox, as the message from Musgrove sat highlighted in bold text waiting to be opened. "Yes... it's from Muzzy!" he exclaimed and his finger twitched nervously, as he hovered the curser arrow over the message. Bradley took a deep breath before clicking on the item. He quickly scanned the contents and then composed himself to read it slowly with anticipated excitement;

To: bradleybaker1@hotmail.co.uk
Cc/Bcc: serenyugbrooke@aol.com
From: muzzythesurfingdude@live.co.uk
Subject: "A New Adventure"

....

Hey Brad, sorry to hear about K2... that really sucks dude! But it's fantastic news that you're coming down here to live, mate! Just spoken to Sereny and she's really excited too. We're meeting in town later for a coffee and a chat. We'll get ourselves prepared for another adventure just in case we have to act fast when you arrive! lol... Can't wait to see you again buddy! :) When you travel down on Saturday, give me a call (damn you can't cos you lost your phone in Pathylon) ahh... just use your Mum's phone when you're getting near to Sandmouth, I'm sure she won't mind! lol. Be sure to call me! Hope everything goes ok with K2 and all that before you leave Ravenswood. See you at the weekend... can't wait! Muzzy ;-)

Bradley smiled, as he printed off the email and then directed the curser to close all the windows before shutting down the computer. He appreciated Musgrove's comments about K2 and he wiped away a few more tears before leaving the confines of his bedroom. He rushed onto the landing and made his way hurriedly downstairs, as he jumped the last few steps.

The excited boy turned so fast that he failed to notice his father, who was standing in the hallway that led to the kitchen. Patrick held out his arm to stop his enthusiastic son in his tracks. "Hey... slow down sunshine - what's the rush?"

"Oh, err, hi Dad... sorry – I didn't see you there!" replied Bradley, as he hooked into his father's arm lock. "I've got to get some things together... I want to make sure I don't forget anything for the journey to Sandmouth!" he expressed, as he released his arm and pushed passed his amused father.

Patrick was pleased to see a positive spring in Bradley's step. The death of K2 had created a traumatic atmosphere within the household but it was good to witness an enthusiastic mood return to his son's demeanor. "You okay, Son?"

Bradley reached the kitchen doorway and turned to acknowledge Patrick's concerned tone. "If you're referring to what happened to K2... then no - I'm not okay, Dad!" he replied and then cast a raw smile. "But I am okay that Uncle Henley will be here to make sure he is buried beneath the blue light before we travel down to Devon!"

Patrick shrugged his shoulders then sighed and nodded. "It's good of my brother to look after K2's burial... but I still don't understand why it has to wait until Saturday," he insisted. "We will be travelling to Devon straight afterwards... I thought you would want to bury him sooner and get used to the idea that he's gone – it would seem more logical to say your farewells to the old fella properly?"

Bradley paused before replying. He knew it was only a matter of time before someone questioned the reason for the delay in putting the family pet to rest. His father had now raised the question so he had to divert the topic of conversation away from the fact that it was due to the importance of a full moon appearing in the sky on Saturday evening. Grog's release depended on it and the quick-thinking boy retorted. "Well our neighbour Mrs. Knowles told Mum that the lady at the local council has approved K2's burial for Saturday!"

Patrick scrunched his face and afforded his son a puzzled look. "Thanks funny... you're Mum never mentioned anything!"

"She's probably too wrapped up in the move down south, Dad," replied Bradley and seized the opportunity to change the subject. "Must admit, I'm pretty excited about living in

Sandmouth... can't wait to see Muzzy and Sereny again - I've just emailed them and we're all going to meet as soon as we arrive on Saturday!"

"That's great news, Bradley... I'm relieved that you are happy with our decision to move to Devon - but what about all your school friends and teachers?" asked Patrick. "Aren't you going to miss them?"

Bradley aborted his dash to the kitchen and walked back towards his father. "It's not like I've been there that long... I only started at Maulby Grammar in September - I will miss Mr. Flowers the rugby coach though!"

"Yeah... he seems like a nice bloke and you have just secured the scrum half position - still, I'm sure Sandmouth has a school team you can play for!" assured Patrick.

"I'll check it out when we start the new term in January... I'll tell you one thing though, Dad - there's one person I won't miss!" exclaimed Bradley.

Patrick shrugged his shoulders and asked. "And who would that be?"

"One of the prop forwards... a thuggish idiot called Ethan Darke or *Ed-Case* as he's commonly known!" retorted Bradley and then laughed nervously. "He's been giving me some grief lately... I've handled him so far but I will be glad to get away from him!"

Patrick assumed an over-protective fatherly stance and adjusted his posture, as he pushed out his chest. "Glad to see you've been sticking up for yourself, Son!"

"No worries in that department, Dad... I can look after myself," replied Bradley with a confident repose and teased his father. "I'm the *eternal chosen one*... didn't you know?"

"Oh yeah... referring to one of your make-believe adventures again are you - thought you'd have grown out of those by now!" chuckled Patrick.

"Something like that!" replied Bradley and a smug smile broadened across his face, as he offered his father a cheeky wink of an eye.

Patrick afforded his son another puzzled look. "I do worry about what goes on in your head sometimes, Bradley... go on with you - carry on with what you were doing!"

Bradley turned away from his father and looked up to the ceiling, as he sighed and muttered to himself. "That was close... now, what was I doing?" he thought. "Ah, yes... Mum's mobile phone - I need to call Uncle Henley and speak to him about Saturday!"

9

The Emerald of Yeldarb

Meanwhile deep underground in Rekab, the Witch and the Shadow Druid had successfully negotiated the twisting tunnel that linked Hooked Point to the flowing sewers below Crystal City. They had safely dismounted from the primitive wagon and the old lady scooped up her nervous cat, as they made their way towards a large pair of oak doors.

The Witch placed the fidgeting feline on the floor and pulled out another smaller glass container from beneath her cape. She removed a cork bung from the neck of the jar and then revealed a small wooden bowl from a hidden pocket. "Here you are, my dearest Truffles... a nice tipple of Hoffen milk for my pretty little kitty."

The Shadow Druid groaned at the old hag's peculiar antics and rolled his dark eyes beneath his hooded robe. "Just how many glass jars and dishes have you got under that cloak of yours?" he quipped and continued his outburst before the Witch had a chance to reply. "Never mind... forget I even asked - I'm not really interested!" he retorted and quickly averted his attention away from the hag, as he lifted his head slightly to view the great ancient doors that stood tall and imposing. "This is the first time I have seen this entrance... I didn't even know it existed – do you know what lies behind them?" He asked, as the Witch finished pampering the cat and scurried over to where the dark figure stood.

"This is a very special entrance, my lord... and these doors will definitely look familiar to Bradley Baker - should he get this far that is!" revealed the Witch. "The boy hero will recognize their similarity to those that hang within the forbidden caves on the outskirts of Pathylon.... like them - a vortex lies waiting behind these great timber monuments to transport its passengers to the next leg of their journey!"

"Ah, yes... I remember you mentioning the vortex before – my head is still a bit fuzzy after that very uncomfortable ride in the coal wagon!" The Shadow Druid growled and then continued impatiently. "So tell me... how do we get through the doors and where will the vortex lead us?" he questioned and then held out his arms to push against the solid oak gateway.

The cat brushed up against the Shadow Druid's leg again and purred gently. The Witch picked up the empty bowl and wiped it with her thread-bare cardigan before placing it back beneath her cape. She tapped her pocket to celebrate the dish's safe return and then cackled, as the cat scratched at the doors. "Truffles will show you how to get through... go on fluffy-kins find the hidden stone!"

The hooded being grunted and moved his shaded eyes, as they followed the tiny footprints made by the cat in the dusty floor. Truffles walked casually over to a small mound of sand, which was illuminated by a burning torch that hung from the wall next to the great doors. The animal started to claw at the floor and the Shadow Druid calmly strode over to help the excited animal remove the remaining sand that covered a pyramid-shaped stone with an aluminum tip.

The Witch joined them and instructed the Shadow Druid to lift the metal top from ornate rock, as she cackled again. "This is the key to the vortex that will lead us straight to pyramids beyond Crystal City… the blood from the dead dwarf is waiting for us there and your future path lies beneath that stone!"

The Shadow Druid grunted in delight, as he started to lift the miniature prism. He emitted a more sinister growl, as he revealed a green sparkling gem on one side of the carved stone that glistened from the reflection of the burning light. "The *Sacred Emerald of Yeldarb*… so it does exist!" he exclaimed.

"Yes… of course - now press the gemstone into the side of the pyramid!" ordered the Witch, as she let out a continuous chortle of laughter that echoed around the cavern walls. "Your destiny awaits you, my dark lord!"

The Shadow Druid stared at the huge sparkling emerald and pushed down with both his shovel-like hands, as a stream of green coloured light began to appear around the circumference of the sacred stone. The aluminum tip glowed and the ground began to quake, as the haunted figure was sent flying backwards by the force generated from the sacred gemstone. An arc of lightning maintained a connection between his hands and the stone, as he travelled through the air. His back crashed against the side of the cavern. "Aaaaaaaaarrrrgghhhhh!" he groaned loudly, as he landed on his rear. He quickly regained his composure and watched in amazement, as another series of lightning strikes shot out from the centre of the emerald.

"Meeooooowwwwww!" shrieked the cat, as she jumped back into the protective arms of the Witch.

The excited sorceress retained a calm demeanor amid the chaos and stroked the trembling feline, as the parallel streams of energy blew her crooked hat from her head. She furrowed her crinkled brow to shield her black eyes from the powerful gusts of green strikes that twisted within the energy field. The hag shook her head to prevent her hair tangling around the cat's studded collar and she whispered gently in the terrified animal's ear. "Don't worry, my dear Truffles... it won't be long now!" she revealed, as the iron hinges that secured the huge oak doors started to creak.

The ground continued to shake, as the Shadow Druid steadied himself and got to his feet. The energy blast began to subside and he rubbed his sore behind. The dark stranger readjusted the lie of his heavy robes and stretched out his cloaked arms to maintain his balance, as he witnessed the enormous doors begin to move. Then suddenly the lightning flashes ceased, as the emerald gemstone stopped glowing and the doors scraped to a standstill leaving just a small gap to peer through. "Something's wrong!" he roared, as he tried to force his hooded head through the gap. "It's no good... the gap is too small - I can't get through!"

"Be patient, dark lord... the doors will continue to open when the time is right – we'll just have to sit and wait," replied the Witch, as she cushioned her skinny behind on a raised stone. The cat started to lick its paws and the hag called over to the intolerant warlock. "You may as well settle down for a while... I've got a feeling we are going to have to wait for the young Baker boy to make his appearance before the doors open fully!"

The Shadow Druid took another peek through the slight opening and noticed a dull glow behind the doors. "I think I can see the entrance to the vortex!" He exclaimed in a frustrating tone. "I can't believe we have to wait!" The Witch closed her eyes and ignored the dark figure, as he flicked back his robe and sat as far away from her as possible. The Shadow Druid accepted that he would have to delay his advance and he contemplated his first confrontation with the eternal chosen one. He rested his staff against the large oak door frame and pulled his hood forward to cover his whole face. He muttered a few choice words under his breath. "Bradley Baker... I hope you are ready to meet your end – the Shadow Druid waits for no-one!"

Back in Frey, King Luccese paced the full length of his royal quarters. "Where are they?" he fumed, as his tolerable wife prepared to leave the room. "Meltor told me that he and the General had something important to tell me... I can't abide lateness and they know it!"

"Please calm down, my dear Luccese... I am sure there is a valid reason – it's not normally like Meltor to be late for a meeting," reasoned Queen Vash, as she opened the door. "Especially with you... and speak of the devil - here they come now!" she exclaimed, as the two commanders fast approached along the icy corridor.

"Your majesty," bowed Meltor to acknowledge the Queen, as the General tipped the peak of his furry cap with his huge white paw.

"The King is waiting for you both inside... I'll leave you to calm his impatient disposition," smiled Vash and held the door ajar. "Good luck... I think you're going to need it!"

Meltor pushed open the door and looked embarrassed, as he entered the room followed by the Freytorian. The King was standing with his back to them leaning against the hearth, as the heat from the flames melted the edges of the icy mantelpiece. He turned round looking very exasperated and moved his royal eyes to stare at the clock. "I expected the meeting start five minutes ago!"

"That's my fault, my lord... I was feeling a little unwell and I..." reacted Meltor and was quickly interrupted by the unreasonable King.

"Meltor, please forgive me... I forget about your condition," apologized Luccese. "You rush around as though nothing has happened and I still expect you to jump through hoops!"

"Please, Sire... I understand your expectations – now, please if we may talk to about our plans to invade Pathylon and overthrow Varuna's illegal reign over your land," requested the Galetian, as the General remained silent.

The King was taken aback by his High Priest's assumptive manner. "Plans... what plans?"

Eidar broke his silence and assured Luccese that it was his idea to formulate the plan. "Your majesty, we knew you would feel aggrieved and I suppose slightly betrayed at the thought of Meltor and myself discussing some options to invade Pathylon... but I assure you Sire, we have done this in the best interests of both our lands!"

King Luccese sat his imposing frame down on a nearby settee and responded in an unexpected way. "Go on... enlighten me with your battle plans."

Eidar and Meltor looked at each other and wasted no time in informing the King that the new fleet of ice-submarines was just about ready to be put into service. They proceeded to tell the interested monarch about their idea to build a second bridge to join the southern part of Krogonia to the Galetis Empire and asked permission to send the last surviving Klomus Hawk to inform the allies.

Luccese rose to his feet again and nodded. "I am impressed… you have both formulated an excellent plan and I wish I had thought of it - we should act at once!" he responded and summoned a guard by ringing a small handheld bell.

A member of the royal entourage entered the room and stood to attention, as he waited for the King to offer his instruction. "My lord, you rang?"

"Yes… send word to the bird whistler in Tor and inform him that Ploom is needed again – I believe she is still in Devonia on a spying mission!" ordered Luccese. "It is imperative that the great bird travels to Krogonia upon her return… she has a very important task to fulfill - please ask the bird whistler to liaise with Meltor, when the Klomus Hawk arrives back in Freytor."

"At once, my lord!" replied the guard and left the royal quarters immediately.

"Thank you, Luccese," said Meltor. "And I have another request."

"What is it?" asked the King.

"I intend to journey down to Rekab to seek further help, my lord," suggested the Galetian.

"Help… from whom?" asked Luccese, as he moved over to the fireplace again and wiped a melting line of water droplets from the edge of the icy mantelpiece.

"I feel the Black Squirrels knowledge of the forest would come in very handy against the Tree Elves of Haldon!" replied the High Priest. "And it is quite possible that if I can persuade them to help... there is a good chance that the Wood Ogres will get involved too!"

King Luccese wiped his wet hand on his cloak and pondered for a few moments. "It's a very good suggestion... but do you feel well enough to travel to Rekab?"

"Yes, my lord... my new heart is growing stronger by the day and I am ready to make the arduous journey across the Red Ocean!" assured Meltor.

"Very well, but I insist you take General Eidar with you!" suggested Luccese. "In fact the Queen and I will travel with you as well!"

The Freytorian stepped forward and pleaded with the King. "But Sire... who will command the fleet of ice-submarines?"

"You will lead the fleet, General!" replied the King in a smug tone, as a confused look appeared across the ice-bear's face.

"And how do you expect me to be in two places at once?" replied Eidar, as he quipped sarcastically. "You must have forgotten, my lord... my twin brother is no longer with us!"

"Come now, General... I have not forgotten about your unfortunate loss – I simply suggest that we take the fleet with us to Rekab and then attack Pathylon from there!" suggested Luccese, as a broad smile replaced the scowled look on the ice-bear's face.

Meltor pitched in excitedly. "That's a brilliant idea, Sire... the distance across the ocean to the Galetis Empire is much shorter from Rekab – ingenious!"

"Thank you Meltor, but I suggest that we leave the southern route of attack via the Galetis Empire to Pavsik and Gun-yin... we can add an extra element of surprise by coordinating a sea-strike from the north by sailing around the top of Krogonia and invading Devonia from its eastern coastline – ice-submarines will afford us the speed we need to accomplish or goal," recommended the King.

General Eidar released a roar of laughter and placed his paws on his hips, as he stuck out his muscular chest. "And the goal is to get rid of Varuna?" he vowed. "Well gentlemen… I believe between us - we have formulated a brilliant battle plan to achieve that goal!"

The three orchestrators cheered and each held out an outstretched arm affront to invite a united act of agreement. They placed their strong palms one by one on top of each other's creating a heaped pile of unified strength, as Luccese landed the last decisive hand to issue a royal seal of approval. "Yes indeed… we have a great plan – now, let's get moving!"

They released their individual grips in one congratulatory upward motion and General Eidar was quick to head towards the door. The Freytorian held the door handle and then paused momentarily, as he turned to address his fellow comrades. "I will have the ice-fleet ready within two hours… then we will be able to set sail for Rekab immediately!"

The King acknowledged Eidar and the ice-bear closed the door behind him, whilst Meltor held his head low. Luccese approached his trusted friend and asked him what was wrong. "Are you feeling unwell again, Meltor?"

The High Priest delayed his reply at first and then finally explained his anguish to the concerned King. "No Sire, it's not that… I just wanted to ask you another question before I go – it's something the General mentioned when I met with him in his office earlier today."

"Go on, my friend," insisted Luccese. "Ask me the question and if I have the answer… I will deliver it to you truthfully – as I always do!"

"It concerns Bradley Baker!" replied Meltor. "Eidar mentioned something about the eternal chosen one returning to Pathylon because he has to… is this true, my lord – is there something I should know?"

The King turned away and held his horned forehead in one hand, as he rebuked the meddling Freytorian. "Damn… I wish Eidar hadn't mentioned this to you – I told him not to say anything until you had fully recovered from the heart surgery!"

"I am well enough, Sire… so it is true – Bradley Baker is coming back to our world!" confirmed Meltor.

"Yes… he is - but he's not returning to Pathylon," explained Luccese. "I am in no doubt that we will be meet our young friend again… very soon - when we visit Rekab!"

"Bradley is travelling to Rekab?" queried the puzzled Galetian. "But why Rekab and how do you know all these things?"

King Luccese asked the High Priest to sit down before he became too upset and he explained that Turpol the Gatekeeper had informed him about Bradley's predicament. "Apparently, the young boy hero became contaminated when he saved us all from the ice-cloud… the kratennium inside his body is transforming the boy into a Werebeast."

"And all this happened because I was lying in a health-pod in Frey Hospital… I wasn't there to help Bradley!" exclaimed Meltor, as he smashed his fist into his chest and then on the arm of the huge sofa. "I could have prevented this… if it wasn't for my stupid heart deciding to pack up on me!" raged the Galetian. "Poor Bradley… he must be going through hell right now!"

"You must not feel that way… and remember, Bradley isn't the only victim from the last battle to save Pathylon –

think of that precious heart beating inside your chest before you crash your angry fist of frustration onto your ribcage again!" sympathized Luccese. "Rathek's gift of life enabled you to face the difficult days ahead and as for Bradley... there was nothing you could have done to stop the infection taking over his body - Bradley did what he did because he is a true hero!" insisted the King. "That's why you entrusted him with the sacred grobite – now, I am confident that he will succeed in his task to find the antidote he needs to rid himself of the poison."

"You're right, my lord... I should be more appreciative of Rathek's kind offering that enabled me to live," agreed the humble Galetian, as he stroked his chest. "And I should also acknowledge that Bradley will always put others needs before his own in a selfless act of bravery... after all he is the eternal chosen one and he no longer needs my guidance - but where is the antidote and is there anything I can do to help him when we reach Rekab?" asked Meltor in a desperate tone.

The King informed his High Priest that Turpol knew the location of the antidote and suggested. "I will ask the bird whistler to tell Ploom to bring Turpol back with her... there's no reason why the dwarf can't join us in Rekab – Pavsik and Guan-yin are more than capable of leading the attack from Krogonia."

Meltor wiped a few stray tears away from his heavy eyelids and shook the Kings royal hand. "Thank you, Luccese... the dwarf's knowledge of the antidote's whereabouts should provide the young boy with the help he needs!"

Luccese nodded. "It's the least we can do for the eternal chosen one... let's just hope he finds the antidote in time!"

10
Laid to rest

Saturday had finally arrived in Ravenswood and the Baker's family estate car was packed to the brim with personal affects in readiness for the journey to Sandmouth. Bradley had managed to force an over-filled back pack into the rear compartment before his father slammed the door shut.

The car was overshadowed by a huge container lorry, which was parked parallel in front of the house and two removal men were carefully loading the last few items of furniture. One of the men approached Bradley's father, as Patrick took hold of a pen and signed the scruffy piece of paper presented to him. The transportation of the lorry's precious cargo had now been authorized and the shutters on the back of the vehicle were closed so the contents could start their long trip to a new destination in Devon.

There was one last task to complete before the family set off and Frannie ran over to a crowd of onlookers that had gathered around the cenotaph. Some of the neighbours on Braithwaite Road were helping Bradley's uncle dig the grave in readiness for K2's burial. Henley had travelled over from Sheffield to stay in the family home until the new tenants arrived later that evening. He would be handing over the keys to the house long after his brother's family had reached their new seaside home.

Frannie tapped her uncle on the shoulder and wiped away an icy tear, as the cold wind swept like a small tornado around the war memorial. Henley's coat was too thick and he did not respond to the delicate touch of his four year old niece, as he continued to drive the blade of his shovel into the hard ground. The persistent girl sniffed heavily and this time prodded him in the side of his face causing the startled grave digger to drop the shovel into the unearthed soil.

Bradley grasped the opportunity to help and rushed over to pick up the tool and started to dig while Henley tendered to Frannie's tears. "Now, now, little cherub... there's no need to cry - K2 is going to a really nice place," he reassured the girl and waved to her mother to come over. "Frannie's getting a bit upset, Margaret... it's to be expected though - it's a lot to take in for such a beautiful little girl," he explained and rubbed her button nose with the back of his gloved finger. Henley offered more words of comfort to benefit Margaret in her attempt to ebb the flow of tears that were now streaming down the red-head's face. "What with moving to a new home in Devon and losing K2... it's no surprise angel-face here is upset," he explained and hooked the back of his glove to catch a stray tear, as it ran down the girl's cheek. "Now, you have a good cuddle with your Mum while me and your brother get things ready for the old fella... we want to make sure he has the best send-off possible - don't we?"

Frannie responded by nodding with a slight reluctance to her uncle's reassuring words and the distraught girl pushed her face into Margaret's midriff. She held on tightly to her mother's slim waistline and continued to sniff into the soft woolen fabric of her jumper. Margaret's attention to her daughter's weeping was interrupted by the arrival of a familiar car and she called over to Bradley. "I think you have a visitor!" she shouted, as her son stopped digging and reluctantly handed the shovel back to Henley. "It looks like your friend Jefferson has come back to see you!"

The car stopped in front of the Baker's front garden and the passenger door swung open. Jefferson spoke a few words with his father before climbing out of the vehicle. Mr. Crabtree waved to Margaret and then wound his window down, as he started to drive slowly along the edge of the pavement. "Hello again… apologies for interrupting but it's been a bit manic at home this week and Jefferson was unable to speak with Bradley on the phone," he explained, as the car continued to move forward at a snail's pace. "So he asked if I'd drop him over… he wanted to say goodbye properly before you all head off on your new adventure to Devon!" he concluded and watched his son walk over to where Bradley was standing. "Hope you don't mind?"

Margaret held Frannie closer and replied. "Not at all, he's very welcome to stay with us for a little while... you've arrived at a pretty emotional time and I think Bradley will appreciate his friend being here."

"What's wrong?" asked Mr. Crabtree and stopped the car from moving forward.

Margaret looked down at the top of Frannie's head and stroked her hair, as she explained to Jefferson's father that they were just preparing to bury K2 under the blue light before they headed off to Sandmouth. "Not sure if Marian had said anything to you... when I met her for a coffee yesterday - I did mention to her that we were laying K2 to rest today."

"No... she never said anything - but to be fair, we've been like passing ships in the night recently!" explained Jefferson's father, as the vehicle started to hedge forward again.

Margaret could feel herself turning with the car's forward movement and adjusted her stance, as she cupped her hand under Frannie's chin. She attempted to make it clear that it was time to end the conversation, as she knew that Mr. Crabtree would keep her talking all day if he could. "Frannie's getting a little upset, so we're just going back inside the house to get a few of K2's toys... aren't we Frannie?" She insisted and turned her cupped fingers to caress her daughter's cheeky face.

The little girl lifted her head and afforded Mr. Crabtree a shy glance then pulled her arms tighter around Margaret's waist, as she looked up at her mother's caring smile. Frannie nodded and acknowledged the obvious sign to make a move, as she started to steer her mother's body in the direction of the house. Margaret reacted by reciprocating her daughter's intention and instinctively raised her arm to wave.

Mr. Crabtree lifted his foot off the brake and allowed the car to move freely, as he winked at Margaret to acknowledge the situation. "I'll let you guys get on with it... you sure it's okay for Jefferson to stay?"

"Absolutely," insisted Margaret, as she continued to wave like a contestant at the end of a TV game show.

"Okay then... I'll pick him up in about an hour?" he procrastinated and waved to his son, as he carefully pulled away from the pavement's edge.

Margaret sighed with relief and ushered Frannie away from the graveside, as they disappeared into the house to find K2's favourite toys.

Jefferson was left alone with Bradley and he waved to his father, as the car headed back down Braithwaite Road. Henley climbed down into the newly dug grave and planted the shovel firmly into the ground. He finished scooping out the last few loose bits of soil and asked Bradley to pass him the wooden box that he had constructed earlier. Jefferson offered to help. "That looks quite heavy... let me give you a hand."

Bradley smiled and welcomed his friend's assistance. "You've made a really good job of this, Uncle Henley... K2 is really going to like it - he would have been very proud!" commended Bradley, as the two boys picked up the box and carefully eased it over the edge of the grave side.

Patrick was standing in the front doorway of the house and shouted over to Henley. "Can you give me a hand, bro!"

Henley finished positioning the makeshift coffin in the grave and levelled it out by pushing soil under the corners of the box. "I guess it's time!"

Bradley and Jefferson held out their hands simultaneously and helped Henley out of the hole. Bradley smiled at his uncle and they all walked back towards the house. As they approached, Patrick patted his son's shoulder and acknowledged his friend's arrival. "Thanks for coming over, Jefferson... it's good to see you," he sighed and instructed them to follow him into the conservatory. "Let's go and get the dear fella... he's quite heavy so it's definitely going to take all four of us to lift him!"

Margaret had found some suitable items to offer the family pet and she stood with Frannie in front of the cenotaph, as the cold air bit into their faces. The front door of the Baker household opened. A large crowd had gathered to pay their respects and a selection of the neighbourhood looked on forlornly, as the four bearers appeared from the house. A blanket covered the body of K2, as he rested peacefully on their shoulders and just a single limp paw could be seen hanging down from the protective covering.

Henley, Patrick and Jefferson crouched awkwardly to counter Bradley's lack of height, as they walked across the front lawn. The fresh fall of snow crunched beneath their feet and the three taller males looked uncomfortable, as they made their way towards the war memorial.

Bradley's neck cushioned K2's heavy head and he could feel the dog's jowls moving under the soft cloth, as they strode carefully across the slushy road. The boy whispered into the tartan printed blanket and aimed his message into K2's ear. "Nearly there, old boy... you'll soon be on your way into the vortex and I really hope one day you'll return to me – as you promised."

Patrick looked down and followed his son's footsteps, as he concentrated his efforts on maintaining a steady balance on the ice-covered Tarmac. He thought he heard Bradley talking and tapped his shoulder. "You okay, Son?" he asked in a sincere tone. "Did you say something?"

Bradley sighed and replied politely. "Yeah, I'm fine... just wishing K2 a good journey - that's all."

"Journey?" questioned his father. "What journey?"

"To heaven… where else?" exclaimed Bradley.

"Oh yes... of course - sorry, Son," replied Patrick and at last they reached the crowd of mourners who had gathered around the war memorial.

Bradley looked up at the blue glass housing atop the cenotaph and crooked his neck to catch his uncle's attention, as they lowered K2's body to the ground next to the open grave. Henley offered his nephew a reassuring smile and raised his brow, as a faint cry from Frannie echoed in the still air causing a fresh mumbling of concern amongst the crowd. Henley acknowledged the boy's look and he knew why Bradley was looking at the lamp. He leant over and spoke quietly to his anxious nephew. "When we lay K2 to rest, the blue light should flicker... this will indicate that his soul is safely on its way to the Vortex of Silvermoor."

"Then what?" asked Bradley.

Henley whispered. "We will have to wait a little while to be sure that his soul has reached the vortex... by the time you are in the car and ready to set off for Devon - we should know."

"How will we know?" insisted Bradley in a frustrated tone.

"Calm down... be cool - your Dad is watching," replied Henley. "You will know... trust me!"

Patrick looked on, as Bradley and his brother parted their heads. "Everything alright, you two?"

Henley responded. "No probs, Bro... Bradley and I were just debating which side to lift K2."

"Oh, okay... well I guess we better get on with it - everyone's getting cold," replied Patrick, as he bent down and patted the top of the blanket. "Time to send you on your way, old boy!"

Bradley felt a tear roll down his cheek and thought privately to himself. "Appropriate words, Dad... if only you knew where he was going."

Jefferson stood next to his friend and they both reached down and took hold of one corner of the blanket. Patrick and

Henley did the same and together the four of them lifted the heavy bundle over the top of the hole. Frannie let out a high-pitched scream, as K2 was lowered into the handmade box positioned in the grave.

Margaret pulled her daughter close and gently protected her face from the cold breeze, as tears welled up in her eyes too. She fought through her own emotion and selflessly managed to offer some words of comfort to the distraught little girl. "K2 is going to a very special place, my darling... now be strong and think of all the funny things he used to do - think of the time he stole Bradley's birthday cake and ran round the garden with it in his mouth."

Frannie responded with a forced smile, as she wiped her running nose with the back of her sleeve. An image conjured in her mind and the sight of the clumsy Burnese Mountain Dog bounding around the ornate pond with butter cream all over his slobbering chops made her smile even more. She looked up at her mother and they hugged each other even tighter, as K2 disappeared into the ground.

Patrick asked Frannie if she would like to say anything and his daughter just shook her head, as she threw one of K2's favourite chew-toys into the grave. The bone-shaped object squeaked, as it hit the blanket and she turned back into her mother's arms to seek more consolation.

Margaret held out K2's collar and lead, as Patrick calmly reached out to retrieve them and immediately held them to his nose. He smelt the worn leather, which afforded a distinct reminder of just how much the canine's odour dominated the scene of remembrance. He muttered a few words and threw them into the hole, as he looked over to his son for his parting contribution.

Bradley responded by reaching into his pocket. Everyone watched in anticipation, as he pulled out a small plastic figure. Unbeknown to everyone except his uncle, it was the green toy soldier that had journeyed into Pathylon on his first adventure down the plug hole. He threw the World War Two American Infantry captain into the hole and it landed on top of the blanket that shielded the dog's head. The brave boy held back his tears and croaked his final farewell, as the binoculars moulded into the plastic figure's face peered up at him. "The soldier will help to protect you during your brave journey... take care K2 - I hope you reach your intended destination!"

Patrick did not question his son's passing comment and simply afforded him yet another perplexed look. Bradley's father picked up the shovel and handed it to Henley. "Would you mind looking after things while I get the family ready to leave?"

"Yeah... you lot go ahead and get yourselves sorted - you've got a long journey ahead of you," replied Henley, as the crowd began to disperse. "I'll wrap things up here and make sure the old fella is covered up okay!"

Patrick thanked his brother and led Margaret and the children back towards the house.

Bradley turned to Henley and drew a blank expression across his face, as he mouthed the question he had asked his uncle earlier. "How will we know?"

Henley wrested his chest on the handle of the shovel, as the blade carved a parallel line in the frozen ground. He winked at his nephew and mouthed back in silence. "Be patient!"

Bradley nodded and shrugged his shoulders, as he turned to continue his walk back towards the front garden. Jefferson appeared at his side and thanked his friend for allowing him to attend the funeral. Bradley smiled and invited his fellow rugby team player into the house. "Your Dad will be here soon... you can wait inside if you like - it's far too cold to stay out here."

"That's good of you," thanked Jefferson and could not resist enquiring about Bradley's comment at the grave side. "If you don't mind me asking... what did you mean back there when you said to K2 - I hope you reach your intended destination!"

"It's complicated, mate!" reacted Bradley in a defensive tone. "There's no time to explain now... I have to get ready to leave - anyhow, you probably wouldn't believe me even if I did have time to tell you the whole story."

Jefferson stoked up a broad New York accent and promised not to tell anyone if Bradley gave him a brief explanation. "Now I'm intrigued, dude... you can't leave for Devon without telling me what's just gone on!"

"Shusssshhhhh!" insisted Bradley. "Keep your voice down."

Jefferson looked over to Bradley's parents, who were busy tending to Frannie and making their way into the house. The American boy apologized. "Sorry, Bradley... your Mum and Dad didn't hear me, so come on - give me something to chew on once you've gone!"

Bradley sighed and stopped, as they reached the path that led to the front door. He turned to face his inquisitive friend. "Look, it really isn't that simple... I'll tell you mor..."

Jefferson interrupted. "No kidding... I agree with that much buddy - has this something to do with your little fracas in the shower block with Ethan Darke?"

Bradley rolled his eyes and replied tentatively. "Sort of... now listen, I promise I'll tell you more when I get down to

Sandmouth - I've arranged a meeting with my friends as soon as I arrive," he explained. "Once I've made some important arrangements and sorted out a few things... I'll give you a call and I will explain everything - arrrrrghhhh!" he cried and bent forward, as he held his stomach.

"Bradley... are you okay - what's wrong?" asked Jefferson in a concerned tone, as he helped his troubled friend along the path.

Bradley straightened his body and coughed a few times, as the cold air misted from his mouth to exaggerate the depth of his breathing. "It's the reason I need to get down to Sandmouth... and as I said, I promise to tell you everything - trust me!"

Jefferson hesitantly agreed, as the two boys shook hands and entered the warm hallway inside the house. He had just noticed a slight change in his friend's appearance and he was now even more intrigued.

Bradley made his way into the kitchen, as Jefferson cautiously stopped at the bottom of the stairs and held onto the bathroom door handle. He waited till his friend was out of sight and then contemplated his next move. He was not prepared to give up that easily and was determined to find out why Bradley had acted so weirdly at the graveside.

There was a sudden bang, as Margaret appeared from the lounge and accidentally slammed the door behind her. "Oops!" she exclaimed. "I must close some windows... there seems to be a draft coming from somewhere." She noted and looked at her son's friend standing awkwardly outside the toilet door. Jefferson had a forlorn expression on his face and she asked. "Are you alright... you seem to have a bit of a lost look about you – where is Bradley?"

The startled boy stuttered. "Oh, err... he's just gone into the kitchen, Mrs. Baker," he replied and excused himself, as he pulled on the handle and entered the under stairs bathroom. Jefferson could hear Margaret's feet climbing the stairs above his head and then caught his reflection in the mirror. He stared deep into his own dark brown eyes, as he muttered a comment with reference to his friend's unusual behaviour. "You're up to something, Bradley Baker... and I'm going to find out what it is!"

11
The New Queen of Pathylon

Back in Trad, Varuna paced back and forth across the ballroom inside the royal palace. The weasel-like Hartopian was dressed in full regalia and waited impatiently for his new queen to arrive. He adjusted the afresh Pathylian crown that adorned his puny head and looked around at the strident assembly of seated onlookers in the galleries.

The reluctant addressees were ordered to gather for the inaugural ceremony, which had been hastily arranged to join Varuna and Flaglan together in matrimony. The occasion would also affirm the pair of rebel's unlawful claim to the throne, as King and Queen in the absence of Luccese and Vash.

Varuna stopped pacing and tossed back his purple velvet robe, as he stared arrogantly at the audience of witnesses. The viewing gallery above the main hall was mainly made up of senior Tree Elves and fellow Hartopians. There was an obvious non-attendance of Devonian noblemen. Most of them had fled to Krogonia and those that had been captured were deliberately kept away from the proceedings. Varuna ordered their absence as a precautionary measure just in case they were to perform an embarrassing display of incompliance. He secretly feared the Devonians would rebel against him during the inauguration process and the Hartopian was not prepared to take the risk, as he addressed those present. "Thank you for attending, my people... it will not be long now and I will be crowned as your King!"

The crowds murmured quietly in reply but were soon enthused into rapturous applause, as a scruffy clothed and hunched-backed creature threatened them with his raised sword. "Cheer for your new leader... you rabble of low-lifers!" instructed Ulan-dem, the newly appointed High Priest for the Blacklands.

The intimidating Hartopian had also been invited and Varuna approached the uncouth military veteran, as he devoured the remains of freshly caught flax. "I see you haven't lost any of your charming appeal!" He quipped sarcastically.

Ulan-dem wiped his long-whiskered snout and exhibited a decayed set of yellow teeth that still bore remnants of the shredded flesh from the blood-stained flax carcass. "Don't mock me, Varuna... if you showed a fraction of the fear I instill in people - you wouldn't have lost control of Pathylon the last time you tried to knock Luccese off his perch!"

Varuna frowned and held on to the greasy fur waistcoat that adorned the uncouth creature, as he pulled his fellow Hartopian towards him. He whispered aggressively in Ulan-dem's pointy ear. "Keep your voice down, you idiot... and don't get too cocky - I dragged you out of retirement to lead the Blacklands populous and not to insult me in front of my guests you insolent weasel."

Ulan-dem snarled and pushed Varuna's paw away, as he stared at the shiny hook attached to the end of his other arm. "Calm down, Varuna... all this King and slushy Queen stuff is going to your head - just remember who I am and don't insult me like that again!"

"Or what?" retaliated the disgruntled monarch-to-be, as he nestled the sharp tip of the curved metal peg between the brow of the Hartopian's eyes.

The position of the hook caused Ulan-dem's eyes to cross, as he stared inward at the intimidating hand-weapon. "Or, I'll remove that hook of yours and shove it so far up you're..."

Before the veteran lieutenant could finish his derogatory remark, a palace servant interrupted the irate confrontation. "My lord... I don't mean to disturb you – but your future Queen is waiting outside in the foyer."

Varuna was keen not to upset Flaglan and he acknowledged the servant by pulling his hooked limb away, as he cast his fellow Hartopian a wrathful look. "We'll finish our conversation later, Ulan-dem... right now I have a beautiful enchantress to marry and a throne to sit on!"

Ulan-dem sniggered his retort, as Varuna turned and was led by the palace servant towards the two thrones that stood ornately on a raised platform at the end of the huge room. The crowd had witnessed the uncomfortable exchange of words between the two Hartopians and they continued to hum their disapproval, as Varuna took his place in the larger of the two chairs.

The mumbling ceased, as a fanfare of horns drowned out the disquiet and announced the arrival of Flaglan. She had been upstairs in the bed chamber dressing and preparing herself impeccably for the coronation ceremony. Her appearance was imminent and the large ballroom doors opened majestically, as the beautiful buxom Tree Elf entered the chamber. She moved elegantly with a drifting motion, as the base of her large domed dress hid her petite feet. The attractive sorceress continued to glide effortlessly across the floor to an appreciative welcome from the open-mouthed audience, as the outstretched arm of a palace aid supported her majestic pose. Beams of sunlight broke through the windows of the splendid ballroom and hit the sparkling jewels that twinkled in her small crown, as the resulting light reflected onto the walls like dancing stars.

Varuna was totally overwhelmed by Flaglan's beauty and he stood up from his throne to make his way down the few carpeted steps to greet his future queen. "You look stunning, my dear!"

The sorceress produced a bewitching smile and blinked her large green eyes, as she curtsied politely in front of her future husband. "Thank you, my lord... you are most kind."

Another fanfare of horns sounded out, as Flaglan placed her delicate hand on Varuna's good paw. They grinned simultaneously, as they both remembered a very different situation in the same ballroom when the Hartopian lost the end of his limb. The uncomfortable memory of the brief recollection was quickly dispersed, as Varuna displayed the hook and they walked carefully up the steps to take their positions on the lavishly decorated seats.

Flaglan sat on the wrong throne and a dull hum of gossip quickly spread through the crowd, as Varuna smiled and ignored the mistake. He was still overwhelmed by the stunning beauty of his bride-to-be and he made no reference to her unforced error, as the crowd settled down again.

The fanfare stopped, as Ulan-dem sniggered again and muttered to himself. "Varuna is such an idiot... I'll just need to bide my time - his own incompetence will be his downfall and then I'll simply pick up the Pathylian crown and his gorgeous Queen to boot!" he sniggered and tore his razor sharp teeth into the remains of the dead flax. Blood dripped down his hairy chin, as a sudden movement at one of the ballroom windows attracted his attention.

The Klomus Hawk peered through the multi-coloured glass and adjusted her position to achieve a better view. Ploom looked horrified to witness the joint coronation and wedding of Varuna in full flow. The disgusted bird looked around the room and his eyes caught sight of a piercing look from Ulan-dem.

The Hartopian pointed a blood-covered finger straight at the spying hawk. "Guards!" he shouted, as the proceedings came to a swift halt and the audience focused their attention on the ranting of the raging Blacklands leader. Ulan-dem threw the carcass on the floor and wiped his blood-stained paws on his worn tunic, as he struggled to climb onto the seat of his chair. The out-of-breath disrupter continued to point at the window, as the startled bird launched its six legs off the ledge. "Varuna... you are being spied on - that is a Klomus Hawk!" he declared, as the bird spanned her great wings and flew out of site.

Varuna lifted his paw from the back of Flaglan's slender hand and walked over to where Ulan-dem stood, as the Hartopian climbed awkwardly down from his lofty position. "What is the meaning of this?" he roared. "Why have you interrupted my coronation and wedding... just because some stupid bird looked through the window?"

Ulan-dem pressed his bloody snout against his fellow Hartopian's jaw and cast him an evil grin, as the foul stench of decay escaped through his smelly breath. The Blacklands leader snarled a cutting reply. "You're really stupid aren't you... do you not know what relevance the presence of the Klomus Hawk has on your continued reign over this kingdom?"

Varuna lifted his arm again in a threatening manner and placed his hooked limb hard against the side of Ulan-dem's face. "Do not speak to your new King with such distain... your insolence offends me!" he shouted and this time pressed the point of his hook into the trembling Hartopian's cheek.

"You haven't officially received your crown yet, Varuna... so that makes it difficult for you to be my King!" sniggered Ulan-dem, as Varuna frowned in response to his quip. "You've no idea why that bird was here... do you?"

Varuna responded by pushing Ulan-dem into the seat of his chair and pressed his knee into the Hartopian's chest, as he penetrated the point of the hook through his slobbering jowl. Blood started to flow from the open wound and Varuna asked the embarrassed lieutenant to address the crowd. "Now, I obviously do not know the relevance of the bird... so why don't you enlighten me and our wonderful audience!"

Flaglan approached and placed a gentle hold on Varuna's arm, as she smiled persuasively. "Remove your hook from the poor lieutenant, my dear... our friend here cannot speak while the metal at the end of your precious limb continues to penetrate his mouth."

There was a deathly silence in the huge ballroom, as Varuna heeded the sorceress and removed the hook from Ulan-dem's snout. "Well... stop looking at me like a deranged Wartpig and speak to our honoured guests - you insolent moron!" he demanded.

Ulan-dem cast Flaglan an admiring glance and smiled, as he turned to address the unsettled crowd. "That was Ploom...

the only surviving Klomus Hawk left in Pathylon – she was most certainly sent here to spy on our new beloved leader!" he roared, as he offered an open-handed gesture to Varuna. "The bird will now be on its speedy way back to whoever sent it… King Luccese I suspect!"

Varuna interjected. "Luccese no longer holds the title of King… I am to be crowned as your new King of Pathylon!" he boasted and held up the royal scepter. "Now forget about the hawk and let's finish the coronation… we have some serious celebrating to do and I'm ready to party through the night with my new bride!"

Flaglan approached the scruffy Hartopian and asked what relevance the Klomus Hawk's presence would have on the current situation. Ulan-dem pushed his smelly snout against the beautiful sorceress's face and gloated in her attention towards him. He spoke with a spine-tingling groan in his husky voice. "Your future husband does not take the bird's actions seriously… you on the other hand obviously feel threatened – that's bodes well for a future Queen."

"Get on with it Ulan-dem… what ramifications will come of this?" demanded Flaglan.

Varuna cast the curvaceous Tree Elf a disapproving look and moved over to separate the Hartopian from his bride. "What's going on, Flaglan?" he snarled, as he pushed Ulan-dem away. "Why are you fraternizing with this filthy heathen?"

"I'm trying to find out why the bird was spying on us… why aren't you taking this seriously, Varuna?" questioned the frustrated sorceress. "What happens if Luccese mounts an attack?"

The Hartopian flung his head back, as the crown slipped and crashed on the wooden boards. He started to laugh uncontrollably, as the gold head piece rolled across the ballroom towards the steps in front of the waiting thrones. "See how that crown rolls easily across the floor?" he asked, as Flaglan nodded ignorantly. "That's what our armies will do to Luccese if he dares to tread on Pathylian soil again... we will roll straight over him and crush his pathetic allies too – now, enough of this nonsense and lets finish the formalities!"

Varuna walked away and bent down to retrieve the crown, as Ulan-dem whispered in Flaglan's ear. "Don't say I didn't warn you, my pretty little Tree Elf."

The sorceress did not respond to the Hartopian's retort and rejoined Varuna to complete the coronation and wedding ceremony. The onlookers unwillingly applauded the confirmation of Varuna as their new King, as Ulan-dem starred out of the window at the fading silhouette of the Klomus Hawk. The bird sped away in the direction of the Red Ocean and the veteran Hartopian muttered to himself. "You have a long journey back to Freytor, Ploom... and I wonder how long it's going to take before your beloved owner makes his move – I just hope Luccese decides to bring his trusty sidekick along with him!" he sniggered. "I quite fancy giving the old Galetian a good beating... Meltor still blames Basjoo Ma-otz for the death of his beloved Granddaughter – wait till he finds out it was me who slaughtered her!"

It took the Klomus Hawk just thirty minutes to cross the Red Ocean and reach the capital of Freytor. Ploom had flown the fastest time ever recorded from Pathylon and she confidently landed her six legs on the harbour wall in Frey. King Luccese was there to meet the fatigued bird and she was handled carefully by the bird whistler, as he placed the huge hawk onto a waiting ice-cart.

The King walked by the side of the carriage, as Ploom rested her weary wings. "Are you okay to talk?"

"Certainly, Sire!" replied the exhausted bird, as Meltor and General Eidar approached the wagon. "I have lots to tell you!"

The ice-cart was pushed by the bird whistler towards the senate building and the Klomus Hawk talked continuously, as she informed them of what she had witnessed inside the royal palace. By the time they had reached the main entrance to the senate, King Luccese had all the essential information he needed to know about Varuna and his new bride.

Meltor asked Ploom how long she would need to recuperate from her long journey and then informed the bird that they required her to travel back to Pathylon. Ploom listened intently about the plans to build a new bridge across the Satorc Estuary from Krogonia to the Galetis Empire and she agreed to leave immediately. The High Priest was most impressed with the bird's stamina and he requested that she deliver Turpol straight to Rekab in time for their arrival.

"Why do you need me to deliver the dwarf to Rekab?" asked Ploom, as they entered the main reception hall of the senate building.

King Luccese intervened. "It relates to a situation involving Bradley Baker."

The Klomus Hawk jumped off the ice-cart and fluttered her wings. "Has the boy hero returned to our world?" she asked and exuded a very excited squawking sound, as she ruffled her feathers. "Has the eternal chosen one come back to save Pathylon again?"

General Eidar spoke sternly. "Calm down, hawk... no, he has not returned – but we think he is about to!"

"Why would he return so soon to our world again... is Bradley aware of your plans to build the bridge?" asked Ploom, as she afforded the uncouth General a displeased glare.

The King replied in a down beat tone. "No... the young hero is not aware of our battle plans - this time, I'm afraid the troubled boy is coming back for his own sake!" Declared Luccese and concluded. "Bradley Baker is returning to save his own life!"

12
The Beacon Shines

Back in Ravenswood, Bradley's parents busied themselves around the car in readiness for the start of their journey to Sandmouth. Jefferson had made a call earlier to be picked up and he had since offered his farewells and informed them that he preferred to meet his father at the entrance to the housing estate.

Margaret had just finished saying her goodbyes to a few of the neighbours, who had missed the burial ceremony earlier and they offered their condolences. They sensed that the stressed mother needed to tend her fidgeting daughter, who was now wrestling with the fastener on her pink hold-all in the back of the car. Margaret smiled politely, as the well-wishers departed gracefully and she popped her head through the window to make sure Frannie's seat belt was securely fastened. "Not be long now, sweetheart… just waiting for Daddy and Bradley."

Patrick was speaking with his brother and they discussed the arrangements for handing over of the house keys to the new tenants. Henley must have cracked a funny joke because their laughter echoed over to where Bradley was standing next to the cenotaph.

The boy smiled at the two male siblings, as they bantered and he then focused his attention on the wooden cross that his uncle had made from two pieces of architrave. The cross marked the spot where K2 had been laid to rest and Bradley knelt down to offer a final farewell. "We're going to be heading off in a few minutes," he said in a soft and caring tone, as he straightened the makeshift crucifix in the soil. "When I get to Sandmouth, I'll be going on another amazing adventure and I wish you were coming with me... you know why I have to return and I just hope I'm not too late!" he concluded and stared at the back of his hand. "It's starting again... I'd better go and find something to hide these hairs – now you take care, K2 and have a safe journey into the Vortex of Silvermoor!"

Bradley ran over to the car and lifted the boot lid. He pulled out his back pack and removed a pair of black woolen gloves. He quickly pulled one of the gloves over the affected hand and slammed the lid shut.

Margaret called over to her son in an inquisitive tone. "You okay, Bradley?" She enquired and noticed the boy dressing himself with the second glove. "Are you cold?"

"Err, yeah... s - something like that!" stuttered Bradley and climbed into the car to find his sister patiently waiting, as she played with her favourite doll. Bradley smiled at Frannie and held her hand, which was very uncustomary for him, as he tried to take his mind off the agonizing changes that were rushing through his body. "Here we go then... off to our new home in Devon - I bet you're excited aren't you?"

Frannie nodded and offered her older brother a look of surprise, as she stared at his hand resting on hers. "Err...hermmm!" she exclaimed, as the cheeky little girl cleared her throat. "Hands off, please!"

Bradley chuckled and pulled his aching arm away. "Sorry, Frannie... for a moment there I imagined I was an older brother who really cared about his little sister!"

Frannie scrunched up her freckled nose and chose to ignore Bradley's sarcastic quip, as she continued to play with her vampire-chick doll. Bradley smiled, as he allayed his attention away from his cheeky sister and looked over to the war memorial again. The boy focused on the blue light and he fell into a slight trance, as the departure procedures carried on around the car.

Patrick climbed into the driver's seat and the engine roared into life, as he turned the key in the ignition. Bradley's concentration was interrupted and his passenger window lowered without his interaction, as his father pushed a button on the dash board.

Bradley's view of the cenotaph was impeded by Henley's upper body, as he appeared at the window. The spellbound boy shook his head to clear his dazed condition, as his uncle leant into the vehicle. "Oh... hello… I wasn't expecting that!"

Henley released a short burst of laughter, as he reached out his hand to ruffle his nephew's hair and just missed touching his wolf-like ears. "Didn't mean to startle you... just wanted to say bye and to reassure you that things will be okay - take a look!"

Bradley corrected his hairstyle and looked beyond his uncle's head, as Henley moved to one side. The light at the top of the memorial had burst into life and the blue glow shone like a beacon of hope. The boy smiled and turned his attention to his uncle's smiling face. "Does that mean?"

"Yes!" replied Henley in an excited tone. "The old fella's made it... K2's soul has reached the vortex!"

"Brilliant!" exclaimed Bradley, as his mother got in the car and mumbled a few words to her husband.

Patrick replied. "Don't know what they're chatting about back there... something about the cenotaph and K2?"

Margaret looked over to the blue light that was still shining brightly, as the cold misty air enhanced its glow atop the memorial. "Look, Patrick... the light - it's come on!"

Bradley's father turned and looked out of his son's window. "That's strange... the light sensor must have broken!" he declared in a confident manner. "I'm sure the neighbours will call the council to sort it out... I may have maintained the blue light whilst I was an electrician at Silvermoor Colliery but it's not my job anymore - anyhow, we better get going!"

Henley gripped Bradley's shoulder and winked at his nephew, as he whispered. "Have a good trip to Sandmouth... and into Pathylon - looking at that gloved hand of yours, you need to act fast and you have to reach the chalice before the Shadow Druid gets his filthy mitts on you!"

Bradley nodded and held his affected hand again, as he squeezed his throbbing fingers through the glove. He offered his uncle a final look of reassurance. "I'll do my best... just make sure Grog gets out of that vortex - otherwise K2's death will have been in vain."

"I'll check it out as soon as you've gone," replied Henley, as Patrick grunted to indicate that it was time to leave. "Sorry Bro... I'm keeping you all waiting - better let you get off!"

Patrick displaced the handbrake and the car started to move away, as Bradley exhibited a thumbs up signal to his uncle.

Henley reciprocated and the car sped out of the estate to deliver the Baker family on their journey to a new life in Devon.

The car's brake lights shone brightly, as the vehicle stopped at the end of Braithwaite Road. There was a slight delay because of traffic and then the vehicle pulled out of the estate, as it disappeared from view. At that moment, the blue light distinguished and Henley made his way back into the house.

Bradley's uncle finished writing the letter he had started earlier and placed it in an envelope, which was addressed to his brother at the Haytor Hotel. He reached for his wallet and pulled out a booklet of first class stamps and peeled one away, as he placed it on the envelope. He attached a yellow post-it note asking the incoming tenants to kindly post the letter and then left the house. Henley locked the front door and put the keys in another brown envelope, as he carefully placed the package under the doormat.

Unbeknown to Henley, a figure had been watching proceedings for some time from behind the tall vent pipe at the end of the Baker's driveway. Bradley's uncle was unaware of the stranger's presence and he walked straight past the crouching body, as he made his way over to the war memorial.

K2's ghostly form had now fully entered the vortex below the cenotaph and at the same time Grog's mortal hand had successfully grabbed the release key, as the Krogon started to materialize from the abyss. The Lizardman opened his eyes and felt a warm grip around his webbed claw. A broad grin spread across his orange-coloured face, as he looked up and recognized the smiling face staring down at him. "Thank you, my dear friend... you kept your promise - you came back for me and I see you have your face back too!"

Henley laughed and pulled the giant reptile out of the hole, as they both stood for a few moments inside the small room beneath the cenotaph. Bradley's uncle removed his cap and scratched his fingers through his thinning hair. The two Devonian horns that adorned his head caught Grog's attention and Henley explained that he too originated from the arcane world of Pathylon. He also went on to explain about K2's death. "Bradley is pretty cut up about it but he will be pleased to hear that you have escaped the vortex safely!"

The Krogon sighed and offered his condolences. He then enquired after his young human friends. "How is Bradley... and of course, Sereny - I didn't get a chance to say hello to her when we passed in the vortex."

"Sereny didn't see you inside the time portal... however, she is aware that her actions released you from your crypt," explained Henley. "As for Bradley, he is in a bit of a bad way but he is really looking forward to seeing you again," he continued. "Hopefully, you'll get a chance to thank them both when you next see them - after all, if it wasn't for their joint efforts you wouldn't have been released from your tomb on the Flaclom Straits."

"What is wrong with Bradley?" asked the Krogon.

"He was contaminated with kratennium when he visited Pathylon last time... his body is transforming into a Werebeast!" replied Henley, as he went on to explain the boy's predicament.

Grog sighed and then offered an expression of regret, as he held his head low. "It's a shame I won't be able to thank K2 for his act of sacrifice... I will be indebted to him forever!"

Henley touched the Krogon's scaly arm and offered some supporting words of reassurance. "Don't worry about that... K2 is aware of your gratitude – anyhow, his death was pre-ordained and hopefully you may get an opportunity to thank him personally, should his soul escape the vortex someday," he explained. "For now... your strength and bravery is needed back in Krogonia to lead the depleted Lizardmen against Varuna's army - King Luccese will be glad of your help and you need to get back to Pathylon as soon as possible."

"I cannot wait to see my people again... its sounds like they are in serious trouble - I just hope it's not too late!" replied Grog, as he looked around the damp room. "So let's not waste any more time... show me how we get out of here!"

"Follow me, Grog!" instructed Henley, as he felt the sides of the wall for the secret lever. "Ah, here it is... now don't be alarmed but we have to go back into the vortex - Sereny took the same route when she discovered your tomb so hopefully it will lead us straight back to your crypt in Krogonia!"

Grog took a deep breath and looked down, as Henley pulled the lever. The Krogon cleared his throat and declared his fear with a sense of trepidation in his voice. "This feels weird... but if it's the only way back then I guess we'll have to take the risk – the future of Pathylon depends on it!"

The trap door opened and Henley placed his flat cap back on his head and then held out his hand in a polite gesture. "After you... Grog!"

The orange reptile stared into the swirling portal and hesitated for few seconds. He then gently lowered his bloated body and sat on the edge of the opening, as he shuffled his large bottom forward. Grog held on tentatively to the sides of the trap door and then declared his intention. "Here goes!" he shouted and launched his heavy frame into the centre of the hole. "Arrrrrrrrrrrrrrrrghhhhhhhhhh!" he yelled, as his fading cry disappeared into the abyss.

Henley quickly followed and managed to pull the trap door behind him, as the sound of wood crashing against the metal frame echoed into the void. Bradley's uncle could see Grog drifting aimlessly some fifty metres ahead, as he span out of control inside the tubular vortex. The fork in the time portal was around the next turn and the Krogon would have to make the crucial maneuver that would ensure the correct route was negotiated. Henley straightened his body and placed his arms by his side, as his streamlined form accelerated him to within a few metres of the disorientated Krogon. He held out his hand and grabbed the Lizardman's body armour to steady his trajectory. Within a few seconds they had both reached the fork and with a slight shift in body movement they were catapulted into the correct path that would take them to the Flaclom Straits.

Henley breathed a huge sigh of relief, as he looked over to Grog and smiled. "That was close!" he exclaimed and the two weary time travellers settled into a steady holding position, as they followed the colourful jet stream of energy that flowed through the vortex.

Unbeknown to Henley and Grog, the strange figure that had hidden behind the vent post outside Bradley's house was also inside the vortex. Jefferson Crabtree had not actually made the phone call to his father and instead he had doubled back around the housing estate to watch Bradley Baker's departure with interest. The inquisitive American boy was still intrigued about his friend's parting comments and he was determined to find out what was really going on.

As soon as Henley had disappeared through the doorway at the base of the old war memorial, Jefferson had made his way over and waited outside until the old mauled miner and the Lizardman had entered the vortex. He had then sneaked into the base of the cenotaph and managed to jump into the hole before the trap door had fully closed.

To add even more mystery to the proceedings, the boy was unaware that he had also been followed. The Shade Runner that struck the fatal blow to the deceased Burnese Mountain Dog had been spying on Jefferson. Even though the trap door had sealed the entrance to the vortex, the dark being had summoned the powers bestowed upon him by his master to locate the secret lever. The Shadow Druid's apprentice used this to great effect and he had also successfully entered the swirling abyss to pursue all three time travellers from a safe distance.

Jefferson was unaware of the evil that now followed him, as he concentrated all his efforts on maintaining his balance inside the time portal. He could just make out the Krogon and Bradley's uncle, as they successfully negotiated the fork in the vortex ahead. The boy muttered to himself, as he neared the junction. "I knew there was something weird about Bradley Baker and it looks like I'm going to find out what's going on pretty soon!"

Just then there was a loud bang and the vortex shuddered violently. Jefferson was thrown off course and his limp body was tossed around like a bouncing ball, as he ricocheted off the sides of the time portal. He yelled out for help, as the fork in the tubular cyclone appeared in front of him. "Oh no!" he shouted. "I'm going to be pulled the wrong way!"

Within seconds a cold hand grabbed his arm and pulled Jefferson back onto the correct trajectory, as the petrified boy stared into the faceless hood of a darkened leather cloak. The piercing red eyes of the Shade Runner narrowed, as the evil creature laughed in a haunting tone. "I have you at last!" he sneered, as Jefferson struggled to break free from the strong grip around his waist. The dark creature roared out another harrowing scream of laughter. "Struggle all you want, boy… you are staying with me and you're going to come in very useful when we reach the other side!"

Jefferson was powerless to resist the freezing grip of the Shade Runner's grasp and he mustered up enough courage to ask the strange being what he meant. "Where is this tunnel taking us and what are you going to do with me?"

"Silence, you pathetic mortal... Pathylon awaits us at the other end and as for you - you will be used as bait to lure the eternal chosen one!" replied the evil creature, as he grabbed Jefferson by the throat and pulled the frightened boy towards his muscular body. "I have already witnessed how Bradley Baker protected you... so it's quite probable he will do so again - but this time his act of chivalry will result in a slow and painful death!"

An uncomfortable realization struck Jefferson like a hard rugby tackle, as he stared into the hood of the strange being. "It can't be you... it's not possible!" he exclaimed, as he plucked up enough courage to reach up and pull on the creature's cloak.

"Hahahahahahahahaha!" The Shade Runner laughed again uncontrollably, as the vortex twisted and turned ahead. He ceased his evil cackle and insisted the boy continue to reveal his face by encouraging him to lift the hooded veil that disguised his true identity. "Go on then... satisfy your curiosity - uncover your worst nightmare if you dare!"

Jefferson's legs trembled and they splayed outwards, as the swirling vortex vibrated again. He clung on to the Shade Runner's cloak and hesitated for a few seconds, as the coiling flow of the portal twisted their bodies around in a circular motion. He waited until they levelled out again and then swallowed deeply, as he started to pull back the creature's hood. The Shade Runner released his grip on the boy's throat then grinned and his red eyes continued to glow, as Jefferson's jaw dropped. The boy from New York took an exaggerated intake of breath then exclaimed in his Hudson Valley accent. "Oh my god... no - not you again!"

The vibration inside the Vortex of Silvermoor had summoned Henley and Grog's curiosity. The overweight Krogon called over to his new friend. "I wonder what caused the portal to vibrate so fiercely."

Henley paused for a brief moment, as he concentrated on keeping his unsteady pose on a horizontal plain. "Not sure!" he replied and looked ahead. "Maybe we can discuss it when we get off this damn roller coaster!"

The two weary passengers were now approaching the exit from the time portal and they readied themselves to alight the vortex through the sparkling lights about twenty metres ahead. The two time travellers had been unaware of the activity that had previously played out some hundred metres and more behind them. Unbeknown to them, the vibration in the vortex had been caused by the additional personnel travelling with them and they were in for a shock, as Jefferson and the Shade Runner were now closing on them at a very fast pace.

The presence of evil inside the vortex radiated a cold gust of air that wafted over Grog's huge frame. The Krogon struggled to keep his balance, as he instinctively turned his broad head to look back down the spiraling tunnel. "Arrrrgggghhhhhh!" he exclaimed, as a sharp pain ran through the scar on the back of his neck.

"You okay, Grog?" called Henley.

"Yes, I'm fine... just an old wound providing me with a gentle reminder of why I ended up in this damn time-tunnel in the first place!" he replied. "Anyhow, never mind that... you'd better take a look behind us - we have company and it doesn't look very friendly!"

13

The First Supper

Meanwhile in Sandmouth, the journey to Devon had taken just over five hours and included two motorway service station breaks. The Baker family had just arrived in the seaside town and the car pulled on to the gravel car park that fronted the Haytor Hotel.

One of the passenger rear doors flung open, as soon as the car came to a halt. Bradley excused himself immediately and ran across the car park, as he made his way back out of the hotel's entrance. Margaret shouted after him. "Don't you even want to see what the house looks like inside?"

"Later, Mum… later – I have to meet Musgrove and Sereny in town – I'm late as it is!" replied the excited boy and he disappeared down the hill that led into the main shopping area of Sandmouth.

"But it's got a massive kitchen!" she replied sarcastically.

As expected, no reply came from her disinterested son and Margaret sighed, as she picked up her handbag from the front seat of the car. This prompted Frannie to get out of the vehicle and she ran over to the large open garden area, as Patrick lifted the boot lid and remarked. "I don't know what's got into him… he's been acting really strange since K2 died – I just hope the surprise we've arranged for him on Christmas day will be okay."

Margaret wrapped her slender arms around her husband's waist and made sure Bradley's little sister was out of earshot. "I think we've got Bradley the perfect Christmas present and I'm certain he will love it… now, let's get the suitcases inside – I can't wait to see what the hotel looks like before our Vera arrives!"

"Good idea," agreed Patrick, as he lifted the baggage out of the estate car. "We'd better make the most of our new found freedom before you sister gets here… still it's good of her to accommodate your Mum till she finds a new place – anyhow, what time does the kid's Grandma arrive?"

"Margaret checked her watch, as a slight breeze wafted through her long dark brown hair. "Brrrrrrr… it's getting quite cold!" She shivered and rubbed her hands up her arms. "Her train arrives in Sandmouth in an about an hour so we timed our journey perfectly… Vera has agreed to pick up her and the cat from the station so that means we can concentrate on unpacking – can you bring Mum's suitcase in first so I can put it somewhere safe for when she arrives later?"

"I forgot all about Sky… I hope she has travelled okay in her cat basket on the train!" responded Patrick, as he pulled out the largest suitcase and placed it on the gravel drive, as Frannie ran past to join her mother inside the hotel's front porch. He then quipped at his wife's request to carry in her mother's luggage. "No problem, dear… taxi driver, butler and general dogs-body - at your service!"

Margaret issued a quick retort to her husband's sarcastic remark and responded in a joking manner. "Oh, just get on with it Jeeves … it's too cold for me and Frannie out there – come on little lady let's check out that scrumptiously big commercial kitchen!"

The next hour soon passed and Vera's vintage Morris Minor pulled up outside the front door to the hotel. Frannie ran out to greet her aunt and Grandma, whilst her parents finished unpacking the remaining suitcases and carried the cat basket inside.

"Helloooooooooo my little lovely!" shrieked Aunt Vera, as the tubby woman afforded her niece a brief hug and then waddled into the hotel's reception hall in search of her younger sister. "Anybody home!" she shouted, as Frannie and Grandma Penworthy followed the eccentric woman down the hallway.

Frannie gave her grandmother a peck on the cheek and then went off to explore the ground floor of her new home. The four year old looked out of the bar lounge window and saw her brother walking across the car park with the two friends he had met in town earlier. "Bradley's back!" she shouted and disappeared into the adjacent dining room.

Bradley invited his two friends into the entrance hall of the Victorian villa. Musgrove and Sereny obliged and they made their way through the hallway into the bar lounge.

Sereny looked around and upwards, as she admired the white plaster-mouldings on the ceiling. "This is a lovely house, Bradley... you are so lucky to live here - a friend of my Mum's used to work here as a cleaner."

Bradley replied. "Thanks... I'm really looking forward to investigating the whole house – apparently it was built in the

1870's and there are lots of little rooms and cupboards to explore!"

"Why don't we start exploring the house now?" insisted Musgrove, as he reached up to retrieve a glass. He then pretended to draw a measure of whiskey from one of the optics, as Bradley and Sereny looked on.

"Don't let my Dad catch you doing that... anyhow, come away from the bar - you're not aloud near it because you're under-age," ordered Bradley, as Musgrove heeded his friend's advice and moved away from the counter. "Before we start exploring the hotel... I think we'd better check out the grobite - it's been vibrating on and off in my pocket all morning!"

Sereny squeaked a little cry of excitement, as she bounced on the edge of one of the leather lounge settees. "Brilliant... it must be time for us to go on the adventure you were talking about in your email!"

Musgrove laughed and aimed a sarcastic comment in the excited girl's direction. "Calm down, Sereny... you sound like a strangled hamster!"

Bradley intervened, as he felt another vibration against his leg and instinctively reached into his pocket to grab the coin. He held the gold object between his thumb and forefinger, as the grobite started to glow. "Here goes!"

Sereny asked. "Can I be the first one to check what the message says?"

Bradley smiled and offered the coin to his enthusiastic friend without hesitation. "Of course... read it out loud to us!" He insisted, as Musgrove moved in closer to listen to the pretty girl recite the new message that had just started to appear around the edge of the coin.

The boys waited, as Sereny swallowed nervously and took a deep breath. She turned the coin slowly between her slender fingers and prepared herself to read out the mysterious line of text imprinted along the serrated rim of the gold disc.

The children were interrupted by an old lady's voice, as Grandma Penworthy entered the bar lounge. "Ah, there you are… hello, Bradley."

The revealing of the coin's message would have to wait until Bradley performed a welcoming ritual for his endearing grandparent and he quickly introduced his friends. "Oh, hi there, Grandma," he replied and gave her a hug. "You didn't get to meet Musgrove and Sereny when they came up to Yorkshire in October did you?"

"No, dear," she replied and turned to face her grandson's friends. "But Bradley has told me all about you both and it's very nice to meet you at last… anyhow, I'll leave you three to get on with whatever it was that you were doing – your Aunt Vera is here as well and I'd better see what she's up to!"

Bradley's eyeballs moved in an upward motion. "Oh god… my Aunt is here!" he exclaimed and looked out of the bar window at the Morris Minor. "I didn't even notice the car outside when we came in… quick Sereny – read out the message before she finds us!"

Sereny giggled and lifted the coin, as she recited the message. "*Find the map that leads to Rekab and align the prisms of blood to stop the Yeldarb Beast*!" she exclaimed. "It doesn't make any sense!"

"They never do at first!" quipped Musgrove.

Bradley held out his hand and asked to see the grobite. "Let's have a look... it sounds like some kind of riddle." He suggested, as Sereny handed over the shiny object. "It's obviously another message that will take us on another amazing adventure down the plughole... let's head to the bathroom - there's no time to waste!"

"Which one?" exclaimed Sereny, as she looked through the bar entrance at the winding staircase that led to the three floors of guest rooms in the hotel. "Every bedroom in the hotel must have an en-suite bathroom."

Bradley noticed Musgrove had gone very quiet but he ignored him and suggested they start with the owner's accommodation. "Some have showers and some have baths... anyhow, it's probably the bathroom next to my own bedroom - come on, let's head on through the kitchen!"

"Wait!" shouted Musgrove. "The message mentions a map... I've got an idea - I think another visit down to Amley's Cove is in order!"

"Why waste time in Amley's Cove?" asked Sereny. "Shouldn't we do what Bradley says and check to see if the plughole in his bathroom is the right one?"

Musgrove paused and combed his fingers through his blonde disheveled hair, as he perched his sunshades above his tussled fringe. "Bear with me guys... before we even think about going down a plughole again - I think we're going to need the map that the coin's message refers to."

Bradley agreed. "Muzzy's right, Sereny... it's no good jumping down any old plughole without knowing where we're going when we get to the other end - the journey could lead us anywhere and I don't recognize the name Rekab on the edge of the coin either," he explained, as he handed the grobite back to Sereny and asked her to read out the message again.

The girl took the coin and lifted it up, as she held it nearer to the light emanating from the lounge window. Sereny started to read the message again. "*Find the map that leads to Rekab and align the prisms of blood to stop the Yeldarb Beast!*"

Musgrove interrupted. "Like I was saying... we need to find the map - I definitely recall something my brother Simon said after our first adventure in Pathylon in the summer holidays," he explained. "You know... when the search party followed us into Pathylon but didn't remember anything about it afterwards?"

"Yes... go on," insisted Bradley.

"Well... even though Simon was not aware he had played his part in that adventure - he still keeps going on about a secret cave with a primitive map painted on a carved-stone wall," replied Musgrove. "A cave located somewhere along the cliffside in Amley's Cove!"

"Interesting... tell us more," encouraged Sereny. "It sounds like you're onto something, Muzzy!"

Bradley interrupted. "Sorry, Muzzy... but before we go looking for caves and wall paintings of maps in Amley's Cove - let's analyze the message on the coin in more detail."

Sereny handed the coin back to Bradley and agreed. "Good idea!" she said, as the three children left the confines of the bar lounge and made their way into the hotel kitchen.

Bradley surveyed the area and reported no sign of adults or four year old sisters. "Coast is clear!"

"Wow!" exclaimed Musgrove, as he looked around the huge commercial preparation area and opened the door that led into a very roomy cupboard full of shelves. "This is a very big kitchen and look at the size of this larder... it's stacked full of food - you lucky sod, Brad!"

Bradley laughed and insisted that his impressed friend came over to the table where he and Sereny had started to examine the message on the coin again. "Dad arranged it with the estate agent for when we arrived… apparently we have a couple of guests booked in by the previous owners over Christmas – Mum's not very happy but they didn't want to let the guests down." He explained. "So Dad asked if someone could fill the larder before we got here… they went to the cash and carry yesterday - Mum said she thinks they may have overdone it a bit on the initial stock!"

Musgrove chuckled, as he closed the larder door and walked over to the table. "You're not kidding, Brad… there's enough breakfast cereal in there to feed a year's worth of guests at the five star Imperial Hotel - never mind a little guesthouse like the Haytor!"

Sereny laughed. "You're so funny, Muzzy."

Bradley picked up a hotel receipt pad, as he frowned and insisted Musgrove sit down so they could finish examining the grobite. He didn't like the fact that Sereny laughed at his quip, especially because it was at the expense of his father's over-indulgence at the wholesalers. "Right, Muzzy… grab that pen and *write* the coin's message on this note pad before it disappears!" He insisted and slid the jotter across the table.

Musgrove smiled. He knew very well why Bradley was so wound up and he winked at Sereny. The girl shrugged her shoulders and looked bemused. She was totally oblivious to the perceived jealousy displayed by the eternal chosen one and instead concentrated her attention on the end of the pen nib, as Musgrove wrote down the message.

Bradley quickly put his lapse of emotional control out of his mind and let out a cry of pain. "Arrrrrgggghhhh!" he shouted and collapsed with his head striking the table top.

Sereny jumped out of her seat to tend to the stricken boy, as Musgrove finished writing down the message and dropped the pen to help. They stood either side of Bradley and lifted his head back slowly, as a look of shock emanated from the girl's face.

Musgrove stared at Bradley in amazement and the petrified girl stepped back from the table, allowing him to take the weight of their friend's unconscious body. He finally acknowledged the weird occurrence and declared. "Oh my god... look at his face - it's starting to change shape and he's got hairs growing out of his cheeks!"

"I can see that!" replied Sereny. "What's happening to Bradley?"

Musgrove was aghast, as he witnessed Bradley's pointy ears sprout out from the sides of his head through his thick brown hair. "Look at the size of those lugs... the message on the coin mentioned the Yeldarb Beast - do you think this has anything to do with it?"

Sereny stepped back towards Bradley and put her arm around him, as she answered Musgrove's question. "Yes, I do... what does Bradley's name spell backwards?"

Musgrove paused for a moment, whist he worked it out. "Yeldarb!" he exclaimed and took a tighter hold of Bradley's upper body.

Bradley remained unconscious throughout the ordeal and was totally unaware of what was happening to him, as his two friends cupped their lower arms under his armpits. They lifted the insentient boy up from his seat, as the dining chair toppled over and crashed onto the tiled floor. They avoided tripping over the fallen chair and guided him past the line of heavy duty cooking equipment, as the toes of Bradley's white trainers dragged along the surface of the non-slip floor. The two exhausted teenagers finally negotiated their way through the back door and pulled the boy's limp body outside onto the paved area, at the rear of the kitchen.

Sereny noticed a wooden bench close by and they carefully sat the boy down, as they steadied his upper body from falling to one side. As soon as Bradley's bottom hit the seat of the bench, a series of parallel sunbeams broke through the grey clouds in the sky above and struck his hairy wolf-like face like a spray of laser shots. "Look, Muzzy... his face - it's starting to change back!"

Bradley's frontal facial features and his ears gradually reverted back to normal, as the sun's rays continued to beat down. Then the wintry clouds moved across to block the sunlight and the boy remained unconscious. Sereny stroked his soft face, as she turned to Musgrove to exclaim. "The sunlight must have helped to cure him!"

"Well, that's pretty obvious... but why is he still unconscious?" stated Musgrove.

"I don't know... but we can't just leave him here!" insisted Sereny, as she ran back into the hotel to retrieve the coin from the kitchen table. She reappeared and looked towards the end of the courtyard at a small brick building. She quickly placed the sacred grobite back in Bradley's trouser pocket and announced. "I've got an idea."

"What is it, Sereny?" asked Musgrove, as he followed the girl's stare towards what looked like a storage building. "Are you thinking what I'm thinking?"

Sereny smiled. "Hope so!"

The two teenagers were on the same wavelength and they supported Bradley's body, as they carried him towards the old wooden door that secured the white-painted building.

Musgrove pulled on the padlock and the hasp fell away from the rotten frame, as Sereny pulled the door open.

"It's an old laundry room... he'll be safe in here!" exclaimed Sereny, as they gently lowered Bradley onto a pile of bed linen. "When he wakes up and finds us gone... he'll wonder what the hell has happened!"

Musgrove smiled and suggested they get going. "Come on then... let's head down to Amley's Cove and find that cave before he wakes up - it will be a nice surprise for Bradley."

"Okay... hopefully we can locate the cave pretty quick - I've got a camera on my mobile phone so we can take a picture of the map!" replied Sereny, as she closed the laundry room door. "There's lots of spiders in there... do you think he'll be okay?"

"Are you serious... if that boy can battle with giant ants - a few incy-wincy spiders aren't going to hurt him," laughed Musgrove, as they ran around the side of the hotel and across the car park.

Sereny reached the roadside first and turned to shout back. "Keep up, Muzzy... we've no time to lose!"

It did not take long for the two teenagers to reach the shoreline and Musgrove held on to Sereny's hand, as they negotiated the rock pools in Amley's Cove. The tide was out so it made it easier for them to move across the short stretch of rocks. A shallow pool led the teenagers to a pile of fallen boulders at the cliff bottom.

Musgrove pointed his arm toward a ledge on the cliff side, as a flock of cackling seagulls flew above their heads. "That I believe is the spot where my brother thought he had remembered seeing a cave... do you see that narrow ledge on the side of the cliff?"

Sereny lifted her hand to shield her eyes from the sun that had just reappeared from behind the dark clouds. "Yes... I see it - but how are we going to get up there?"

"Stay there... I've got an idea," replied Musgrove, as he walked forward towards the cliff bottom and disappeared behind a large rock. He reappeared instantly holding a length of hemp rope. "We can use this!"

"How did you know the rope was behind that rock?" asked Sereny in a curious tone.

"There was a good chance that a length of rope would have been left here somewhere from last time... the tide doesn't affect this part of the cove so it couldn't have been washed away and my brother must have scaled the cliff to find the cave - so hey presto!" explained Musgrove an a very succinct manner.

"I know I'm going to regret saying this, but... Musgrove Chilcott - underneath those long blonde locks of yours there is the brain of a genius!" stated Sereny and she laughed at his smirking grin. "Come on then, superman... let's find that cave you've been banging on about!"

14

A Familiar Face

Meanwhile back at the Haytor Hotel, Aunt Vera sped out of the car park following a futile search for Bradley. She thought that her nephew was very rude not to have greeted her and she remained silent, as Grandma Penworthy sat quietly in the front passenger seat with the cat basket on her lap. The Morris Minor indicated to turn right out of the hotel grounds and the rear wheels screeched, as it moved away at pace in the direction of Aunt Vera's cliff top cottage.

Bradley was not ignoring his aunt at all and he lay still on top of the laundry pile where Sereny and Musgrove had left him about an hour earlier. The door to the room opened and a tall figure stood in the doorway, as the boy opened his eyes to focus on the stranger.

The height of the person encouraged Bradley to instinctively call out his friend's name. "Muzzy... is that you?"

"No!" replied a female voice. "But it's great see you again, Bradley!"

Bradley adjusted his position and used the edge of the washing machine to lift himself up to face the stranger, as the girl offered her hand to help. He pulled himself up and then rubbed his eyes to accustom his sight to the daylight in the doorway that surrounded the girl's familiar face. He recognized the sequined word that was emblazed across the busty chest of the girl's t-shirt beneath her denim jacket. "*ELVIS*... that shirt could only belong to one person that I know, Jules - is that you?"

"Yes it is... hello, Bradley - but what are you doing in here with the door closed?" asked Simon Chilcott's attractive girlfriend. "I've just seen you're Aunt Vera race off in her old banger... with a terrified cat meowing its head off in a basket - being clung onto for dear life by a white-faced old lady!" she exasperated. "Anyhow, getting back to why I'm here... I'm looking for Simon's brother and you're Mum just told me that Muzzy was supposed to be with you - apparently they've searched the hotel high and low but couldn't find either of you."

"Yeah, well... err, I thought Muzzy *and Sereny* were with me too!" retorted Bradley and rubbed the side of his head to make sure his ears had returned to normal. "I must have passed out."

"Well, I need to find Muzzy... his brother is back from fighting in Afghanistan and his mother wants him to come back to the house to have some tea - Simon's waiting with Bomber and Tank," explained Jules. "Apparently they are all heading back to Lympstone Barracks in a couple of hours... so it's important I find Muzzy real quick," explained Jules. "Have you any idea where he might be?" she asked, in a concerned tone.

Bradley stepped out of the laundry building and looked around the courtyard. "Muzzy was here with Sereny not long ago," he explained and then remembered the conversation around the kitchen table. Bradley acted swiftly, as he changed tact and realized that his two friends had probably gone down to Amley's Cove to search for the cave. The boy's face coloured a slight shade of red and he diverted the conversation to a fictitious tome. "Oh, I remember now... we were playing a game of hide and seek and I must have dozed off in the laundry room - they obviously couldn't find me so Muzzy and Sereny must have got fed up with looking for me," he concluded. "They've probably gone off somewhere else by now... have you tried the school playing fields?" he asked. "They told me they hang around up there quite a bit!"

Jules acknowledged Bradley's explanation with a look of doubt and chuckled. "I thought you three we're a bit too old for playing hide and seek... oh, whatever lights your candle I suppose - anyhow, come round to the front of the hotel!"

"Why?" asked the curious boy, as he followed Jules back through the kitchen and into the hotel foyer.

"Just wanted to introduce you to a couple of my new work colleagues," explained the pretty nineteen year old. "I started my new job at Costa Coffee in Sandmouth this week!" she continued and led Bradley out of the hotel into the car park.

"Didn't see you in there earlier," replied Bradley and he coloured up again, as Jules introduced him to her two female companions.

"It was my day off today but you'll probably recognize these two beautiful ladies!" she replied, as the boy politely held out his hand and both women gently accepted his friendly handshake. One of them had very distinctive white blonde hair and she whispered in Jules ear, as the three females started to giggle in an affectionate kind of way. Jules afforded Bradley a friendly nod and pointed to the woman with the blonde hair. "This is Lobke and the other lady is Tara... I told them that this very handsome young man was moving down to Sandmouth from Yorkshire and they have been dying to meet you!"

Bradley's face reddened for a third time and rubbed his finger across his mouth to shield his embarrassment. "Yeah, I did see them both earlier... in fact Lobke made my Cappuccino – and it was very nice by the way." He said and found himself staring into the blonde girl's striking blue eyes before plucking up enough courage to acknowledge both women's compliments. "It's really nice to meet you ladies... but I have to go back inside now - my Mum wants me to peel some vegetables ready for our guests evening meal," he fibbed and started to walk backwards on his heels in the direction of the front entrance.

Jules laughed and the two women waved, as they started to walk away. "Well it's great to see you again, Bradley!" shouted Jules. "Hope you settle in to your new home and as soon as you've finished peeling your veg - why don't you pop round later?" she suggested. "Simon and Muzzy's Mum would love to see you!"

"What about Muzzy's Dad?" asked Bradley, as he stepped back inside the safety of the hotel porch.

"If you do come round... it would be best not to mention anything about that - especially in front of Muzzy!" she suggested. "Thomas Chilcott left the family home about three weeks ago and nobody has heard from him since!" shouted Jules, as the three females reached the main entrance to the car park. "Muzzy's Mum is in a bit of a state... still it's good that Simon is home on leave - at least it will take her mind off it a bit!"

Bradley waved, as the women disappeared out of sight and he thought. "Well that's a turn up for the books... fancy Muzzy not mentioning anything about his Dad disappearing again - I'd better choose my moment carefully when I next speak to him about that bit of bad news!"

Margaret appeared in the hallway, as Bradley made his way through the entrance porch. "Oh, there you are... did Jules find you okay?"

"Yes, Mum... just been talking to her and her two friends - they seem quite nice," he replied nonchalantly and put his hands in his trouser pockets, as he squeezed past his mother.

"Your Aunt Vera wasn't very happy that you didn't come and find her to say hello!" retorted Margaret.

"Yeah, I heard… Jules just told me she went off in a huff – and it sounds like Grandma and Sky were treated to a few wheel spins on the gravel car park!" he replied. "Still… that's Aunt Vera for you and it's nothing new – is it?"

Bradley's mother smirked and ruffled his hair. "Cheeky sod… anyhow, enough about your Aunt's predictable tantrums – you've not even looked at your bedroom yet and where do you think you are you going now?"

"I thought I'd take a walk down to Amley's Cove to meet Muzzy and Sereny," suggested Bradley, as he grabbed his puffer jacket from the bottom of the stair banister.

"Oh, so that's where they are... Jules was looking for Muzzy a few minutes ago," said Margaret, in a concerned tone. "When you see him... make sure you tell him to go home as soon possible - apparently his brother has just got back from Afghani..."

Bradley stopped his mother in mid-sentence. "Yes, Mum... I know - Jules told me!"

Margaret frowned and rolled her eyes. "You know I don't like it when you interrupt me like that!"

"Sorry, but I've got to go... Muzzy and Sereny will be waiting for me," explained Bradley, as he felt the gold coin in his pocket vibrate again and smiled. "Bye!"

Before Margaret had chance to open her mouth and reply, her energetic son had disappeared out of the hallway. She sighed and stared at the front door to the hotel reception, as it swung back and forth on its heavy hinges.

Patrick appeared from the bar lounge drying his hands on a beer cloth and put his arm around his wife, as she scrunched her shoulders. "You look a bit shocked, my love... is everything okay?"

Margaret reacted instinctively and brushed her husband's arm away. "Your hand is still wet... what were you doing in the bar?" she asked.

Patrick rubbed his hands in the beer towel again and quipped. "Just been connecting a new barrel of lager to the pump... thought I'd get some practice in before our new guests arrive later - I'm hoping they will partake in a few pints after we've fed them our first dinner in our new hotel!"

"Well, we'd better get in that kitchen then and make a start!" replied Margaret and afforded her husband a nervous smile, as the novice hoteliers kicked open the door and walked arm in arm towards the kitchen larder to choose the vegetables for their first evening meal at the Haytor Hotel. "Christmas tree is being delivered later... as well - so there's another job for you to do after preparing the dinner, Jeeves!"

Patrick sighed and jokingly pinched his wife's bottom. "You've got a cheek woman... well two actually!"

Margaret slapped he husband jokingly and responded to his playful banter. "Patrick… behave!"

Bradley had reached the dirt track that led down to Amley's Cove. The excited boy looked out at the splendid view in front of him, as he stood transfixed at the top of the cliff. The wind blew effortlessly through his hair and he blinked occasionally, as the cool winter breeze glanced his face. He still could not quite believe that he now lived so close to the sea and he stared out to the ocean, as it glistened like one of his mother's iced cakes.

Bradley's concentration was interrupted by another sharp pain that pierced through his torso like a bolt of lightning. He grimaced and bent forward to intercept the churning in his stomach, as he thought out loud. "Arggghhh, that hurts so much... I'm running out of time and it feels like I am starting to change again - I have to find Muzzy and Sereny before it's too late!"

At that moment the sound of familiar voices shouted up from below and Bradley refocused his attention down to the cove, as the incoming tide brushed a gentle cluster of waves over the rock pools. Musgrove and Sereny were stood atop a large boulder and they waved their arms frantically. The stricken boy held his midriff with one hand, as he raised his other arm to acknowledge his friends.

Musgrove cupped his hands around his mouth and shouted. "Stay there, Brad... we're coming up!"

Sereny lifted her voice and shouted in a very excited tone. "We found the cave!"

Bradley managed a raw smile, as he keeled over and collapsed. His friends looked up in shock and witnessed the eternal chosen one disappear from view.

Sereny screamed. "He's fallen!"

"Oh my god!" exclaimed Musgrove, as he move quickly to negotiate the rock pools. "It's a sheer drop at the other side of the track... I think he may have fallen over the edge of the cliff!"

Sereny screamed again and cleared the last rock, as she jumped onto the pebbled beach. The crunching sound of the shingles was absorbed by the cushioned soles of her sneakers, as she quickly regained her balance and headed straight for the dirt track. "Muzzy, you go round the blind side of the cove to check the bottom of the cliff and I'll head up to the top... hopefully it will be me that finds him!"

Musgrove nodded and changed direction, as he continued along the edge of the cove. "No problem!"

Sereny continued to run as fast as she could up the dirt track and it didn't take her more than a few minutes to scale the sharp incline. She reached the top and placed her hands on her knees, as she rested momentarily to catch her breath. She then frantically searched the spot, where Bradley was last seen and called out. "Bradley... where are you?"

Musgrove arrived at the base of the cliff and looked up to make sure he had reached the right spot. He saw Sereny walking along the cliff top and then started to explore the gaps between the jagged rocks.

Sereny carefully shuffled her feet to the extreme edge and held onto a stray sapling that had rooted into the cliff side. She secured a good footing and slowly leant out to look down, as she saw Musgrove below and shouted. "Any sign of him?"

Musgrove looked up and reacted to the girl's voice. "No... nothing!" He replied and held his arms out-stretched to indicate that there was no sign of Bradley at the base of the cliff.

Sereny increased her grip on the small branch, as she pulled herself back towards the cliff side. As she tugged on the sapling, the sound of cracking wood preceded yet another scream, as the soil filled roots appeared in her hand.

Musgrove heard the girl's cries and stared up open-mouthed, as the girl fell backwards. This time Sereny's screaming tones were due to her impending plummet onto the sharp rocks below and he stood helpless, as her horrified face looked down at his. "Sereny.... nooooooooooooooo!"

Then Sereny's fall came to an abrupt halt, as her body jolted and her arms flopped downwards. The girl screeched out an exclamation of relief and her pigtails curled around her face to obscure her vision, as a strong hand gripped her ankle. She shook her head and looked down at a smiling Musgrove, who was now jumping up and down on the rocks below.

"Got you!" revealed a familiar voice, as Bradley Baker hung by his bent knees over another much stronger branch. "You okay, Sereny?"

"Bradley... thank god you're okay!" cried the shocked girl and held out her hand, as the handsome hero pulled Sereny up towards the safety of the extruding tree stump.

"Yeah... that was a close call for both of us... not sure how we're gonna get back up though?" replied Bradley, as he eyed the rocky canopy above their heads.

Sereny shuffled her bottom onto the branch and Bradley pulled himself back up to sit behind the girl. He then placed his arms around her petite waist and the two children sat awkwardly, as if they were riding a horse.

Musgrove could see his two friends from below and shouted up. "Wait there and don't move... I'm coming to get you!"

Bradley chuckled at Musgrove's expense. "Not sure where we're going!"

Sereny slapped the boy's thigh and responded. "That's true... but don't make fun of Muzzy - after all, he does have a rope!"

"Owwww... that hurt!" shouted Bradley, as he rubbed the top of his leg. "Anyhow, where did he get the rope from?"

"He worked out that his brother must have used a rope to scale the cliff to reach the secret cave... he found it hidden behind one of the rocks," replied Sereny.

"Fair enough... and fair play to him!" replied Bradley. "So you found the cave then?"

"Yes... and take a look at this!" said Sereny, as she reached into her pocket and pulled out her mobile phone. "I took a few pictures with my camera."

Bradley rested his chin on Sereny's shoulder, as he watched the girl's slim fingers negotiate the keypad on the mobile device. She didn't react to the boy's touch and continued to locate the app on her *Blackberry* that contained the pictures.

"Here you go... take a look at that!" revealed Sereny, as she lifted the screen so they could both view the image.

"Wow!" exclaimed Bradley, as the map on the cave's wall stood out so clearly. "That's brilliant and you can see all the detail... it will be even better when we download it to a computer - then we can print it off to get a better look!"

Sereny smiled and was very pleased with her work. She was about to boast some more about her achievement when the end of a rope appeared in front of her face. "Ah... I guess Muzzy's up top - shall we?"

"After you... ladies first!" replied Bradley.

Sereny smiled and slipped the phone back into her pocket, as she grabbed the rope. "I enjoyed our little chat... it was nice spending time with you - even though we were sitting a hundred feet up on the side of a cliff!"

"Yeah, me too... see you at the top!" replied Bradley, as he released his hold on the girl's waist.

At last all three children were safe and they stood at the top of the cliff to congratulate each other on their joint heroics. They agreed to return back to the hotel immediately so they could print off some pictures of map.

They walked along the roadside and talked continuously until they reached the entrance to the Haytor Hotel. Bradley paused for a brief moment and suggested. "Once we've printed the map... we will need to go straight down the plughole."

"What's the rush?" asked Musgrove.

Bradley held his stomach again. "I felt another sharp pain at the cliff side and it was the most severe one I've had yet!" He explained. "It was so bad... it caused me to fall off the cliff - if we don't get to Pathylon soon, who knows what will happen to me next!"

Sereny agreed and ushered Bradley in the direction of the hotel entrance. "Come on then... let's get going!"

The three friends entered the hotel and made their way through to the kitchen where Bradley's parents were finishing their preparation for the evening meal. Patrick shouted over. "Here they are... the wanderers return - so what've you lot been up to then?"

Bradley was quick to reply and dilute the conversation before it turned into an interrogation. "Can we talk later,

Dad?" he suggested and headed straight for the door to the owners accommodation. "We need to print off some pictures we've taken of the rock pools in Amley's Cove and Muzzy has to shoot off in ten minutes... so no time to chat at the minute!"

Patrick look bemused and did not get the chance to reply, as the three children started their evacuation procedure through the doorway into the owner's accommodation. As the door started to close behind them he turned to his amused wife, who was now putting a tray of meat pies into the oven. "Is it me or do kids live in their own world nowadays?"

Margaret chuckled and replied. "It's probably you, dear... it's most definitely you!"

Unbeknown to Bradley's parents, the children had just caught the end of their conversation, as the door slammed shut. They all started to giggle, as Bradley pointed out the obvious to his fellow time travellers. "We certainly do live in our own world... don't we?"

"Sure do!" quipped Musgrove. "If only they could remember Pathylon too... after all – they have been there!"

Sereny laughed and pulled out her phone, as they entered Bradley's bedroom. "Have you got a USB cable that will fit my mobile?" she asked, as Bradley grabbed a connector lead to sync her phone to his computer.

"Sure have... now, let's get those pictures downloaded so we can finally see the full extent of the map inside the secret cave!" declared Bradley, as the images started to appear on the monitor's large screen. "Wow... look at the detail," he exclaimed and pointed to the bottom right of the map. "You guys have done a brilliant job... and look - I don't even recognize that part!"

Musgrove followed the end of Bradley's finger and read out the word that the boy was indicating. "Rekab... that's the same word that appeared around the edge of the gold coin!"

Bradley reached into his pocket and pulled out the sacred grobite. It began to glow immediately and the words appeared again, as he read them out loud. "*Find the map that leads to Rekab and align the prisms of blood to stop the Yeldarb Beast!*"

"Musgrove's right," said Sereny, we spoke about this when you passed out in the kitchen earlier. "Rekab is your surname spelt backwards," she explained and examined the map further, as she pointed to a cluster of trees. "And look... there's a forest with your first name spelt backwards too - Yeldarb!"

Bradley replied. "Oh my god... both the map and the coin confirm that I am turning into the Yeldarb Beast!

Musgrove nodded. "I'm afraid it looks that way, buddy... so I guess we have to get you to Rekab - there has to be something there that can stop your transformation!"

Sereny took the coin from Bradley, who looked very downbeat and worried. She afforded him an affectionate glance and examined the message again. "It also mentions something about *aligning the prisms of blood*... that must refer to those pyramids on the map – after all, a pyramid is a prism."

Bradley's eyes lit up again, as he took the coin back from the startled girl. "That's it, Sereny... I think you've got it - we have to find our way to Rekab - there must be something inside one of those pyramids that can help me!"

"What if you have to drink some blood?" suggested Musgrove.

"I don't care if I have to eat Hoffen poo!" declared Bradley.

Sereny reacted by giggling. "Sorry, Bradley... I didn't mean to laugh but that was very funny!"

"That's okay... it does no harm to make light of the situation - it's important for me to stay positive or I'll never survive the journey back to Pathylon!" replied Bradley. "Now it's time to find the time portal!"

Musgrove interjected. "I disagree, Bradley... going directly back to Pathylon isn't the answer - you haven't got time."

"What do you mean?" asked Sereny.

"I mean... we have to go straight to Rekab!" replied Musgrove.

"That's what I meant!" replied Bradley in a stern tone.

"Okay... calm down, Brad!" insisted Musgrove, as the two boys squared up to each other.

Sereny pushed her arms between them, as Bradley's chin rested on Musgrove's chest. "Calm down, you two... this is not getting us anywhere," she suggested, as they parted reluctantly. "It doesn't matter who said what... you're both right - we have to find a time portal that will take us straight to Rekab."

15

Back Home to Krogonia

Henley and Grog were conscious of the evil that was closing fast, as the two time travelers from the outside world prepared for a heavy landing. The energy streams at the exit of the Vortex of Silvermoor wrapped around their bodies and catapulted them into the cramped space that had previously held the Krogon's lifeless body.

Grog smashed against the side of his old tomb and quickly recovered, as the nine foot reptile regained his balance. He then used all his strength to push the heavy slab of stone off the top of the ornately decorated burial chamber. The burly Krogon warrior wrapped his webbed fingers around the edge of the opening and pulled his rotund frame out of the crypt. "Give me your hand, Henley!" he croaked and leaned down, as he gripped the Devonian's hand. The Lizardman eased his fellow journeyman effortlessly out of the constricted chamber.

Henley's feet cleared the edge of the frame, as the Shade Runner appeared still holding on to the petrified boy. The two latest arrivals hit the side of the small undercroft and

Jefferson seized the opportunity to pull free, as he escaped his captor's evil grip.

Grog shouted down, as the Shade Runner tried to grab the boy's ankle. "Give me your hand!"

The evil aggressor had hurt his leg and Jefferson lifted his foot to avoid the hooded being's reaching grasp, as the injured fiend crawled across the tomb and just managed to grab the boy's trouser leg.

"Get away from me, Darke!" yelled Jefferson and kicked out, as he reached up to grasp the Krogon's slimy hand.

Henley picked up a nearby ornamental vase and threw it into the pit, as the Shade Runner reeled back. Ethan Darke roared, as he released his hold on Jefferson's clothing. "Arrrrrrrghhhh!" he screamed and swept the broken fragments of pottery from his hooded cloak.

Grog spotted his opportunity and pulled the boy clear, as the Shade Runner swiped his arm in desperation. He rose to his feet and stared up at Jefferson's smug face, as Henley helped Grog to lift the heavy lid.

Jefferson called down, as the shadow from the torchlight moved across the tomb. "What were you saying about using me as bait for Bradley Baker?"

Ethan Darke's face appeared from beneath his hood and he shouted out a warning, as the lid moved across the top of the crypt. "I'll find you Crabtree and you can tell Baker that we have some unfinished business!" he threatened, as the stone slab clunked heavily into the edge of the square frame to silence the Shade Runner and seal the tomb once again.

Grog rubbed his webbed hands together in a satisfied manner and encouraged his two new friends to follow him out of the inner chamber of the tomb. He pushed a burning torch upwards and a cloud of dusty sand poured out of a crack in the wall, as a sudden stream of daylight pierced through the dust.

A hidden door grated, as it slid sideways to reveal a row of Krogon warriors with spears at the ready. The Lizardmen were knelt forward in a precise battle-ready formation with the ends of their weapons secured in the ground, as the canvasses from an uncompleted camp site formed a colourful background to their military stance. A look of aggression covered the war-torn faces of the reptiles but this was soon displaced with warm smiles and loud cheers, as they recognized Grog immediately.

Pavsik and Guan-yin also spotted the familiar tangerine frame of the region's popular champion and they ran forward to welcome the Krogon back to his homeland, as Henley and Jefferson appeared from the tomb.

Pavsik left Guan-yin's side and called over to Henley. "My dear fellow Devonian… it is great to see you again after all these years – are you here to stay this time?"

"We'll see!" replied Henley. "I suppose it depends whether we can defeat Varuna and his bunch of traitors… the three of us are here to help – so tell us what you need us to do!"

A small grey figure pulled on Henley's coat tails and the Devonian turned round expecting to come face to face with someone. Instead he lowered his head and looked down at the dwarf, as Turpol held out his short arm. The Gatekeeper grinned smugly and offered his welcome. "We'll accept all the help we can muster to fight Varuna and Flaglan… welcome to Krogonia – and you are?"

Henley removed his cap to reveal his horns and the dwarf smiled, as the stranger introduced himself to the little Gatekeeper. "My name is Henley Baker!"

"Ahhhh… you must be the mauled miner – Bradley Baker's uncle!" replied the dwarf. "Bradley has told me all about you… and who is the dark coloured boy speaking to Grog and Guan-yin?"

Henley looked over to the chatting group and replied. "That is Jefferson Crabtree… he managed to get himself involved in all this chaos and was followed by a Shade Runner."

"Ethan Darke by any chance?" asked Turpol.

"Yes… apparently so!" replied Henley. "How did you know?"

"He is the Shadow Druid's apprentice… I knew he was at large but did not realize he had ventured as far as the outside world – I wonder why he was there and why he followed you back into Pathylon?" puzzled the Gatekeeper, as Jefferson approached.

The boy had overheard the dwarf's question and he informed Turpol about K2. "Bradley's dog has been killed… and Grog has been released!"

The dwarf responded in a nonchalant manner. "I was aware that would happen… and I feel for Bradley but was relevance does that have to Ethan Darke?"

Jefferson revoked Turpol's flippant retort and lowered his head in a display of sadness, as he delivered the bad news. "It was Darke who killed K2!"

The Gatekeeper's demeanor changed immediately and he offered the boy an apologetic look. "Oh no… that's not how it was meant to be – I expected K2 to die of natural causes so Grog could be released from the Vortex of Silvermoor but not at the hands of an evil Shade Runner!"

The difficult conversation was interrupted by a solitary cry from one of the Krogon warriors. He was pointing to a cloud in the sky, as the silhouette of a large bird appeared in the centre of the nebula. Everyone lifted their heads to witness the Klomus Hawk circling above and it suddenly swooped down and stretched out its huge wingspan.

Guan-yin ran over to where Ploom had landed safely and the bird immediately aimed one of its wing tips in the direction of the dwarf. The exhausted hawk explained her reason for travelling to Krogonia. "I need to speak with you, Pavsik and Turpol at once... Luccese has sent me from Freytor to relay a message - there has been a change to the battle plan and I also need to take the Gatekeeper back with me!"

The Hartopian High Priestess acknowledged the Klomus Hawk and nodded, as she guided the great bird over to the waiting group. She informed Turpol and Pavsik that the King had sent Ploom to advise a change of plan and the Gatekeeper suggested they finish making camp and discuss the situation in private.

Before Turpol retired with the others to chair the planning meeting, he approached Grog. "I am pleased you have returned to Krogonia and I would like to take this opportunity to hand over command of the Lizardmen ... I feel the time is right for you to assume your rightful role as Krogon Champion and take up the deserved mantle following your defeat of Zule!"

Grog was speechless and immediately summoned a nearby group of his fellow reptiles, as he commanded the legion of warriors to erect a large canvass marquee alongside the many tents and banners that were covering the Flaclom Straits.

Pavsik and Guan-yin congratulated Grog and then followed Ploom, as the dwarf spoke briefly to Henley. "I suppose you are wondering whether or not your nephew has arrived from the outside world?"

"Yes... it is a question I was going to ask of Ploom when you had all finished talking about the new battle plan," replied Henley, as a small group of noblemen joined their fellow Devonian.

Turpol shouted over to the Klomus Hawk and the bird waddled across. "When you left Freytor... was there any news of the eternal chosen one's arrival?"

Ploom replied. "No... I'm afraid I have no news for you – but Meltor and King Luccese were both confident that Bradley's arrival would be imminent!" he declared, as Henley accepted the bird's explanation. "I was told that Bradley Baker has to return at some point... there was talk that he may materialize in Rekab – but don't quote me on that!"

Henley moved away to digest Ploom's account of the situation, as Jefferson walked by his side and the boy offered some words of support. "Don't not worry about Bradley... when he left Ravenswood he seemed pretty determined to accomplish whatever it was he was planning to do – I'm sure he is doing everything possible to locate a time portal that will deliver him safely to Rekab!"

Bradley's uncle smiled at the boy and admired the confidence this young American had in his brave nephew's ability. "You are turning out to be quite a character, Jefferson Crabtree... and I very much appreciate your support – Bradley is very lucky to have you as a friend!"

The planning meeting was over within the hour and Turpol appeared drained, as the others were now fully aware of the new task they had to complete. Pavsik appointed a combined group of Galetian and Devonian surveyors, as he asked Henley to oversee the building of the new bridge.

Ploom had already informed the Gatekeeper that he was needed in Rekab to aid the eternal chosen one's search for the antidote. The bird explained that King Luccese and Meltor had already set sail from Freytor aboard the fleet of ice-ships. The bird also suggested to the dwarf that Jefferson should travel back with them to assist his human friend when he eventually arrived from the outside world.

Turpol agreed to Ploom's suggestion and Jefferson was informed that he would be travelling to Rekab to be reunited with his school friend. Everything was happening so fast and the boy said his goodbyes, as the Klomus Hawk prepared for the journey. Turpol climbed onto the bird's back and Guan-yin helped the excited boy up, as he sat behind the dwarf.

Henley arrived to bid them farewell and he called up to Jefferson. "When you see Bradley... give him my love and wish him good luck in his quest to find the antidote!"

"I will... and happy bridge building!" replied the boy, as the great bird lifted off the ground and launched her solid frame into the air.

16
The Hidden Room

Bradley sat down in front of the computer screen to recompose himself, as he started to analyze the map again. He pointed to the Forest of Haldon. "Okay, well we know that Aunt Vera's plug hole will lead us to the Forbidden Caves... but as far as we are aware - that way is still blocked anyway!"

Sereny joined in the analysis. "And we can't go via the secret cave in the cliffside because the Vortex of Souls died during the first adventure into Pathylon."

Musgrove suggested. "What about the old mine workings... we know we can get into the unknown land by travelling through the Vortex of Silvermoor!"

Sereny also mentioned the cenotaph and the route she took via Grog's crypt. Bradley quashed both suggestions quickly and replied. "They're both good ideas but it would take too long to travel back to Ravenswood… in any case, neither route wouldn't take us directly to Rekab – one vortex leads to the Flaclom Straits in Krogonia and the other would take us into the unknown land," he concluded. "So there has to be another way in!"

Sereny made another suggestion. "Bradley, your location always seems to have something to do with where you travel from... so surely it has to be one of the plugholes in this hotel - the coin is glowing, so why don't we let it guide us to the correct one!"

"Great thinking, Sereny!" exclaimed Bradley and held the coin out in front. "And you suggested... let's start with the bathroom in the owner's accommodation."

The three adventurers made their way into the bathroom and Bradley placed the coin in the plug hole. They waited for a few moments but the grobite stopped glowing.

Bradley prized out the coin and held it in the palm of his hand. "Well, it's obviously not that one."

"How many guest bedrooms do you have in the hotel?" asked Musgrove.

Sereny answered. "It's not necessarily the number of bedrooms... it's the number of rooms with en-suite baths."

"Sereny's right, Muzzy... not all rooms have baths - most of them have showers."

Musgrove corrected his line of questioning. "Okay then... how may *baths* are there in the hotel?"

Bradley suggested they go through to the reception. "Not sure, exactly... I haven't been here long enough but there is a poster on the wall in reception that informs visitors about the hotel's bedroom facilities... that should tell us which rooms have baths in them."

"Good thinking!" declared Sereny, as they made their way through the rear entrance of the owner's accommodation to avoid the prying eyes of Bradley's parents.

The children walked down a side path that twisted through the garden and around to the front of the hotel. They re-entered the building through the main entrance, as Bradley led his two friends down the hallway and straight to the poster. "Here it is!" He announced and started to assess the room layouts on the chart. "Well, according to this diagram... only bedrooms four, six and twelve have baths in them!"

"Where's room thirteen?" asked Sereny.

Bradley's father appeared. "There isn't a room thirteen," he said calmly. All three children jumped and Patrick began to laugh. "Sorry... I didn't mean to startle you."

Sereny and Musgrove held their beating chests, as Bradley responded. "That wasn't funny, Dad!"

Patrick waited for the stunned children to recover from is prank and then asked. "So tell me... why are you looking for hotel rooms with baths in them?"

There was a deathly silence and then Musgrove came up with the most bizarre answer. "We need to measure the force of the water that comes out of the taps!"

Bradley and Sereny stared at each other with a disbelieving and very puzzled look. It was if they were telepathically thinking the same thoughts. Of all the answers that Musgrove could have provided, why did he come out with that amazing pearl of wisdom.

Patrick furrowed his brow, as he looked beneath Musgrove's puffer jacket and stared at the camper van emblazoned on the teenager's t-shirt. Bradley's father couldn't think of a good enough reason to ask why they wanted to measure the force of the water coming out of the hotel's taps so he just replied. "Nice shirt!"

"Thanks Mr. B!" replied Musgrove and the three children walked past the confused hotel owner, as he returned to the kitchen.

Bradley whispered. "I don't think my Dad knew quite what to say to you, Muzzy... I bet he's gone back in there to tell my Mum you're a right loony."

Musgrove grinned, as Sereny stopped them both and held out her hand to reveal the keys for the bedrooms that contained the en-suite baths.

Bradley gasped. "Where did you get those from?"

"Well, while your Dad was trying to figure out Muzzy's crazy reply... I took the liberty of helping myself to the bedroom keys," explained Sereny, as she handed them to the new boy hero. "Shall we make a start in room four?"

The children entered all the rooms with baths but none of them contained a plug hole that initiated the coins power of transportation. The three explorers reappeared from room twelve and stood on the second floor landing, as they stared at each other in disbelief.

Sereny looked to her left and noticed another door. "What's behind there?"

Bradley reached out and tried the handle. "Not sure... it might be a linen store - but it's locked!" he replied and noticed Musgrove staring at the door, as if he were in some sort of trance. "You okay, Muzzy?"

Sereny snapped her fingers in front of Musgrove's face and the boy blinked his eyes. He then walked over to the door and rubbed his fingers over the surface of the paintwork. "Feel this?" he suggested to the others.

Bradley and Sereny took it in turns to rub their hands over the uneven surface and both acknowledged that the paintwork wasn't smooth but still did not understand why their friend was referring to a blemish on the door.

Musgrove asked. "Does that feel like the shape of two numbers to you?"

Bradley placed his fingers over the area again and replied. "Now you mention it… the first part does feel like a number one!"

Sereny confirmed the second number. "And this bit feels like a three!"

All three children shouted out at the same time. "Thirteen!" They exclaimed in a very excited tone.

The faded remains of the number thirteen on the door afforded them some fresh hope. So far, their search for a bathtub with a plug hole that would trigger the sacred grobite's magical powers had proved fruitless.

Bradley insisted that his two friends stay outside the door. "I'll get the key to the linen cupboard!" he exclaimed and descended the three flights of stairs before they had the chance to acknowledge his request.

Sereny rubbed her fingers over the number again and turned to Musgrove. "Do you suppose there may be something hidden in here?"

Musgrove shrugged his lanky frame and answered in a matter of fact way. "I think Brad is over-reacting slightly... it's just a store cupboard for heaven's sake - we need to be looking for a bath not shelves full of bed sheets!"

Before Sereny could reply, Bradley reappeared at the top of the staircase panting heavily. The boy paused for breath, as he opened the palm of his hand to offer the key to his friends.

Sereny reached out and grabbed it before Musgrove could pull his hands out of his pockets. She glared jokingly at the teenager and challenged. "Well, Muzzy... let's see if we can prove you wrong!"

"What's that?" asked Bradley, still panting after his rapid ascent of the ornate staircase. "Prove me wrong... about what?"

Musgrove insisted that they were wasting their time, as Sereny placed the key in the lock. "I just said we should be searching in other parts of the hotel... maybe one of the bedrooms with showers in them could be what we're looking for - after all, shower trays do have plug holes!"

Bradley did not comment and watched Sereny, as she turned the key in the lock. She pushed the door open and felt for a light switch on the wall but instead found a cord hanging from the closet ceiling. The nervous girl pulled the thin cord and the switch operated with a loud clunk, as the light bulb flickered before illuminating the cobweb filled store cupboard.

Musgrove commented. "Told you... it doesn't look like anyone's been in there for a while - look at the state of those bed sheets!"

Bradley ignored his tall friend, as he brushed past him and headed along the landing to the adjacent door of bedroom twelve.

"What's he doing now?" asked Musgrove, as Sereny picked the dusty cobwebs from her sleeve and followed Bradley into the adjoining room.

Musgrove sighed. "Is anyone going to answer me or am I just invisible?" He declared and pursued his inquisitive friends into room twelve.

Bradley disappeared into the en-suite bathroom. "Come in here, you two... see what you think of this!" he revealed and placed both hands on the wall above the bath tub. He then started to tap gently every few centimetres with his knuckles in a horizontal direction, as Sereny and Musgrove watched his systematic inspection of the hollow sounding wall.

"What are you thinking, Bradley?" asked Sereny.

Bradley continued to knock on the tiles and replied. "The closet next door is tiny... but if you look at the distance between the door of that store cupboard and the door of this bedroom in the hallway - it would mean this bathroom should be much larger than it actually is!"

Musgrove left the bathroom and walked back onto the landing to assess the distance between the two doors, as Bradley described. He shouted back a statement of confirmation. "He's right, Sereny... Brad's right - the bathroom should be about two metres wider!" He estimated. "There must be a void or something hidden behind the wall!"

Sereny patted Bradley on his back. "Well done you!"

Bradley failed to turn around and acknowledge Sereny's congratulations. The predictable smile that normally followed the thought of proving Musgrove wrong did not materialize. Even the girl's adulation towards him did not summon a response and instead he grimaced and released a cry of agony. "Arrrrrrrrrrrrggghhhhhh!"

Musgrove heard his friend's outburst and rushed back into the room to find out what all the commotion was about. He appeared in the doorway of the bathroom to witness Sereny holding her hands affront an open mouthed expression. They both stood helpless and unable to stop their troubled friend, as Bradley held his stomach and fell unconsciously forward into the bathtub. "Brad!" yelled Musgrove, as the striking pain returned to haunt the eternal chosen one.

"Urrrrrgghh!" moaned Bradley, as he hit his shoulder on the side of the tub and landed head first in bath. This time the pain was much more acute and fired through his torso like an industrial boiler. He instinctively reached out and took hold of the handle grips on the side of the bath, as he lifted himself upwards. Then the pain twisted violently in his gut and caused him to turn with a rapid motion to face his startled friends. He stared at them with a look of dread streaming from his bloodshot eyes and let out another agonizing cry, as he fell sideways back into the bath. "Arrrrrggghhhh!" he exclaimed, as he cracked his forehead on the cold water tap.

"Bradley!" screamed Sereny, as blood splattered across the wall tiles from the open wound and she grabbed the back of his shirt. Musgrove recovered his composure and reached over to help lift the unconscious boy out of the bath tub. The two worried children dragged Bradley carefully into the bedroom, as they and lay him on the bed. Sereny retrieved a towel from the bathroom and used it as a make-shift bandage to stem the flow of blood that was oozing from the deep gash on his forehead. "Is he going to be okay, Muzzy?"

"I think one of us should go and get Brad's Mum or Dad!" insisted Musgrove. "That cut looks really bad... this is serious - he needs to go to a hospital!"

"Wait!" exclaimed Sereny. "Look!"

The two teenagers watched in amazement, as the shape of Bradley's face started to change. The eternal chosen one's jawline began to elongate and coarse brown hairs sprouted from his cheeks, as his canine teeth started to grow. His ears became pointed again and emerged from his thick brown locks like new plants shooting out from the soil. Then to Musgrove's and Sereny's astonishment, the cut on Bradley's forehead began to close and the blood stopped flowing.

Musgrove took a step back and declared. "The wound has completely healed and look at his legs, Sereny!"

The startled girl stared at Bradley's ankles and inhaled a deep breath of shock, as the boy's transformation continued at a rapid pace. "His feet are growing and starting to split his shoes!"

"Arrrrrrrrrrrrrrgh!" cried Bradley, as he arched forward and opened his eyes to reveal two flaming red marbles in place of his friendly hazel-coloured eyes.

Musgrove grabbed Sereny's sleeve and pulled her off the bed, as he forced her to hide behind him. The lanky teenager continued to protect the petrified girl, as he witnessed Bradley's shin bones crack and his hands developed into sharp hooked claws.

The lower limbs of the boy hero curved into the shape of two hairy canine hind legs and he stood upright in front of Musgrove. Bradley was now the same height and he placed one of his large claws around the helpless boy's neck, as he opened his snout-shaped jaw to reveal a set of pristine razor teeth.

Beads of sweat streamed down Musgrove's face, as the creature placed its paw beneath his chin and slid him up the side of the bedroom wall by his neck. The transformed Bradley growled and then lifted his snout upwards. "Hoooooowwwwwwl!" he cried and then pulled the helpless boy towards his raging jaw before tossing him like a piece of disused garbage across the room.

"Arrrrrrgggghhh!" exclaimed Musgrove, as he landed heavily against the wardrobe doors and then crumpled to the floor.

Sereny dropped to her feet and hid her face in her hands, as Bradley's wolf-like form stood tall above her crouched defensive position. His torn cloths hung off him with ragged edges and he released a muffled snarl. The girl flinched, as he brushed the back of his claw across her blonde hair and lifted one of her blue-ribbon pigtails. The girl moved her head to release his hold and stared up at the creature. "Oh, Bradley... what's happened to you?"

A tear rolled down Bradley's hairy face and he appeared to struggle with a faint smile, as it reluctantly spread across his pointed jawline. He then slowly lifted his paw away from the girl's head and jumped to one side, as he disappeared out of the bedroom.

Sereny rushed over to where Musgrove was lying unconscious and lifted his head up from the carpet. "Muzzy... wake up - please wake up!"

The disorientated boy shook his head and groaned, as he looked into the girl's worried eyes. "Owwww... that hurt - where is he?"

"He just ran out of the room... it was really weird, though - after he threw you against the wardrobe, he just stood over me," replied Sereny, as Musgrove held his throat and gasped for breath. "It was as though the real Bradley inside was trying to get out and he attempted a smile!"

Musgrove coughed uncontrollably and clenched the girl's clothing, as he came to terms with his near escape from certain death at the hands of his young friend.

Sereny waited for his coughing fit to stop and asked. "Are you alright now... shall I get you a drink of water?"

"No... I'm fine - I just need to catch my breath!" exclaimed Musgrove, as he rubbed the marks on his throat to ease the discomfort caused by the creature's sharp nails. "I can't believe that Bradley turned on me like that... he certainly didn't offer me a smile!"

"I'm sure he didn't mean to hurt you, Muzzy," replied Sereny calmly. "The wolf-like thing he's turned into must be controlling his mind... we have to find him - we have to get Bradley back to Pathylon before it's too late."

Musgrove nodded and held onto the girl's slight shoulders, as he maneuvered himself back to his feet. "Did you see where he went?"

Sereny pointed to the top of the staircase. "He ran in that direction... so I guess he must be downstairs somewhere," she replied, as Musgrove pushed the closet door open to inspect the linen cupboard. "What are you doing, Muzzy?"

"There's no point looking for more trouble... if we find Bradley still in the same state - who knows what he might do to us," assumed Musgrove and started to move some old dusty bed sheets off the shelves. "I think it would be best to let him calm down... I don't think whatever it is that's affecting his body has taken full control yet."

"What makes you think that?" asked Sereny and helped him remove more linen to reveal a plastered wall at the back of the cupboard.

Musgrove paused for a moment, as he stared at the bare wall beyond the empty shelving. "Because... I believe if the beast inside him had fully manifested itself - he would have killed me for sure!" He paused again, as he pulled on the loose shelving and then suggested. "The best way to help Bradley now is to find the plug hole that will transport him to Rekab... and I have a feeling he was on to something before he turned in to that monster - now, help me remove these shelves!"

The two teenagers quickly cleared the wooden shelving and the remaining linen to reveal the full wall that at first glance appeared to adjoin the bathroom of room twelve.

Sereny stepped back out of the closet and judged the distance between the two doors again. "I think you're right, Muzzy... Bradley was onto something!" She exclaimed "Now that the shelves have been taken down... you can see a definite difference - we need to get behind that wall!"

Musgrove looked around for a heavy object and noticed a fire extinguisher at the top of the landing near the staircase. He ran over to unhook the red cylinder from its wall bracket. "This should do!"

Sereny exclaimed. "Where's the fire... that's no good - we need some kind of crow-bar or something!"

Musgrove laughed and entered the linen cupboard. "Nah... this will do just fine!" He declared and smashed the bottom of the fire extinguisher against the wall. The heavy device crashed through the plaster with little effort, as a small cloud of dust filled the closet. As the airborne plaster cleared, a large hole in the wall revealed itself. "There... told you it would do the job!"

"Wow... yeah - you're not kidding!" she agreed and stared at Musgrove, as he hesitated. "Well... are you going to take a look inside?"

The boy stepped back and placed his hands on his hips. "The last time I peered through a hole like that... I ended up being chased by a giant ant deep underground - there's a blummin good chance that another man-eating creepy crawler could be hiding behind that wall!"

"Stop being such a wimp, Muzzy!" teased Sereny.

"Well you take a look then!" insisted Musgrove, as the girl brushed past him.

Sereny nervously approached the hole and tentatively placed her head through, as a cold chill blew against her face. She waited for her eyes to adjust to the dim light on the other

166

side of the closet wall. Her body trembled in anticipation and Musgrove couldn't resist the temptation, as he placed his hands on her slender hips. As he squeezed her sides, the girl instinctively screamed and jumped, as she hit her head on the top of the hole. "Owwww!" she cried and swung round to hit the boy, as he burst into uncontrollable laughter "You idiot, Muzzy... that wasn't funny!"

"Sorry... but I couldn't resist - it wasn't fair of me!" he apologized and held up his hands to stop the girl's playful slaps to his chest. "Move over and let me take a look."

Sereny obliged and landed another thump on Musgrove's arm, as he bent down and placed his blond locks through the opening. "See anything?"

"Nope... not yet!" he replied and then the tone of his voice turned to a delighted pitch. "Hang on... ignore that last comment - I think we've found what we're looking for!"

Sereny struggled to push her head upwards past the boy's chest, as her hair tangled with the beads around his neck. She pulled free to adjust her view and joined his observation, as she released an enthusiastic cry. "That's brilliant... Bradley was right!"

17
The Victorian Slipper Bath

Back inside the linen cupboard, Sereny was clearing away more shelves to make it easier to access the hole in the wall. Musgrove pulled at the fragile plaster to make the hole bigger and he noticed a power socket conveniently located above the skirting board. Sereny anticipated his next request and nodded, as she disappeared into room twelve.

The girl returned within seconds and handed Musgrove a shaded lamp that she had retrieved from a bedside table, as the boy plugged it into the mains. "Thanks, Sereny... now let's get a proper look in here!" exclaimed the excited teenager and held the lamp through the hole. The light revealed an amazing discovery and he cupped his hand to invite the girl to take a look. "We've definitely found what we're looking for!"

Sereny pushed her head through and squeaked a gleeful outburst of excitement. "Wow... that is amazing - it must be Victorian!"

"Yeah, I think you're right!" agreed Musgrove, as the two children stared at the old freestanding bath tub in the corner of the room. Musgrove moved the lamp to reveal more features on the bath. "Look at the feet... they've got claws - it looks very old!"

Sereny detailed the design of the old tub. "It's a Victorian Slipper bath!" exclaimed the girl and pushed passed, as she entered the small room. She looked around at the old-fashioned decor and Musgrove squeezed through the hole to join her, as they both stood open-mouthed in ore of their find. Their brief viewing was disturbed by the noise of wooden planks crashing together inside the linen cupboard.

Musgrove bent down to place the lamp carefully on the floor and stepped back, as he held Sereny close to his side. "What was that?" he whispered.

"It came from the closet," replied Sereny, as a shadow moved over the hole in the wall. "There's someone in the linen cupboard!"

Musgrove reached down again, as he flicked the lamp switch to the off position and quickly stood back up to feel the trembling hold of his female companion gripping his waist. He whispered to Sereny again in a gentle tone. "Stay still and try not to make any noise."

The girl responded by standing rigid and pushed her face into Musgrove's clothing, as the shadow moved over the hole again. She lifted the side of her face to take a peak and a head appeared through the opening in the wall. The sudden appearance of the silhouetted figure caused Sereny to jump and she broke the silence inside the hidden bathroom by screaming. "It's coming for us!"

The sound of laughter emanated from the stranger's mouth and it filled the room, as the figure reached for the lamp to turn it back on. The light revealed the familiar presence of

Bradley Baker, as he stood in front of his friends. "Sorry to startle you, guys... I see you've found the bath then!"

Sereny reached out and hit Bradley on the arm. "You're as bad as you're Dad... I can't believe you just did that - you nearly frightened me to death!" she shouted. "However... you're forgiven and I'm so pleased to see you're back to normal!"

Bradley smiled and offered Sereny an apologetic look, as Musgrove released his hold on the girl. The eternal chosen one handed his friend the lamp and revealed his latest transformation experience. "Yeah... it's good to be back - don't remember much about it though."

"Where did you go?" asked Musgrove. "And look at your shoes... they're in shreds!"

Bradley looked down at his feet and replied. "They do look a bit of a mess... don't they?" he exclaimed. "It must have happened when I transformed, but... as I said - I don't remember too much about it!"

Sereny commented. "You turned into a wolf-like creature and that made your legs grow quite long... your feet would have split the leather."

Bradley shrugged his shoulders. "Wow... that must have been quite a show - I hope I didn't hurt either of you!"

"Well, you did give Muzzy a bit of a hard time!" replied Sereny and pointed at Musgrove's throat.

The teenager approached Bradley and took the lamp, as he lifted it to reveal the marks on his neck. "Yeah, you certainly summoned up some strength when you turned into that creature, Brad... you actually picked me up with one hand by my throat and then threw me across the room like a helpless kitten!"

"I'm so sorry, Muzzy... I don't remember any of that!" he replied in a regretful tone. "After I left you, I must have passed out again... I found myself crouching in the downstairs toilet - I do remember leaving you guys here though and I remember looking for this hidden room."

Musgrove placed the lamp on the floor again and patted his young friend on the arm. "Please don't worry yourself about it, Brad... I know you didn't mean to hurt me - now, we have to get you to Rekab before it happens again."

Sereny agreed and urged Bradley to find the portal key that would send them on another incredible journey down the plug hole.

Bradley reached inside his pocket and pulled out the sacred grobite. The gold coin was glowing and it started to vibrate, as he threw it into the air. The spinning disc hovered for a few seconds and then moved towards the bathtub. "It would appear the coin has found the correct bath... and it looks very familiar – it's the same shape as the one in Aunt Vera's cottage," he explained and declared. "Well it certainly looks impressive and it's time to try it out... I guess we should go back down the plug hole!"

The three adventurers grinned at each other simultaneously, as the coin continued to hover over the bath tub. The room began to fill with a fine mist and the familiar green haze appeared around the base of the bath. Bradley cast off his torn shoes, as he headed back through the hole in the wall to retrieve the closet key and closed the linen cupboard door behind him. He turned the key in the lock and returned to his friends to explain his actions. "We don't want to attract any unwanted attention, whilst we're away... do we?"

"Too right!" replied Musgrove and turned the lamp off again, as he offered the usual gentlemanly gesture to Sereny. "Ladies first!"

Sereny smiled and suggested. "I think we've forgotten something!"

"What?" asked Bradley.

"Our jackets!" revealed the girl. "If the weather in Rekab is anything like it is outside... then it will be very cold when we arrive - we're going to need something warm to wear."

Bradley nodded. "Good thinking... wait here, you two!" he ordered and made his way out of the bathroom to unlock the linen cupboard door again. He shouted back to his friends. "Where did you leave your puffer-jackets?"

Musgrove answered. "They're hanging on the banister at the bottom of the stairs... near the reception desk - do you want me to go and get them?"

"Nah... I'll pick'em up, don't worry - I'll be back in a minute!" insisted Bradley, as he started to descend the stairs. As he reached the bottom floor he noticed the two jackets strewn over the handrail. "Ahhh, there they are," he muttered and headed for the hotel's kitchen. "I'll grab those on my way back!"

Bradley rushed quietly through the kitchen past his father and mother, who had their backs turned. They had just finished prepping for their first evening meal and he tried to avoid eye contact. The clumsy boy failed in his mission and Patrick's attention was caught by the noise of his son tripping over a box of potato peelings. The soggy scraps of disused vegetables left the confines of the plastic container and covered the floor like a layer of stone chippings.

"Bradley!" shouted Patrick. "Be careful... what are you rushing through a busy kitchen for?" He scolded. "There are hot pans and all sorts going on in here!"

"Sorry, Dad... I'll tidy it up," replied Bradley, as he bent down and started to pick up the peelings.

Margaret opened a cupboard and located a dust pan and brush. "Leave it, Bradley... I'll do it - carry on with whatever you were doing and don't forget your Aunt Vera is coming over later to look after Frannie, while your Dad and me serve the dinners."

"Thanks, Mum!" exclaimed Bradley and demonstrated a quick show of affection by glancing his flushed cheek against hers. The boy hero then had to think of something fast to excuse him from his aunt's restrictive clutches that evening. He crossed his fingers behind his back and replied. "I know it would be nice to spend time with Aunt Vera... but is it okay if I give that a miss tonight - it's just that Muzzy has invited me over to his house to see Simon before he goes back to Afghanistan?"

Patrick afforded his wife a disbelieving look and Margaret nodded. "Yes... that's fine but don't be too late home - nine o'clock latest."

"Great... thanks, Mum - I'll just get my jacket," replied Bradley, as a broad smile appeared across his face and his cheeks reddened even more.

Patrick observed his son entering the owner's accommodation and waited for the door to close before offering his thoughts to his wife. "He's up to something!"

"What makes you think that," said Margaret, as she swept the potato peelings back into the box.

"Bradley never says it's nice to spend time with your Vera... that's why!" he stated and held the box lid open, while

Margaret emptied the dust pan. "He's definitely up to something!"

Margaret smiled. "Oh leave him be... you know what he's like – I think it would be good for him to spend the evening with the Chilcotts," she continued. "It means we only have to worry about Frannie winding up our Vera... that will be bad enough!"

Patrick sighed and watched his wife put the last few pieces of potato peelings in the box. "I suppose you're right... he has been chomping at the bit to spend more time with Muzzy and Sereny since we left Ravenswood - so I'll try not to be so distrusting."

Bradley reappeared with his violet-coloured puffer-jacket covering his favourite blue checked shirt and wearing a new set of training shoes.

"Why are you wearing your new sports shoes?" asked Margaret. "You'll get them filthy... they were supposed to be for when you start your new school after the Christmas break."

"I can't find my others!" replied Bradley, as he edged nearer the exit door to the reception. "Haven't got time, Mum... don't worry - I won't get them dirty!" He concluded and left the confines of the kitchen to avoid another onslaught of interrogation from his over-protective parents. He leapt up the first few stair treads and grabbed his friend's coats, as he sniggered to himself. "Sorry, Mum... but they might get a bit dirty - especially when I go down the plughole!"

Bradley scaled the three flights of stairs and re-entered the linen cupboard. He handed the matching puffer-jackets to his friends and turned the key in the lock for the last time.

Sereny stretched her slender arms into her jacket and asked. "What took you so long... the room is full of smoke and coin has been hovering for some time!"

"Yeah," continued Musgrove. "We thought we'd have to go without you!"

Bradley climbed through the hole in the wall and looked over to the bath to witness the coin still spinning in midair. "Mum and Dad kept me talking... at one point I thought they were going to make me stay to see my Aunt Vera."

"Thrilling!" laughed Musgrove.

"Exactly!" replied Bradley and made his way over to the bathtub.

"So how did you get out of that awkward situation?" asked Sereny, as she held out her hand to be helped into the tub by the eternal chosen one.

Bradley smiled and informed his fellow adventurers that he had to tell a little white lie. "I said we were all going round to Muzzy's house to see his brother!"

Musgrove exclaimed. "What if your Mum rings mine?"

"She won't," insisted Bradley, as he climbed in the bath after Sereny. "She's too busy fretting about the evening meal and there's only four guests staying in the hotel... anyhow, she'll avoid speaking with your Mum for a while - with your Dad not being around and all that."

Musgrove's chin dropped onto his chest and he looked a little upset. Bradley's mention of his father disappearing again had reminded him that all was not right back in the Chilcott household. He lifted his head and faced his two friends, who were now sat waiting in the bath. He then explained. "I can't go with you... you'll have to go without me!"

Sereny pulled on Bradley's shoulders and stood up, as she held her hands out to the tall boy. "Put your jacket on and get in this bath, Musgrove Chilcott... that's an order!"

Bradley offered an apology. "I didn't mean to upset you, Muzzy... please get in - the coin's slowing down and it's about to fall."

Musgrove stared at the girl, who was still standing with her hands on her hips and affording him a stern look. He then responded to both requests. "I know you didn't mean anything, Brad and by the look on Sereny's face... I don't think I have any choice!" he quipped, as the athletic surfer jumped sideways into the tub and landed behind the girl's feet. "Sit down then, Sereny... it's time we were on our way!"

Bradley started to laugh, as Sereny's bottom landed heavily in Musgrove's lap and the teenager let out a painful cry as his private parts received a crashing blow. The coin stopped spinning and it was if it knew it was time to act, as it fell into the tub.

Bradley turned on the hot and cold water taps to release a flow of discoloured water, as the rusty liquid poured into the bath. Musgrove had now recovered from Sereny's retaliatory action and he nudged the smug girl in her back. He then peered over her shoulder, as all three children waited in anticipation for the coin to make its final move. The sacred grobite did not disappoint the three time travellers and as expected, it flipped onto its edge to roll slowly towards the plughole.

"Get ready to start shrinking!" shouted Bradley, as the tension between the three children inside the bath intensified. "Any second now!"

Sereny gripped the side of the tub and closed her eyes, as Musgrove wrapped his arms around her waist. Bradley stared at the taps and the expression on his face changed from excitement to surprise. He turned round to see his female passenger with eyes tightly shut so he expressed his concern to his older friend. "Muzzy... something strange is happening!"

"What is it, Brad?" replied Musgrove, as Sereny opened her eyes to witness the shocked look on Bradley's sullen face.

"The water is slowing down... there won't be enough to take us through the plughole!" declared Bradley, as the taps ran dry. "Oh no... the water has stopped altogether!"

The green smog in the bathroom began to clear and the bath started to vibrate, as the ornate feet broke away from the floorboards. Sereny looked over the edge of the bathtub and screamed. "We're moving upwards... the bath is lifting away from the floor!"

Bradley noticed the coin starting to spin again but this time it stayed in the plughole. The sparkling object continued to glow brightly through the smoky atmosphere, as it increased in size substantially. "Something's happening to the sacred grobite... it's getting bigger!" he declared, as the magical power within the metal disc caused it to expand the plughole by twice its diameter. "We're not shrinking this time... it would appear that the coin and the plughole are getting bigger!"

Musgrove pointed at the tiles on the bathroom wall, as they started to shift position to form a series of triangular shapes. "Look... what's happening to the wall?" he exclaimed, as beams of yellow light shot through the cracks between the reformed tiles. "The tiles have turned into three pyramid shapes!"

Bradley agreed. "You're right, Muzzy... and I'll hazard a guess that those things they have something to do with the message on the coin - they must represent the Pyramids of Blood!" he shouted, as the creaking of bending metal vibrated through the bathtub. Bradley noticed the tops of the bath taps starting to twist and change shape. "The taps are also increasing in size!" he yelled, as they formed into two propeller-like blades that began to spin at a rapid speed. "The bath is being pulled towards the pyramids!"

Sereny screamed, as the bathtub lifted higher into the air and tipped forward at a thirty degree angle to face the wall. The brightness from the beaming lights between the tiles illuminated the inside of the bath and the three children instinctively shielded their eyes. The girl let out another cry. "I wasn't expecting this... I'm really frightened, Bradley!"

The new boy hero pushed his feet against the front of the bath to steady himself, as he held on to Sereny's feet. "Don't worry... I won't let anything happen to you!" he replied in a reassuring tone. "Now, brace yourself... I think we're about to go through!"

Bradley was right and the sound of rushing air whistled around the room, as the green smoke thickened. Shooting yellow stars danced within the smog and the twisting smoke built into a twirling tornado that caught the bathtub in its turbulent grip. The sacred grobite shone more brightly and the taps turned even faster, as the bath was propelled forward into the centre of the pyramid shaped tiles.

There was a massive explosion and the tiles shattered into tiny pieces, as they turned into powdered dust. The howling winds dispersed the tiny fragments of ceramic particles around the three children's faces and they closed their eyes again. The bathtub crashed through the wall and entered a swirling vortex that pulled the time travellers into its vacuum.

Musgrove opened his eyes and shouted ahead to his two friends. "Here we go again... this is going to be one hell of a ride!"

Bradley looked forward into the kaleidoscopic void ahead, as the bathtub jolted sideways. "Well it's certainly going to be different... that's for sure!"

Sereny finally mustered enough courage to open her eyes and see what the boys were shouting about. "Wow!" she exclaimed, as the bathtub travelled further into the vortex. "Where do you think this will lead us?"

Bradley turned to look at the pretty face of his female companion. "Rekab, I hope... and most probably the Pyramids of Blood - if the shape of those tiles has anything to do with it!"

"Let's hope you're right, Brad!" declared Musgrove, as he held onto the side grips. The vortex twisted and turned the bathtub in a corkscrew motion, as the teenager fought for his breath. "Jeeeeze... that was scary - just hope we get there in one piece!"

The three children huddled closer together and lowered their heads to avoid the flying debris that had followed them through the time portal. The stray fragments of wall tiles and discarded plaster bounced off the side of the bathtub, as the broken pieces collided with the propelling taps. The spinning metal blades chopped the shards of ceramic splinters into smaller shapes and they crashed against the prism-shaped walls of the twisting vortex. The sharp particles created multi-coloured ripples, as they penetrated the pliable structure of the time tunnel and the resulting turbulence catapulted the bathtub deeper into the unknown.

18
A Crash Landing

The Victorian rolled-top bath had been travelling through the time portal for some time, as Bradley and his two friends were readying themselves for departure. A white light appeared in the distance and it was a familiar sight to the three adventurers.

Bradley knelt and avoided the spinning taps that were still propelling the bath forward through the prism-shaped tunnel. The kaleidoscopic effect produced by the time portal mesmerized the eternal chosen one and he exclaimed. "It never ceases to amaze me just how fantastic our adventures are... we are so lucky to experience such a brilliant journey each time we travel into these strange worlds!"

Sereny pushed herself against the side of the bathtub and knelt behind Bradley, as she peered over his shoulder. "I agree... and this particular journey is even more amazing - the shape of this tunnel is so unusual."

Musgrove joined the conversation, as the white light in the distance grew bigger. "Why do you suppose this vortex is shaped like a triangular tube?"

Bradley turned round to face his inquisitive friend. "Maybe it has something to do with the Pyramids of Blood... everything we've come into contact with during this particular adventure seems to be connected with them!"

"I think you're right, Bradley," agreed Sereny, as she pointed towards the bright light. "And we're just about to find out... prepare yourselves, fellas - the tunnel is coming to an end!"

Bradley and Musgrove heeded the girl's observation and stared ahead, as an explosion of shooting stars cascaded over the bathtub. The taps started to reduce in size and the propeller blades reverted back to normal, as the coin in the plughole began to shrink.

Bradley noticed the sacred grobite had stopped glowing and he prized it out of the plughole. He put the coin in his trouser pocket and focused his attention back to the portal exit. "Get ready... we're about to go through!"

The turbulence inside the vortex increased, as the three children lowered their heads and braced themselves for a heavy landing. The bath pierced through the bright light and a cold rush of air brushed over the children's faces, as a cascade of small rocks showered them from above. This was followed by a loud rumbling noise, as the bath appeared out of the cliffside. The tub continued its midflight trajectory, as it powered itself forward about thirty metres or so above a small stretch of coastal seawater.

Bradley peered over the side of the bath, as the tub nosedived towards a wooden platform. He looked behind at the tall rocky structure that they had just emerged from and noticed a small rickety cottage perched at the summit. "Hey, Sereny… take a look at that house at the top of that hooked-shaped island!" he shouted, as the girl held on tightly to the sides of the bathtub and slowly turned her head.

"Where has the bath taken us this time, Bradley?" she exclaimed, as Musgrove alerted his friend's attention to an imminent landing place on to the sea-worn surface of the decked area.

"Hold on tight!" shouted the teenager, as the bathtub hit the wooden platform hard and veered towards the entrance to the small shack. Sparks ricocheted off the metal feet, as the tub scraped over the rusty board nails that held the platform together. Musgrove screamed in an assumptive tone, as he braced his knees into the girl's slender waist. "I think we're about to find out where it's taking us, Sereny!"

The bath crashed through the rotten door and landed on top of the trap door that led to the underground railway. Another loud explosion erupted outside the shack, as Hooked Point and the Witch's cottage crumpled into the sea. The impact of the debris caused a large wave to lift high above the shack and it crashed down like a tsunami, as seawater smashed through the wooden hut.

Bradley grabbed hold of Sereny's jacket. "Hold on tight!" he shouted, as the water filled the shack and splinters of wood swirled around the children's heads.

The weight of the bath and the sudden inrush of water caused the trapdoor to give way, as the tub hurtled down the stairwell that led to the rail track below. The flow of water carried the upturned bath along the underground passageway and the children reacted instinctively by leaning in the same direction to upright their makeshift boat.

The torrent of rapids carried the rudderless craft along the winding passageway and all three adventurers gasped for breath, as their heads finally reached the surface. Bradley immediately shouted out a warning to his two startled friends. "Keep your heads down, guys... this tunnel is quite low and there could be lots of sharp objects sticking out!"

"That's easy for you to say!" replied Sereny, as she frantically cupped her hands and began to scoop the water sideways out of the bath. "This thing keeps filling up with water... if we keep our heads down we'll all drown – give me the coin and I'll block the plughole again!"

Bradley responded and reached into his pocket to retrieve the grobite. He handed the sacred coin to the girl and she held her nose, as she dipped her face back under the salty water.

Sereny's first attempt to lodge the coin proved futile and she continued to struggle to keep the grobite in the plughole. She gave up and returned to the surface, as the bath smashed against the sides of the tunnel. "It's no good... I can't get it to stay in the plughole!"

"That's the problem!" replied Bradley. "The coin will only secure itself when there is a need... look – it's not even glowing!"

Musgrove fell to one side and hit his head on the side of the tub, as the bath collided with the rocky passageway again. He composed himself and agreed with his young friend. "Bradley's right... the coin is not going to help us – this tunnel can't go on forever so I suggest we hold our breaths and get under the water before we lose our heads!"

"Watch out, Bradley!" exclaimed Sereny, as she pulled the eternal chosen one back by his hair.

Water rushed up Bradley's nose and he shook her hand free, as he rose to the surface again. "What happened?"

Sereny explained in a rushed voice. "There was a sharp jagged rock sticking out of the roof of the tunnel… it would have taken your head straight off!"

"Then I suggest we do what Muzzy said!" insisted Bradley, as he pinched his nose. "Right you two… hold your breath and let's keep our heads under the water for as long as we can!"

The long wait in front of the large oak doors had finally bore fruit for the Witch and the Shadow Druid. They had been resting for quite some time and the sorceress had now fully recovered from the jolting rollercoaster ride along the underground rail track.

The Shadow Druid jumped to his feet, as the emerald began to glow again and the creaking of the hinges emanated an eerie sound within the tunnel. The Witch opened her eyes, as the cat brushed up against her wrinkled face and witnessed the great doors completing their grand opening.

The Witch struggled to find her balance and pushed herself upwards against the rocky wall, as she eventually steadied her footing in the soft sandy floor. She waited for her head to clear and then walked over to where the Shadow Druid was standing. The stranger paid her no attention and the two dark figures prepared to enter the swirling vortex that spun continuously behind the wooden gateway. The spiraling entrance enticed them forward, as the cat dug its claws into the Witch's cardigan. A multitude of yellow stars shot out from the edge of the twisting cyclone that would transport them to the underground river beneath the great pyramid.

The Shadow Druid paused for a brief moment, as he turned back to look down the dark eerie passageway from which they had travelled. The metal track began to vibrate, as the small coal truck bounced off the rails and landed on its side. "Something is happening inside the tunnel up ahead... we have to move quickly – it sounds like rushing water!"

The Witch cackled a predictable reply. "Right on cue... that will be the infamous Bradley Baker – we had better get a move on!"

"No wait... if it is the meddling boy hero – I might as well get it over with and kill him now!" roared the hooded being.

"No!" shouted the Witch. "You are not ready to fight him yet... we need to complete the potion – your time will come very soon, my lord!" she insisted and pulled on the shadowy figure's cloak sleeve. "I know it is frustrating for you... and you may think he's just some meddling kid - but you must not underestimate the power of the eternal chosen one!"

The Shadow Druid growled in an exasperated tone and turned to face the vortex, as a trickle of water flowed under the base of the oak doors and began to lap around the soles of his boots. The sound of gushing water grew louder in the distance, as the sides of the passageway began to shake and tremor. Slithers of splintered rock began to cascade from the crumbling ceiling, as the rumbling intensified. Without any further hesitation the hooded stranger jumped into the swirling void, as his long robes spread out behind him like the wings of a raven to aid his flight.

The Witch took one last look down the tunnel, as the bathtub appeared at the front of the sprawling wave. She caught the eye of the leading child and smiled, as she held her trembling cat close to her boney chest. The sorceress rubbed her hand down the feline's back and muttered under her breath. "See that young boy in the silly bath... that's *the* Bradley Baker that everyone's been talking about," she grinned. "Well... *we* will be meeting him again very soon – won't we, Truffles?" she screeched and let out a deafening shriek of laughter. "Heeeeheeee... hahahahahaha!" The cackling Witch then turned to dive forward, as she leapt towards the curling stars within the vortex and followed the Shadow Druid into the time portal.

Bradley could not believe what he had just seen in front of him, as he gasped for air following the record breaking breath holding competition. He rubbed his eyes and then looked around to witness his two friends surfacing from beneath the water, as they too gasped for breath. "You just missed it!" he exclaimed, as the wave carrying the bathtub on its crest finally crashed down and the tub landed against the enormous oak door frame.

The three flustered children managed to hold on to the sides of the battered tub and were lying in a crumpled heap with their legs and arms intertwined. Musgrove cried out a moaning sound, as he pushed Sereny's hand from his face. "I think I've broken every bone in my body!"

Sereny pulled her leg from between Bradley's groin and apologized for the inconvenience. "That could have been a bit awkward!" she giggled and rubbed her head, as her pigtails danced in front of the multi-coloured background created by the swirling vortex.

Bradley smiled and stood up, as he proceeded to climb out of the bath. He cricked his neck to one side to release a faint clicking sound within his spinal cord and then straightened his head, as he stared up at the gigantic open doorway. "This all looks very familiar!" he declared. "Muzzy, Sereny... come and look at this!"

The Sandmouth duo followed Bradley's request and stood by his side, as all three children gazed into the kaleidoscopic effect of the rotating time portal's entrance. Musgrove responded with a familiar retort. "The great doors that formed the entrance to Pathylon looked just like these... and the vortex is exactly the same!"

Bradley nodded and confirmed Musgrove's observation. "I wonder if there is a link... I wonder if this portal joins the one that leads to the Forbidden Caves in Forest of Haldon!"

Sereny had moved away, whilst the boys were discussing the possible connection between the two vortexes. She remembered the ruby at the centre of the Pathylon star and she shouted over for them to check out her discovery. "Come and look what I've found, boys!"

Bradley and Musgrove ran over to where Sereny was kneeling and looked over either shoulder to witness the girl rubbing some loose sand away from a sparkling green gemstone. She dislodged the crystal from its housing inside the stone pyramid-shaped rock and held it up to the light being emitted from the vortex. "Isn't it beautiful?"

"Yes it's absolutely wonderful!" admired Musgrove. "You obviously remembered the ruby at the centre of the star of Pathylon that triggered the opening of the other doors – is that what made you look for the key to these doors?"

"Yes... I have a feeling the gems may be linked – this is our third adventure together and we have always encountered a gemstone every time we have travelled into these strange worlds," she surmised. "Do you think they are linked, Bradley?"

"You may be onto something, Sereny... but I'm not sure if it means anything!" replied the eternal chosen one in a nonchalant manner and raised his hairy hands, as a slight tremor shuddered beneath his feet. "Anyhow, by the look of my fingers... we need to get a move on – I think I'm starting to transform again!" He warned and watched Sereny as she continued to admire the emerald. "Do you think it was a good idea to take the gem out of the rock?" asked Bradley, as the ground began to shake more violently. "You must have triggered something!" he assumed, as the gigantic hinges emitted a heavy creaking sound and the oak doors began to move slowly. "Quick, Muzzy... help me drag the bath in front of the portal entrance – the doors are closing!"

Unbeknown to the boys, Sereny slipped the emerald into the lining of her puffer-jacket and helped them to push the bath tub through the colossal doorway. The gateway slammed shut and Bradley felt a vibration in his pocket. "The coin!" he exclaimed and reached in to pull out the grobite, as it glowed as brightly as ever. "Now it's time to lodge the sacred coin in the plughole... looks like we're about to continue on our quest – jump in folks!"

19
Dragon Spirit

Preparations had begun to transport the dead dwarf to the River of Blood than flowed beneath the great pyramids. The funeral parade made its way slowly along the main avenue that ran through the centre of Crystal City.

Six of the small grey creatures that inhabited the emerald coloured capital steadied the glass coffin, as they mounted the translucent box onto the back of a waiting carriage. A burly pair of agitated Lurgs were being calmed by two other dwarves, as the scaly mounts reared up in readiness for the ceremonial journey ahead. The broad-shouldered animals had bodies shaped like Hoffen but had no tails and their bird-feathered heads were adorned with a row of sharp horns that differed in uniform length. The over-excited animals scratched their double-toed hoofs on the crystalized roadway, as the stout equestrian driver mounted the carriage and lashed his whip to continue the procession.

The funeral cortege moved slowly along the brightly lit streets, as the cart made its final turn onto the east bound road that led out of the city.

The fifty or so relatives of the dead dwarf walked in pairs behind the carriage, which was led by a winged bearded-dragon called Ryuu. The friendly lizard creature was an ageless being that had lived on Rekab for as long as anyone could remember. He normally resided alone inside the Emerald Caves and only appeared when a dwarf had perished. His main role was to protect the entourage on their dangerous journey between Crystal City and the Pyramids of Blood. Ryuu was traditionally a friendly dragon but he was capable of inflicting a ferocious burning flame from his huge mouth. Up to now no one had dared to attack a funeral parade on its way to the great pyramids. The giant bearded-reptile's name stood for *dragon spirit* and he ensured the dwarves safety against all the evil creatures and dangerous species that lived on Rekab.

It did not take long for the entourage to arrive at a crudely built stone building at the side of the main route about two hundred metres from the pyramids. The lead mother dwarf walked ahead of the procession, as Ryuu bowed his head. The female dwarf held out her short stubby arm and stroked the dragon's long neck, as she made her way over to the derelict structure.

The building looked like an old barn and a pair of wooden doors that fronted the stone shelter were pulled open by the dwarf. She waved at the driver to steer the Lurgs towards the open doorway and the carriage was then carefully reversed into position, as the harnessed creatures stamped there hoofs on the dusty ground. A few drops of rain began to fall as the glass coffin was lowered onto a table inside the single dwelling. The carriage was driven back out and a select group of ceremonial dwarves entered the structure, as the doors closed behind them.

Ryuu's job was done and he raised his clawed front leg to bid the rest of the funeral party farewell, as he spread his giant wings and launched is huge scaly frame into the air. The remaining dwarves waved, as their protector soared higher into the sky and headed over the nearby woodland to return to his mountainous home.

Inside the building, the coffin was secured to the top of the table and the mother dwarf lifted it, as it swung upright on a central pivot. Each side of the glass coffin folded back against the wood and the sheet-covered head of the dead dwarf was revealed. The mother dwarf then tilted the table top so that the head was at the lowest point and a fellow dwarf held a large axe aloft.

With a swift accurate blow the head was severed from it stumpy body and the blood began to trickle down a single blood stained channel that led to a hole in the ground. The opening formed the top of a vertical tube that was connected to a series of pipes than ran away from the building and through the forest undergrowth before angling down beneath the foundations of the pyramids. The blood flowed along the interconnecting tubes, as they twisted and turned the few hundred metres to the river below *Talum*, the tallest of the three sacred monuments.

Deep underground, the blood from the dead dwarf started to emerge from the end of the pipe and a boney hand held out a glass test-tube to collect a small measure of the precious red liquid. The old hag cackled as she pressed the bung into the top of the narrow vessel. "At last... we have it!" declared the Witch, as she held the container up against the naked flames of a nearby burning torch. She teased the Shadow Druid, as he attempted to grab the tube. The Witch evaded the warlock's sweeping hand, as she jumped down from the rock that she had used to reach the pipe and allowed the blood to glisten in the torch lit cavern.

The Shadow Druid moved across the swirling entrance of the vortex that had carried them to the underground river beneath the pyramids. He shouted at the Witch. "Stop playing with me… I will tear your head from your scraggy body if you don't stop messing around – now mix the blood with the potion before Bradley Baker gets here!"

Unbeknown to the Shadow Druid, he was not in any imminent danger from the eternal chosen one. The bath tub carrying Bradley Baker and his two fellow adventurers had taken a different route within the vortex and they were now travelling northward to a place called Wolf Town.

The bath burst out of the time portal and landed perfectly on its ornate metal feet, as it stopped in front of a husky wolf-like creature. The ugly looking beast licked its yellow fangs, as it stood intimidatingly over the startled children. "We have been expecting you!" roared the Werebeast and stepped back to allow the children to depart the bath.

"Who are you?" asked Bradley.

"No matter… that does not concern you!" replied the brown hairy creature and pointed to the straw lined doorway that led outside. "Go that way… Karn is waiting to see you!"

The three exhausted children walked out of the dark room and covered their eyes, as the daylight poured down over the primitive village square. The straw huts were crudely built and were secured on bamboo stilts. Musgrove commented. "This reminds me of the Mece Village… but they didn't have one of *those*!" he exclaimed and pointed to the enormous structure that formed a backdrop to the tiny houses.

"Wow!" cried Sereny. "Now that's impressive!"

Bradley asked the growling escort what the building represented and the Werebeast explained that it was an arena. "That is the coliseum!" he confirmed. "And it is where you will fight the Shadow Druid in the duel of destiny!"

Bradley looked shocked, as he stared openmouthed at the emblazoned flags flying some hundred metres above the stadium. He thought back to what K2 had told him and pictured the Burnese Mountain Dog, as he lay dying in his arms; *"The Shadow Druid has returned and he wants you out of the way... if he successful he will take your powers and Pathylon will be destroyed."*

"Get a move on!" ordered the impatient Werebeast, as he guided the children into a large straw hut. "Here they are, Karn!"

The muscular animal approached the three nervous visitors, as his ornamental feathered headdress flowed down his hairy back. The leader of the Werebeasts thrust his sharp claws through his pristine hair line and addressed the eternal chosen one, as Sereny and Musgrove sat down next to the guard.

Musgrove whispered. "I don't like this, Sereny."

"Stay calm, Muzzy... Bradley will handle things," replied the confident girl, as she held Musgrove's trembling hand. "Don't worry... and don't forget – Bradley is almost one of them so let's listen to what the Werebeast has to say!"

Bradley remained standing and waited for Karn to speak. The fierce looking creature sniffed the boy's head. "You are changing into one of our kind... and you don't have much time left!" The creature's action felt unpredictable and Bradley decided to remain silent, as he froze in fear of the great wolf man striking out at him at any moment. Karn spoke again. "You must find the antidote before the duel of destiny can commence!"

Bradley thought back to what the guard had said to him outside. "I think you may be mistaken... no one said anything about fighting the Shadow Druid in a duel!" he exclaimed and took a pace back.

"I'm afraid you have no choice... you are Bradley Baker – the eternal chosen one!" declared Karn. "It is written in the ancient archives that a person not of this world would be contaminated with the Werebeast virus that is carried inside the kratennium layer!"

"But why do I have to fight the Shadow Druid... why can't one of your Werebeast guards fight him?" he asked in a desperate tone. "They look much more powerful than me!"

Karn laughed. "I don't think I have explained myself clearly enough... the Werebeast in you will weaken your chances against the dark lord – that's why you must drink the antidote first," he continued. "It is your powers as the eternal chosen one that stands you in good stead against the Shadow Druid... while ever the kratennium runs through your veins – you will not only turn into one of us but your powers will remain weakened!"

"I understand," replied Bradley, as he lowered his head and the girl approached to offer him a caring touch. "Thanks Sereny."

Musgrove stood and asked. "Where is the antidote?"

Karn shook his head. "That I do not know."

Bradley replied. "We need to find Turpol... K2 said he will know where to find the sacred chalice!"

"Ahhhh... you speak of the Gatekeeper of Pathylon – we are expecting him to arrive later today," revealed the Werebeast. "He has been summoned by King Luccese and is being transported from Krogonia by the Klomus Hawk... I am expecting Meltor to arrive by sea too – and I believe you know the Galetian High Priest?"

All three children nodded and looked very pleased indeed. At last some familiar names and friends were about to enter the fold and Bradley commented. "Thank you for advising us of their arrival later, Karn... that makes all of us feel so much better about the whole situation." He declared, as Musgrove patted him on his shoulder. "I don't know about you guys... but I can't wait to see Meltor again."

Sereny smiled and agreed. "Yes it will be lovely to see him and I'm so looking forward to seeing Turpol again, as well... what time do they arrive?"

Karn looked over to the guard and requested an approximate time. The Werebeast raised his paw and held up two claws. "In about two hours... so please take the time to rest!" he suggested and the guard escorted the children to a nearby eating hut to relax.

Meanwhile the Shadow Druid had persuaded the Witch to mix the blood with the rest of the potion. "We need heat!" she declared and held the glass container over the wall mounted torch.

The heat from the flame caused the mixture to bubble, as the Shadow Druid watched with interest. "Is it ready yet?"

"Patience... just a few more minutes and it will be ready!" replied the old hag, as the cat meowed and rubbed its fur against her ankle. "Hello Truffles... isn't the Shadow Druid impatient and bossy?"

The dark stranger had grown tired of the Witch's sarcastic comments and he kicked the cat out of the way, as it screeched a howling meow. "Give me the potion!"

The Witch was taken by surprise at the sudden outburst of anger from the warlock and she ran towards the entrance to the vortex. "Come any closer and I will throw the container into the time portal… I told you it's not ready!"

"Enough talking hag!" bellowed the Shadow Druid and summoned his powers, as he moved his arms across the path of the vortex. The Witch was lifted off the ground and flung against the wall, as the glass container rolled across the floor. The dark hooded stranger picked up the potion and held it against his wrinkled lips.

The Witch regained her balance and shouted. "Noooooooo… it's too soon – the mixture is not hot enough!" she warned and a group of dwarves from the funeral cortege appeared behind her, as the Shadow Druid tipped back his head and poured the liquid down his throat. He wiped his mouth and smashed the empty container on the floor, as he turned quickly to run passed the entrance to the vortex.

"Stop him!" shouted the mother dwarf.

"It's too late!" cackled the Witch, as she nursed her sore back. "He is heading for Wolf Town… he has drunk the potion and now has the power he needs to fight the eternal chosen one – the duel of destiny must now take place!"

The mother dwarf shrugged her shoulders and grabbed the Witch's cloak. "That is of no concern to us… we must let the leader of the Werebeasts sort it out – we dare not interfere with Karn's arrangements!" she exclaimed and ordered that the injured cat should be collected too, as she ushered the old hag towards a stairwell that led up to the surface. "You are coming back with us… we have waited for this moment for a long time – at last the Witch of Rekab has been caught and there is a very cold dungeon waiting to secure you back in Crystal City!"

20
Arrival in Wolf Town

The ice-submarine carrying Eidar, Meltor and the royal couple had just arrived off the north coast of Rekab. The other ice-vessels in the fleet anchored nearby in readiness to collect the Black Squirrels and Wood Ogres from Yeldarb Forest.

Bradley and his two friends were there to witness the influx of a united hierarchy from Freytor and Pathylon step onto the mainland of Rekab for the first time. They kept out of the way intentionally, as they allowed the VIP's to complete their initial welcoming revelries.

The hospitalities were interrupted briefly by the perfect timing of the Klomus Hawk's arrival in Rekab, as Ploom landed safely with his passengers and the convivial formalities proceeded.

Karn was there personally to greet the royal Devonian's, the Galetian High Priest and the Freytorian General and he invited them back to his village. The imposing Werebeast then made his way over to the exhausted bird and helped the dwarf alight. Turpol the Gatekeeper brushed himself down, as he strode by the side of the Werebeast leader. Meltor joined them and Karn made pleasant conversation, as he asked the dwarf. "So what's it like to return to your homeland after all this time?"

The Gatekeeper smiled and replied, as the entourage walked between the village huts. "It feels good… but I sincerely wish it was under much better circumstances!"

King Luccese and General Eidar also joined the conversing group, as Meltor added. "Yes… we need to meet with Captain Dray to ask for his help as soon as possible – the attack on Varuna's forces depends on the help of the Black Squirrels and indeed their fellow forest dwellers, the Wood Ogres."

"That's all in hand… I have already spoken with the Black Squirrel leader and he is happy to help – he also told me that a senior Wood Ogre called Spew has commissioned ten other giant trolls to make the voyage to Pathylon and they will all make their way to board your ice-ships before first light," explained Karn, as he escorted the royal party into a large reception room inside his straw-built headquarters. "Therefore… I am pleased to announce that none of you need suffer the treacherous expedition to Yeldarb Forest and I am more than happy for you all to stay here in Wolf Town to rest before your onward journey."

Meltor overheard the conversation and conveyed his relief. "That's great news!" he retorted and passed the news to King Luccese, as General Eidar nodded in agreement. The Galetian's attention was then averted to the three smiling children standing patiently at the back of the group. "Bradley Baker!" he shouted and ran over to the eternal chosen one, as he wrapped his white cloak around the boy.

Sereny and Musgrove shook Meltor's hand, as Karn turned to King Luccese and commented. "I didn't realize that Meltor was so close to the boy!"

Luccese replied. "Bradley Baker is Meltor's protégé… if it wasn't for his initial recruitment of the chosen one's – Pathylon would have been destroyed a long time ago."

Turpol approached Bradley and interrupted his warm reunion with Meltor. He explained to the eternal chosen one how the Klomus Hawk had been commissioned the collect him from Krogonia and deliver him back to reveal the location of the antidote. "I'm sorry to break up this happy reunion… I have just had to endure the most uncomfortable flight and the speed of that bird has made me feel quite sick," moaned the dwarf. "But I do have some interesting news for you and I also have a message for you from a few of your friends – but first I have to inform you that I am aware that K2 is dead and I am very sorry for your loss?"

"Yes, I'm afraid so," replied Bradley. "And thank you for your condolences… please, tell me the news you have."

"Well you will be pleased to know that Grog is very much alive and well because of your dog's brave sacrifice… the Krogon arrived with Henley and a coloured human boy called Jefferson – your Uncle and Grog both told me to tell you that they hope to see you again very soon."

"What are they doing in Pathylon?" asked Bradley. "And what about, Jefferson… where is he?

"According to your Uncle… the Jefferson boy arrived by mistake - I believe he was being too curious!" chuckled Turpol. "However, it was great to see Grog and Henley back in Pathylon again… when I left with Ploom - they were busy preparing to help Pavsik and Guan-yin plan the bridge build from Krogonia across to the Galetis Empire."

"That's amazing and so much information to take in… but I asked where Jefferson was!" cried Bradley, as he turned to Sereny and Musgrove. "Did you hear what Turpol just said?" he asked. "Grog is alive again and my Uncle Henley has travelled into Pathylon with him… I can't believe Jefferson has travelled through the vortex as well!"

"Who's Jefferson?" asked Musgrove.

A stranger appeared from behind King Luccese and called over to the group. "I am!"

Bradley turned round and he immediately recognized the African-American boy's familiar broad smile, as it lit up the room. "Jeffers!"

The two school chums hugged each other and Bradley introduced the boy to his two Sandmouth friends. "You will have no doubt gathered by now that this is Jefferson Crabtree… we played in the same school rugby team at Maulby Grammar – I can't believe you didn't tell me about this straight away Turpol!"

The Gatekeeper smiled. "I thought the surprise would be a welcome boost to your morale and that you would be pleased to receive some extra help… and I'm glad to see that I wasn't wrong," he joked and then his demeanor changed. Turpol's face turned to a pale shade of grey and his solemn look was followed by a stern warning, as he relayed some bad news to Bradley and the others. "There is a down side to Henley and Grog's arrival… as indeed Jefferson here can verify - they were accompanied by a dark force inside the Vortex of Silvermoor!"

"Yes," confirmed Jefferson, as he nodded and prepared himself to explain about why the Shade Runner had been following him. "When I…!"

The nervous boy was unable to continue his explanation and was inconveniently interrupted by Luccese. "Sorry young man, but I insist the battle plan preparations begin immediately!" ordered the King, who was keen to start talking about the impending attack on Pathylon and the leaders started to disperse.

Turpol stayed with the children and picked up where he had left off after the awkward intervention by the King. "Right… err, anyway, enough about dark forces," he continued. "That can wait for now… and anyhow I'm sure it will all sort itself out in time!" waffled the dwarf and turned to face Bradley. "We need to talk about the main reason why I am here… you need to find the antidote?"

"Yes, Turpol… you mentioned that and K2 advised me to speak with you – he said you may know where it is located!" declared Bradley in a hopeful tone.

The Gatekeeper smiled. "Yes, I do know where it is but unfortunately you will have to go alone… this is a quest that you must complete by yourself I'm afraid and you must face the biggest challenge of your life – you must destroy the fearsome creature that guards the altar inside the Pyramids of Blood!"

Bradley swallowed loudly as he took a deep breath. "If that is what I must do… then so be it – where is the chalice?"

Turpol paused momentarily. "You need to find a hidden chamber inside the great pyramid, *Talum*… there you will locate the altar and the antidote – but be careful not to choose the most obvious clues!"

Sereny and Musgrove crowded round their worried looking friend, as the concerned girl asked. "Are you sure you don't want us to come with you?"

Bradley shook his head. "Thanks guys... but no – I have to do this by myself and rid this poison from my body once and for all!" he declared. "Then I suppose I'll have to come back and face the Shadow Druid in the duel of destiny that Karn was going on about!"

Word of Bradley's new quest spread around the room very quickly and a pretty female Werebeast approached and offered the boy a drink. Even though she had wolf-like features, he was taken aback by her show of kindness. "Thank you...err?"

"I am Nika – one of Karn's servants and I just wanted to offer you my best wishes and to tell you that all the Werebeast people will be praying for your safe return from the great pyramid." She conveyed and stroked Bradley's hairy hand. "I see you are changing into one of us... I too used to be human like you but unfortunately I never got to drink the antidote and go back home – you on the other hand are strong and you are the eternal chosen one!"

"What was your human name?" asked Bradley, as Sereny's facial expression changed and her brow started to frown.

"I was known as Nicole but I can never go back to my real home," she replied in a soft voice. "Anyhow, my destiny has been set... but your plight is not over and you are well known to be a brave hero - I just wanted to say good luck, *Bradley Baker*."

Sereny looked on with a hint of jealousy, as the smitten boy continued his conversation with the attractive wolf creature and Musgrove chuckled. "Leave it alone, Sereny... Bradley is talking to a *Werebeast* – for god's sake!"

Karn was curious to find out why one of his servants was talking to the human boy and he pushed passed Musgrove and pulled Nika away. "There are guests with empty glasses… now stop fraternizing with these humans and get back to your work!" He scolded and the female Werebeast offered the boy hero a farewell smile, as she turned to leave.

Bradley held up his glass and muttered under his breath, as the wolf girl left the room. "Thanks again, Nika… and I hope one day your destiny will change for the better."

Karn demanded to know what they were talking about but Bradley dismissed the Werebeast leader's unnecessary outburst and put his arm around Jefferson. "Well… it looks like you'll have to go with Musgrove and Sereny to Pathylon without me!"

The King and Queen had now joined the group, as Meltor intervened in Bradley's conversion with his friend. "I'm afraid it's not as simple as that!"

"What do you mean, Meltor?" asked Bradley.

Karn butted in rudely to explain. "No one leaves Rekab until you have drunk the antidote and returned from the pyramid… the battle for Pathylon and Varuna's demise is not the number one priority – first your quest must continue here in Wolf Town in a duel of destiny with the Shadow Druid!" he growled.

Bradley declared. "Alright… it's bad enough having to defeat some fierce creature inside the pyramids never mind being reminded that I face an even more daunting challenge upon my return – that's providing I don't get myself killed in the process!"

Karn confirmed. "You have to return from Talum… the dark lord is here on Rekab and you are the only one that can defeat him - only the eternal chosen one can summon the necessary power needed to suppress his evil manifestation!"

21
The Pyramids of Blood

Many hours had passed and Wolf Town seemed like a distant memory, as the eternal chosen one battled his way through the dense undergrowth to reach the base of the great pyramid. He remembered the look on Sereny's face when the female Werebeast was speaking to him and he chuckled to himself, as he assessed his next task.

Bradley started to climb the hundred or so steps that led to the main entrance and by the time he had reached the top he was out of breath. The twelve year old boy stood motionless with his hands on his hips, as he looked up at the huge torch lit doors. He looked down and noticed a raised stone on the floor, as he instinctively placed his foot on the rock to push it down. The stone disappeared into the ground and the base of the pyramid began to shudder, as a loud creaking sound emanated from behind the doors. "Here goes!" he exclaimed, as the doors opened and he stepped forward into the unknown.

Bang! The ancient doors slammed shut behind him causing the ground to tremor and the resulting draft blew the solitary flame hanging from the wall a few metres ahead. Bradley readjusted the water flask on his belt and approached the burning torch, as he took hold of the cold metal shaft. He held the flame aloft and pointed it forward, as he squinted into the dead air along the winding passageway. The torch light danced across the dusty floor revealing dark inscriptions scrawled along the pyramid's walls. Gingerly he crept along the tunnel, making sure he stepped carefully to avoid the irregular lumps in the ground.

All of a sudden, a cloud of dust filled the air and a row of fatal-looking spikes shot out from the floor and pierced the ceiling of the tunnel just ahead of where Bradley was standing. The horrified boy's eyes widened and he instinctively shouted out a cry of distress, as the spikes disappeared back into the stone floor. "It looks like I'm about to encounter a few challenging tasks before I reach the antidote," he declared and looked around for another way passed. "It doesn't look like I have a choice... there doesn't appear to be any other way through!" He despaired, as he gripped the torch tightly in his grasp and contemplated his fate. "What have I let myself in for... how can I get over those spikes?"

Still shaking, he placed a foot forward and felt around the beginning of the spear laden trap. The spikes did not reappear and he spotted a vent in the wall. He stepped back again and lifted his hand in the air and waved it in front of the round hole. A sharp piercing sound was followed by another cloud of dust, as the spikes shot out of the ground again.

Bradley repeated this several times and he was now convinced that if he bent down to avoid passing in front of the vent, the spikes would remain in the ground. His summation proved correct and he moved forward tentatively.

As Bradley's narrowing eyes adjusted to the dark, he approached a second obstacle. He lifted the torch light and noticed a gap in the floor. He moved closer to the edge and peered down into what seemed to be an infinite drop. He thought back to when was seeking out the Mece back in the Unknown Land. "This reminds of the abyss in the caves at the base of Mount Pero!"

Directly above his head, there was a row of evenly spaced bones suspended between two parallel ropes and bound together with old bandages. Bradley stared at the makeshift hanging rope ladder, which simulated the one he liked to swing on in the park back in Ravenswood. He smiled and his heart was filled with courage, as he threw the burning torch to the other side of the abyss. He then leapt up to the first bone and noticed that his hands were already thick with fur, as razor sharp claws started to appear from the ends of his padded fingers.

Bradley swung his body and as he grasped the second bone, there was a loud cracking noise. The startled boy was caught unawares, as the wrung snapped and the resulting splinters of bone cascaded into the void below. He held on tightly with his other hand, as the broken pieces clattered against the sides of the gaping hole causing echoes to bounce off the walls. Sweat poured down his forehead, as he swung round and grasped the third bone. He regained the momentum he needed to battle his way across the void. After what seemed like hours, Bradley was safely on the other side and he bent down to pick up the torch. "Phew... that was close!" he breathed heavily and proceeded to wipe the sweat from his hairy face.

Bradley's reddened eyes sparkled with excitement. The exhausted boy was proud to have tackled the first two obstacles and he was sure that there would be many more challenges ahead. He paused for a few moments to catch his breath and then trudged on. Little did he know what he was about to come up against and at that very moment, an unusual screeching noise emanated out through the passageways. It sounded like it was a fair distance away and it was now quite obvious to him that he was not alone. There was something else inside the pyramid and by the sound of the hallowing cry; Bradley feared that he could be facing something far worse than his impending transformation into a Werebeast. A cold shudder ran through his aching body and he thought out loud. "Whatever that thing is... I'm in for the fight of my life - there's no way back so I have keep moving deeper into the pyramid!"

Bradley swallowed slowly and took another deep breath. He reached down and unfastened the flask from his belt and removed the stopper. The petrified boy shook the bottle and then took a swig of fresh water, as he quickly refastened the flask securely. "Sounds like there's not much water left," he muttered and wiped the residue of liquid from his face by brushing it with the back of his familiar check-patterned shirt sleeve. He peered ahead into the darkness in search of the strange being that had just released it's a spine-tingling cry. It was quite possible that his imminent encounter with the malicious creature was about to result in a gruesome finale, which would render his fate beyond death itself.

The stillness in the air was interrupted by another strangled roar in the distance. The noise from the unidentified creature was getting closer and Bradley span around to check the passageway was still clear behind him. The boy was now becoming very nervous and picked up a steady pace, as he raced along the ancient tunnel. The torch light danced on the uneven walls and the passageway seemed to be inclining. As he ran, the eternal chosen one had realized an observation and he continued to venture deep into the centre of the great structure. "It feels like I'm climbing... the passageways seem to be guiding me towards the upper part of the pyramid!"

Many twists and turns later, the carved tunnel started to level out and Bradley reached the base of a steep incline of stone steps. He stopped to catch his breath again and looked over his shoulder to make sure the coast was clear. He pointed the burning torch in the direction of the primitive stairwell. It seemed to go on up infinitely and he took his first few tentative steps forward. "This is it then!" he exclaimed, as another screeching roar echoed from an upward direction. "I guess I'm about to meet whatever lives at the top of these steps... I have no choice - I have to defeat this creature and find the antidote before I permanently turn into a Werebeast!" he declared. "Risking death seems to be the norm for me... so I'd better get on with it - but at the hands of god knows what?"

Bradley's self-sermon summoned the courage he needed to start his ascent of the ancient staircase and he took a few more steps with his back held close the wall. He kept the torch aloft and trailed his other arm behind, as he spread the palm of his hand flat against the damp surface. He took another deep breath and edged his way closer to an inevitable duel with the fearsome creature.

At last he reached the final step of the staircase and looked ahead into another musty dank passageway. There was a foul smell of rotting food wafting towards him and then the silence was broken again by another almighty roar. Bradley whizzed round and noticed another tunnel entrance to his right and in a split second he found himself face to face with the perilous monster. The ugly creature was standing no more than a few metres away and it was immensely taller than him. It must have measured some ten feet high and it let out another ear-piercing cry, as it displayed a distortedly misshaped mouth full of glistening teeth.

Bradley instinctively pushed the burning flame ahead to ward off the creature and he took a few exaggerated strides back. He felt the top step of the sand covered staircase under his heel and immediately lost his footing, as the helpless boy stumbled backwards. He crashed heavily on the gritty surface and let out an agonizing yelp, as his the arch of his back landed awkwardly on the edge of one of the stone steps.

The impact caused the torch to fall from his wolfish grip and it hurtled down the stairwell. The flaming beacon clattered against the walls and the dancing embers disappeared from view, as the clanking of metal against stone echoed into the distance. Now there was a deathly silence and complete darkness, as both the creature and the boy simultaneously kept still in anticipation of who would make the next move. The two competitors were temporarily on an even keel with the pitch blackness delaying their confrontation slightly until they had both adjusted their eyesight to the dim surroundings.

Bradley was still in immense pain from the fall but he managed to hold his silence and edged his aching body sideways until he was able to sit up against the wall. He could hear the creature moving around at the top of the stairwell and sweat began to pour down the side of his face.

The frightened boy's lungs felt heavy and he managed to control his breathing to avoid the creature's attention, as his heart pounded like a base drum within his chest.

The darkness inside the tunnel at the top of the stairs was diminishing and wall mounted torches burning in the distance created a backlight, which placed the creature's form in a silhouette. Bradley could now make out its ugly features, as it stood menacingly looking down in search of its prey. The creature tilted its head and released another screeching hallowing sound, as it spread out a multitude of limbs affront of its scaly body. One of the monster's brittle arms held aloft a club-like weapon and the boy gulped. The roof of Bradley's mouth was dry and he swallowed quietly, as the bug-like being continued to scan the steps leading down to where he was resting.

The creature was a sullen looking giant scarab-like beetle with emerald green wings tucked tightly behind its leathery torso. Its angry eyes peered out like sparkling rubies from its skeletal head and tied around its spiny neck hung a necklace made of flesh-eaten bones. Bradley noticed something glistening at the centre of the necklace. As the creature continued to survey the steps, the boy muttered to himself. "That looks like a key of some sort... and I bet your bottom dollar that I'm gonna need it - if I'm able to get passed this disgusting thing that is!"

Bradley was right. It was a bronze key in the shape of round insect that resembled a glittering beetle with two pincers sticking out of its head. The boy knew from the depths of his heart that he had to get his hands on the key so he gathered enough courage to stand up and confront the creature.

The giant scarab was taken by surprise and shouted out. "Ha, ha... to whom do I owe this unexpected pleasure - who dares to venture inside my pyramid lair?"

Bradley was startled by the fact that the creature had spoken and he pushed out his chest. "My name is Bradley Baker... and I am the eternal chosen one - now step aside and let me pass!"

The repulsive insect threw back its head again and released a roar of echoing laughter that caused a shower of sand to rain down from the roof of the tunnel. The giant scarab levelled its boney head and stared piercingly at the young boy through its evil red eyes. "You obviously do not know who I am and what I am capable of?"

"Well, tell me... who are you?" replied Bradley, in an attempt to buy himself some time to think of a plan to get passed the creature.

"I am King Tok... the Pharaoh of REKAB!" replied the scarab creature, as it lifted one of its eight limbs to reveal the club-like weapon with hazardous spikes sticking out of its bulging end. "You have disturbed my sacred period of rest inside my sarcophagus and woken me from my hibernation... you are trespassing inside my pyramid - for all these reasons you will now die a slow and painful death!"

The creature's voice sounded like it was filled with dust and every move it made caused the bones around its neck to clatter. The sight of the disgusting leathery scales on its body made Bradley tremble inside but he was determined not to display any fear towards the giant beetle. The boy felt a small rock on the floor next to his foot. It wasn't big enough to cause the creature any harm but he needed something to create a distraction. He bent down and pretended to tie his shoelace and carefully retrieved the object, as he cupped the stone in the palm of his hand.

The creature stared at Bradley's wolf-like paw and shouted. "What are you doing, boy?" roared the pharaoh and waved the spiked club from side to side. "You must think of me as a stupid insect... I saw you sneakily pick up that stone - do you think that pathetic weapon is any match for my bone battering-batten!"

Bradley's snout was starting to take on the form of the Werebeast's features and a smirk appeared along his hairy pointed jawline. He was no longer fearful of the affects caused by the kratennium rushing through his veins, as he cast a raw smile and stared at the creature's neck. He was prepared to put his unwanted strength to use and had noticed a possible flaw in King Tok's huge frame. The way the scarab's head was attached to its cumbersome broad shoulders looked the most fragile part of its body. The boy hero pulled back his arm and cringed, as another striking pain shuddered down through his bruised back. He struggled through the piercing ache and released a deafening howl of adrenaline filled anger. "Arrrrrrrgggghhhhhh!" he roared and drew back his arm. He spun the stone out of his now fully-formed paw and the boy wolf growled a defiant cry. "Take this *beetle-juice*!"

The stone flew through the air and missed its target by some margin. King Tok let out an amusing snipe of laughter, as the stone hit the side of the passageway and ricocheted off the hard surface. Bradley was to have the next laugh, as the stone took a sharp deflection and struck the creature's neck bone at the exact point that the boy had intended. There was a momentary silence, as the insect pharaoh stopped bellowing and the sides of its mouth pulled downwards in a distressed droop. Then the giant scarab's head detached from its body like a heavy weight and crashed to the ground. The creature's motionless frame stood upright and the club-like weapon remained clasped securely in its claw, as the lifeless skull rattled across the floor shattering into tiny pieces.

What happened next completely flawed Bradley's hopes of retrieving the key and thwarted his attempts to get passed the creature alive. The boy hero looked on in amazement as two newly formed heads grew out in parallel from inside the pharaoh's body. Within a matter of seconds four red eyes appeared in the sockets of the blood covered skulls and sparkled into life to stare out at the startled boy. This time each head was much bigger than the original and King Tok looked more terrifying than ever.

22
A Riddle to Solve

Bradley's transformation into a Werebeast was almost complete and time was running out for him to find the sacred chalice that contained the antidote. He pulled at the long coarse hairs on his forearm and a solitary tear rolled down his canine cheek. He stared at the huge scarab creature and for the first time a feeling of doubt entered his mind. He cast his thoughts back momentarily to his mother and father in Sandmouth, as he contemplated the end of his short-lived existence. Continuing his quest to find the goblet all seemed pointless to him now, as he had failed to destroy the scarab creature and he lowered his head to accept defeat.

King Tok spread his legs evenly to balance the heavy weight of his winged frame and stood in front of the deflated young hero. The creature recognized the boy's submission and he lifted his clubbed weapon into the air in readiness to kill the eternal chosen one. Bradley raised his furrowed brow and resigned himself to the fact that he had run out of time. Getting passed the powerful pharaoh was now an impossibility and he looked up at the spiked weapon, as his eyes closed in readiness for the fatal blow. He felt it would be better for his life to end now rather than endure an eternal existence as a wolf-like being.

The club lowered and in that split second Bradley cast his mind back again. This time the images in his head pictured the family house in Ravenswood and a dinner with his parents. Frannie was running around being as mischievous as ever chasing K2, who had just grabbed a piece of chicken bone from the table and his mouth was slobbering. Bradley's father shouted at the naughty hound and the Burnese Mountain Dog dropped the bone, as he proceeded to lick Grandma Penworthy's hand. She was sitting in one of the fireside chairs knitting an umpteenth cardigan for a non-existent relative, as she watched her favourite gardening programme.

CRASH! A thunderous noise was followed by a cloud of dust, as the particles of stone filled the tunnel. Bradley's thoughts of home were drastically interrupted, as he reacted instinctively by holding up his hands to protect his head. He cowered down and waited for the impact. With a surprised feeling derived from not receiving the resulting blow, he opened his eyes slowly with a slight squint. Still expecting to feel a crunching thud being delivered to his head, he retained his protective crouching position. His fears were proven wrong and to the contrary, King Tok had disappeared and in his place was the front of a brilliant white object. Inside were two very familiar friends. "Hiya Brad!" shouted Musgrove, as he jumped out of the bathtub and quipped. "Looks like we got here in the nick of time!"

Sereny energetically climbed out of the bath and brushed the dust from her clothes. She caught Bradley's eye and smiled. "Hello... I see you've nearly changed into that wolf creature again - are you feeling okay?"

"Not really!" Bradley replied and looked totally shocked at the appearance of his friends in the same bath tub that had transported them all to Rekab. He looked around for a third passenger. "Where's Jefferson?"

Sereny told Bradley that the American boy was helping Turpol and Meltor prepare for the duel of destiny. "King Luccese insisted that Jefferson stay behind and arranged with Karn for us to travel back through the vortex to help you."

Bradley afforded her reply with a roll of his eyes and then summoned a response to their unexpected arrival. "Speaking of kings… where the hell is King Tok?"

"Who?" replied Musgrove, as he adjusted the taps on the bath.

Sereny spoke softly. "Do you mean that nasty looking beetle thing with green wings and two heads?"

"Yeah... he's a giant scarab thingy called *King Tok*!" exclaimed Bradley. "He was just about to bash me over the head with his *bone battering-batten* before you guys turned up... did you see it?"

Musgrove ignored Bradley's question for a moment and he did not look very happy. He completed his inspection of the bathtub and then looked over to acknowledge his young friend to confirm that they had just seen the creature that the eternal chosen one spoke of. "The ugly brute didn't look too happy when we sent him flying!"

"What happened?" asked Bradley, as he got to his feet and rubbed his back.

The lanky teenager laughed and combed his fingers through his think blonde hair. "He took a bit of a pounding from the bath when we crashed through the side of the tunnel, Brad... I think this *King Tok* bloke you are going on about is lying over there in a crumpled heap - there's not much left of him I'm afraid!"

Bradley tried to move but he was in too much pain. "I thought Karn said I had to do this alone... why did the Werebeast and King Luccese send you to help me?"

Sereny put her arm around his waist and helped the injured boy. "Apparently Meltor put Karn right... you were only supposed to get inside the pyramid on your own – and according to Turpol there's nothing in the rule book to say we can't help you find the antidote once you're physically inside!" she explained and guided the wounded adventurer over to where the scarab creature lay.

"Well if that's the case there maybe something that could help us to complete the task," said Bradley, as he remembered the bronze key and reached down to pull at the cord around the dead pharaoh's neck. The necklace of bones detached easily and he held up the crucial scarab-shaped key in a triumphant pose. "I've got a feeling we might be needing this now you two have arrived with the bath... hopefully we'll be able to escape this damn pyramid the same way you guys came in - we just have to find the chalice first so I can drink the antidote!"

"Not so fast, *Sherlock*!" insisted Musgrove, as he pointed to the bathtub. "This thing's going nowhere I'm afraid... the taps are absolutely wrecked and that means we won't get any propulsion - we'll have find another way out!"

Sereny stepped forward. "So how are we going to get out of here if the bath has broken?"

Bradley offered some words of reassurance and held up the bronze object. "I really feel this key is important... it could be what we need to escape, so I suggest we head further up into the pyramid - we have to find the secret tomb that contains the sacred chalice," he suggested. "And there's bound to be more obstacles and challenges ahead... so let's go – we have no time to waste procrastinating about the state of the broken bath tub!"

"Brad's right, Sereny... let's get going - there's some equipment in the bath that might be useful to us!" agreed Musgrove, as he reached into the tub and pulled out a tatty hessian back pack.

"What's in the bag, Muzzy?" asked Bradley.

Musgrove opened the dusty cloth sack to show his friend the contents. "It's just a length of old rope, a printed copy of the map from the cave wall in Amley's Cove that Sereny took with her mobile phone and a bottle of water... thought you might be thirsty, mate!"

Bradley instinctively reached down for his own flask of water and pulled out the bung. He tipped the top of the container downwards and a few drops appeared around the rim. "Thank goodness you brought that with you, Muzzy... I've run out and I don't know what I'd have done - it's so hot inside this pyramid!"

Muzzy handed his friend the bottle and Bradley emptied the contents into the flask. "There... that should see us alright - now, shall we proceed?"

"Sounds like a plan!" replied Musgrove.

"Oh... I forgot to ask - why did you bring a copy of the map?" enquired Bradley, as he reattached the flask to his belt.

Musgrove replied in a confident tone. "It's always good to keep a map... especially when you don't know where you're going to end up - after all, we do seem to be having a lot of unexpected adventures lately!"

Bradley laughed, as Sereny stepped over the felled scarab-creature and she pointed down the tunnel. "I guess we should head this way... look, there's an arrow etched into the wall and I'm assuming its directing us to where we need to go."

"Well spotted, Sereny!" exclaimed Bradley, as he placed the bronze key in his jacket pocket and pulled the zip fastener across to secure the object. "Come on Muzzy, let's go before I complete my full transformation into the Werebeast... who's knows what I'll do to you guys if I change completely before we reach the antidote!"

Sereny giggled and reminded the boys about the incident in the Haytor Hotel bedroom. "Well, the last time it happened you picked poor Muzzy up by the neck and threw him across the room... so you're right - we'd better get a move on!"

"Yeah... I'm still really sorry about that, Muzzy!" said Bradley in a very apologetic tone.

"Stop fretting about it, Brad... there's no hard feelings!" replied Musgrove, as he slung the back pack over his shoulders and tied it securely around his chest.

Bradley attempted a smile through his extended jawline and looked down at his hairy hands, which had now formed into perfect killing paws with razor sharp claws. His canine teeth were protruding from his upper lip and his ears had now grown outwards in a pointed fashion from beneath his thick brown hair. The new shoes that his mother had asked him not to wear were starting to feel very tight and the backs of his legs had begun their transition into the hind legs of a wolf, as the pupils of his eyes began to take on a vibrant shade of crimson red.

Sereny noticed a confused look on Bradley's face, as if he had forgotten something important. "What is it... have you lost something?"

"Wait there you two!" insisted Bradley, as he ran down the stairwell to reach the step where the metal torch had landed. The embers were still glowing inside the reservoir and he lifted the torch into the air to allow the humid atmosphere to rekindle the flames. The torch began to glow brightly and the dancing flames created shadows that bounced off the sides of the stairwell, as the boy hero ran back up to join his friends. "I think we'll need this!" he smiled and the three adventurers headed up the tunnel, as it inclined steeply towards the centre of the pyramid.

The children had walked only a few hundred metres before they noticed a glow in the distance. Bradley ran ahead and peered through an opening in the side of the passageway. His eyes grew wide, as he discovered a pool of shining gold liquid through the entrance to a small chamber.

Musgrove and Sereny caught up with their friend and peered over his shoulder to witness the splendid sight. All around the edge of the pool were scattered the most brightly coloured jewels you could imagine. A treasure trove of rubies, amethysts, emeralds, sapphires and diamonds sparkled vibrantly, as Bradley moved the burning torch from side to side. The flame flickered momentarily and then intensified to reveal the full magnitude of the enchanting contents inside the chamber. A wooden chest edged with brass rivets and filled with gold ornaments was tilting slightly. Ornate jewels were embedded inside antique necklaces that hung over the side of the chest and its base was buried in a pile of silver coins.

"It's so beautiful," said Sereny in a bewitching tone. "Let's go inside!" she insisted and attempted to push passed the eternal chosen one.

"No... wait, Sereny - it might be a trap!" exclaimed Bradley, as he held out his arm to stop the pretty girl from entering the chamber. "Look over there!"

Musgrove and Sereny turned, as Bradley held the torch above their heads in the tunnel. The light revealed another entrance to a second chamber but this particular room appeared very dark and gloomy. Sereny heeded Bradley's advice and the explorers moved carefully up the passageway and approached the black opening in the stone-carved wall. They immediately caught the whiff of a disgusting smell and all three stepped back simultaneously, as they shielded their noses from the repulsive odour.

Musgrove pulled his hand away to reveal his distaste for the rank aroma. "Something must have died in there... it smells like rotten eggs!"

Sereny laughed at the teenager's quip and insisted they go back to the room that contained the sparkling treasure. "Come on let's go inside the other chamber... there's bound to be a chalice in that treasure chest."

Bradley held a strong sense of foreboding beneath his rib cage, as his heart began to beat faster. The two entrances to the chambers were abreast and he revealed his thoughts. "One chamber is dark and smells of death... the other is enchanting and full of riches!" He grinned and continued to explain his suspicions. "It's definitely a trick!"

"What makes you think it's a trick?" asked Musgrove.

Bradley continued to explain, as the shimmer from the golden pool of liquid inside the first chamber continued to mesmerize the inquisitive girl. "Anybody in their right mind would go for gold... wouldn't they, Sereny?"

"Err, yes... err sorry - I was just looking at the..." she stuttered and struggled to take her eyes off the glistening contents of the small tomb.

"That's just the point I'm trying to make," explained Bradley. "As I was saying... anybody in their right mind would go for gold but I know exactly where we should go!" He retorted and tentatively crept inside the dark room.

"Wait!" shouted Musgrove. "Be careful... we're coming in with you!"

Bradley nodded and his two friends followed behind slowly. The burning torch revealed a shelf at the far end of the chamber and in the centre of the room there was a large crypt. The boy hero described the contents on the shelf. "There's only three bottles and they look like they have something inside them!"

The children walked around the crypt, which was shaped like a church altar with a heavy slab of granite covering a stone-carved box with hieroglyphics etched into its sides. Sereny pointed out the images. "This looks like some kind of sacrificial table... look - the carvings depict beetle-like things killing other kinds of creatures!"

Bradley turned his attention away from the three bottles and moved the flame closer to the crypt. "I think you're right, Sereny... those beetle creatures look like King Tok!" he declared. "It would appear that our gruesome foe has been very busy and he must have used this altar to carry out most of his sacrifices… this must be the altar Turpol was referring too!"

Musgrove tapped his friend on the shoulder and pointed at an old discoloured scroll on the shelf adjacent the third bottle. "Look at that, Bradley!" He observed and picked up the fragile rolled piece of paper.

The scroll was secured with a piece of old bandage and tied with a slip knot. Musgrove pulled on the delicate threads and particles of dust created a small cloud, as the boy unravelled the piece of stiff paper. He coughed and then sneezed, before reading out a message that was neatly scribed in italics. "It's in English... very strange - surely it would have been written in some kind of Egyptian language or something, don't you think?"

Sereny nodded. "Yeah... it does seem unusual - you would have thought something that old would have some hieroglyphics or ancient pictures like those on the altar!"

Bradley scratched the back of his large ear with a sharp claw, as he agreed with the observant girl and then politely asked Musgrove to read out the message on the scroll. "It's as if we were meant to be able to understand it... please tell us what it says, Muzzy!"

Musgrove caught sight of his friend's unusual pawed hand and smiled obligingly, as he held out the scroll beneath the flame of the torch. "It looks like a riddle... and I think it refers to the three bottles." He assumed and started to read the message. "*Before you gulp a substance here... look around then stop and peer, until you find a cup of cheer.*" He paused momentarily to clear his throat and then swallowed before continuing to recite the riddle. "*Over time the potion holds, overall the antidote... the future has told!*"

Bradley and Sereny remained silent, as Musgrove finished reading the message. "*Dose the right liquid and you will live!*"

Sereny looked at Bradley's wolfish face and hunched her shoulders. "What are you thinking?"

Bradley politely asked to see the riddle again so he could condense its meaning. "Please pass me the scroll, Muzzy... I need to see if I can decipher the message - reading the words is much better than listening to them and it might spark an idea!"

Musgrove nodded and handed it over, as he stood next to Sereny. They waited in anticipation for Bradley to puzzle over the message. The eternal chosen one muttered the first line again. "*Before you gulp a substance here...* this line must refer to the contents of one of the three bottles!"

"Good thinking, Brad!" replied Musgrove and picked up the bottles individually from the shelf and carefully placed all three of them on the altar. The three children stared at the bottles side by side, as Musgrove revealed the colour of each liquid. "One is full of a thick dark blue substance... another has a bright red liquid in it and the last one looks like it has a greeny sort of colour to it!" he revealed, as he picked up the third bottle and held it near to the naked flame of the torch. "Yeah... it's definitely green and it looks like its got lots of dead insects lying at the bottom!"

"Urrrrghhh... that sounds disgusting!" declared Sereny, as Musgrove shook the bottle in a spiraling motion to send the dead insects into a mini whirlpool and then placed it back on top of the altar.

Bradley continued to decipher the riddle. "The second line of the message says... *look around then stop and peer, until you find a cup of cheer*!"

Musgrove started to scan the chamber for clues and Sereny caught him unawares, as she reached over swiftly to untie the knot securing the back pack to his chest. The determined girl grabbed the hessian bag and ran out of the chamber, as she wandered quickly down the tunnel a few metres towards the entrance to the glowing room. She called back to the two boys. "I'll just take a look in the other chamber... I'm sure I'll find the chalice in that treasure chest - that's probably the cup of cheer in the riddle!"

"Noooooooooo!" shouted Bradley, as he dashed into the passageway to stop Sereny. "It's a trap... don't go in there!"

Musgrove rushed out to follow Bradley but it was too late, as they witnessed the over-inquisitive girl disappear into the chamber full of treasure. She entered the lustrous tomb and a multitude of bright flashes filled the room, as the overspill of shimmering light flooded out into the passageway. This was followed by a loud explosion, as Bradley instinctively protected his friend by pulling on Musgrove's jacket. The teenager fell backwards, as streams of shooting sparks shot out of the entrance. The resulting effect filled the narrow corridor with a simulated firework display, as Bradley covered his reddened eyes.

"That was close!" exclaimed Musgrove and he pushed himself up off the hard floor. "Thanks, Brad... you saved my life!"

"No problem, mate!" Bradley responded with a heroic retort. "I'll always be here to protect you, my friend... now let's get in there and save Sereny!"

The ground was unsteady and still shaking, as they waited impatiently for what seemed like a life time. It took a few more moments for the eruption to die down and for the light to diminish inside the chamber. At last the boys were able to peer through the entrance but they were too late to save their female friend. The frustrated duo stood helpless, as they witnessed Sereny's arm sticking upwards out from the centre of the gold pool of liquid. She had managed to remove the length of rope from the back pack and she was clinging on to it. Bradley dived forward in a vain attempt to grab the end of the rope but it slipped out of his claws into the pool, as the girl's arm lowered further. Bubbles appeared on the surface, as Sereny's hand let go of the rope and she finally disappeared from sight beneath the golden liquid. A few more gulps of air reached the surface and popped, as the pool rippled to indicate the capture of its latest victim.

Bradley pulled himself back and offered Musgrove a look of anguish, as he sighed heavily. "I can't believe it, Muzzy!" exclaimed the eternal chosen one. "It's happening all over again... just like when we were in the base of the cenotaph at the start of our last adventure down Silvermoor!" He raged. "Why does Sereny keep doing this to us... she decided to do her own thing and disappeared that time and now she's done it again!" he exclaimed and punched the air in frustration. "This time we might never find her... for all we know she may have drowned in that blasted pool of liquid gold!"

23
Locating the Chalice

Meanwhile back in Trad, Ulan-dem had called a meeting with Varuna and Flaglan inside the Royal Palace. The veteran Hartopian was very unhappy about his current role within the new regime. He had been instructed to oversee the construction of a new stronghold to replace the felled Shallock Tower next to the River Klomus.

He could not believe that Varuna was still ignoring the implications that could arise from the recent uninvited presence of the Klomus Hawk during the inauguration ceremony. The newly appointed High Priest for the Blacklands was keen to eradicate the nonchalant approach that his irresponsible King had adopted and he waited impatiently at the bottom of the grand staircase inside the main entrance hall.

A fanfare sounded, as Varuna held Flaglan's delicate hand aloft and they descended the crimson-carpeted marble steps in a majestic pose. The waiting servants and guards bowed nervously, as the royal couple stepped onto the mosaic floor and the sound from their elegant footwear echoed around the grand hall. The Hartopian kissed his wife's hand and bid her farewell, as a group of Devonian ladies-in-waiting escorted the new Queen out of the palace.

Ulan-dem cringed at the sight of the newly crowned couple and urged Varuna to join him in private. "I must speak with you... I am not happy about my new role – I seem to be spending all my time as a glorified building site manager!"

Varuna looked around and noticed a few of the guards sniggering. "See what they think of your outburst... you are making a fool of yourself – is that all you called me here for?" asked the angry Hartopian. "I could be with my beautiful wife right now... she has gone shopping for new furniture and you are wasting my precious time – get back to the construction site and make sure the new tower is ready!"

Ulan-dem growled under his breath and insisted Varuna tell him why the construction of the tall battlement was so important. "You seem to be focusing all your attention on that blasted turret and not facing the fact that Ploom will have told Luccese what she saw!" he fumed. "Why do you need a tower anyway... you have no one left to imprison?"

"Listen to me, Ulan-dem... I know the Klomus Hawk will have fed Luccese and his cronies with information about my coronation!" replied Varuna, as he led his fellow Hartopian away from the prying eyes of the guards and into a nearby alcove. "You think I'm unaware that they are planning an attack... I'm not an idiot, you fool – I spent many days locked away in the Shallock Tower before it was destroyed and I am keen to exact my revenge on Luccese!" he roared. "I want the new tower built in time for when he mounts his pathetic attack... when he fails and is captured again - I intend to lock him inside my new iconic monument and throw away the key so he can rot inside a cold cell!"

Both Hartopians were unaware of the current status of their enemies advance and support for the deposed rebels was growing. The senior members of the alliance had left Freytor behind and they had now reached Rekab. Varuna was unaware of the ally's movements and subsequent battle plans to re-invade Pathylon, as Ulan-dem sighed in frustration. "Varuna, you are deluded... while Luccese languishes in Freytor, the Galetians and the Lizardmen will have regrouped in Krogonia by now – they could attack within days!" he explained. "The tower will never be ready in time and in any case when they get over the Satorc Bridge you won't need a tower... Luccese won't even need to leave his safe haven inside the Freytorian senate – so he will be laughing at your demise from a great distance!"

The new King tilted his head back and laughed. "Did you not hear the explosion this morning?"

"Yess, but I thought that noise was made by my workers when they were shot-blasting some stones for the new tower," replied Ulan-dem in an assumptive tone.

"No... that was the sound of the Satorc Bridge crumbling into the estuary!" replied Varuna, smugly. "So you see... no Krogons or Galetians will be stepping foot on the mainland of Pathylon for some time – they are trapped on Krogonia!"

"I see," said Ulan-dem, as he lowered his head.

"I am so glad you can *see*, you old fool!" taunted Varuna. "That's why you are over*seeing* the building of my new tower... and as you are now reliably informed - we have plenty of time until Luccese and Meltor get their lazy backsides off that frozen island and set off to help their isolated countrymen!"

The disheveled Hartopian quickly changed his demeanor and offered his apologies. "I seemed to have underestimated your cunning defense strategy, my lord!" groveled Ulan-dem, as he backed away. "The destruction of the Satorc Bridge is an ingenious move and I apologize for wasting your time... I will return to the construction site immediately and continue to oversee the building of your tower!"

Varuna smirked and insisted that Ulan-dem remove his filthy presence from his pristine palace, as he summoned two palace guards. "It would appear Ulan-dem is just about to leave!" he announced, as he cast a nonchalant quip in the hunched Hartopian's direction. "And don't forget to close the door behind you... now, I must find my beautiful wife – I have some important shopping to attend to!"

The undermined veteran was reeling inside from his belittling ordeal at the hands of Varuna. The palace doors slammed closed and he dared not look back, as the irate weasel strode towards the river in the direction of the construction site. He muttered to himself. "If Varuna thinks that by blowing up a bridge will delay an attack by Luccese and his armies... then he is a fool – if I know Meltor, he will have anticipated that already," he surmised. "But I can't see how they will manage to invade, so maybe Varuna does have reason to feel relaxed... still it is not my concern – I better get on with building the tower for my gullible King!"

Back inside the great pyramid, Musgrove comforted his wolfish friend. He placed his arm around Bradley's young shoulders and insisted they return to the dark chamber. "There's nothing we can do here... let's go back and work out the rest of the riddle to make sure we can stop your transformation into a Werebeast - then we can concentrate on finding Sereny."

Bradley nodded and reluctantly accepted Musgrove's suggestion, as they walked away from the golden chamber entrance and returned to the gloomy atmosphere of the darkened tomb.

Bradley knew he had to push the thoughts of Sereny to the back of his mind, as Musgrove handed him the scroll. The distraught boy fought back his tears and tentatively read out the second line again. "*Look around then stop and peer, until you find a cup of cheer.*" He coughed quietly and cleared his throat, as he looked up towards the top of the chamber. He then noticed some more hieroglyphics etched into the domed ceiling. "Can you see what I see, Muzzy?"

Musgrove followed his friend's line of sight and noticed an engraving of a goblet in the hieroglyphics. "It's just an etching of an ancient cup... wait - *cup of cheer*!" He shouted and jumped up onto the altar to take a closer look. "Hey, Brad... it's no etching either - it's the real thing!" shouted the excited teenager. "It's an actual goblet set in the stone!"

Bradley picked up the torch and climbed onto the altar, as he stood next to Musgrove. He steadied his balance by holding onto the taller boy's belt, as he held up the burning flame to take a closer look. "You're right, Muzzy... it must be the chalice we've been looking for and just look at those rubies set into the side of it - they're magnificent!"

"We need to find something to remove the chalice from the stone," suggested Musgrove, as the two boys forgot about the loss of Sereny for a while and scanned the tomb for a sharp implement. "Over there, Brad... on the shelf where we found the bottles - it looks like hook or something!"

Bradley spotted the rusty looking metal object and jumped down from the altar. He picked up the hooked shaped pin and handed it up to his friend, as Musgrove grabbed the makeshift tool. "Be careful, Muzzy... don't damage the chalice!"

It took about ten minutes for Musgrove to ease the goblet out of the rock face and at last he was able to hand it to his friend. "Here you go, Brad... safely removed and undamaged - as requested!"

"Brilliant!" exclaimed Bradley and quickly examined the chalice more closely. "I thought it would be made out of metal... but it seems to be some sort of granite - it's very heavy!"

Musgrove jumped back down and watched Bradley, as he placed the goblet on the altar next to the three bottles. "What now, Brad... what does the riddle say?"

Bradley unravelled the scroll again and read out the next line. "*Over time one potion holds*!" He scrunched his elongated snout and then noticed another inscription, this time on the stone slab that formed the top of the altar. "Look, Muzzy... there's the face of an old clock - maybe we should place the chalice on top of the clock face?"

"Well done brain box!" replied Musgrove and patted his friend on his back.

Bradley growled and showed the first signs of anger towards his friend. The transformation was reaching its final stages and at that moment both his training shoes burst, as his feet grew in size to reveal the hind limbs of a wolf. "It's happening, Muzzy... I'm turning into a fully formed Werebeast - we have to hurry!"

Musgrove placed the chalice on top of the clock face and then snatched the scroll from Bradley, as the eternal chosen one fell to the ground holding his stomach.

Now it was up to the nervous teenager to solve the riddle and he quickly scanned the writing again on the torn piece of paper. He started to mutter out loud what they had deciphered so far. "Okay, we've found the potion - it has to be in one of the bottles," he surmised. "And we've found the cup and I've put that over the clock to represent time." he read the last part of the riddle again. "*Overall antidote... the future has told - dose the right liquid and you will live!*" recited the confused boy, as he paused for moment then he shouted out in delight. "Now all I have to do is choose which bottle has the right ingredient and pour the liquid into the chalice... this should make the potion that Bradley needs to change back into his human form!"

Musgrove looked at the three bottles and could not decide which to choose. He kept flipping from reading the riddle to looking at the bottles. The boy continued to shift his focus from one to the other until he experienced the eureka moment he was looking for, as he let out a loud cheer. He slammed the scroll onto the altar and realized that the clue was in the riddle all along, as he recited the first letter of each line of the message. "B, L, O, O, D!" he exclaimed. "The potion must be in the bottle that contains the red liquid... blood red - I'm a genius!"

Musgrove pulled out the bung and tilted the bottle. Suddenly, a slight hand slapped his back and a familiar voice shouted. "Stop!" the startled boy turned round to witness a female covered in gold liquid. "Hi!" she said calmly.

"Sereny... how - where, err?" stuttered Musgrove and then burst in to uncontrollable laughter. "You look like that spray-painted girl out of one of the old *James Bond* movies!"

"Ha, ha... very funny - surf boy!" retorted Sereny. "Well it's a good job I managed to get out of that pool of gold in time - that rope in your back pack came in very handy!"

"I wondered where the bag had gone... so did you enjoy your quick dip in the plunge pool?" teased Musgrove. "That will teach you to go off looking for blingy treasure!"

"I didn't go looking for treasure... I was trying to locate the chalice but I see you've found it!" observed the girl and then looked over to where Bradley was lying on the ground, as the wolf boy started to regain consciousness. "Looks like we need to hurry... looks like he's about to wake up again."

Musgrove began to tilt the bottle with the red liquid, as Sereny snatched it out of his hand. She repeated her warning. "I told you to not to do that... it's not the right bottle!"

"But it's got blood in it!" insisted Musgrove. "The message clearly spells out the word BLOOD!"

Sereny agreed. "You're right... but not human blood - remember the images on the side of this altar?" she remarked, as Musgrove picked up the torch and bent down to examine the side of the crypt. Sereny continued. "This is where King Tok carried out his sacrifices... the blood of a scarab creature has to be green - now pass me the bottle with the creepy-crawlers in it!"

Musgrove stood upright and handed the glass vessel containing the green substance to the insistent girl. "Here you go Professor Plum... or should I say *Goldilocks*!"

"Oh... shut up, Muzzy and hold the chalice steady while I pour this in!" she replied in a tiresome tone and proceeded to empty the green slimy liquid out of the bottle. As the substance hit the surface of the goblet, the rubies started to glow and a green haze of steam rose up from the sacred cup. "There I told you this was the correct bottle... now let's get this down Bradley's throat before it's too late.

Sereny had spoken too soon. Bradley was no longer lying on the floor. The boy had finally transformed into a fearsome Werebeast and he stood hauntingly in the corner of the dark chamber with his head hung low. Bradley was now a wild creature and he raised his head slowly to stare at the two petrified children through his evil glinting red eyes.

Musgrove and Sereny froze on the spot, as the fearsome creature stood hauntingly still in front of them inside the darkened chamber. The red glow from the beast's piercing eyes created an eerie glow inside the tomb that resembled a photographer's processing room. But instead of photographic paper trays, the three bottles and the chalice remained standing on the sacrificial altar.

Vertical clinging lines of saliva dripped from the beast's hungry mouth, as Sereny cried out in a desperate voice. "Bradley Baker!" she shouted. "We have the antidote... we can save you - all you need to do is take a drink from the sacred chalice and the evil will disappear!"

"Who is this *Bradley Baker* you speak of?" roared the newly formed creature. "My name is *Yeldarb Rekab* and I am a Werebeast!"

24
Confronting the Werebeast

The evil presence inside the chamber sustained an eerie atmosphere and it grew even more hallowing, as the fully-formed wolf creature stared menacingly at the two teenagers.

Musgrove tried to avoid the Werebeast's heated glare, as he muttered under his breath to Sereny. "Bradley has finally adopted his alter-ego and now recognizes himself as *Yeldarb Rekab*... so by assuming the same names as the places on the map – it's given me an idea."

"What are you two whispering about you ignorant humans?" growled the angry wolf-like creature.

Sereny nudged Musgrove and secretly handed him the hessian bag behind his back. The teenager responded and took hold of the gold-covered back pack, as he attempted to keep the conversation going by insisting that they were just trying to be helpful.

"What are you holding behind your back?" roared the Werebeast. "Show me at once or I will tear off your head!"

Musgrove placed the bag on the altar and encouraged his old friend Bradley to approach by using the creature's alter-ego. "Take a look at this, *Yeldarb Rekab*... this will be of interest to you."

"What is it?" demanded the curious wolf boy.

Sereny could see that Musgrove had made a connection with the real Bradley Baker and she quickly took the opportunity to intervene. "Look at the map!"

"Who asked you to speak, female?" growled the young Werebeast uncharacteristically, as another stream of saliva dripped from the huge sharp fangs that had now grown even further down from his upper jaw.

Sereny quickly realized that she had no connection with this thing that called itself Yeldarb Rekab, even though she had deep feelings for the true Bradley. She now risked jeopardizing the plan, so the disappointed girl heeded the creature's response and stepped back to allow Musgrove to continue reasoning with the annoyed Werebeast. She had an idea what Musgrove was up to and she grabbed the chalice while the creature was distracted.

Musgrove braved an approach and leant over, as he laid the map down flat in front of the creature. He then pointed to the pyramids. "This is where you will find the blood that will make you stronger than any other Werebeast in Wolf Town... so forget about the contents of the chalice - you need to drink the red liquid in order to attain these special powers!"

The creature looked puzzled and a little anxious. He pushed Musgrove away and grabbed the bottle with the red liquid inside it. "Make me stronger you say... stronger than any other Werebeast in Wolf Town?" He growled and smashed the bottle on the stone slab, as the crimson liquid splashed across the surface of the altar. "Rubbish... you must think I'm a fool - the power I need must be in this bottle!" he declared and pulled out the stopper in readiness to drink the blue coloured potion. "Good health!" he roared and gulped the bottle dry.

Musgrove exclaimed. "Damn... what have I done?"

Sereny started to giggle, as the Werebeast reeled backwards holding his throat. "Don't worry, Muzzy... I had a feeling he would do that!"

"What's happening to the creature?" demanded Musgrove.

"He's drinking the antidote... watch and see what happens," replied Sereny calmly, as the gold substance on her body glistened from the dancing torch light that had now replaced the red glow from the creature's eyes.

"But he drank the blue liquid from the bottle... I witnessed it with my own eyes!" insisted Musgrove, as the Werebeast fell to the floor in a crumpled heap.

"Whilst you were showing him the pyramids on the map I switched the liquids and poured the contents of the chalice into the wrong bottle," explained the cunning girl.

"Brilliant... well done you!" replied Musgrove and kissed Sereny on the cheek. "Oops... sorry!"

Sereny blushed beneath the gold covering on her face, as they stood in anticipation and watched Bradley transform back into the boy they both recognized. The antidote gushed through the reeling boy's veins and every wolfish hair and claw fell to the floor, as his body returned to a more familiar form.

Bradley opened his eyes and smiled, as his two friends approached. "You did it... you saved me!" He exclaimed and wrapped his arms around both their necks.

"Welcome back, Brad!" cried Musgrove. "Thought we'd lost you there… for a minute!"

Sereny looked into the boy's hazel eyes and stroked his youthful face. "Hello, Bradley Baker... so glad to see those awful red eyes have gone!"

The reunion was short-lived, as the ground began to shudder. A loud rumbling noise was immediately followed by a series of tremors, as the quake began to reverberate through the floor of the chamber. Bradley let out a painful cry, as a piece of stone fell from the ceiling and hit him on the head. "Arrrrggghhh... I should have known!" he gasped, as the wall behind the shelving opened to reveal a cascade of dead scarab skeletons.

A sliding stone panel slammed down to block the entrance to the tomb and the skulls continued to fill the chamber. Gripping the dusty bones, the three children scurried and clambered upwards using the skeletal heads to reach the top of the chamber, as the ceiling began to open above. Then a gust of fresh air blew in Bradley's face, filling what was left of the musty chamber with a cool breeze.

The scarab skulls continued to push the three adventurers upwards out of the tomb and they found themselves situated outside the vibrating structure at the summit of the great pyramid. Bradley punched the air again and yelled. "Yes... we did it!"

The three children held on to whatever they could grasp to secure themselves from falling the hundred metres and more to the forest floor below. Bradley looked out at the wondrous sight and commented on the panoramic view. "Wow... you can see right out as far as the Red Ocean - and look, there in the distance," he cried. "You can just about make out the remains of that curved rock we blasted through in the bath... when we arrived in Rekab - there's not much left of it and the little cottage has been totally destroyed!"

Sereny capped her shiny gold hand above her brow and peered in the direction that Bradley was pointing. "Oh dear… I believe the cottage belonged to a Witch – apparently she is preparing a potion for the Shadow Druid!"

Bradley replied. "Who told you that?"

Turpol mentioned something back in Wolf Town before me and Muzzy set off in the bath to help you," explained Sereny. "The Gatekeeper told us that if the Witch manages to retrieve the dwarf's blood to complete the potion and the Shadow Druid gets to drink it - he will become more powerful than anyone in Pathylon, including you Bradley!"

The boy hero nodded and confirmed the girl's fears. "It's a good job we survived the dangers inside the pyramid... we have to get back to Wolf Town before it's too late - and you're right, the odds of me defeating the Shadow Druid will be severely reduced if he manages to drink the potion!"

Sereny smiled and offered a vote of confidence to the brave twelve year old. "You'll beat him in the *duel of destiny*, Bradley... you have to - the future of Pathylon depends on it!" She then turned to Musgrove, who was looking down at the tops of the trees. "You okay, Muzzy?" she asked in a caring tone.

The teenager was holding on precariously to a slight gap between the blocks in the square stonework and replied nervously. "Not really... I was just wondering how the hell we're gonna get down from here - it's no good whittling on about Witches and beating Shadow Druid's, if we're stuck at the top of this blooming pyramid!"

Sereny attracted Bradley's attention again, as he resumed his admiration of the view and asked the eternal chosen one. "Muzzy's right, how do we get down... we can't go back inside the pyramid - the scarab skulls are blocking the way!" she exclaimed. "We're stuck here and it's freezing!"

Bradley stopped his assessment of the surrounding landscape and stared at Sereny. His eyes became transfixed on the girl. Inside the pyramid, he hadn't really noticed the shimmering gold that covered her from head to toe. Now they were outside in the fading daylight, the extremity of the shining liquid that had coated her body was very intense. He smiled and remembered that she had ventured into the chamber of treasures. "I hope that stuff washes off!"

"Me too... I don't fancy looking like an *Oscar* statuette for the rest of my life!" replied Sereny and laughed at her own expense. "Anyhow, have you got any ideas how we get down from this thing?"

Bradley returned a gesture of laughter in a kind sort of way and then edged himself around the ridged aluminum sheath that covered the top of the pyramid. The structure continued to vibrate, as he removed the bronze key from around his neck. "Well, to answer your question, Muzzy... I think I might have found a way down - now hold on!" He shouted and placed the key inside a perfectly carved beetle-shaped hole at the very tip of the prism. Not really knowing what to expect, he turned the replicating key and then stood back to take a firm grip on the side of the apex.

Nothing happened at first then after a few seconds the whole pyramid started to vibrate more intensely and the aluminum sheath began to glow, as the giant prism trembled beneath the three terrified adventurers. Bradley shouted to his friends. "Are you two okay?"

Musgrove and Sereny both replied together nervously. "Yessssss!"

Their voices were drowned out by the noise of a swirling wind that had rapidly whisked up around the summit and large pieces of stone began to cascade down the triangular sides of the huge structure. The whole pyramid started to bend and twist with a spiral of polished granite steps emerging from the four angled slopes of cracked stone. The stairwell continued to curve around the structure, working its way down in a twisting fashion until it reached the base of the pyramid.

The vibrating stones set into the prism settled and the wind stopped howling, as Bradley shouted out a descriptive response. "The pyramid has turned into a perfectly formed cone... it's just like the *helter-skelter* ride in Clifton Park back home but with steps instead of a slide!" The ecstatic boy was jubilant and he retrieved the key to place it back around his neck. He then edged over to join his two friends, as they began their long descent.

Sereny was still glowing like a golden statue and she followed Bradley and Musgrove down the cascade of perfectly formed footholds. She giggled to herself and called ahead. "Try and guess what I'll be doing when we get back to Wolf Town?"

Bradley turned round and looked up at the shining girl. "That's obvious... having a bath by any chance?"

"You bet ya!" she replied.

Musgrove stopped and joined in the conversation, as he realized something very important. "Speaking of baths... how are we going to get back home?"

Bradley replied. "How do you mean?"

"The slipper bath is still trapped inside the pyramid!" explained Musgrove.

Sereny realized the implications and held her hands up to her cheeks. "Muzzy's right, Bradley... how are we going to get home?"

"Let's try not to worry too much about that right now... it's important that we all get down from this thing safely - so I can get back and meet the Shadow Druid in the *duel of destiny*!"

"That's all very well, Brad... but then what?" insisted Musgrove. "So we get back... you kill the druid and everyone in Pathylon is happy - but what about us?"

Bradley was starting to get a little impatient and called upon his calm demeanor to settle Musgrove's concerns, as they continued to descend the spiral staircase. He decided to conclude the conversation and pacify his friend by offering him a few words of hope. "After I have fought the Shadow Druid, we'll head back to Freytor with General Eidar and Meltor... the Freytorians will probably have some kind of time machine to get us back home safely - the old stream powered locomotive might still be in use," he explained. "Now let's just finish the quest... I'm sure they're still plenty of strange things that are bound to test our resolve – so let's make the most of this amazing adventure - are you up for it, Muzzy?"

Musgrove smiled and admired his young friend's courage. "Too right... I'm definitely up for it, Brad - now let's find that Shadow Druid so you can kick his butt!"

Bradley turned to continue his descent, as he looked down at the last few steps that led to the sandy ground below. He noticed that the final step was bronze in colour and it had an image engraved at the centre. He carefully strode over the metal plate, as he crouched down to examine it further and then called up to his two friends. "Hey... there's a picture of the scarab key on the last step - what do you think it means?"

Musgrove jumped down and landed in the soft sand, as he regained his balance quickly to look at Bradley's discovery. He gently brushed the dust away from the step to reveal some writing above the scarab. He started to read out the message, as Sereny took her last few steps down the spiral staircase. "Place your weight to reverse the effect and beware the…!"

Before Musgrove could finish reading the inscription, Sereny stepped onto the bronze plate and a loud rumbling shook the ground. The three children jumped into the forest undergrowth and peered out through the grass reeds. The spiral staircase began to ascend back up the side of the huge monument, as each step disappeared effortlessly back into the slabs of the stone structure. Within seconds the gigantic cone transformed back into the pyramid, as the aluminum cap rotated into place at the apex of the monument.

Bradley turned to Musgrove and started to laugh. "Nothing like putting your foot in it… eh, Muzzy?"

"You're not wrong there, Brad… and that was well and truly executed!" replied Musgrove in a fit of laughter and rolled onto his back, as he held on to his ribcage.

Sereny afforded the two giggling boys a scorned look and responded accordingly. "Oh well… I preferred it as a pyramid, anyhow!"

Bradley smiled and winked at the girl. "Well said, Sereny… and no matter – it's not like we'll ever need to go back in there again!" he reprised and lifted his aching body out of the damp undergrowth. "Come on… we'd better start heading back to Wolf Town - I've still got another battle to fight and a date with an evil druid to keep!"

25
The Contest Must Go Ahead

Back in Wolf Town, Meltor and General Eidar had arrived at the coliseum. They entered the royal enclosure to receive word that the Shadow Druid had mysteriously reached the perimeter of the arena. The two commanders were waiting for King Luccese to appear with Queen Vash in readiness for the planned *duel of destiny.*

Karn arrived before the royal couple to congratulate the High Priest and the Freytorian. "A delayed communication from Krogonia has been received at my headquarters... Pavsik has confirmed your prediction, Meltor - Varuna has destroyed the Satorc Bridge!" he revealed and growled out more information. "And you'll both be pleased to know... construction of the new bridge in the south of the region is still on schedule for completion - in readiness for the allied reinforcement's arrival!"

Meltor nodded and acknowledged the Werebeast. "Thank you for the update, Karn... I am glad to hear that the vital the link from Krogonia to the Galetis Empire is almost finished!"

"Everything seems to be going to plan," remarked General Eidar, as the King and Queen appeared in the doorway of the royal enclosure. Luccese entered the balconied room that overlooked the great arena stage below and he shook everyone's hand, as he declared. "Just heard about the good news from Pathylon... you must be very pleased, Meltor?"

"Yes, my lord... we were just discussing it," replied the Galetian, as he accepted a firm handshake from Luccese.

Queen Vash offered further welcoming news. "Bradley Baker has just arrived back in Wolf Town with Sereny and Musgrove," she announced. "They have returned triumphant and Bradley managed to drink the antidote... so the infectious strain of kratennium inside his body has thankfully been suppressed."

"That's excellent news!" remarked Karn. "The eternal chosen one will have regained the strength he needs to fight... and hopefully defeat - the Shadow Druid!"

Meltor commented, as he released his strong grip of the King's hand. "Not so fast, Karn... the boy will be tired following his ordeal - he will need to rest!"

"Nonsense... the contest must go ahead, as planned!" insisted Karn. "The Shadow Druid cannot be kept waiting any longer!"

Luccese frowned at the Werebeast's selfish retort and then averted his stare to look around the impressive coliseum. It was a breathtaking view from the royal enclosure and the excited noise among the waiting crowds of spectators had reached a deafening crescendo. The stadium was packed to full capacity with a mixed species of differing creatures that had travelled from far and wide to witness the great event.

The enormous arena boasted upwards of two hundred thousand seats with row upon row of brightly coloured stalls forming a perfect oval. Parallel strips of canvass tied atop the grandstands created a uniform canopy that contrasted against the stunning sunset on the Rekab horizon. The impressive outline of the stadium fashioned a harmonious fusion of colour and created the illusion of an impressive seamless spectacle. An array of brightly coloured flags representing various regions within Pathylon, Rekab and Freytor were flying proudly around the circumference of the uppermost tier. The setting was complimented by a fan of parallel sunbeams that formed a vibrant backdrop and continued to pierce the skyline from the setting sun that had now disappeared behind the distant mountain range. The shaded areas of the arena were supplemented with light reflecting from cleverly positioned mirrors that directed the dying sun's rays onto the centre stage.

A fanfare of horns sounded and quieted the masses, as King Luccese and Queen Vash appeared uncomfortable in the presence of such a baying crowd. They offered each other a disapproving glance and hesitated slightly before sitting down in their designated thrones next to Karn. The Werebeast leader maintained a respectful stance, as they took their seating positions. He then turned to face the unsettled audience and outstretched his arms in a welcoming gesture in order to calm the impatient crowd. The onlookers responded by reducing their chanting to a dull mumbling, as the disgruntled voices faded into a gentle hum around the stadium.

The spectators sensed that the battle between the Shadow Druid and Bradley Baker was about to commence. A solitary voice shouted out from the terraces. "Kill the druid, Bradley... and save us all!" A deathly silence followed the isolated outburst and a cohesive group of Black Squirrels responded to the lone cry with a chattered roar of approval, as the crowd reacted to their supportive chant with an endorsed cheer.

Karn turned to speak with Luccese. "The boy you have nominated to challenge the Shadow Druid seems to be quite popular with the audience."

The King covered his mouth with a close-fist gesture, as he gently bit his forefinger in frustration and then politely cleared his throat in readiness to counter the Werebeast's comment. His reply was subsequently drowned out by the infinite din, as the crowd started to recite the name of the eternal chosen one in a unified chorus. Luccese indicated with a graceful wave of his hand that they should retire to a more private setting to discuss the ensuing battle between the boy hero and the evil warlock.

The royal couple stood to disguise their discomfort and waved at the crowds, as Karn followed them into a room behind the enclosure. They were joined by Meltor and General Eidar, as the door slammed shut and the noise from the stadium was reduced to a dull background anthem.

King Luccese invited everyone to take a seat around the large round table and he addressed the leader of the Werebeasts. "Karn... firstly let me make it very clear - neither I, nor any of my people nominated Bradley Baker to fight with this *Shadow Druid* character!" He continued before the irritated Werebeast could interrupt. "And secondly... I do not agree with the ceremonial charade you have organized... the masses out there are baying for blood and it's pretty certain that the young boy will be killed by that evil druid - this whole thing is ludicrous and I insist you stop this so-called *duel of destiny* before it's too late!"

Karn stood and carefully placed his hairy paws on the table. "King Luccese... I have the utmost respect for you and the people of Pathylon but I am not prepared to stop the duel of destiny!" He roared and lifted his arm. The angry Werebeast proceeded to slam his fisted claw on the wooden surface, as Meltor raised his muscular frame in a threatening pose. Karn pointed a sharp talon at the High Priest in response to the Galetian's retaliatory action. "And don't you even think of trying to stop me, Meltor ... I am aware that the young Baker boy is your protégé but it is written in the ancient archives that the eternal chosen one will challenge any evil that threatens our lands – and this particular evil just happens to be the Shadow Druid!"

King Luccese raised his hand calmly and asked Meltor to sit back down, as he responded to Karn's statement. "There has to be another way... surely we can all stand together and defeat the Shadow Druid - we have armies that can overcome this villain without offering young Bradley to be slaughtered in front of the marauding hordes you have amassed for your own amusement!"

"That is utter gibberish, Luccese... the boy was destined to be one of us - he may not have transformed into a Werebeast permanently but he still has the strength of one!" exclaimed Karn. "I am honoured to be hosting such a life changing event here in Wolf Town... and this contest is definitely *not* for my amusement - both Rekab and Pathylon will benefit from the warlock's death!" he raged and waved his arm at a low-ranking officer that was guarding the door. "Now... I insist we continue with proceedings and if you've all finished with your unjust demands - I would like to return to the arena at once!" he roared and raised his clenched fist in the air. "The duel of destiny will go ahead, as planned!" he proclaimed and recovered his composure. Karn then strode passed the King of Pathylon without making eye contact with the frustrated monarch and marched in an aggressive manner towards the door. The wolf-like creature paused for moment, as Meltor stepped into his path and the stubborn Galetian formed a defensive stance by crossing his robed arms. The angry Werebeast responded aggressively by expanding his chest and snarled, as an evil grin appeared across his snout. The awkward standoff was interrupted by a loud fanfare from inside the coliseum, as Karn teased the obstinate High Priest. "Ahhhh... the ceremony is about to start – the time has come for your young apprentice to prove his worth, Meltor!"

The fuming Galetian moved aside to allow the Werebeast to pass and brushed his shoulder across Karn's headdress, as he headed out of the room.

Luccese stepped forward to calm his friend's anger. "I am pleased that you didn't get drawn into his provocative ways, Meltor... we Pathylians are much better than that," confirmed the King and ushered the High Priest through the doorway. "It would appear we have no choice... the contest must go ahead – let's just hope Bradley has what it takes to defeat the Shadow Druid."

The resounding atmosphere of the arena above the darkened room was met with a nervous reception from Bradley Baker's friends. They were preparing the exhausted boy for his impending duel with the Shadow Druid inside a dungeon-like chamber beneath the oval stage. A metal suit of armour hung forlorn on a wooden manikin in the corner of the room, as rays of dust-filled light streamed in through the barred window in the ceiling.

The splayed parallel beams reflected from the metal shoulder plates of the armour to cast horizontal stripes across the boy hero's worried face. Bradley turned to Jefferson and offered thanks to his Maulby Grammar School friend. "I really appreciate you being here with Sereny and Muzzy… Turpol told me that a Shade Runner nearly killed you when you travelled into Pathylon – you never mentioned it when you first arrived in Wolf Town."

Jefferson smiled and replied, as Muzzy helped him lift the suit of armour from the wooden stand. "I began to explain but didn't get the chance to finish because everyone started talking about the plans to invade Pathylon," he clarified. "I didn't want to push the issue… anyhow, I wasn't going to say anything till after the duel of destiny because I didn't want to upset you - but now you've mentioned it, I think I should explain what happened!"

"Go on," requested Bradley.

Jefferson continued from the start. "It's probably all my fault… when I entered the time portal below the cenotaph - a hooded figure followed me!" he explained. "The Shade Runner grabbed me but I managed to escape… he must still at large somewhere in Pathylon though!"

"Have you any idea where this Shade Runner is?" asked Sereny.

"When we exited the vortex… Bradley's Uncle and the Lizardman managed to trap it inside Grog's old tomb in Krogonia - I guess the creature must have jumped back into the time portal," replied Jefferson.

"That means he could be anywhere!" declared Bradley. "And who is this Shade Runner you speak of and why should I get upset about it?"

Jefferson cleared his throat and then delivered the devastating news. "You already know who the Shade Runner is… you've encountered him before – and it's the same evil character that killed K2!"

Bradley gritted his teeth and his eyes widened, as he raised his eyebrows. "Jefferson… stop avoiding the question and just tell me the truth – who is the Shade Runner?"

Jefferson paused nervously and then looked to Sereny for support. The girl's body was still covered in a glittering coat of gold powder, as she stood open-mouthed below the roof light and reacted in an outraged manner. "I can't believe you have broached such a sensitive matter just before the biggest fight of Bradley's life… you idiot – oh, just tell him will you!"

Bradley repeated his demand, as he grabbed the boy by the collar. "Jefferson… I'm beginning to lose my patience – who killed K2?"

"Okay, okay… it was Darke - Ethan Darke!" he replied and bowed his head.

"*Ed-Case* is the Shade Runner?" shouted Bradley, as he released his grip on the petrified boy. "Why would Ethan Darke want to kill K2?"

Jefferson bowed his head and moved aside, as Musgrove put his hand on his friend's shoulder. "Calm down, Brad."

Bradley shunned his affection, as the anger spread through his aching body and he held his face in his hands. "Ouchhhh!" he yelled, as the sharpened nails on his hairy fingers scratched his forehead. "Oh no… it's happening again – I'm transforming back into a Werebeast!"

Sereny screamed. "But that's impossible… you drank the antidote from the chalice!"

The door to the chamber burst open and the familiar outline of a small figure appeared in the doorway. The little Gatekeeper stepped forward into the light and addressed the distressed group of children. "What's going on... the crowds are waiting – why aren't you dressed for battle, Bradley?" asked Turpol and then noticed the hairs growing on the boy hero's face. "Oh, that's why... something must have angered you to trigger the transformation again and it's just what I feared would happen - where is the chalice?"

The wolfish features on Bradley's tortured face blushed slightly in response to the dwarf's comment. "Do you mean *this*!" he replied and reached over to retrieve Musgrove's hessian back pack. He pulled a cloth-covered object out of the bag and revealed the sacred goblet to the stunned onlookers. The boy's arm slumped by his side and he held the chalice tightly, as it hit his thigh. A line of regretful tears rolled down his cheeks and he looked deep into the dwarf's eyes. "What have I done, Turpol... what have I done?"

The Gatekeeper rushed over to the distraught boy and looked up at his saddened face, as he held out his hand. "Give me the chalice, Bradley... its presence here is the only reason why you are turning into a Werebeast again."

Sereny asked. "Can you explain to me why he's changing back into the creature if he's already drunk the antidote?"

"The healing effects of the potion have only been made temporary... the chalice should never have been removed from the great pyramid – Bradley will complete his transformation if we don't return the sacred goblet back to its original resting place!"

Musgrove intervened. "What about the duel of destiny... if Bradley fights the Shadow Druid there will be no time for him to go back to the pyramid – he will end up as a Werebeast forever."

Bradley dropped the chalice, as it clattered against the hard floor and he shouted. "Never mind the Shadow Druid… take me to Ed-Case – Ethan Darke will pay with his life for what he did to K2!"

Sereny and Jefferson reacted and held on to both Bradley's arms, as the boy fell to his knees sobbing. Jefferson released his hold and picked up the sacred goblet. He handed it to Turpol, as the girl insisted that they move Bradley into a nearby chair. "He's in no fit state to go into battle with the Shadow Druid… never mind kill a Shade Runner – what are we going to do, Turpol?"

The Gatekeeper rubbed the edge of the dusty chalice with his sleeve and stood in front of the chair, as the boy continued to regenerate into the wolf-like creature. He carefully placed the ancient cup inside his cloak and positioned his small wrinkly hand beneath Bradley's chin, as he lifted the boy's head. The dwarf peered into his red eyes and spoke gently. "Bradley… I know you can hear me – now listen to me carefully," he explained. "You have to forget about the Shade Runner for the time being… you have much more important things to consider - if you try to find this Ethan Darke you speak of, you will run out of time and transform into a Werebeast." The dwarf continued. "If you fight the Shadow Druid… you will also lose the precious time that you need to prevent you from turning into the wolf creature – I'm afraid you only have one option if you want to retain your true identity and avoid living the rest of your life as *Yeldarb Rekab*."

Jefferson interrupted. "What do you suggest, Turpol?"

254

The dwarf paused and then turned to face the three children. "This is my plan… and don't challenge it because it's the only way we can save Bradley and also fulfill the duel of destiny at the same time," he insisted, as he stared at Jefferson and Sereny. "You two will help me to get Bradley back inside the great pyramid."

"But what about the Shadow Druid?" asked Sereny.

"I'll come to that in a second," replied Turpol.

Musgrove added. "But all entrances to the pyramid are blocked and the bathtub is still trapped inside there… even the spiral staircase has disappeared thanks to Sereny - so how are you going to get into the pyramid?"

Sereny afforded Musgrove a scowled look, as the dwarf smiled. "That's the easy bit!" declared the Gatekeeper. "There is another way into *Talum*," he revealed and pulled the bronze scarab key away from Bradley's neck. "And we'll probably need this little beauty to help us get inside!"

"So what part do I play in your plan?" asked Musgrove.

The Gatekeeper paused momentarily and then walked over to the suit of armour. He pushed a wooden stool in front of the manikin and reached up to remove the shining metal suit, as he threw it on the ground in front of the lanky teenager. "You'll need to put that on!"

"Ehhh… why?" asked Musgrove.

Bradley stood up from the chair and held his stomach to steady the pain that churned inside his torso. "Arrrrrgggghhh!" he yelled and then mustered enough energy to approach his dear friend, as Sereny offered the boy much needed support by hooking her shoulder under his trailing arm. "Muzzy… as much as I want to confront the Shadow Druid – I'm in no fit state to fight!" he took a deep breath, as he looked over at the dwarf for confirmation and

Turpol nodded in agreement. Bradley took another deep breath and sighed in a defeated manner. "I'm relying on you, my dear friend... you must now take my place and fight in the arena above!"

The room fell silent, as Musgrove bent down and picked up the suit of armour. He looked at his reflection in the mirrored chest plate and then stared at the group of waiting onlookers. "But surely they will know it's not Bradley out there... I'm taller than him!"

The Gatekeeper reassured the teenager. "You will be too far away from the royal enclosure for them to notice... they won't be able to judge how tall you are from that height." Musgrove clutched the armour close to his chest and his eyes met with the collective stare from his hopeful colleagues, as he nodded tentatively. Turpol took the boy's action as an affirmative response, as he smiled. "Then you will do it, Muzzy?"

"Of course I'll fight the Shadow Druid... I can't let Bradley Baker down – besides, I owe him my life ten times over!" replied Musgrove in a nervous tone, as he pulled his friend towards his side.

Sereny reluctantly released her hold on the eternal chosen one, as she handed Musgrove the helmet that would disguise his face from the Shadow Druid and the audience. "That arena is full of blood-lusting spectators and they will be watching your every move, Muzzy!" she exclaimed "You'll need this... and by the way – it's not just about letting Bradley down," she stated. "You will be making us all very proud... and *when* you *beat* the druid – you will become the new saviour of Pathylon!"

Musgrove offered the girl a raw smile. "*If...* I *beat* him - you mean!"

Bradley mustered enough energy to pat Musgrove on the shoulder and uttered a confident retort. "No, Muzzy... *when* you *beat* him!"

Turpol reached into his cloak again to retrieve the chalice and spoke to Muzzy in a hopeful tone. "There's one last thing we could do for you before we go... it may help to protect you against the Shadow Druid's magic powers – hand me the sacred coin, Bradley."

Sereny asked. "What are you going to do with the grobite?"

Bradley reached into his trouser pocket and pulled out the coin. "It's not glowing... it's of no use to you, Turpol!"

"Wait and see," replied the dwarf, as he turned the chalice upside down. "Now, Bradley... I want you to place both your thumbs and index fingers on the four horned Lurg heads that are depicted around the sides of the sacred cup – can you see the rubies inside their eyes?"

"Yes," replied Bradley, as he placed his hands on the goblet. "What are Lurgs?"

"No matter... just make sure you cover the jewels, whilst I place the coin in the clawed foot of the chalice," explained the Gatekeeper. "We are going to extract what's left of your eternal powers and transfer them through the ancient cup and hopefully they will pass into the coin!"

Jefferson and Sereny watched on with interest, as the dwarf summoned Musgrove to wrap his hands around Bradley's fingers. "Now, whatever happens... do not let go of the chalice!" ordered the dwarf and he placed the grobite on top of the upturned goblet.

The four claws on the base of the granite cup curled around the coin, as a haze of crimson smoke escaped between Musgrove's clasped fingers. The goblet began to vibrate and it became very hot to handle, as Bradley screamed out a painful cry. "Arrrrrrrrrrrggggggghhhhhh... I can't hold on any longer – my hands are burning!"

"Keep your hold steady!" shouted Turpol. "It's not really burning you... the coin is trying to reject the chalice – keep your faith and summon all your strength!"

The smoke grew thicker and the room was soon engulfed with a cloud of warm mist, as the rubies set in the goblet began to glow. The radiance from the fiery gems beneath Bradley's fingers created a scarlet haze within the smoggy chamber and the coin began to illuminate brightly to compliment his piercing red eyes.

"It's working!" shouted Jefferson.

Turpol clenched both fists and urged the boys to keep hold of the chalice. "It won't be long now!"

Musgrove released an agonizing cry, as the burning sensation passed through Bradley's fingers into the palms of his hands. "Arrgggggghhhhhh... Turpol, the pain is too much!"

"Muzzy... you must keep your grip - or the eternal powers from Bradley will not pass into you!" replied the dwarf in a desperate plea to the exhausted teenager.

The brightness of the coin intensified and the clawed base of the chalice released its grip on the grobite, as it shot into the air. Bradley and Musgrove lifted their heads instinctively to watch the glowing disc hover above the blanket of smoke, as the sacred cup stopped vibrating. The coin fell like a leaden weight and everyone in the room watched in silence, as the coin rolled slowly across the floor.

The grobite span and finally settled in front of Bradley's feet, as Turpol took a firm hold of the smoking chalice. The face of the coin had been cleverly imprinted on the base of the white hot goblet and the dwarf approached Musgrove, as he waved at Jefferson. "Help Muzzy to get dressed… and when he has adorned the armour I can stamp the inscription of the coin onto the chest plate to cover his heart – as I said, hopefully it will help to protect him against the warlock's special powers!"

Jefferson lifted the metal chest plate and secured it around Musgrove's shoulders, as he clipped it into place. Turpol carefully positioned the goblet so as not to burn himself and then held the rim of the chalice to use it as a makeshift branding iron. He stood on a nearby stool and asked Musgrove to step forward, as the dwarf held the sacred cup in front of the boy's chest. The spitting of molten metal sparked from the clawed feet, as the burning sound of smelting crackled against the body armour. "There… it is done – the imprint of the coin has been mirrored onto your battledress!"

Bradley struggled to bend down, as he picked up the coin and offered it to the dwarf. "Do you still need this?"

"No… probably be best if you keep it – you might need it again when we return to the great pyramid," replied Turpol.

Bradley placed the coin in his pocket, as he fought back the dull pain inside his aching body and thanked the dwarf. "It is good of you to help me, Turpol… I owe you big time!"

"You owe me nothing… the danger is far from over and it's the least I can do – helping the eternal chosen one is a great honour and I'm just glad I can be of assistance!" he replied in a humble tone, as he called over to Sereny and Jefferson. "Okay, let's get Bradley back to the pyramid!"

Sereny stroked her fingers against the back of Musgrove's trembling hand, as she walked past the anxious teenager. "Good luck, Muzzy… and please don't be afraid!"

26
The Duel of Destiny

Musgrove was now fully equipped for battle in his shiny suit of armour, as he stood alone and afraid. The barred window in the ceiling cast an eerie light over his lanky posture, as he waited in the centre of the basement room.

Turpol led the three children out of the chamber and Bradley was the last to leave, as he turned to face his brave friend. "We both have daunting challenges ahead of us and there's a pretty good chance that neither one of us will make it through... in case anything bad should happen, I just want you to know that it's been a pleasure knowing you – I truly mean that!"

"Thanks, Brad... that means a lot – now you'd better get going before you transform into that creature again," insisted Musgrove, as Bradley picked up a sword that was leant up against the door frame and threw it towards the armour-clad gladiator.

Bradley prepared to leave his friend and cast his mind back to his encounter with Aunt Vera, when he accidentally poked a straw up her nostril. He had likened that particular incident to a scene from the *Gladiator* movie and the digitally re-mastered coliseum in Rome, as he referred to the same scenario again. "Just like in the film, eh… but this time it's not in my imagination and you're not facing my Aunt or a bunch of prowling tigers – this is for real and you have to fight the Shadow Druid!"

"Don't worry, Brad… I have the power from the chalice and the imprint of the coin to protect me – so hopefully I'll get through this ordeal in one piece!" replied Musgrove in a nervous tone. "Now, go… and try to salvage the bath if you can – we might still need it if we get the chance to escape from this blasted place!"

"Oh yeah… the gold coin may come in useful after all – I'll do my best to try and recover the old bathtub!" chuckled Bradley and his smile turned to a grimace, as he then winced at the shooting pain that travelled up his spinal cord. He managed to summon another raw smile and encouraged his friend. "No worries, Muzzy… and you just make sure you kick that druid's butt for me – okay?"

"Deal!" replied Musgrove, as Bradley finally left the confines of the chamber. With his best friend gone, he immediately placed the helmet on his head and inserted the heavy sword in the sheath hanging from his side.

A fanfare sounded from the arena above and Musgrove waited a few minutes, as he held an emblazoned shield in his other gloved hand. He carefully hooked his arm into the handle grips and pulled the shield close to his armour, as the trembling teenager reacted to the cheering crowd. The noise from the bawling hordes evolved into a deafening crescendo, as he walked slowly out of the chamber and made his way up a stone flight of steps.

The startled boy emerged from the darkened basement and instinctively raised his metal-clad arm to shield his eyes from the fading sunlit skyline. He emerged at the far side of the arena and peered through the thin slits in his helmet, as the noise from the spectators increased to a higher level. The trap door behind him crashed down and sealed the opening to the chamber below.

The cheers for the disguised hero quickly turned to boos and hisses, as the Shadow Druid appeared at the opposite end of the stadium. The dark figure moved eerily sideways, as the correlated hatch slammed to the ground. The hooded being kept his staff close and his head down to shield his face, as his long black cloak glided across the dusty floor.

Another fanfare sounded, as Musgrove and the evil warlock reacted to the instructions from a stadium announcer and they walked slowly towards the centre of the battle zone. The pair of combatants stopped within a few metres of each other and they waited for the next announcement, as the noise from the crowd erupted again. This time the instructions came from the royal enclosure and the familiar growling voice of the Werebeast leader bellowed out, as he rose from his throne.

Karn addressed the masses. "Silence, people... and please formally welcome our two contenders – who will fight to the death in the long awaited *duel of destiny*!"

The baying audience needed little encouragement to erupt into yet another frenzy, as they started to chant the boy hero's name over and over. "*Bradley, Bradley, Bradley, Bradley...*"

The real Bradley Baker and the others were now running through the dense undergrowth, as they approached the edge of Yeldarb Forest. Turpol led the way and was keen to get through the dark woods and onward to the Pyramids of Blood before nightfall.

Bradley reacted to the chanting sound of his name, as he stopped and turned to listen. The booming noise from the coliseum's audience was so loud that the others also stopped to pay attention to the distant hum.

Sereny stood next to Bradley and put her arm around his waist. "Listen to that chorus of noise… they are shouting your name, Bradley – you are their hero!"

"No… I'm not!" he declared. "I know I should be there… but it's poor Muzzy that will have to bear the terrifying responsibility of defeating the warlock - and assume the title of *hero* on this occasion!" he replied in a disenchanted tone, as the sound from the spectators inside the arena summoned a current of fear that ran through Bradley's throbbing bones. The boy lifted his hand to his head and felt his pointed ears sprouting out from his hair again. He snarled frustratingly and then muttered a tome of optimism for his isolated friend, as he focused his line of sight in the direction of Wolf Town. "I have to go, Muzzy… fight well, my dear friend – fight well!"

Back inside the coliseum, the announcer held up his arm to instruct a solitary horn blower to sound the signal to start the contest. The resonance from the brass instrument made Musgrove jump, as the scrawny Werebeast creature blew the guild-draped trumpet and the Shadow Druid remained motionless with his hands still hidden.

The crowds encouraged the fighting to start and Musgrove summoned a fragment of courage, as he pulled the heavy sword out of his sheath. "Come on then, hoody… let's get this over with!"

The Shadow Druid lifted his head slowly to reveal the bottom of his chin and his long grey hair hung sullen, as it rested on his broad shoulders. The warlock held his staff in front and pulled back one of his legs, as he knelt down in front of the disguised boy. He lowered his hooded head again and muttered a few words. "Prepare to die… eternal chosen one."

"I don't think so!" shouted Musgrove, as he lifted the sword above his head and prepared to administer the first crushing blow.

The Shadow Druid responded with rapid speed and before Musgrove could react, the warlock somersaulted over the boy's aerial weapon. He landed neatly behind the teenager and instinctively crouched to avoid another swipe of his blade.

The Shadow Druid readied himself for another trailing swing of the sword and he drew in his stomach to avoid the boy's pathetic attempt. The end of Musgrove's blade just sliced through the warlock's cloak and the dark lord swerved effortlessly, as he swept his staff in a full circle. The wooden pole made contact and unbalanced the boy, as the long staff clipped his ankles.

Musgrove fell backwards and a unified hush spread around the terraces, as the spectators grew quiet. Their hero had faulted and he attempted to swing his sword again but the druid rotated the staff like a spinning propeller. A multitude of accurate blows caused the brave fighter to hit the ground hard and his winded rib cage felt the weight of the imprinted chest plate upon it. The back of Musgrove's helmet hit the floor and the resulting jolt to his head produced an array of shooting stars that danced in his eyes like a twisting galaxy. He completed his unceremonious fall by swinging his sword again in self-defense but his feeble attempt missed the dark stranger by some distance.

The Shadow Druid released an evil laugh from beneath his hood, as he sensed the boy was growing tired. The warlock's plan to tire his opponent was working, as he held his staff aloft to inflict the fatal strike. As he prepared to thrust his wooden shaft into Musgrove's body, the injured boy noticed a gap in the druid's cloak and thrust his sword forward into the dark void. The blade penetrated the tormentor's abdomen and this instigated a loud cheer from the crowd, as the protagonist reeled backwards and dropped his weapon.

The boy jumped forward and strode the warlock, as he held the sword tightly by its jeweled handle and pointed the blade in a downward vertical position. Musgrove was panting heavily and he paused for a few seconds, as he offered his fallen opponent a parting comment. "Back luck… I guess this time you lose – this is for my friend Bradley Baker!" He stated and lifted one of his hands away from the sword handle, as he removed his protective helmet to reveal his true identity.

The masses reacted in a shocked manner and a loud hum resonated around the coliseum, as Musgrove prepared to lower his blade. The Shadow Druid was confused and was unaware who the brave gladiator was, as the triumphant boy stood in silhouette against one of the deflecting mirrors. The reflection from the sunset-strewn sky continued to disguise his opponent and the warlock took advantage of the boy's hesitation. The blood continued to ooze out of his side, as he reached out his hand and pulled his staff forward. Before

Musgrove could react, the warlock thrust it into the boy's chest.

The crowd's mumbling turned to groans of disbelief and a feeling of disappointment spread around the terraces, as Karn rose to his feet. King Luccese and Queen Vash followed the Werebeast leader's reaction, as they rushed to hold the balcony's rail in the royal enclosure. Meltor stood and joined his King's side, as the Galetian shouted down to the arena floor. The concerned High Priest's voice was drowned out by the noise inside the stadium and Musgrove reeled back, as he fell heavily to the ground.

The Shadow Druid jumped to his feet and his hood slipped to reveal his reddened eyes, as he stared down at the stricken boy. Musgrove held his chest and his face turned to an ashen shade of grey, as the warlock's hood rested on his shoulders to reveal an equally shocked face. The boy exhaled a distressed exclamation that overcame the pain he was feeling inside his bruised ribcage, as tears welled up in his eyes "Father!" he screamed.

The Shadow Druid instinctively dropped his staff and stumbled backwards, as he realized that the brave gladiator lying on the ground was not the eternal chosen one. He could not believe that he had just thrust the end of his staff into his own son's chest in an attempt to kill the boy. Thomas Chilcott dropped to his knees, as Musgrove crawled over to comfort his stunned father.

The members of the royal enclosure had already made their way down to the arena floor and a silenced crowd watched on, as the proceedings unfolded. King Luccese was first to the scene and lifted Musgrove's head off the floor and rested it on his knee. "Are you alright?"

The boy groaned and nodded, as he felt the imprint of the coin on his chest plate. "Yes, I'm fine... thanks to this – but I can't believe that my father is the Shadow Druid!"

Thomas groaned, as blood poured from the open wound in his stomach. "Musgrove!" he cried. "I didn't know it was you... I would never have fought you if I had known!"

Meltor assisted the King and helped Musgrove to sit upright, as the boy leant over to place his arm across his father's broad neck. Queen Vash and Karn watched on, as the boy stroked the distressed face of the newly identified Shadow Druid.

Thomas Chilcott released a huge sigh, as he groaned in pain. "Musgrove... please don't be sad – it's time for me to leave and I am so pleased it is you that finally released me from my living hell."

"Don't die... I miss you, Dad – please don't go!" he cried, as he reached down to feel the warm blood seeping into the sand on the dusty arena floor. "I want you to come home... Mum needs you!"

"Good bye, Muzzy... make sure your Mum and Simon stay safe – and please don't blame yourself for my death," replied Thomas, as he declared. "You have provided the biggest gift a Son could ever give his Dad... you have given me my freedom back and now my soul can rest peacefully."

Musgrove cried out and then collapsed on top of his father's blood-stained cloak, as Queen Vash tried to comfort the stricken teenager.

Meanwhile, Bradley and the others had ventured deep into the heart of Yeldarb Forest. The shimmering silver bark that adorned the trees glistened, as the sun set over the mountains in the distance. Turpol led the children and they made their way along a beaten path through the centre of the haunted woods.

Sereny heard a scratching sound and instinctively pulled on Jefferson's jacket. "What was that?"

"What was what?" replied the boy in broad New York accent.

"That sound… its coming from those trees over there!" indicated the girl, as she attracted Bradley's attention. "Can you see anything?"

Bradley peered into the thick mass of twisted trunks and replied. "No… nothing but trees!" he declared. "I'm glad we didn't come this way before – taking the longer route around the forest after we left the great pyramid was a wise move," he confirmed and then suddenly spotted some movement in the branches ahead. "Wait… there is something out there!"

Turpol joined the three children and asked why they had stopped. "We have to keep moving!"

Sereny positioned herself behind Bradley, as Jefferson bravely walked towards the moving branches and called. "Who goes there?"

A screeching voice replied. "Get out of our forest… you are trespassing!"

Bradley looked around and made Turpol aware of the many black sparkling eyes that appeared in the gaps between the branches. "It appears we are completely surrounded… what are these creatures?"

Before the Gatekeeper could reply a swarm of black furred animals with long bushy tails jumped down from the branches and scurried around the four strangers. All the creatures had tightly strung bows wrapped around their chests with sheaths to hold primitive arrows on their backs. Each Black Squirrel had a crude red cloth around its waist and a cross canvass strapping that braced their muslin footwear. The lead squirrel stepped forward and asked the dwarf to explain why they were in the woods. "These trees are sacred... only those who are invited by Captain Dray are allowed to tread the paths that lead through Yeldarb Forest!"

Turpol apologized and revealed the sacred goblet. "Please let me explain... we need to take the quickest route to Talum – we have to get the eternal chosen one back inside the great pyramid so this chalice can be repositioned."

The lead squirrel stared at the granite cup and looked puzzled. "The eternal chosen one, you say... don't you mean Yeldarb Rekab?"

Bradley stepped forward and introduced himself. "Yes... I am Yeldarb Rekab or at least I will be if I don't get back inside the pyramid!"

To everyone's surprise the lead squirrel crouched to his knees and all the other black creatures followed suit. Turpol insisted that they all get to their feet but they retained a worshipping position with heads bowed.

Bradley walked towards the kneeling lead squirrel and spoke softly. "What is your name, my friend?"

The creature remained silent and kept his eyes focused on the leafy ground. Bradley repeated his question but still there was no response. Then the ground began to shudder, as the trees in the distance began to sway.

Sereny and Jefferson shouted simultaneously, as the huge giant pushed his way through the trees. "Bradley... watch out!"

Their warning came too late and the enormous ogre picked Bradley up in its shovel-like hand, as the boy's legs frantically kicked out at the ugly brute. Turpol ran over and insisted that the giant creature put the boy down. "You must be Spew… release the eternal chosen one!"

The Wood Ogre responded by glaring at the dwarf, as the Black Squirrels remained in their crouched positions. Spew realized what the other forest creatures were doing, as he let out a bellowing laugh and then lowered Bradley to the floor. "You must be Yeldarb Rekab… only the great Werebeast can command such respect amongst the squirrel clan!" roared the ogre.

Bradley was amazed that all the woodland animals were still worshipping his every move and politely asked the Wood Ogre if he could request that they stop kneeling. "This is very humbling but also quite embarrassing… please ask them to stand up."

"I'm afraid they will not listen to me… but I know someone who can influence them!" he yelled and cupped his large hands around his broad mouth. The Wood Ogre released a deafening call that penetrated the depth of the forest. "Drayyyyyyyyyyyyyy!" he roared and declared. "That should do it!"

Within minutes the trees ahead started to move again but this time the branches much higher up in the roof of the forest started to rustle. Bradley and the others all stepped back a few paces, as the largest of the Black Squirrels landed in front of them. The muscular animal puffed out his chest and spoke in a dulcet tone. "I am Captain Dray and I assume by the look of my worshipping army of Black Squirrels… you must be Yeldarb Rekab - or should I say Bradley Baker!"

27
Mummified Skeloyds

The worshipping Black Squirrels began to disperse and retreated into the forest, as they heeded their captain's command. Dray started to build a fire to keep the children warm, as the Wood Ogre picked up a stone and threw it into the dark trees. The accurate shot produced a felling sound and an innocent woodland creature yelped, as it felt the full force of the rock.

Bradley sat next to Dray, as the squirrel poked a stick into the flames and he began to explain his predicament. The Captain already knew about his transformation glitch and he informed the group that Karn had been in touch earlier. Spew returned with the dead prey and mounted it over the fire on a spit, as they continued to discuss why the group had ventured into the forest.

Turpol asked how Karn knew where they were and the Black Squirrel replied. "They all worked it out when a boy called Musgrove was discovered to be deputizing for young Bradley in the duel of destiny... it was Meltor who realized that the eternal chosen one must be in danger or he would not have allowed his friend to fight on his behalf," explained the captain. "The old Galetian worked it out and assumed the chalice must have been taken from the pyramid... is this true?"

"Yes!" replied the Gatekeeper and retrieved the scared goblet from his cloak again. "This is the reason why we are here... and we have to return it before Bradley does indeed turn back into Yeldarb Rekab forever."

Jefferson interrupted. "How is Muzzy... I take it he must have won the contest?"

Bradley and Sereny listened in hope that Captain Dray's reply would yield the news they hoped for, as the squirrel paused for a few seconds. "He did indeed!"

"Phewwww!" sighed Bradley, as he high-fived his American friend and then hugged the girl. "I knew he wouldn't let us down!"

Captain Dray put an end to their celebrations and revealed the identity of the Shadow Druid, as the three children stared with open mouths. "It turns out that the dark lord was the boy's father!"

Turpol broke the shocked silence and spoke calmly. "Musgrove must be devastated... he must be in a terrible state!"

Bradley moved away from the fire and wandered off to a nearby clearing in the trees, as he looked up into the night sky. The stars were twinkling and Sereny followed, as she touched his arm. "You okay, Bradley?"

"What do you think?" he replied in a sullen voice. "Who would have thought that Thomas Chilcott was the Shadow Druid?"

Sereny held on to the boy's trembling arm and placed her rosy cheek against his blue-checked shirt sleeve. "Nothing surprises me any more... but I guess it does answer the question why Muzzy's Dad disappeared from home a few weeks ago – and now we know why!"

Bradley stiffened his stance and shook off the girl's affection. "Don't mean to dismiss you, Sereny... but we have to get moving – I want to get back to Muzzy, as soon as possible!"

"No problem... no offence taken, Bradley – I'm with you on this one!" she exclaimed and they both returned to the others.

Bradley's canine teeth were starting to appear out of the corner of his elongated snout and he suggested that they set off for Talum immediately. Turpol noticed that the boy's finger nails had grown somewhat sharper and he agreed, as the Wood Ogre groaned at the waste of good food.

Captain Dray suggested that Spew bring the freshly cooked animal with him, as he decided to go with Bradley to help him return the chalice. "You may need our support... I believe you killed King Tok on your last visit?"

"Yes... well, it was Musgrove and Sereny who actually achieved that brave feat - with the bath tub!" replied Bradley.

"What is a bath tub?" asked Spew, as he sunk his uneven teeth into the roasted carcass.

Sereny intervened. "Never mind... it's a long story." She replied and dismissed the greedy ogre to ask the Black Squirrel why he mentioned King Tok's demise.

Captain Dray informed Sereny and the others that a bunch of very nasty creatures dwell in the pyramids and they will be looking for revenge.

"What are they?" asked Jefferson.

"They are dead, really... but inside the confines of the pyramid they remain part mortal," replied the Black Squirrel. "Their souls were taken away by King Tok and now they will be looking to seek revenge on those that have taken their only hope of living again away from them!"

"Skeloyds!" shouted Bradley, as Sereny looked at Turpol.

Spew threw the stripped bone on the ground and asked. "How do you know of these creatures?"

The dwarf's response was predictable. "We have come across them twice before but I didn't realize they existed on Rekab!"

Captain Dray confirmed Bradley's outburst but explained that they were not quite the same skeletal creatures that they have fought against before. "These are not normal Skeloyds... that's if you can call a Skeloyd normal!" he laughed. "No... these are called Mummoyds!"

"Mummoyds?" questioned Jefferson and started to laugh.

"You may mock, but yes... they are a result of King Tok's experiments at the sacred altar inside the great pyramid – they are mummified Skeloyds!" explained the Captain.

The conversation had reached its conclusion. It was agreed that Dray and the Wood Ogre would join the quest to return the stolen chalice. The group armed themselves with primitive weapons and gathered their belongings, as they headed south towards the Pyramids of Blood.

Over an hour had passed and the exhausted dwarf requested a short break to catch his breath. The walk from the edge of the forest to the base of the great pyramid had tired Turpol's short legs and he suggested that the children start looking for the secret entrance into Talum.

Bradley was standing at the bottom of the hundred or so steps that led up to the oak doors that he had entered previously. He called over to the Gatekeeper. "Why don't we just go up here and make our way up to the main entrance?"

"The Mummoyds will no doubt be guarding the main entrance... we need to enter the pyramid without them knowing – that way, we still retain an advantage and have the element of surprise," replied the dwarf.

"So what exactly are we looking for?" asked Sereny.

Turpol pulled the sacred goblet from his cloak and held it up so the three children could see the markings around the cup. "As you can see, there are four symmetrical heads depicted on the chalice... they look like dragons with beaks but they are actually horned creatures called Lurgs!" he explained. "You asked me back inside the coliseum what these creatures are... well, we dwarves use these animals as mounts just like Galetian's ride Hoffen and Krogons utilize Koezard!" he revealed. "You need to look for a pair of parallel paths that lead to the base of the pyramid... just like the shape of the horns on the chalice – where the paths meet you should find the clue to open the secret entrance!"

Bradley nodded and he suggested that Sereny and Jefferson each take one side of the pyramid base. "We should systematically search the immediate circumference around the structure," he explained. "You go that way, Sereny... and you round that way, Jeffers – I'll search the far side and we'll meet back here in ten minutes if we can't find it."

The search for the hidden entrance ensued, as Captain Dray tensioned his bow and sat down next to the fatigued dwarf. Spew was busy sharpening the end of his spear then suddenly a shout of excitement could be heard from the far side of the great pyramid.

Turpol disregarded the pain in his aching legs and stood up. "That sounds like Bradley... let's hope he has found the clue!" he exclaimed and started to run through the undergrowth. The Gatekeeper was so small that just his pointy ears could be seen bobbing up and down in the long grass. The dwarf ran past Jefferson and encouraged the boy to follow him. "Come on... I think Bradley has found what we're looking for!"

Captain Dray and Spew soon caught up with Turpol and Jefferson just as Sereny rounded the pyramid from the opposite side. They all stopped suddenly and watched in disbelief, as they witnessed Bradley balancing precariously on one leg at the top of a long vertical pole.

The boy hero had found the clue but was stuck at the top of it, some thirty metres off the ground. He shouted down. "So now what do I do, Turpol?"

The dwarf chuckled and scratched his head, as he hunched his shoulders. Everyone looked at him for an answer or some gestured indication of what the next move should be but he offered no immediate explanation. The Gatekeeper walked around the bottom of the pole, as he continued to scratch his bald grey head and then shouted. "Give me a minute or two... I'm thinking!"

Bradley groaned and yelled back down, as he kept his arms out-stretched to stop himself from wobbling. "That's not good... *I'm thinking* means you don't know what I need to do next – I guess I'll have to work this one out for myself!"

Sereny shouted up and asked. "Can you see anything ahead of you on the side of the pyramid?"

"What am I supposed to be looking for?" replied Bradley.

"Is there anything unusual or *out-of-character* on the pyramid... the pole's supposed to be the clue and it has sent you up there for a reason - so there must be something at that height to help you find the entrance!" explained Sereny, as she scanned the surrounding area for any other clues.

Jefferson commented. "Or maybe it's just a trap?"

Captain Dray looked at the bottom of the pole. "No... it's not a trap – it's definitely the clue," he claimed and asked Turpol to hand him the chalice. He pointed with his paw at one of the Lurg heads. "Look at the shape of the two paths leading up to it... they are exactly the same as the horns on the goblet!"

Jefferson accepted the squirrel's observation and joined Sereny in a search for more clues. They both kicked around in the dense undergrowth at the base of the pole and then the boy hooked the end of his shoe around a metal ring that was sticking out of the ground. He shouted over to Turpol. "I think I've found something!"

The Gatekeeper stopped circling the pole and reached down to pull the ring but nothing happened. "It's stuck!" he exclaimed and tried again. "It's no good... I can't move it!"

Captain Dray called over to Spew. "Can you try to pull this out?"

The Wood Ogre paced over in three large strides to join Turpol's side and lifted the dwarf out of the way. He then placed his huge forefinger through the ring and with a single effortless jerk he lifted the object out of the ground.

Bradley nearly lost his balance, as he shrieked with delight. "I don't know what you just did but there's a gap opening up in the side of the pyramid... and I've got an idea!" He yelled and held his balance as he pulled the bow from around his shoulders. "Sereny... see if you can join together some strands of grass – I need you all to make a rope of some kind!"

"Why?" she asked.

"You'll see why… when I have the rope - I'm not very steady up here and I'll fall off this thing in a minute if you don't hurry up!" shouted Bradley and his face grimaced, as he carefully removed an arrow from the leather sheath on his back. "I can feel the pain inside my body getting worse… so ensure the rope is long enough to reach between me and the side of the pyramid with a bit more to spare!"

Everyone could see that Bradley was in trouble. The boy was rapidly changing back into a Werebeast and this time his form was taking on that of more disheveled creature. He was also struggling to keep his balance on top of the tall pole. The group quickly amassed enough lengths of grass, as they hurriedly began to weave a single piece of rope long enough to meet the boy's request.

Captain Dray attached the end of the rope to one of his arrows and launched it towards the top of the pole. The accuracy of the squirrel's aim was inch-perfect and the arrowhead penetrated the timber post just below Bradley's foot, as the boy carefully reached down to retrieve the arrow.

"What is he doing?" asked Jefferson.

Turpol affirmed. "You'll see… clever boy, Bradley!"

Sereny asked the dwarf to confirm his thoughts. "What are you thinking?"

The Gatekeeper rubbed the coarse stubble on his chin and replied. "It looks like he's going to use the arrow to attach the rope to that small plinth… you can just make it out if you look carefully inside the gap on the side of the pyramid!" He directed and held out his pointed finger to guide the girl's line of sight to the tiny plaque.

"He'll never hit that… it's no bigger than a tennis ball!" exclaimed Jefferson.

278

They watched in anticipation, as Bradley secured the rope to his arrow and pulled back the bow string. The boy steadied his one-footed stance and released the arrow, as the flight path of the rope veered slightly to the left. The end of the arrow clipped the side of the stone pyramid, as sparks flew from the broken arrowhead. "Damn!" he exclaimed, as the unsuccessful attempt also received a disappointed hum from the frustrated spectators below.

Bradley readjusted his balance and reeled the rope back up, as he detached the splintered piece of wood. He only had a single arrow left to complete the task and he pulled it out of the sheath to attach it to the rope. "Here goes!" he shouted and stretched the bowstring. "This time I'll allow for the swerve!" he exclaimed and moved his aim to the right of the object.

Whoooooooooooosh! The arrow was released and everyone held their breaths, as the projectile flew towards the target. An accurate thud followed, as the arrow hit the plaque dead centre and Bradley held the end of the rope tightly. He shouted down to the relieved onlookers. "Get away from the pole!" he ordered and cried. "Except you, Spew... can you stay and get ready to catch me?"

The Wood Ogre heeded the boys request and held out his huge muscular arms, as the rest of the group moved back. Bradley pulled the rope and the wooden plate was drawn out of the gap, as a crack started to appear in the side of the structure. The pole began to sway and the gap grew wider, as the end of a horizontal metal beam appeared.

The girder continued to move outwards at the same level towards the top of the post and Bradley prepared to jump. "Get ready Spew... I'm coming down!" he yelled, as the beam struck the pole. "Arrrrrrrrrrrrhhhhhhhhh!"

"Make sure you catch him!" shouted Sereny, as the Wood Ogre focused on the falling boy.

"I got him!" replied Spew, as he moved in motion to the boy's landing and clutched him safely in his arms.

Bradley applauded the giant creature. "Good catch!" He remarked and held on tightly to Spew's leather braces, as the Wood Ogre trudged through the undergrowth to rejoin the others. He placed the wolf boy on the ground and they all watched in amazement, as the metal beam interconnected perfectly with the wooden pole.

The girder hinged inside the gap to create a fulcrum on the pyramid wall and then started to move slowly down the side of the pole until it reached the ground. The upper surface of the beam was made up of wedge shape grooves and had now formed a makeshift staircase that led up to a small entrance in the side of the pyramid.

A loud creaking sound followed and the pole began to sway again, as the base started to splinter. Bradley warned the others. "Get further back… the pole is about to fall over – the weight of the girder must have weakened the base!"

The unstable post leaned severely and the weakened base splintered even more, as the post finally gave way. The heavy column came crashing down like a felled tree, as Jefferson made a light-hearted quip. "Timber!"

"Very funny!" responded Sereny, as the post crashed into the nearby trees and snapped the branches like brittle twigs.

The group waited for the flying leaves to settle and then ran over to the angled girder. Turpol placed his hand inside his cloak pocket and felt the scarab key, as he muttered under his breath. "Well I guess I didn't need to use the bronze talisman after all."

Captain Dray asked. "What was that you said?"

The Gatekeeper smiled. "Oh, err... nothing!" He replied and released his hold on the key to let it fall to the bottom of his pocket, as he held out his gestured hand to direct the Black Squirrel. "After you!"

"Thanks!" replied the captain, as he placed his foot on the narrow beam.

Bradley pulled back on the squirrel's belt and insisted that he should be the first to enter the pyramid. Captain Dray did not hesitate, as he lifted his foot off the girder and moved aside.

The boy hero had almost transformed into the weakened Werebeast creature and he addressed the dwarf. "Hand me the chalice, Turpol and come with me... everyone else wait here until we have checked the gap!"

Turpol nodded and handed over the sacred goblet, as he followed Bradley up the inclined beam. They reached the small entrance in the side of the pyramid and the boy peered into the dark void. "The coast is clear!" he shouted and waved for the others to join them.

Once all inside, the explorers found themselves at the beginning of a long passageway that led into the centre of the pyramid. They stayed close together, as they ran along the torch lit corridor until they reached a stone stairwell that led upwards and they continued their journey.

As soon as they reached the top of the stairs, Sereny nudged Bradley and said. "This corridor looks familiar... we are in the same passageway where we discovered the two chambers but it looks like we have entered from the opposite direction – look at the golden glow in the distance!"

"Yes, you're right... but this time, don't fall in the pool – you're still covered in gold paint from last time!" laughed

Bradley and winked at the frustrated girl. "Don't worry... we'll get you back to normal when we get out of here!"

Turpol heard their conversation and suggested that Bradley put the chalice back inside the correct chamber.

"I can't... it's full of scarab skulls – that's how we escaped before," he explained. "We'll have to leave the chalice somewhere else!"

"Okay," replied the dwarf and pulled his hand out of his cloak pocket. "Then I suggest we use this!"

Sereny shrieked. "The scarab key... I wondered when you were going to use that!"

Turpol replied. "Well it was supposed to be used to help us get into the pyramid but Bradley didn't need it," he explained. "Clip it into the base of the chalice and place the goblet in the golden chamber... I'm sure that will be enough to reverse your transformation – let's give it a try."

Captain Dray confirmed that the dwarf's suggestion was a good idea. "I thought I heard you mention the bronze talisman... I have seen that key used many times before - it has very special powers, so it should provide the assistance you need!" he claimed, as he stood to one side with Spew and Jefferson.

Bradley, Turpol and Sereny entered the shimmering tomb. The treasure inside the chamber was still glistening and the girl made sure she stayed well clear of the pool this time. She carefully handed the chalice to Bradley and he placed it on the floor, as they all stepped back to wait.

The frustrated boy held out his hairy hands. "Nothing's happening!" cried Bradley.

"Be patient!" insisted the Gatekeeper, as he reached down to move the chalice into the treasure chest and the scarab key began to glow. "The bronze talisman is responding to the goblet's sacred powers… let's see if that makes any difference."

Captain Dray heard a distant rumbling noise. "What was that?"

Sereny commented, as the uniform tremors beneath the floor intensified. "It's probably all related to the chalice and the key being placed inside the chest!"

Jefferson noticed the first change in Bradley's form, as the eternal chosen one's pointed ears began to retract into his thick brown hair. "It's working!"

Everyone cheered, as they too noticed the reverse transformation begin to take affect and Bradley's hands quickly changed back to human form.

The celebrations were short-lived, as the sound of marching boots echoed down the corridor. Captain Dray commanded Spew to check what all the commotion was about and the ogre turned around to witness an assembly of bandage-torn creatures sprinting along the passageway. The Wood Ogre roared in response. "Those tremors were nothing to do with the chalice… we've got company – the Mummoyds have arrived!"

28
The Journey to Pathylon

Meanwhile back in Wolf Town, Musgrove had fallen into a deep depressive silence since killing his father in the duel of destiny. The unmindful boy was being consoled by Queen Vash, as the hierarchy waited patiently for Turpol's return.

King Luccese had arranged a meeting with Meltor, Karn and General Eidar to discuss the launch of the iceberg-ships and the ice-submarines. "We can't wait for Turpol and Bradley forever... time is moving on and we have to start our seaward journey to Pathylon."

Meltor was conscious that Luccese wanted to launch the attack on Varuna's armies as soon as possible and he attempted to buy more time by reassuring the King that the group would be back in time. The Galetian afforded the Freytorian General a concerned look and then spoke softly to the King. "They must have found their way into the pyramid by now... as soon as Bradley repositions the chalice they will be back before you know it."

Luccese stared out of the window, as the Klomus Hawk appeared in the distance. "It will not hurt to prepare the ships ready to sail... and we will have a progress report from Ploom very soon – my royal messenger has just arrived back from Pathylon!"

Luccese had ordered the giant bird to carry out another spying mission in Trad and she returned full of energy and with some revealing news. Meltor, General Eidar and Karn joined the King, as he made is way out of the Werebeast's headquarters. The Klomus Hawk landed in the village square and waddled over to the waiting leaders, as he squawked in an excited tone. "Greetings your majesty... and my lords – I have some information that will be of great interest to you!"

Luccese welcomed the over-worked bird onto the decking of the large straw-covered hut and urged her to reveal her findings. "What is this interesting news you bring, Ploom... we are all eager to know!"

"Varuna has commissioned the building of a new battlement to replace the Shallock Tower... and he plans to imprison you inside it, my lord – should you dare to attack his kingdom!" disclosed the Klomus Hawk.

A stern look appeared on the face of the deposed King and he replied in a confident voice. "Let's get one thing straight... I do not want Pathylon referred to as Varuna's kingdom!" he insisted. "And as for building a new tower to imprison me... the Hartopian fool is only erecting his own jail cell – by the time our armies have finished with him and his bunch of traitors, no tower would be tall enough to hold them all!"

Ploom apologized to the King for her fraudulent slip about the ownership of the kingdom and then turned to Meltor. "I also have some information for you."

The Galetian looked surprised and asked. "What is it, Ploom?"

The bird paused and rubbed her beak, as she requested that Meltor be seated. The inquisitive High Priest insisted that he stay standing, as Ploom delivered her news. "It's something that Ulan-dem said... I overheard him bragging to a Devonian prisoner, who was working on the new tower – he mentioned Basjoo Ma-otz and the death of your Granddaughter."

Meltor instinctively sat down at the mention of this delicate subject. "Why do you bring this up again?" He asked, as he placed the palm of his hand over his sullen face to rub his moustache with his thumb and fore finger. The High Priest continued the same stroking action down his long white beard and exclaimed. "Basjoo Ma-otz is dead and I never got the chance to enact my own revenge on the evil Hartopian for killing my Granddaughter... but that is of no matter – what is it that concerns Ulan-dem about her unlawful death?"

King Luccese and the General could see that Meltor was getting upset. Karn approached the bird. "Why have you mentioned something with such irrelevance?"

Ploom insisted. "It is not irrelevant... on the contrary - it has great importance to Meltor because he has a second chance to settle an old score!"

Karn reacted. "What do you mean?"

Meltor mirrored the Werebeast's inquisitive request and asked. "Please explain... what has Ulan-dem's comments got to do with my Granddaughters sacrifice?"

"The veteran Hartopian was boasting that he was the one that slaughtered her... not Basjoo Ma-otz!" replied the hesitant Klomus Hawk, as a deathly silence filled the decked area. "I'm sorry to have to tell you, Meltor... but I thought you would want to know!"

The Galetian's brow furrowed and produced deep lines of hatred along his forehead, as he looked at the King. "Luccese?"

"Yes... Meltor," replied the consoling monarch, as he waited for the High Priest's response.

The revealing news had greatly influenced Meltor's decision to delay the launch of the ice-ships and a burning desire to face his old foe influenced his next suggestion. "Bradley and Turpol will have to find their own way to Pathylon if they wish to join the fighting... I suggest we set sail immediately – it would appear we both have old scores to settle with two gloating Hartopians!"

"Your intentions to leave with such anger and haste are not what I anticipated going into battle... but I understand your feelings and I agree - Varuna and Ulan-dem need to be taught a lesson!" responded King Luccese and asked General Eidar to prepare the ships. He then turned to Karn. "Please send a message to the leaders of the Black Squirrels and the Wood Ogres... we need them here as soon as possible!"

Unbeknown to Luccese and Karn, Captain Dray and Spew were facing a very awkward situation inside the great pyramid. The mummified Skeloyds were fast approaching the entrance to the golden chamber, as they wielded a combination of swords and hatchets above their bandage covered skulls.

Bradley shouted. "We have to get out of here... if they reach the entrance we're done for!"

The Gatekeeper asked. "Which way are they heading?"

Spew answered. "The same way we just came in… we will have to go this way!" He roared and pointed in the direction where Musgrove and Sereny had killed King Tok during their previous visit.

Sereny insisted. "We have no choice… if we stay here we will die – but we know there isn't a way out that way because that's where we left the broken bath tub!"

Bradley had now fully transformed back into a human being and grabbed the girl's arm, as he confirmed her suggestion. "Sereny's right… we don't stand a chance against them outside this chamber – there's a lot more room to fight down there, so let's go!"

The furious Mummoyds quickened their pace along the passageway and neared the entrance to the golden tomb. Jefferson was the last to leave the sacred chamber and just managed to evade the out-stretched hand of one of the groaning zombie-like creatures.

Bradley and the others ran as fast as they could down the narrow corridor and he turned to make sure his friend was safe. "You okay, Jeffers?"

"Right behind you, Bradley… just keep running – they're closing on us fast!" warned Jefferson, as a flying axe flew passed his head. "Wow… that was close!"

Sereny looked ahead and revealed. "I can see the old bath tub… maybe we should stop here and fight them off!"

Spew heeded the girl's suggestion, as he stopped and turned to raise his huge wooden club. The chasing Mummoyds closed in on the Wood Ogre and five of the bandaged creature's leapt into the air, as they landed on the shoulders of the giant troll.

Captain Dray angled his body to reverse direction and launched his muscular frame towards the struggling ogre. He pulled his bow from around his chest and tightened the string, as he fired a multitude of piercing arrows. The Black Squirrel maintained the continuous firing mechanism whilst running, as he pulled arrow after arrow from his back sheath.

Bradley and Jefferson copied the captain's advance, as they too tethered their bows and started firing their barbed missiles at the frenzied creatures.

Spew was still struggling to pull the clinging zombies from his body, as the friendly arrows whizzed past his head and struck the resilient Mummoyds. The screeching echoes of the felled creatures wailed down the passageways, as they slumped to the ground one by one.

Turpol shouted to Sereny. "I have an idea... Bradley and the others seem to have the situation under control - come with me."

"Where are you going?" asked the girl reluctantly. "We can't just leave them!"

The Gatekeeper made his way over to the bath and brushed the fallen debris away to reveal the taps. He spotted a small length of metal that looked like it had once belonged to the bars of an old doorway. "That will do... please pass me that iron rod – I'll be able to use it as a wrench."

The fighting continued along the corridor and Sereny shouted down the passageway. "Bradley... I need to help Turpol - can you hold them back?"

The boy turned and acknowledged the girl's request, as more and more Mummoyds appeared. "We're killing them off slowly... but I don't know how long we can keep it going – carry on with whatever it is you're doing and try to be as quick as you can!"

Sereny picked up the metal bar and handed it to the dwarf. "I hope you know what you're doing... they can't keep those things back for too much longer – there are hundreds of the damn things!"

Spew finally cast off the last clinging Mummoyd and he rejoined Captain Dray, as the two forest dwellers ploughed through the remaining creatures. The Wood Ogre wielded his club and smashed some of the erratic zombies against the walls, as they reached the far end of the passageway. They were now separated from Bradley and Jefferson with about thirty or so Mummoyds trapped between them, as they managed to contain the fracas. The creatures could now be attacked from both ends of the corridor, as the Black Squirrel yelled over the continued fighting. "We have secured this end of the passageway… can you get through?"

The two exhausted boys were punching their way through the baying army of skeletal beings and the eternal chosen one replied, as he fended off another irate creature. "Not a chance… there's still too many of these things!"

The heated scuffle continued as the Gatekeeper placed the metal bar between the taps and pulled, whilst Sereny watched her friends continue their battle with the Mummoyds. Turpol shrieked with delight and tossed the bent shaft onto the floor. "That should do it!"

The clanking of metal on the ground alerted the girl's attention and she turned round to witness the dwarf climbing into the bath. "What are you messing around with now?"

Turpol's head disappeared momentarily as he fiddled with the plughole inside the tub. His face resurfaced and he asked the irritable girl. "Go and get the coin off Bradley… we're going to need the sacred grobite!"

Sereny was growing tired of being the fetcher and carrier, as she sighed deeply and ran over to where Bradley was fighting. The boy hero knew the girl was behind him but he kept his concentration on the sword wielding Mummoyds. "What it is, Sereny… what does Turpol want now?"

"The coin!" she replied, as a stray hatchet came crashing down near her face and hit the side of the stone corridor. "He needs the grobite!"

"Reach into my trouser pocket!" instructed Bradley, as the girl pushed her hand into the left side. "No not that one… the right side – that's it!" he exclaimed, as Sereny pulled out the gold coin. "Now, please be quick... whatever Turpol is up to – he had better get a move on!"

Sereny ran back to the dwarf, as a loud rumbling sound shook through the pyramid. The girl fell to the floor and dropped the grobite, as dust started to fall from the roof of the passageway. Cracks began to appear in the walls and large boulders started to fall from the roof of the corridor.

Bradley turned around to see a cloud of dust engulf the area where Turpol was working and there was no sign of Sereny or the dwarf, as more rocks fell down above his head. He shouted over to where Jefferson was swinging his bow to protect himself against the last few mummified creatures. "We have to retreat… this roof is going to give way at any minute!"

Jefferson thrust the end of his bow into the face of another bandaged zombie, as he replied. "But we'll be trapped… we have to try to reach Captain Dray and Spew!"

Before Bradley could answer, the roof of the passageway completely collapsed and the remaining Mummoyds were crushed, as the sound of undignified squeals emanated from beneath the fallen rocks. The boy called over to Jefferson again. "Get back… there's no way through – we have to go and help Sereny and the Gatekeeper!"

At the other side of the rock fall, the Black Squirrel leader and the Wood Ogre stood helpless, as the route to the others was blocked with fallen rubble. Captain Dray pulled Spew back, as the ogre tried to lift the heavy rocks. "It's no use... they are trapped in there and if we don't get out fast – we'll end up in the same predicament!"

The ogre looked forlorn and nodded, as he turned to follow the fleeing squirrel and they made their way back to the gap in the side of the trembling pyramid. They rapidly ascended the inclined girder and ran over to a safe distance in the trees, as the great pyramid imploded and then rapidly collapsed into a derelict heap. A thick cloud of dust covered the aluminum prism that had once adorned the tip of the great structure, as it landed upright with a loud thud on top of the crumpled pile of stone.

Spew wiped a large tear from his haggard face and declared. "So that's the end of the eternal chosen one... it's a great shame that Bradley and his friends should perish like that – *Talum* has claimed yet another four victims inside its evil lair of tombs."

Captain Dray looked up at the distraught Wood Ogre and declared. "There is nothing that we could have done to save them... we must now return to Wolf Town and inform the others that they must set sail for Pathylon without Bradley Baker and his brave friends!"

29

Dead or Alive

The impressive fleet of Freytorian ice-ships were moored in fixed parallel berths and now fully prepared to set sail from the northern coast of Rekab to the designated regions of Pathylon. Weapons and provisions had been loaded, as the walkways connecting the vessels to the dock side carried busy personnel back and forth.

General Eidar had been designated to take overall command of the three ice-submarines that would make the longest journey across the Red Ocean to the coastline of Devonia. In the absence of Captain Dray, Karn had volunteered to join the final battle to save Pathylon and was appointed as commander of the two iceberg ships. The surface floating vessels would set off ahead of the faster submersible craft to arrive in Krogonia via the Satorc Sea at approximately the same time.

The arrival of Luccese and his entourage was imminent and a fanfare of horns sounded, as the royal party approached the port. A primitive wooden chariot pulled by two Lurgs carried the King and Queen, as they fronted a convoy of carriages. Flags and banners waved, as the line of ornately coloured carts swept down the cobbled streets that joined the quayside along the raised sea wall.

Meltor was travelling in the second carriage and was listening intently to a Lurg-mounted Werebeast, who had just ridden alongside his moving cart. The Galetian put his head in his hands, as the messenger pulled on his reigns and galloped away.

The trail of wagons reached the port side and another fanfare sounded, as the royal couple dismounted their chariot. Queen Vash allowed her husband to go ahead alone and meet the waiting spectators while she waited for Meltor to alight his carriage. She looked concerned, as the Galetian remained seated and appeared to be in a dreadful state.

Vash approached the wagon and could see that the High Priest had been weeping, as the whites of his eyes had reddened in reaction to the news he had just received. "Meltor... what is it that has upset you so greatly?"

The old Galetian lifted his head and faced his Queen. "Your majesty... I have just been informed that Captain Dray and the Wood Ogre have arrived back in Wolf Town!" he exclaimed and struggled to explain further. "I... I can't believe it –"

The King observed his High Priest's body language and rushed over to enquire. "What is it, Meltor... what has happened?" asked Luccese, as Queen Vash climbed into the carriage and held the trembling High Priest. The King followed and sat down next to his inconsolable friend. "This is not like you... something terrible must have happened!"

Meltor cleared his throat and wiped his face with his large sleeves. "It's Bradley and Turpol… and the other two children – they have been trapped inside the pyramid!"

Queen Vash attempted to raise any hopes of the four still remaining alive. "Surely Captain Dray can take some of the Black Squirrels back to the pyramid and get them out?"

Meltor shook his head. "The pyramid has totally collapsed… they have been buried alive – the Captain and the ogre witnessed the explosion!"

The Galetian could not speak any more, as the sound of two approaching Lurgs grabbed the attention of the shocked King and Queen. It was Captain Dray and Spew galloping down the cobbled road, as they pulled up next to the chariot. The exhausted squirrel looked into the carriage to witness the High Priest being consoled. "It looks like you have just received my message… I am so sorry about your loss – there was nothing we could do to save them!"

King Luccese acknowledged the two riders and suggested that they start to board the vessels. "Captain Dray, please tell Karn that you will be assuming command of one of the iceberg ships… be as tactile as you can and don't upset him – we still need him to sail with you and his legion of Werebeasts will come in very handy when we launch our attack via the Galetis Empire!" The squirrel nodded and rode away with Spew, as Luccese turned to his wife. "There is nothing more we can do here for Bradley and the others… please keep the news from Musgrove and stay with him till all this is over – the boy has gone through enough without having to hear of his friends being killed too."

Meanwhile back in Trad, Varuna was totally oblivious to the impending advance by the allied forces. A challenge to his unlawful reign over the four controlling regions of Pathylon was far from his mind, as he observed the building progress for the new tower. The Hartopian was elegantly dressed and was resting on a bench in the palace gardens, as he closed his eyes.

Flaglan was enjoying a picnic on the lawn and she sat on a blanket just a few metres in front of her tired husband. The new Queen of Pathylon looked up at the splendid unfinished battlement, which was increasing in height at a very fast pace. She viewed the definitive turreted upper tiers being winched up the side of the stronghold, as the dulcet roar of an older Hartopian could be heard bellowing instructions on the other side of the walled garden. The annoyed sorceress turned to address her napping husband. "His voice is very annoying!"

Varuna opened his eyes, as he snarled and laughed. "Ulandem is proving very useful… don't worry my dear – as soon as the new tower is built I will send him on his way scuttling back to the Blacklands."

Flaglan joined her husband, as she sat on the bench and placed her petite hand on his arm. She rested her head on his shoulder and enquired about the rest of the kingdom. "What is happening in Krogonia… are you not bothered about extending our rule over that region?"

"What's the point?" replied Varuna. "The Satorc Bridge is destroyed… our enemies are stranded – the Galetians and the Krogon's can't get to us so why should we bother ruling over them?"

Flaglan smiled and replied. "It doesn't feel like we have full control… and talking about control – what are we going to do about the Galetis Empire with its people being forced to live in Krogonia?"

"Haven't given it much thought really," replied the smug Hartopian. "Maybe we can come up with some ideas when the tower is finished… one thing at a time – there's no rush!"

The sultry sorceress looked concerned and asked. "What if Luccese attacks in the meantime?"

"With what… who with and how's he going to get here?" snarled Varuna, as he stood up and strode over to the garden wall. "The old has-been is stuck on that icy island with just a few pathetic Freytorians, as allies… Luccese is no threat to us my darling – now stop worrying and come and have a closer look at my lovely new tower."

Unbeknown to Varuna, the two ice-berg ships had left the port in Rekab and were now sailing across the Satorc Sea. Captain Dray had successfully placated Karn and persuaded his Werebeasts to join the Black Squirrels on board one of the ships. The other wind-powered ice-vessel contained a mixed crew of Freytorians and Wood Ogres led by Spew. Meltor had decided to join the ogre so he could lead his depleted Galetian army when they arrived in the Galetis Empire. The High Priest had recovered sufficiently to focus his emotions back on the invasion. The thought of meeting Ulan-dem filled the High Priest with the rage and purpose he needed to fulfill his important role in the mission.

The three ice-submarines had also departed and were speeding their way in an arrowhead formation deep beneath the waves of the Red Ocean. King Luccese and General Eidar each commanded one of the submersible ice-ships, with the third being navigated by another senior Freytorian naval officer.

The secret new crossing from Krogonia to the Galetis Empire had successfully bridged the narrow stretch of water and Pavsik was busy arranging for the first battalion to make its way over to the mainland.

Henley was still unaware of what had happened to Bradley in Rekab, as he continued to help Pavsik and Guan-yin direct the battle-ready troops across from the isolated Krogon region.

BATTLE PLAN

Hartopia

Black Forest

Ulan-dem leads the Hartopians

King Luccese and General Eidar lead three battalions of Freytorians

Katkaye Idol

Varuna based in Trad

Island of Kestak

River Klonjus

Redis

Forbidden Caves

Satore Estuary

Guan-yin based in Krogonia

FOREST OF HALDON

Flaglan leads the Tree Elves

Mouth of Sayo

Pavsik,& Meltor lead the Devonians and Galetians

Grog & Henley lead the Krogons

Captain Dray leads the Black Squirrels

Karn leads the Werebeasts

Spew leads the Wood Ogres

The Unknown Land

The battle plan was set and detailed on a charted map to be distributed to all the ship's commanders and ground force leaders. The mission was clear to all concerned and the removal of Varuna's control over Pathylon was the goal. King Luccese had given the order concerning the Hartopian's capture and the menacing traitor's fate lay in his own hands, as the instruction was to take him; dead or alive.

Meanwhile back in Rekab, a small group of dwarves from Crystal City were being led by the mother dwarf through the damp foliage surrounding the site where Talum once stood. They had been informed about the destruction of the great pyramid and were keen to find out whether the underground rivers had been affected. Without the flowing waterways, their funeral celebrations would not be able to go ahead and it was important to ensure that they could maintain their sacrificial rituals.

The group was joined by Ryuu the ancient dragon, as they emerged from the forest and approached the ruins. The area where the great pyramid once stood was now an eerie site of destruction with twisted metal and stone slabs strewn everywhere. The aluminum prism was still perched on top of the rubble and the mother dwarf strode over the debris, as she stepped forward to place her grey ear on the huge triangular-shaped apex.

Ryuu joined the mother dwarf, as she placed her finger over her mouth to indicate to the dragon to stay quiet whilst she listened. "I think I heard something underneath the prism... prepare the others – we may need some help to lift it out of the way!"

The dragon flapped his wings and nodded his large horn-dressed head, as he retreated to inform the other dwarves.

Within seconds, the mother dwarf indicated with a thumbs-up signal that there was definitely movement beneath the aluminum profile. Ryuu picked up a heavy log in his mouth and walked over, as the dwarves followed with short pieces of timber to help support the prism.

With very little effort the strong bearded creature pushed his shoulder against the aluminum and the dwarves inserted the temporary props. Ryuu released the log from his teeth and pushed it underneath one of the corners with his outstretched foot to stop the metal structure from collapsing. The mother dwarf peered beneath the cover and exclaimed in a delighted tone. "There's another upturned object underneath... it has four strange feet sticking out of the top – I think it is a bathing vessel of some sort!"

A searching grey hand appeared from beneath the tub and the dragon placed one of his webbed claws between the white bath and the rocky debris, as he lifted it to reveal four trembling bodies huddled together.

The Gatekeeper smiled and welcomed the mother dwarf's intervention. "Thank goodness... we thought we were going to suffocate in here!"

"Turpol?" enquired the female dwarf.

"Yes... and by the look of your ornate necklace – you must be the mother dwarf?" he replied and stared at the impressive dragon. "And you are Ryuu the *Dragon Spirit*... at last we meet – I was so young when my parents told me of your legend before they left Crystal City and I have dreamt of this moment for a long time!"

Ryuu nodded gracefully, as the mother dwarf stared at the three children. "And who are these young ones?"

Bradley sat up and held out his hand to introduce himself. "I am Bradley Baker and these are my friends from the outside world… I came to Rekab to find the sacred chalice but we seem to have made a bit of a mess."

"Ahhh… the infamous Bradley Baker – I have heard so much about you from the Witch!" replied the mother dwarf.

Sereny spoke. "You have met the Witch?"

"Yes… she is imprisoned inside the dungeons beneath Crystal City but unfortunately the Shadow Druid has escaped!" explained the female dwarf.

"Apparently our friend Muzzy, has fought and defeated the Shadow Druid but there are a few complications that we won't bore you with right now," replied Bradley, as he helped to push the bath tub out of the way. "However, we would be grateful if you would help us return to Wolf Town… we need to board the ice-ships and head for Pathylon!"

Ryuu interjected and made a rare statement. "You are too late… the Freytorian vessels have already departed – I have seen them sailing away from Rekab."

Bradley responded to the news. "Can't say I blame them… they probably think we are all dead!" He exclaimed, as Sereny hunched their shoulders in frustration.

Jefferson boldly asked the dragon. "You can fly, right?" Ryuu nodded, as the coloured boy continued. "Well, Turpol seems to have fixed the taps on the bath so would you be able to accompany us to Pathylon?"

Ryuu agreed and Bradley urged Turpol to acknowledge whether it would be possible to launch the bath with the dragon's help. The Gatekeeper responded in a positive manner and the bath was pulled free from beneath the aluminum prism.

The grobite was held aloft by Bradley until it started to glow and the taps were rotated by Jefferson to test their smooth operation, as a tether was attached to the front of the bath. All the dwarves rallied round and strapped the leash to the dragon's tail, as the three children jumped into their new flying machine. Turpol paid a respectful farewell to the mother dwarf and the activated coin was inserted into the plughole.

Sereny held on tightly to Bradley's waist and the bath started to vibrate, as the taps began to spin at a rapid speed. The tub lifted off the ground, as Ryuu flapped his huge wingspan and the makeshift mode of air travel launched into the air. The mother dwarf waved, as the Gatekeeper and his fellow passengers looked over the edge of the airbourne tub. The group of relieved dwarves continued to wave, as they stood in the middle of the pyramid's ruins and soon became a distant dot on the landscape. The dragon pulled the propelled bath into the thick clouds above and headed out across the desert towards the Red Ocean.

Back in Pathylon, the three iceberg-ships had anchored off-shore in their designated positions and all the military personnel had sailed over to the mainland. Meltor was pleased to back in the Galetis Empire and had already been reunited with his Hoffen-mounted countrymen.

Captain Dray was busy organizing the Black Squirrels and Spew was issuing the battle plan details to the Wood Ogres. Karn and his legion of Werebeasts were already camped on the edge of the Peronto Dessert and the Krogons, led by Grog and Henley were mingling with the Galetians.

Meltor approached Bradley's uncle and Grog, as he broke the bad news. The Devonian and the Lizardman held back their emotions and Henley insisted that his nephew knew the dangers of returning to the arcane world to prevent his transformation. "Bradley would want us to carry on without him… I know he would – so I intend to make him proud and help lead the Krogons into battle with Grog!"

The upset Krogon had just been reunited with his trusted mount, as Shatar nudged the tangerine warrior with his snorting nose. Grog's sadness was alleviated by the Koezard's presence and he patted his long neck. The Lizardman then turned his attention to Henley and placed a comforting webbed hand on his friend's back, as he enquired. "What of Turpol and the other children… did they perish too?"

Meltor nodded. "I believe so… the leader of the Black Squirrels informed me that they were fighting some mummified Skeloyd creatures inside the great pyramid and the roof of the passageway caved in on them – thankfully Musgrove didn't travel with them but he ended up killing his father instead!"

Henley exclaimed. "My god… how did that happen?"

"It's a long story," explained the Galetian and he proceeded to tell them about the duel of destiny with the Shadow Druid, as they retreated beneath a canvass awning to continue their conversation. Meltor's version of events was interrupted by a Devonian Nobleman, who delivered a piece of paper and handed it to Henley. He opened the message and revealed that the ice-submarines had just arrived off the coast of Devonia.

The fate of Bradley and others faded into insignificance, as the enthusiastic Lizardman reacted first to the message. Grog hastily made is way out of the tent and summoned Shatar, as a group of his Krogon lieutenants approached. "Prepare the legions… we advance on the Forest of Haldon within the hour!"

Henley followed suit and organized the few noblemen he had to his disposal, as he ordered them to spread the word across the battalions that the attack on Varuna was about to commence. Karn, Captain Dray and Spew were ready and the armies began their advance through the Galetis Empire towards the Forest of Haldon.

Meanwhile on board the leading ice-submarine, Luccese was communicating with General Eidar and the other Freytorian officer aboard the sister ships. The order was given to launch a task force of mini-subs and infiltrate the many coves along the Devonian coastline. Without delay fifty and more underwater landing crafts were released simultaneously from the submarines portholes, as a rush of vertical air bubbles rose to the surface of the calm waters.

The Freytorian armed forces negotiated the rock-laden bays and landed their crafts on the beaches, as they marched on in the direction of Pathylon's capital city.

On the mainland the palace garden in Trad was still peaceful, as Varuna and Flaglan continued to enjoy the morning sun. The oblivious pair of love-stuck honeymooners walked along in a care-free manner, as they strolled through the parallel rows of pruned rose bushes. They were totally unaware of the situation unfolding in Pathylon, as the fast approaching allies advanced through the bordering regions.

The royal couple's peaceful ramble was interrupted by one of the builders who was working at the top of the new tower. "Sire!" he shouted down. "We are being attacked!"

Varuna looked up and shouted. "What was that you insolent fool?" He roared. "How dare you interrupt your King and Queen?"

The tower worker alerted his attention again, as he cast his eyes out at the ant-like armies advancing from all directions. "Pathylon is under attack!"

Flaglan shouted. "What can you see?"

The startled builder froze and continued to stare out to the thousands of troops closing in on the capital, as Varuna cast off his heavy robe and ran through the archway in the walled garden. The Hartopian met Ulan-dem and ordered him to follow, as they made their way up the completed stairwell.

They soon appeared at the summit of the tower to witness the builder's observation and Varuna let out a cry of disbelief. "That's the royal standard of Luccese being carried ahead of legions of Freytorians!" he roared, as the deposed King reached the outskirts of the city. "This can't be happening!"

"I told you he would attack!" stated Ulan-dem. "We're doomed!"

"Silence you imbecile!" roared Varuna, as Flaglan appeared to witness the allied forces moving closer. "Look, my dear... Luccese is attacking our kingdom!"

"You're not kidding...and look over towards Haldon!" she exclaimed. "My beloved forest is being overrun by Black Squirrels and Wood Ogres – my Tree Elves won't stand a chance!"

There was absolutely nothing the three shocked traitors could do but witness the onslaught and they remained at the top of the tower to witness the demise of their rule over Pathylon. Then to add insult to injury the silhouette of the *Spirit Dragon* pulling a propelled Victorian bathtub appeared in the distance, as the boy hero and his friends waved sarcastically at the fuming trio below.

Ryuu dived down when they reached the tower and Bradley Baker winked at Varuna, as the enraged Hartopian waved his hooked arm at the boy's teasing gesture. "You'll pay for this Bradley Baker!" he shouted, as Ulan-dem disappeared down the stairwell.

The veteran Hartopian did not get very far and was met at the tower base by a revengeful Galetian. Meltor glared at Ulan-dem and delivered a precise and threatening statement. "Prepare to say goodbye to Pathylon and accept your punishment!"

"Meltor… can we talk about this?" he pleaded, as the High Priest carried out his retribution and ran the blade of his sword through the trembling Hartopian's chest. Ulan-dem stared into the whites of Meltor's eyes and released a final gasp of breath, as he offered the Galetian dying reparation. "I'm sorry for the death of your Granddaughter!"

"Too late… apology not accepted – this is for her cruel execution by your evil hands!" replied Meltor, as the Hartopian slumped to the ground.

Luccese approached. "Was that necessary?"

Meltor remained silent and then looked over to where the dragon had landed. "Bradley!" he exclaimed and ran over to the boy and his friends.

The King watched Meltor enjoy a happy reunion with his protégé and replied on the Galetian's behalf. "I guess it was!" confirmed Luccese, as he failed to notice Varuna creep up behind him.

The desperate Hartopian was not willing to yield his crown so easily and thrust his sword through the King's crimson robe. "Errrrrrrrrrghhhhh!" moaned Luccese, as he released an agonizing cry and the dull blade entered his side.

Bradley noticed the commotion and quickly excused himself from Meltor's warm welcome, as he grabbed the Galetian's sword and jumped onto Ryuu's back. He kicked his heels into the bearded dragon's side and then leant back, as he swung the blade to sever the rope attached to the bath.

Ryuu soared into the air and turned acutely to face Varuna, as he lifted his weapon in readiness to inflict a fatal blow to the King's neck. The dragon cast his wings back in a single movement and flew above the sword wielding assassin. Bradley dived off the dragon's back and somersaulted several times in the air, as his body leveled out in time to exact an accurate sideways swipe of his sword. The end of the blade scraped across Varuna's face and inflicted a deep gash down the reeling Hartopian's cheek.

"Arrrrrrrrrgggghhhhhhh!" squealed Varuna and dropped his sword, as Bradley completed his heroic sequence. Henley rushed over to congratulate his nephew and was relieved to see him alive and still able to utilize his special powers.

Bradley hugged his uncle and then ran over to Luccese, who was being tendered to by Captain Dray and a small group of Black Squirrels.

The ailing King held his wounded side and looked around in search of Bradley. "Thank you for saving my life, again… that is the second time you have prevented Varuna from assassinating me – I am eternally grateful to you!"

Bradley humbly acknowledged the King's comment, as Meltor arrived on the scene to congratulate his protégé. "That was a very brave thing to do… you are truly a great hero and I am very proud of you – thank goodness you came back in time!"

Luccese struggled to maintain a conscious state of mind and he lay on the ground, as the busy squirrels wrapped a temporary dressing around his deep wound. He suddenly realized that his main ally was missing and he scanned the immediate area. "Where is General Eidar?"

The Freytorian was nowhere to be seen, as Henley approached to offer an update. "Your highness, I'm informed that Eidar hasn't been seen for quite a while but the forest is secured and the surviving Tree Elves have been rounded up!"

"Thank you, Henley... but I am more concerned about the General's whereabouts!" replied the Luccese, as the group looked around in search of the Freytorian.

Spew approached with a despondent look on his face. "I believe you are enquiring after the ice-bear's leader?"

Meltor reacted first. "Yes... have you seen him?"

The Wood Ogre's facial expression crumpled, as he delivered the bad news. "All your allies from across the Red Ocean fought well but I'm sorry to inform you that the brave General didn't make it... and there's more bad news – neither did Pavsik!"

30

Retrieving the Amulet of Silvermoor

Over an hour had passed and the injured King soon found out that the hard-fought battles had taken many lives including his dear friend Pavsik and the Freytorian General.

The Galetian's had incurred many casualties and Karn had lost over a third of his Werebeast clan. Many more Krogon Warriors had also been killed and troops across the allied forces had sacrificed their lives to save the kingdom from Varuna, who had been nicknamed Scarface and ironically imprisoned with Flaglan inside the newly erected tower.

The battle to regain control of Pathylon was finally over and Luccese stood on the steps that led into the royal palace. The proud King scanned the exhausted battalions of differing species that were standing in front of him waiting to hear his righteous words. The blood from the deep wound in his side seeped through the protective chainmail and a red stain spread across his war-torn clothing.

Meltor joined his King and supported him by holding his arm beneath the wound. Luccese struggled to stand, as he held aloft his sword and praised the crowd of brave fighters. "Many have died today to save our land from the tyranny bestowed upon it by Varuna and his fellow traitors!" he shouted, as the High Priest felt the blood seeping into his white cloak.

The crowds cheered their brave leader and the Devonian King was joined by his Queen, who persuaded her ailing husband to sit down. Luccese obliged and asked Meltor to continue addressing the masses.

"I would be honoured, my lord – but what would you like me to say, Sire?" asked the High Priest.

Luccese coughed, as he spluttered blood onto his wife's battle dress. "You know what to say, Meltor!"

Vash afforded Meltor a worried look and waved her arm, as a group of Devonian noblemen were called over to escort the royal couple inside the palace. "Carry on, Meltor," insisted the Queen. "Luccese will be fine… now please execute his request and speak to the brave armies of Pathylon on his behalf!"

Meltor nodded and turned to face the anxious crowd. "Your King is alright… but he needs to rest – as do most of you!" he shouted. "But before you all go about your business and return to your loved ones… Luccese has asked me to thank you all from the bottom of his heart!"

Bradley, Henley, Sereny and Jefferson moved through the crowd and appeared at the front, as they looked up at Meltor standing proud in his magnificent white flowing attire. Bradley spoke softly. "It's a pity Musgrove isn't here to see this."

"Where is Muzzy?" asked Sereny.

"Queen Vash told me he is being guarded by an elite squadron of Devonian Death Troops inside the Forbidden

Caves… he's in a pretty bad way - hopefully, we'll be able to see him soon," explained Bradley.

Jefferson sighed. "We can tell him all about the battle later… there's no way he could have continued in his present state of mind – as you said, he's in a right mess."

Sereny started to cry, as Bradley held her trembling arm. The girl sobbed at the thought of what Musgrove must be going through. "He's never going to get over it… the death of his Dad with his own hands will have left a scar that may never heal!"

Henley gripped his nephew's shoulder, as Bradley comforted the girl and consoled her with some words of solace. "Muzzy wasn't to know… none of us did - the Shadow Druid had to be killed by someone and it's unfortunate that Thomas Chilcott was slain by his youngest Son's blade!"

The children continued to console each other and Henley interrupted their private conversation, as he pointed at the palace steps. "Meltor is about to speak again!" he whispered, as the High Priest's voice raised its pitch to a bellowing retort.

"To my fellow combatants!" shouted the weary veteran, as his white beard moved in the gentle breeze and the Galetian continued his discourse on behalf of Luccese. "Your King salutes you all!" he yelled, as the cheers erupted once more. "To Captain Dray and all the Black Squirrels… and to Spew and his Wood Ogres from the Yeldarb Forest - we recognize your valiant demise of the Tree Elves!" he declared. "To Grog and all the Lizardmen from Krogonia… we thank you for helping to build such a fine bridge and fighting with great courage through the Galetis Empire – also to Karn and his legion of Werebeasts for providing the vital support that made all the difference inside the Forest of Haldon!" he saluted and continued his appraisal. "To the Freytorians, we thank you sincerely for supplying the greatest ice-ships that ever sailed... which enabled us to launch our initial assault on Varuna's armies!"

The crowd cheered again and congratulated each other, as the murmuring grew into a crescendo before Meltor struck the floor hard with the staff acquired from the Shadow Druid. The High Priest's actions silenced the excited audience and he continued with his speech. "And last but not least... I thank the greatest hero of all – the eternal chosen one, *Bradley Baker* for saving our King and not forgetting his trusted friends from the outside world!" he announced and invited the three children and Henley to step forward.

Bradley's name was chanted and Meltor lifted the boy's arm to signify his part in securing the future of Pathylon. The embarrassed boy cupped his hand and spoke up to gain the High Priest's attention. "May I say something, please?"

"Of course, Bradley!" replied Meltor, as he raised his arms to indicate that the crowd should respectfully silence their chants. "The boy hero wishes to speak!"

Bradley walked up a few more steps so he could see the anticipated looks on the waiting crowd, as he cleared his throat. "Thank you for honouring me with your fantastic appreciation... but I cannot possibly accept all the applause!" he proclaimed. "All of you are heroes and let's not forget those that did not make it through this challenging ordeal!" he affirmed. "Please allow me to name those that played an important part in the liberation of Pathylon but who are no longer here to enjoy our celebrations!" he announced and began to name the absent friends. "Pavsik... the High Priest of Devonia!" he shouted, as the crowd cheered in respect.

"General Eidar… a truly courageous veteran soldier that commanded enormous respect from his fellow Freytorian's, who followed him with great conviction!" He continued, as the audience paid their respects to the huge ice-bear. "And I'd also like to mention a special someone that you won't even have heard of… but because of my dog's sacrifice – our dear friend Grog was able to return to his homeland and lead the Krogon warriors into battle!"

A familiar lone voice shouted out from the crowd and the little dwarf finally made his way to the palace steps. Turpol held out his hand to Bradley and then addressed the masses to pay tribute to the deceased canine. "Three cheers for Bradley's faithful pet, K2… hip – hip!"

"Hooray!" roared out the crowd, as the chorus was repeated again and again.

"Thank you, Turpol," said Bradley and bent down to embrace the Gatekeeper.

"It was the least I could do for him… K2 was a good friend of mine too – his brave contribution to Pathylon's continued existence will be remembered always!" he replied and Grog approached Bradley, closely followed by Meltor.

The Krogon stood tall and proud, as he thanked the considerate boy for recognizing the brave sacrifice of the unsung canine hero. "That was a nice touch… K2 would have appreciated that – and just to reiterate I am very thankful for what he did for me!"

Meltor interrupted, as the crowd began to disperse and he placed his large hand on Bradley's shoulder. "The Queen has sent a message from inside the palace… the King's condition has stabilized and he is feeling much better," he conveyed. "Luccese has requested to see you, Bradley… and Grog, please go with him and I'll gather the others he has summoned - we'll meet you both outside the royal chambers in a few minutes."

Bradley and Grog looked surprised and walked towards the main entrance, as they turned to watch the High Priest speak with Turpol, Henley, Sereny and Jefferson. The privileged group followed the Galetian's lead into the royal palace and trailed the eternal chosen one up the magnificent flight of stairs that led to the King's private chamber.

Two Devonian's were guarding the door and clicked their heels together, as Meltor and Bradley approached. They uncrossed their spears to allow the High Priest and the boy hero access to the studded arched door. The Galetian acknowledged the guards show of respect and knocked on the door, as the others waited in line behind him. The door opened and Queen Vash smiled, as she invited the VIP's into the chamber.

King Luccese was sitting upright in his ornate bed and he summoned the group over. "Welcome and thank you for responding to my request to see you… it is important that I make my announcement to you all personally so the Pathylian people can resume their normal way of life."

Meltor asked. "What is it that you wish to tell us, my lord?"

The King looked at Grog and nodded respectfully at the overawed Lizardman. "First, I will start with our Krogon friend, who has returned from the Vortex of Silvermoor to display great courage in the face of adversity," he declared. "Grog… you were once branded a coward for refusing to fight your childhood friend, Zule – you have proved that you are nothing of the sort and your right to be a Krogon Champion was cruelly taken away from you by Harg."

Grog fidgeted uncomfortably, as the others looked on with sincere admiration. The Lizardman was totally shocked by the kind words from Luccese and he had not expected to be recognized in such a fine way by the King of Pathylon. The orange skin on his face turned to a darker shade and he starred precariously at the floor, as he shuffled his large webbed feet.

Bradley moved sideways and elbowed the Krogon in his leathery torso and Grog released a slight outtake of breath, as he reeled from the unexpected nudge. "Urrrggghhh!" he moaned and lifted his head again. "What was that for?"

"I don't think the King has finished speaking to you," whispered Bradley, as Luccese admired the comical antics displayed by the boy hero.

The bemused monarch attempted to retain a serious demeanor and continued his praise for the Krogon warrior. "Your efforts will not go unrewarded and I would be honoured if you would accept an immediate promotion from Champion and serve within the royal congress as the new High Priest of Krogonia!"

Turpol breathed a sigh of relief, as Luccese turned to address the dwarf. "You have served the remote region well in the absence of a Krogon leader and I'm sure you will agree… the time has come for one of their own kind to lead the Lizardmen as High Priest?"

"My lord, your announcement fills me with a huge sense of relief… I wasn't looking forward to telling you this - but the mother dwarf has invited me to Crystal City and spend the rest of my days with *my* own kind!" revealed the Gatekeeper.

Meltor spoke. "My lord… it would appear you have made these two fine representatives of Pathylon very happy – but why have you summoned the rest of us here?"

The King turned to the Galetian High Priest and acknowledged his statement. "Oh yes... let me continue – Henley Baker, please step forward," he requested, as Bradley's uncle moved nearer to the bed. "I want to ask you something and you must answer me with the utmost commitment!"

Bradley looked up at his uncle but Henley remained unaware of his nephew's stare. The short horns on his head started to throb and he had a feeling he knew what the King was about to ask. "My lord... the answer is yes!" he exclaimed and Luccese smiled.

Sereny twisted her shiny gold finger around one of her matching-coloured pigtails and urged Bradley to ask Meltor why his uncle had agreed to something without knowing what it was. "Why did Henley say yes?"

Bradley prodded Meltor and the Galetian anticipated the children's curiosity, as Henley remained stunned by his quick decision. "Luccese... may I confirm the details of Henley's decision on your behalf – so that everyone is aware of the sacrifice he must make in order to fulfill your request?"

The King nodded and insisted that the High Priest continue, as Meltor faced Bradley. "Your uncle has decided to stay in Pathylon."

"Why?" asked Bradley, as he tugged on his uncle's sleeve and Henley looked down at his nephew. "What will I tell Dad... your brother?"

Henley remained silent and could see that Bradley was getting upset, as Meltor continued. "Your uncle will take Pavsik's place in the Royal Congress and join Grog as a High Priest... as you know, Henley was born a Devonian and the region needs strong leadership from a true nobleman!"

Bradley's reaction to Meltor's announcement changed from sadness to joy and the boy sighed with relief, as he congratulated his uncle. "You truly deserve this, Uncle Henley... but what will I say to Dad – that's if we can get back home?"

Henley broke his silence and explained to Bradley that he had already anticipated staying in Pathylon no matter what had happened. "I have longed to return to my Devonian homeland for some time... ever since our last adventure in Silvermoor – I have dreamed of this moment," he conveyed. "I sent a letter to Patrick and Margaret informing them that I was going away for a while... they will think I am taking a year out to travel the outside world – so you don't have to explain anything to them when you get back!"

Bradley exhaled deeply, as he questioned the chances of him and the other children returning home to Sandmouth. "You sound so certain that we will return... Turpol may have repaired the bath but how will it transport us back?"

King Luccese cleared his throat to indicate that he wanted to speak. The monarch shuffled further up the bed, as Queen Vash rearranged the pillows behind his back. "That is why I have summoned the rest of you here," He declared and scanned the faces of the inquisitive audience. "Where is the boy that defeated the Shadow Druid?"

Queen Vash felt it was time to join the conversation. "Musgrove Chilcott is being looked after by the Devonian Death Troops inside the Forbidden Caves, my dear – unfortunately, our young friend has remained distraught following the death of his father and I felt it best that he stay there until the battle was over." King Luccese threw back the covers and swung his legs over the side of the bed, as the

Queen questioned his health. "You are not well enough to leave your bed, my dear… what are you doing?"

The King asked his concerned wife to pass him his robe. "I want to see Musgrove to offer my condolences… the boy must be in considerable pain," he sympathized and pulled the robe around his shoulders. "Also… there's something beyond the Forbidden Caves that the children will need - in order to get back home," he revealed and then spoke to Sereny, as he stared at the shimmering golden coat that still covered the pretty girl from head to foot. "Please pass me the gemstone."

"Sorry!" replied the embarrassed girl in a guilty tone.

"The Sacred Emerald of Yeldarb!" insisted Luccese, as he pointed to the bag around her shoulder. "The one you have hidden inside the sack!"

Everyone looked at the discomforted girl, as she lowered her head and Bradley questioned her integrity. "Did you take the emerald from the prism?"

Sereny nodded in a shameful manner. "I didn't think it would hurt and it was so shiny!" she explained.

Meltor reached over with his open hand. "Please hand over the jewel… you're not in trouble, Sereny – in fact you are going to be pleasantly surprised when you release your unlawful ownership of the sacred crystal!"

Sereny removed the bag and pulled out the sparkling emerald and then passed it to Meltor. As soon as she released the gem, a bright light filled the room and by the time it had distinguished the girl's golden glow had disappeared. She screamed with excitement. "I'm back to normal!"

Bradley punched the air and quipped. "Hopefully that will have taught you a valuable lesson!"

"I guess so," replied Sereny, as she squeaked another expression of glee.

Jefferson concluded. "Yeah... no more stealing sacred gems from strange looking pyramids!"

Sereny saw the funny side and Bradley chuckled, as they both let out a cry of delight. "Brilliant!" they chorused and looked on, as Meltor handed the emerald to Luccese.

The King asked Queen Vash to hand him a glossy black box adorned with ornate silver markings. The box had been sitting on the bedside cabinet and Luccese opened it to reveal a pale gold-coloured diamond, as he placed the emerald next to yellow jewel. "Meltor... please ask the bird whistler of Trad to prepare Ploom for her final mission – we need to retrieve the Amulet of Silvermoor!"

Bradley cried. "But the sapphire is encased in ice at the top of Mount Pero... surely by removing the amulet – Pathylon will be in danger again?"

Turpol understood the King's plan and stepped forward. "Not necessarily... the sapphire will not be needed for too long and by the time it is returned to Mount Pero – Pathylon will only have received the slightest of tremors," he explained. "In order for you to escape and return to your own world... the Amulet of Silvermoor must be aligned with the three other sacred gems – then and only then will your grobite react to the combined power of the jewels!"

"So that makes *four* gems, altogether?" asked Sereny, as she finally calmed down from the relief of changing back to normal. "But with the sapphire... we will only *three*!"

King Luccese interrupted the girl's query and thanked the Gatekeeper for explaining the situation, as he called to the guards outside the royal chamber. "Prepare the Hoffen... and

Meltor, please inform the bird whistler that Ploom is to be sent to the Peronto Alps at once!"

"Yes, my lord... I will arrange it immediately!" he declared. "Everyone else make your way down to the palace foyer and wait for me there... oh, err - Bradley you stay here with me to help the King!"

Sereny looked bemused at not receiving an answer to her observation, as Bradley nodded and the others rushed out of the royal chamber. The girl shouted across the room towards the King and asked Luccese the question again. "What is it beyond the Forbidden Caves that will help us?"

The King continued to get dressed and smiled at the girl's persistence, as she stood in the doorway with her hands on her hips. "The Ruby of Pathylon!" replied Luccese. "The forth jewel that you need to retrieve in order to go home... I will explain the rest when we get to the caves!"

Bradley glared at Sereny and flicked his head, as he silently mouthed his instruction. "See you downstairs in a few minutes."

Sereny smiled, as Jefferson tugged on her jacket and she disappeared from the doorway. Bradley spoke to the King in an embarrassed tone. "Sorry about that, my lord... Sereny is obviously still very excited about shedding her gold coat!"

Luccese laughed and patted the boy on the shoulder, as a dark silhouette appeared behind one of the curtains. No one noticed the imposter and the King picked up the box of gems, as he acknowledged Bradley's explanation. "Please do not feel you have to explain away your friend's inquisitiveness... it is understandable," he sympathized. "Now... let's go and see your other friend, Muzzy - and set the wheels in motion to get you all home safely!"

Finally, everyone including Queen Vash left the royal chamber and the shadowy figure revealed himself from behind the drapes. The Shade Runner pulled his hood down to expose his face and Ethan Darke let out an evil laugh. "Hahahahahah!" he roared and looked out of the window to witness the Galetian High Priest making his way over towards the bird whistler's post. "Go on, Meltor... send the weary Klomus Hawk to retrieve the sapphire and align the four gems inside the caves – you will be saving me so much trouble!" he sniggered and swept his dark cloak around his waist. "But it will be me that will return to the outside world again... and not the famous Bradley Baker and his pathetic trio of friends!"

31

Aligning the Jewels

Bradley looked up, as Ploom soared high and spread her huge wingspan. The entourage reached a clearing in the Forest of Haldon and stopped to wave at the great bird. The Klomus Hawk tipped her beak to acknowledge their support and flew across the Pathylian skyline, as she headed for the Peronto Alps to retrieve the Amulet of Silvermoor.

Bradley followed Meltor's mount and steered his Hoffen out of the clearing along a narrow path that twisted through the dense trees inside the forest. The King was leading the short journey to the Forbidden Caves and he spotted the familiar red suits of two Devonian Death Troops in the distance. The soldiers were guarding the entrance to the caves, which been cleared some time back and they welcomed the entourage, as they held their laser weapons by their sides.

Hoffen hoofs clattered on the hard ground and puffs of hot steam snorted from their flaring nostrils, as the group neared the waiting guards. Grog was proud to be riding his Koezard alongside his King's mount and Shatar reared up, as the two guards approached. The Death Troops calmed the Krogon's reptile steed and then helped the King and Queen to dismount their Hoffen, as the others followed them into the caves.

Musgrove Chilcott was lying very still on a stone slab surrounded by more guards. Sereny ran over and crouched down next to the slab of granite, as she gently stroked the teenager's brow. "Poor Muzzy," she sighed and was quickly joined by Bradley, as Jefferson stood back to let his friends console the bereaved boy.

Bradley called him over to join them. "Don't just stand there, Jeffers… you're part of the team now!"

Jefferson walked over tentatively and noticed the battered Victorian tub in the corner next to Musgrove's stone bunk. "I see the bath has been delivered here okay!"

"Oh yeah… I hadn't noticed – good to see it's still in one piece!" exclaimed Sereny, as a dark shadow rushed passed in the background. The Shade Runner was careful not to be spotted and he hid behind a tall rock, whilst Luccese paced over to the far side of the cave. The King lifted a round disc-shaped stone and called Bradley over to see what he had uncovered.

Henley, Turpol and Meltor joined Bradley and they stood around the King, as he placed the yellow diamond at the centre of a triangular base. "None of the stones can be removed until all four are in place and have been activated." he declared. "That means that once the Amulet of Silvermoor is inserted… we will need to make sure all the other gems are in place before we can remove it again – if the sapphire remains inside the triangle for too long then Pathylon will be destroyed!"

Sereny and Jefferson left Musgrove's side, as he continued to sleep and they muscled their way passed the others to witness Luccese take the emerald out of the black box and position it at the bottom left-hand corner of the three-sided pedestal.

Ethan Darke watched the proceedings from a safe distance, as a few slight tremors released some loose splinters of rock from the ceiling. The debris crashed to the floor, as the fluttering of wings echoed around the cave and the Klomus Hawk appeared. Bradley shouted. "Wow... that was quick, Ploom!"

Turpol announced. "We don't have much time... those tremors indicate that the nuclear reaction within Mount Pero has started – the quakes will grow even stronger if we don't align the sacred gems and then return the sapphire!"

Grog rushed over to retrieve the blue crystal from the bird's claw and stroked the base of her tired neck, as she released the Amulet of Silvermoor into his webbed hand. Grog winked at Ploom and then ran over to King Luccese, as the huge Lizardman offered the King the gemstone.

Luccese placed the stone in the bottom right-hand corner of the pedestal and the yellow diamond glowed even brighter, as he turned his attention to the waiting entourage. "There is no turning back, now... the sapphire cannot be removed until we have retrieved the Ruby of Pathylon!" He looked over to where Bradley was standing and offered his instruction. "You are the eternal chosen one... and it's now time for you to complete the triangle and align the prism of blood!" he stated and pointed to an arched opening at the far end of the cave.

Sereny exclaimed. "The final part of the message on the grobite... so that's what the coin was referring to – not the pyramids on Rekab!"

Bradley held out his hand and put up his thumb to acknowledge his female friend's assessment, as he complimented the smiling girl. "Nice one, Sereny... well thought out – you're getting very good at working out the coin's riddles!"

King Luccese invited Bradley's attention again and continued. "You know what's located through the archway and what lies beyond the vortex... the only way for you and your friends to return to the outside world - is if you collect the Ruby of Pathylon so it can be placed at the top of the triangle!"

Bradley nodded and ran over to Musgrove, who was now stirring. He nudged his friend and spoke with an assertive tone. "Muzzy... wake up – I need you to help me get us out of here and back to Sandmouth!" He pleaded and shook the lanky teenager again. "Come on... we don't have much time!"

Musgrove opened his eyes and starred up at his friend, as his eyes began to well up. "Hey, Brad... did you hear about what I did in the duel of destiny - I killed my father."

"No you didn't!" insisted Bradley. "You killed the Shadow Druid... your Dad disappeared a long time ago – the person that escaped from the Kaikane Idol was not your real father!

"But..." replied Musgrove, as Bradley finished his explanation.

"It was a trick to deceive us... we were all meant to think that your Dad had miraculously returned," explained Bradley. "The Shadow Druid needed a route back to the outside world and we gave it to him... it turns out all he wanted to do was recruit an apprentice – he knew his fate and you sealed it!"

The tears in Musgrove's eyes stopped flowing and he realized what Bradley was saying made sense. He sat up and rubbed his face. "So it's been about Ethan Darke all along... he is the evil force that threatens Pathylon – not the Shadow Druid!" he exclaimed. "So what's happened to him... has anyone seen Darke since he followed Jefferson through the Vortex of Silvermoor?"

Jefferson stepped forward and replied. "No... he's not materialized yet – no one has seen him!"

Musgrove responded by insisting that they stay and kill the Shade Runner. "We can't just return to Sandmouth and let him get away with it and pretend everything is okay!" he declared and jumped down from the stone slab.

Henley shouted, as another quake rippled beneath the caves. "Come on... you're running out of time – get into the vortex!"

Bradley afforded Musgrove an encouraging look and declared. "I promise if we have time... we'll find Darke and make him pay for what he's done – right now, we have to concentrate on finding the Ruby of Pathylon so are you with me or not?"

The teenager nodded and responded by shouting. "Okay...I'm coming with you, Bradley - let's do this!"

Sereny and Jefferson moved out of the way, as the two boys sprinted towards the archway. They kept on running and approached the swirling vortex. The dark shadow moved quickly behind the rocks and followed them towards the entrance, as they jumped into the twisting light.

Luccese and the others had failed to notice the Shade Runner, as he disappeared into the centre of the vortex but one of the Death Troops had spotted something unusual. The guard ran back from the archway that led to the vortex and stood to attention, as he asked for permission to speak. Luccese nodded and guard explained that a strange black shape had appeared within the swirls of the time portal. The whole group rushed through the archway and the King pointed to the dark anomaly at the centre of the spiral. "What do you think it is, Meltor?"

The High Priest studied the twirling shape. "It looks like a misshaped number '5'... what do you think, Turpol?" he asked, as the Gatekeeper squinted his eyes and peered into the heart of the vortex.

The dwarf finished his quick assessment and provided a second opinion. "It's form is too precise and has a uniform shape... it looks more like a letter 'S' to me!"

Henley announced. "A black-coloured 'S'... that can only mean one thing – 'S' stands for *SHADE*!"

Sereny screamed and ran towards the entrance to the portal. "The Shade Runner is inside the vortex... we have to help Bradley and Musgrove!"

"Nooooooo!" shouted Meltor, as Jefferson cast a secure grip on the girl's clothing. "The vortex will be destroyed if you go in there... its capacity was already exceeded when the boys jumped in – and it's even more overloaded now that the Shade Runner is in there with them!"

Turpol comforted Sereny, as Jefferson released his grasping hold. "All we can do, now... is wait!"

Meanwhile inside the vortex, the two boys were being carried along the twisting circular corridor of time. They had steadied their balance and were holding on to each other, as their speed increased to a maximum pace along the multi-coloured tube.

Ethan Darke was fast approaching and by the time the boys had reached the exit, the Shade Runner pounced forward and grabbed Musgrove's legs. All three time travelers hit the ground hard, as they ended up in a crumpled heap against the wall of the receiving chamber.

Bradley kicked out at the flowing cloak that had covered his whole body and Ethan Darke reacted by wrapping part of his cape around the boy's neck. Bradley struggled to breath and gasped for breath, as the cloak was pulled tighter. Musgrove managed to release himself from the fracas and kicked the antagonist in the back but the dark figure kept the tension on his stranglehold.

"Urrrrrrrrrrrghhhh!" gurgled Bradley, as he felt his consciousness ebbing away.

"Die... Baker boy – I told you it wasn't over!" warned the Shade Runner, as he kicked back at Musgrove, whilst retaining his grip on the helpless boy.

Musgrove jolted backwards from the impact of Ethan Darke's heavy boot and smacked his head on the wall. His eyes rolled, as he fell to the ground like a leaden weight.

With his friend out of action, Bradley had to summon an inner strength and he thought back to K2 lying in the road, as he yelled out loud. "Arrrrrrrrrrrrgggggghhhhh!"

"Moan and groan all you want Baker boy... it's no good – you are about to join your precious doggy in hell!" chastised the Shade Runner and made a final attempt to suffocate the exhausted boy by twisting his cape even tighter.

Bradley let out a lung emptying gasp and his body fell limp, as stars filled his head. He slumped to the floor and the Shade Runner released his hold. Ethan Darke tore his cloak and left the lengthy remains of the tattered cloth around his victim's neck. He stood up and walked over to the oak doors, as he pushed them open with ease. Once through he turned and looked up at the plinth that straddled the great wooden entrance. He read out the word inscribed in the oak beam and exclaimed. "PATHYLON... it's where it all began and this is where it all ends!" He paused and then muttered to himself. "Without the ruby... they cannot complete the triangle and align the prism – and without the Amulet of Silvermoor repositioned on Mount Pero!" he continued. "Pathylon will be destroyed... job done – hahahahahaha!"

Meanwhile back inside the Forbidden Caves the entourage was becoming very nervous, as the tremors in the ground grew fiercer. The King summoned his High Priests and Turpol to join him outside the entrance to the caves. He was keen to protect the feelings of Sereny and Jefferson, as the group marched out of the cave.

Meltor, Henley and Grog formed a circle with Turpol, as Luccese shared his concerns. "It's taking too long... I fear that Bradley Baker and his friend have suffered at the hands of the Shade Runner!"

Henley stamped his foot on the ground and clenched his fists. "Damn that Ethan Darke... let me enter the vortex!"

"No... it would be pointless!" replied the King. "If the Shade Runner has killed the boys then he will have already destroyed the ruby... he knows that if we fail to align the prism – Pathylon will be destroyed."

"What do you suggest?" asked Grog.

"I suggest that we all pray that the eternal chosen one is still alive... the existence of Pathylon is solely in the hands of Bradley Baker for the last time!"

32

The Ruby of Pathylon

The Black Squirrels and Wood Ogres had almost completed their homeward journey across the Galetis Empire to the iceberg ships that were waiting to transport them back to Rekab. The exhausted species could feel the underground tremors rippling through the region and hurried their pace to escape the imminent atrocity.

The Freytorians knew there was nothing they could do to change the fate of Pathylon and the impending destruction of the arcane world. The ice-bears had already left the coastline of Devonia on board their fleet of submarines, as they sped away across the Red Ocean. The leading ship was carrying the dead body of Eidar and a heroic reception awaited the brave General upon his return to Freytor.

The five regions of Pathylon were left on a status of red alert, as word of the situation beyond the Forbidden Caves quickly spread amongst the terrified populous.

Meanwhile outside the large oak doors that formed one of the entrances to Pathylon, the Shade Runner searched around for the star in the ground. "The ruby has to be here somewhere… I might as well destroy it to make sure no one ever finds it again," he muttered to himself, as he searched the floor on his hands and knees. Ethan Darke's hand rubbed over a raised stone and he quickly brushed away the dust that covered the ruby at the centre of the star. "There you are… you little beauty!" He exclaimed and began to prize the gemstone from the rock.

The ruby began to glow, as the seal around it was penetrated and the Shade Runner pulled the gemstone free from its ancient housing. He instinctively held the crimson gem above his head and started to laugh uncontrollably, as the jewel was suddenly propelled back towards his face and straight into his sneering mouth. Broken teeth and oozing blood splattered against the cavern wall, as Ethan Darke reeled backwards. He recovered quickly and held his gaping chin, as he looked up at his nemesis.

Bradley Baker stood in front of the Shade Runner and looked down at the injured tormenter, as he held the piece of torn cloak that had tethered his neck in his hand. He was now ready to inflict a revengeful strike and teased the wounded thug. "Hello, *Ed-Case*… it's me again – take this you bully!" he shouted and flicked the cloth at the cowering brute's face.

"Arrrrrgggghhhhhh!" repelled Darke, as the end of the cloth pierced his eye socket.

"You may recall the technique I'm using… what's it like taking some of your own medicine?" chastised Bradley, as he revelled at the sight of the squirming villain rolling around on the dirty ground. Ethan Darke held his hemorrhaging wound, as Bradley kicked him in the stomach. "That one's for killing my dog… you hooligan!" vented the possessed boy and pulled back the cloth for a second strike.

Without hesitation, he repeated the whipping action and took out the Shade Runner's sight altogether by lashing the bloodstained rag at Darke's other eye. "And that one's for using Musgrove's father as a puppet for your own evil gain... it's the last you will see of me - or anyone else for that matter!" he exclaimed and finished his revengeful onslaught by crashing the sole of his training shoe down onto the nose of the screaming tyrant.

The Shade Runner collapsed in a craggy heap, as Musgrove appeared behind Bradley. He tapped his friend on the shoulder and asked. "Need any help, Brad?"

"Nah," replied Bradley confidently, as he lassoed his newly acquired lethal weapon and wrapped the cloth around the Shade Runner's ankle. "Got it covered, Muzzy... everything's under control – now, give me hand to get this scumbag into the vortex."

"No problem!" replied Musgrove and he picked up the ruby. "I guess we'll be needing this little baby too!"

"Sure will... let's get it back to Pathylon – we've got a world to save!" answered Bradley, as they dragged the moaning fiend through the doorway and into the time portal.

Back inside the Forbidden Caves the entrance to the vortex was starting to crumble, as the elite squadron of Devonian Death Troops evacuated the series of inter-connected caverns. King Luccese and the entourage were waiting in the forest a few hundred metres away from the caves.

Meltor was speaking with the group and preparing them for the worst. "We have about five minutes before Mount Pero explodes... does anyone have any last requests?"

Sereny spoke nervously. "I'd like to go home please!"

Queen Vash held the frightened girl and whispered gently. "You must be missing your parents so much... I hope my presence here will afford you the motherly comfort you need during this dreadful experience?"

"Thank you, your majesty," replied the girl, as she started to cry.

"I am not your majesty... I'm Vash – your friend," consoled the Queen and she cuddled the petrified girl, as the ground shook violently again.

Henley commented. "Is it me or did that last quake feel different to you lot?"

Grog nodded. "No... it's not you, Henley – that tremor definitely felt a bit weird!"

"Look!" exclaimed Turpol, as he pointed at the crumbling entrance to the Forbidden Caves.

Everyone turned and witnessed three figures appear from the hollow rock face and Sereny lifted her head from the Queen's lap, as she screamed. "Bradley!"

Grog was the first to reach the two boys, as they dragged the groaning Shade Runner into the forest undergrowth. King Luccese grabbed the eternal chosen one and congratulated the boy hero. "You made it, Bradley... well done!"

Bradley laughed and looked at Ethan Darke, as he rolled in the grass holding his blinded face. "Thought I'd deliver you another prisoner... maybe he can join Varuna and Flaglan in the new tower!"

Meltor chuckled and asked. "Did you find the ruby?"

"Do you mean this one?" declared Musgrove and handed the red crystal to the Galetian.

King Luccese congratulated the boys again and took the ruby from Meltor. "We have no more time to waste... we must insert this into the prism!"

Jefferson spoke out. "The cave is collapsing!"

Bradley did not hesitate and grabbed the ruby from Luccese, as he turned to run in the direction of the dilapidated entrance. The boy hero sprinted through the falling debris and disappeared into the cave, as Sereny yelled. "Bradley... be careful!"

Once inside he fumbled his way through the choking dust, as it showered down from the roof of the caves. Bradley could just make out the glowing diamond at the centre of the triangular-shaped pedestal and he dived forward to insert the ruby into the top corner of the prism. The yellow diamond released a piercing vertical laser beam that penetrated the ceiling above and the three surrounding gems all burst into a bright cascade of dancing light. The four gemstones then rose from the prism and danced in mid-air, as they darted back and forth above the pedestal.

Bradley instinctively grabbed the four crystals and dashed back out of the cave to the waiting group of worried onlookers.

King Luccese approached the exhausted boy and retrieved the blue gemstone, as he threw the Amulet of Silvermoor to Meltor. "Deal with this first!"

"Yes, Sire!" replied the Galetian and ran over to where Ploom was resting. "Fly as fast as your wings will take you... take the precious sapphire back to Mount Pero!"

The Klomus Hawk puffed out her feathers and took the crystal in her beak, as she launched her massive frame. Her red-crested belly shone like a burning torch, as she shot into the air and then disappeared over the tree tops.

Luccese, Queen Vash, Henley and Turpol gathered around Meltor, as the four children stared at the remaining three glowing jewels in Bradley's cupped hands. "Hand me the yellow diamond, Bradley," asked the Galetian, as he reached down to retrieve the brightest gemstone. "It's time to send you all back home."

"How?" asked Bradley.

"Follow me," ordered Meltor and the entourage walked behind the wise old High Priest, as he called on the Devonian Death Troops to lift the bathtub down from a Hoffen drawn cart.

"Ah... I see you managed to pull the bath out of the caves then!" exclaimed Musgrove, as he approached the tub and twisted the gold-plated taps. "Who repaired these?"

The Gatekeeper stepped forward. "I did!"

"Great job, Turpol... I just hope the propellers work again!" replied Musgrove, as he shook the dwarf's hand.

Bradley reassured his friend. "Well they worked okay when Ryuu pulled the bath across from Rekab... so hopefully the rock fall inside the cave hasn't damaged them again!"

Meltor retrieved the gold coin from the plughole and gave it to Bradley. "You won't need the grobite this time!" he declared and placed the yellow diamond into the plughole. "This will do the trick!"

The tremors in the ground stopped and King Luccese announced. "Ploom has done it... the Amulet of Silvermoor must be back in its rightful place on the sacred shelf!"

Queen Vash led the applause and thanked Bradley again for saving Pathylon. "We are so proud of you!"

Henley invited all four children for a group hug and they obliged, as everyone except the Krogon congregated around each other to celebrate. Bradley released the hold around his waist and moved over to where Grog was standing. "Everything okay?"

The Krogon sighed and replied in a saddened voice. "Not really... we have spent little time getting to know each other again – all the fighting has taken precedence and now you are about to leave forever."

"I'll never forget you, Grog," replied Bradley, as Sereny and Musgrove joined their friend. "We have some great memories to hold on to... and you never know – we may meet again someday!"

Sereny wrapped her petite arms around the Krogon's tubby waistline. "I'll never forget you... Mr. Tangerine Man!"

Grog croaked and cleared his throat, as he held back the tears and shook Musgrove's hand. "Go on then... be off with you all – before the diamond stops glowing!"

Meltor suggested to Henley that he bid his final farewell to his nephew and the Devonian heeded the Galetian's advice, as he interrupted the children's parting with the Lizardman. "Bradley... come here a minute – I'd like to tell you something."

Bradley left Musgrove and Sereny with Grog, as he approached his uncle. "Yes, Uncle Henley... what is it?"

"Goodbye, I guess... I'm going to miss you," choked Henley and pulled the boy close to his chest. "Promise me you will give your Aunt Vera a big kiss from me and don't forget to look your Dad in the eye and shake his hand from me too!"

"Shaking Dad's hand... no problem – kissing Aunt Vera, yuckkkkk!" replied Bradley and he started to laugh. "No... seriously Uncle – don't worry, I will!"

The goodbyes were interrupted by the bellowing sound of Meltor's voice. "It's time to leave!"

Bradley, Musgrove, Jefferson and Sereny climbed into the bathtub and the *eternal chosen one* secured the rear seating

336

position this time. He tossed the coin to Jefferson, who was sitting in front of the taps. "Here you go, Jeffers... in case you need it!"

Jefferson felt honoured to be holding the sacred grobite and he slipped the gold coin into his trouser pocket for safe keeping.

"How do we get home?" asked Bradley.

"That way!" replied Meltor and pointed to the entrance of the Forbidden Caves, as he started to laugh. "You know the way!"

Henley, Grog and Turpol stood back, as the King and Queen waved from the side. Meltor turned the taps and the bright yellow laser beam reappeared from the centre of the diamond. The light shot straight into the opening of the tap's mono-faucet and the tub began to vibrate. The tap heads turned to a horizontal position and started to spin, as they increased in size to form two large propellers.

The bathtub moved forward along the dusty forest clearing and built up speed, as it approached the entrance to the Forbidden Caves. All four children waved and Bradley turned around to salute his Pathylian friends, as the tub disappeared into the cavernous void.

Grog looked down at the little dwarf and asked Turpol the obvious question, as Henley listened intently with interest. "Will we ever see them again?"

The Gatekeeper paused for a moment and caught Henley's hopeful stare. The dwarf hunched his tiny shoulders and held his hands up, as he offered his reply. "I doubt it... I think that was Bradley Baker's last amazing adventure in Pathylon!"

33

The Perfect Christmas Present

The children entered the brightly coloured vortex for the last time and the bath held itself steady throughout the twisting journey. They approached the exit and began to congratulate each other, as all four children burst into a combined cheer. Suddenly a jolt in the time portal affected a premature ending to the celebrations, as the bath lifted and turned vertical into an upward driving position.

The bath pierced through the pliable roof of the vortex and carried on rising through the eerie darkness at a rapid pace. Jefferson's back pushed against Sereny's stomach and their collective mass rested against Musgrove. The three children's combined weight squashed Bradley against the elongated back rest of the tub and the eternal chosen one struggled to breath.

Bradley hooked his head backwards to witness the hole in the vortex below moving further way, as the bath continued to climb into the empty void. He pushed against Musgrove's spine to realize a momentary breath, as the conjoined passengers came crashing down on his chest again.

"Urrrrrghhhhh!" he spluttered and an immediate relief followed, as the bath suddenly levelled out again. "What's happening, Jeffers?"

Jefferson looked ahead, as a small dot of light in the distance began to grow bigger and bigger. "Looks like we're heading for another exit!" he exclaimed.

Sereny relayed more information to Bradley, who was now able to breathe freely. She noticed a shape at the centre of the white dot and waited a few more seconds until the image became clearer. "There's something standing in the exit!"

Musgrove turned around to face Bradley and yelled. "It looks like a Witch… what are we going to do?"

Bradley could not believe it and thought to himself. "It must be the same Witch from the cliff top cottage in Rekab." He then spoke aloud. "How could the old hag have got here from Crystal City… the dwarves had her locked away in that dungeon – there's no way she could have escaped." He then replied to Musgrove's question. "It has to be a trick… she must have cast a spell or something – Jeffers, use the coin!"

Jefferson reached into his pocket to retrieve the grobite, as the bath sped towards the white dot and Musgrove's observation was confirmed. The Witch was cackling very loudly, as the cat meowed and nestled in her arm. A cauldron of green slimy liquid bubbled at her side and the sorceress stirred the ingredients, as she aimed her dark eyes at the bath.

"Quick, Jeffers… throw the coin!" ordered Bradley. "Make sure it lands in the potion!"

Jefferson grabbed the sacred grobite and held it firmly in his hand, as the bath jolted from side to side. He aimed and cast the coin into the air, as it flew towards the cauldron. The Witch reacted by swiping her ladle at the flying disc and accidently knocked the cat into the bubbling liquid. The hag dropped the ladle and desperately tried to retrieve the drowning animal from the potion.

Bradley spotted an opportunity to get passed and noticed the Witch's struggling to save the cat, as he shouted ahead. "That will do, Jeffers… now - everyone tilt to the left!" he ordered and the time travellers leant over to steer the bath around the screaming Witch. Bradley leant over the edge of the tub and gave the grappling sorceress a gentle push, as she landed head first into the cauldron to join her feline pet.

"Nice one, Brad!" shouted Musgrove, as he reached out and grabbed the spinning coin. "Got it!" he exclaimed triumphantly and handed it back to Jefferson for safe keeping, as he held the sides of the tub to steady his balance.

The bath passed cleanly through the white hole and the background suddenly reversed, as a small black dot appeared in the distance. Bradley peered into the complete whiteness and released a frustrated sigh. "I can't believe this… when are we going to get out of this monotone nightmare?"

Jefferson thought he had spotted a way out, as he looked to the right hand side of the black dot. "Look over there… I'm sure there's a door – it's difficult to see but you can just make it out if you squint your eyes."

Sereny did as the boy suggested and cried out. "He's right… it looks like a way out!" she confirmed and pointed at a thin vertical strip of light.

Bradley held his arm over Musgrove's shoulder and followed the girl's hand, as he too spotted the narrow opening that edged the door. "Lean to the right, everyone!"

They did as Bradley asked and the bath tub veered off to the right, as the black dot moved out of direct line. Jefferson commended the boy hero on his quick thinking and held the coin tightly in case it was needed again. Then to the surprise of the four exhausted voyagers, the whiteness imploded on itself, as a series of bright lights burst out in all directions.

Musgrove yelled. "I think we're about to find out what lies behind that door!"

Sereny exclaimed. "I just hope its friendly... whatever it is!"

Bradley kept quiet and maintained his focus on the gap around the door. He then stood up and prepared to jump, as Musgrove tilted his head and looked upwards at his friend. The eternal chosen one dove forward over the others and pushed his arms against the door. The bath continued and the gap widened, as the door was ripped off its hinges. Bradley performed a forward roll, as he hit the floor-tiled surface and smashed against the opposite wall.

The bath followed the same trajectory, as the door rebounded against the front of the tub and ricocheted off the taps. Jefferson ducked to avoid the edge of the door and Sereny followed suit but Musgrove was not quick enough, as the blunt edge hit him in the middle of his chest and the teenager was sent flying backwards through the opening.

Bradley lifted his head to see the bath hurtling towards him and he just managed to avoid its full force, as he dived out of the way. Sereny and Jefferson felt the full impact of the bath's heavy landing against the wall, as tiny shards of porcelain tiles showered over their heads. The distraught girl shouted out to Bradley. "Muzzy was hit by the door... I think he's been knocked back into the time portal!"

Bradley reacted immediately and headed for the void, as a powerful stream of air gust through the doorway. He struggled to walk against the force of the jetstream and pulled himself along by using a towel rail. For the first time the boy hero realized where he was and yelled back to

Sereny, as the wind blew against his face. "We're back inside the Haytor Hotel... look at the wall!"

Sereny held onto the side of the bath and the image on the wall became clear, as beams of yellow light shot through the cracks between the reformed tiles. "It's happening again... the tiles are starting to shift position to form a series of triangular shapes - they're turning into the three pyramids just like before!"

The radiating luminance connected with the sparkling diamond in the plughole of the bath and the whole room was filled with a golden glow. Bradley continued to fight against the strong current and reached out to grab the edge of the door frame. He looked down and noticed a pair of hands gripping on to the bottom of the ledge.

Jefferson had managed to join Bradley's side and he held on to his belt. "Reach down and grab him!" he shouted, as Bradley let go of the door frame and held out his arm.

Musgrove looked up and spotted the helping hand from his best friend, as he reached up to grasp it. The force of the wind was becoming more intense and Bradley used all his energy to drag the heavier fourteen year old over the ledge, as Jefferson hooked his arm around the towel rail. With one almighty heave the three boys managed to pull themselves to safety, as the wind grew more powerful.

"Help me to move the bath across the doorway!" shouted Bradley, as Sereny stepped out of the way and held onto the base of the matching Victorian sink unit.

Jefferson and Musgrove reached out and pulled the rim of the bath towards the towel rail, as Bradley pushed the ornate legs of the tub towards the open door frame. The bath tilted upwards, as the wind sucked the solid object into the frame. The gusting vacuum was finally plugged and only the leaking sound of whistling air could be heard pulling at the void, as it sucked through the gaps around rim of the bath.

"That was close," said Bradley in a calm voice. "I'm so glad to be back... come on – let's see what's happening downstairs.

Musgrove and Jefferson simultaneously breathed a sigh of relief and followed Bradley through the hole in the wall that led into the linen cupboard. Sereny had already entered the small room, as she located the key in the lock and realized. "Where do you think we would have ended up if we passed through the black dot?"

A puzzled look appeared on Jefferson's face. "That's a great question, Sereny."

Musgrove offered a casual retort. "Do we really care?"

"Sereny has imposed an interesting thought, Muzzy," argued Bradley. "And I certainly care... but as long as that old slipper bath is blocking the doorway – I guess we'll never need to know!"

"Here, here!" cheered Jefferson, as Sereny turned the key and the four children made their way onto the landing.

Bradley suggested that he should check out what was happening downstairs and everyone agreed. So the eternal chosen one crept down the two flights and heard the sound of laughter coming from the dining room. He completed an about-turn and headed back up to where his friends were waiting. "There's a room full of people down there... not sure what's going on!"

Musgrove heard the sound of bells ringing in the distance. He looked through the landing window and noticed the church spire in the distance. He walked over and placed his hands on the sill, as he scanned the hotel grounds. "Hey, you lot... come over here and look at this – there's loads of cars parked at the front of the hotel."

Bradley, Sereny and Jefferson huddled together and joined Musgrove, as the glass began to steam up. It proved difficult to see, as Jefferson rubbed his sleeve to disperse the condensation and noticed a familiar vehicle parked next to the main entrance. "I think I'm seeing things!" exclaimed the boy. "I'm sure that's my Dad's car!"

"There are quite a few Vauxhall Astra's around," replied Bradley. "Are you sure?"

"Yep... absolutely sure!" declared Jefferson. "That's his license plate, alright!"

Sereny noticed that her parent's car was also parked on the gravel drive. "I suggest we remove our jackets and store them in the linen cupboard... I've gotta feeling we're in for a few surprises when we get downstairs - you know what happened the last time we arrived back in Sandmouth!"

Bradley agreed and they all discarded their coats and made their way tentatively downstairs. They waited a few minutes outside the dining room to see if they could make out what was being said behind the closed door but the sound was too muffled. "I guess it's time to face the music!" He announced and the other three adventurers prepared themselves to receive a grilling from their over-protective parents, as Bradley pushed open the door.

"Ahhhhh... there you are children – we thought you'd got lost!" declared Patrick, as he placed the sharp knife on a large silver tray. "I've just finished carving the turkey and you're just in time... we're about to start the main course – pass me the cranberry sauce please, Margaret!"

Musgrove stood open-mouthed and spoke without thinking of the consequences. "It's Christmas day?"

Sereny nudged the tall boy in the side of his hip with her elbow. "And how we're loving your kind hospitality Mr. and Mrs. Baker... it's been the best Christmas day ever!"

Musgrove reeled sideways and rubbed his boney torso. "Errr, yes... erm – thanks for inviting us over!"

Aunt Vera stared at the four children suspiciously, as Bradley's mother gracefully accepted the fictitious compliments from the two teenagers. "Why thank you... now come and sit back down before your dinners get cold," insisted Margaret, as Grandma Penworthy let out a very loud burp and Frannie erupted into a giggling fit.

Bradley smiled to confirm to his friends that no one in the room had any idea what they had just experienced, as he responded to his Grandma's belching outburst. "Nice one... glad to see the starter hit the right spot, Gran!" he joked and then muttered under his breath to Jefferson. "Whatever the starter was... that is?"

Charles and Marian Crabtree tucked into their dinner, as Jefferson watched them pause every so often to add their contribution to the conversation around the table. His parents looked up at the same time and caught their son staring into space. Mr. Crabtree called across the table. "Everything alright, Jefferson?"

"Err, yes... Dad – just thinking how pleased I am that we were able to make the journey down south to spend time with Bradley and his family," he replied and placed an over-cooked sprout in his mouth by mistake. "Urrrghh!"

Bradley chuckled to himself and winked at Jefferson. "Nice recovery, Jeffers!"

Patrick looked over to acknowledge the four paying guests that had been staying in the hotel and then spoke to the gathering of united Yorkshire and Devon folk. "I'd just like to thank everyone for accepting our invitation to stay at our lovely hotel over the Christmas period… and a warm welcome to our guests from Somerset – oh and if I might say, a special mention to Musgrove's Mum for agreeing to come round after hearing about her sad loss yesterday."

Musgrove froze, as Bradley stared at the guest family and noticed the eldest girl was smiling at him. He instantly recognized her and mouthed a question to confirm. "*Nika?*"

The girl nodded and mouthed back, as she placed her forefinger against her lips. "*Nicole, actually… shhhhhhhhh!*"

Bradley reciprocated by confirming his approval of the girls return from Wolf Town. "*Glad you made it back okay!*" He smiled and indicated his delight with a thumbs-up gesture, as the girl deflected his charm.

Musgrove was still thinking about Patrick's comment, as he muttered to himself. "What loss?" he thought out loud and attracted Bradley's attention, as Sereny and Jefferson simultaneously crashed their cutlery down onto their bone china plates.

Patrick enquired. "Is everything okay, Jefferson… and Sereny - you look a little pale?"

Bradley intervened. "They're fine, Dad… now what were you saying about Mrs. Chilcott's loss?" he asked, expecting to hear that Muzzy's dad had been pronounced dead.

"Oh, I'm sorry… yes – Muzzy, you might be better hearing the news from your Mum," insisted Patrick, as he whispered in Margaret's ear.

Musgrove afforded his mother a sympathetic look and anticipated what she was about to say. "Look, Mum… I know it's a bit awkward and it's going to be difficult for all of us but the circumstances around Dad's death came as bit of a shock to me as well!"

The atmosphere within the room changed dramatically and a murmuring developed around the table, as Mrs. Chilcott began to cry. Simon and Jules had been sitting quietly at the far end of the table and they both got up from their seats to comfort the distraught woman, as Musgrove's older brother asked the outspoken teenager to step outside into the hall.

Musgrove left the dining room and Simon quickly followed. "What are you playing at... you idiot – why on earth did you bring Dad's name into the conversation?"

"I can explain!" insisted Musgrove, as Bradley appeared.

Simon placed his hand on his brother's arm and tried to reason with him. "Look, Muzzy... you've just got to accept that we lost Dad a long time ago – you were only a little kid when it happened so I don't expect you to understand." Bradley pulled a peculiar face at Musgrove behind his brother's back, as Simon continued. "The tides were very strong that day and the waves just took him away from us!"

Bradley winked at Musgrove and flicked his head sideways to indicate that he needed to speak with him alone. The teenager reciprocated by nodding and produced a false smile for his Royal Marine brother. "Sorry... I don't know what came over me and I guess I should be over losing Dad by now – it happened such a long time ago and I promise I'll apologize to Mum when I go back in the dining room."

"No... just leave it for now – we actually lost the cat yesterday," explained Simon. "It got run over but she didn't want to say anything in case it spoilt your Christmas dinner."

"Oh, right!" replied Musgrove and excused himself from the conversation. "Just gotta nip into the kitchen for a drink of water... I'll be back to join the others in a jiffy."

Bradley smiled at Simon to excuse himself and then followed Musgrove, as he punched him in the arm. "I can't believe you said that to your Mum in front of everyone!"

"But I thought…" replied Musgrove.

"I know what you were thinking, but no one knows your father… *or should I say an evil possessed ghost-like creature who posed as your father* - was the Shadow Druid!" explained Bradley. "But that what Simon just said about your Dad disappearing when you were still young… now that was bizarre and a bit spooky!"

Musgrove was confused and lowered his chin onto his chest. "I don't know what to think anymore… the last time we came back from Pathylon my father was alive – now, according to Simon that never happened!" he sighed and rubbed his eyes. "Going on these adventures is driving me crazy and all this time travelling stuff seems to be affecting my father's existence here in the outside world!"

Bradley reassured his friend. "That was our last adventure into Pathylon… so there won't be any more surprises - whatever the situation is here in Sandmouth can't change now," he explained. "You just have to accept that your Dad isn't coming back… and what happened in our last adventure was just part of a whole destiny thing for the folks in Pathylon!"

"You're right, Brad… it's no use me worrying about it anymore – let's go back into the dining room to make sure my Mum is okay," suggested Musgrove and the boys headed out of the kitchen.

As they walked through the reception area, Bradley tapped his friend on the shoulder. "You were so busy wondering about your Dad… you didn't see the girl – did you?"

"What girl?" replied Musgrove, as they stood outside the dining room door.

"I'll fill you in later!" stated Bradley, as he pushed his foot against the door. "So many strange things have happened since we returned from Pathylon... so I think it would be best if we continued our conversation after the Christmas dinner - when everyone has gone!"

The door opened and the two boys apologized for taking so long, as Musgrove sat down next to his mother and gave her a kiss on the cheek.

Nicole smiled at the eternal chosen one again, as Patrick stood up to address the reassembled diners. "Okay... now that Musgrove and Bradley are back in the room – Margaret and I would like to present our Son with an extra-special Christmas surprise, if that's okay with you all?"

A pleasant murmur spread around the table, as Margaret pushed her plate and cutlery to one side. Patrick made his way over to the huge Christmas tree to lift a large box from the floor and he brushed the fallen pine needles away. He then walked back and placed the sturdy brown parcel in the space created by his excited wife.

Sereny smiled, as Bradley maneuvered around the back of the chairs and the curious diners shuffled forward to allow him to pass. At last he reached the box and prepared himself to lift the lid. "This is rather unexpected," he announced, as Patrick encouraged his son to remove the cover. A deathly silence fell upon the proceedings, as the boy placed his hands on the top of the box and a scratching sound emanated from inside. "Well, here goes!" Everyone waited for a reaction, as the boy stared inside the blanket-lined package. He looked up to gaze at an array of open mouths set around the table and then released an ecstatic cry of joy, as he lifted the animal out for all to see. "It's a little Burnese Mountain Dog!" he exclaimed and held the puppy's face in front of his, as it's little pink tongue emerged to lick the end of his nose.

The smell of puppy breath reached the boy's nostrils and he brushed his cheek across the dog's wrinkled snout. A chorus of admiring moans emanated throughout the adoring onlookers, as they all scrambled to get a closer look at the new arrival. Even Mrs. Chilcott managed an admiring glance at the playful hound considering the recent loss of her cat.

The puppy had a distinctive white stripe running from its podgy snout and the end of its wagging tail had a matching white tip. Bradley continued to steady the young dog by holding it under its front legs and noticed immediately that it was a boy. "So what are we going to call you… little fella?" he pondered, as Frannie pulled gently on the dog's hind paws. "We certainly can't call you K2… we've already had one of those!" he stated and a tear rolled down his cheek.

Margaret kissed the top of her son's head and asked. "So… do you like him?"

"Are you kidding me?" replied Bradley. "He's perfect!"

Patrick announced. "Well, we weren't sure whether to wait a little longer… with K2 leaving us just over a week ago and all that."

Bradley grinned, as he cuddled the bundle of rolled fur into his shoulder and needle-like teeth nibbled on his ear. Everyone applauded the little dog's affection towards its new owner and then the boy received an unexpected shock, as the puppy nuzzled into his hair to whisper softly. "I promised you I'd come back… didn't I?"

………..

BRADLEY BAKER

will return soon

in a brand new adventure!

Follow the Author

DAVID LAWRENCE JONES

http://www.facebook.com/davlawjones

twitter: @DavLawJones

"Like" Bradley's Facebook Page and follow his adventures;

http://www.facebook.com/thebradleybaker

Discover more about Meltor the High Priest (pictured) and all the other characters in the Amazing Adventures series;

http://www.bradley-baker.com